private peaceful

*With my thanks to Piet Chielens of
In Flanders Field Museum in Ypres*

michael morpurgo

private peaceful

HarperCollins *Children's Books*

Although the title was inspired by the name on a gravestone in Ypres, this novel is a work of fiction. Any references to real people (living or dead), actual locales and historical events are used solely to lend the fiction an appropriate cultural and historical setting. All other names, characters, places and incidents portrayed in this book are the product of the author's imagination, and any resemblance to actual persons, living or dead, is entirely coincidental.

First published in hardback in Great Britain by
HarperCollins *Children's Books* 2003
First published in paperback in Great Britain by
HarperCollins *Children's Books* 2004
HarperCollins *Children's Books* is a division of
HarperCollins *Publishers* Ltd,
77-85 Fulham Palace Road, Hammersmith, London W6 8JB

The HarperCollins *Children's Books* website address is
www.harpercollinschildrensbooks.co.uk

17

Text copyright © Michael Morpurgo 2003

Michael Morpurgo asserts the moral right to be identified
as the author of this work.

ISBN-13   978 0 00 7150076
ISBN-10   0 00 715007 5

Printed and bound in England by
Clays Ltd, St Ives plc

Conditions of Sale
This book is sold subject to the condition that it shall not, by way of trade or otherwise, be lent, re-sold, hired out or otherwise circulated without the publisher's prior written consent in any form of binding or cover other than that in which it is published and without a similar condition including this condition being imposed on the subsequent purchaser.

For my dear godmother,
Mary Niven

FIVE PAST TEN

They've gone now, and I'm alone at last. I have the whole night ahead of me, and I won't waste a single moment of it. I shan't sleep it away. I won't dream it away either. I mustn't, because every moment of it will be far too precious.

I want to try to remember everything, just as it was, just as it happened. I've had nearly eighteen years of yesterdays and tomorrows, and tonight I must remember as many of them as I can. I want tonight to be long, as long as my life, not filled with fleeting dreams that rush me on towards dawn.

Tonight, more than any other night of my life, I want to feel alive.

Charlie is taking me by the hand, leading me because he knows I don't want to go. I've never worn a collar before and it's choking me. My boots are strange and heavy on my feet. My heart is heavy too, because I dread what I am going to. Charlie has told me often how terrible this school-place is: about Mr Munnings and his raging tempers and the long whipping cane he hangs on the wall above his desk.

Big Joe doesn't have to go to school and I don't think that's fair at all. He's much older than me. He's even older than Charlie and he's never been to school. He stays at home with Mother, and sits up in his tree singing *Oranges and Lemons*, and laughing. Big Joe is always happy, always laughing. I wish I could be happy like him. I wish I could be at home like him. I don't want to go with Charlie. I don't want to go to school.

I look back, over my shoulder, hoping for a reprieve, hoping that Mother will come running after me and take me home. But she doesn't come and she doesn't come, and school and Mr Munnings and his cane are getting closer with every step.

"Piggyback?" says Charlie. He sees my eyes full of tears and knows how it is. Charlie always knows how it is. He's three years older than me, so he's done everything and knows everything. He's strong, too, and very good at piggybacks. So I hop up and cling on tight, crying behind my closed eyes, trying not to whimper out loud. But I cannot hold back my sobbing for long because I know that this morning is not the beginning of anything – not new and exciting as Mother says it is – but rather the end of my beginning. Clinging on round Charlie's neck I know that I am living the last moments of my carefree time, that I will not be the same person when I come home this afternoon.

I open my eyes and see a dead crow hanging from the

fence, his beak open. Was he shot, shot in mid-scream, as he began to sing, his raucous tune scarcely begun? He sways, his feathers still catching the wind even in death, his family and friends cawing in their grief and anger from the high elm trees above us. I am not sorry for him. It could be him that drove away my robin and emptied her nest of her eggs. My eggs. Five of them there had been, live and warm under my fingers. I remember I took them out one by one and laid them in the palm of my hand. I wanted them for my tin, to blow them like Charlie did and lay them in cotton wool with my blackbird's eggs and my pigeon's eggs. I would have taken them. But something made me draw back, made me hesitate. The robin was watching me from Father's rose bush, her black and beady eyes unblinking, begging me.

Father was in that bird's eyes. Under the rose bush, deep down, buried in the damp and wormy earth were all his precious things. Mother had put his pipe in first. Then Charlie laid his hobnail boots side by side, curled into each other, sleeping. Big Joe knelt down and covered the boots in Father's old scarf.

"Your turn, Tommo," Mother said. But I couldn't bring myself to do it. I was holding the gloves he'd worn the morning he died. I remembered picking one of them up. I knew what they did not know, what I could never tell them.

Mother helped me to do it in the end, so that Father's gloves lay there on top of his scarf, palms uppermost, thumbs touching. I felt those hands willing me not to do it, willing me to think again, not to take the eggs, not to take what was not mine. So I didn't do it. Instead I watched them grow, saw the first scrawny skeletal stirrings, the nest of gaping, begging beaks, the frenzied screeching at feeding time; witnessed too late from my bedroom window the last of the early-morning massacre, the parent robins watching like me, distraught and helpless, while the marauding crows made off skywards cackling, their murderous deed done. I don't like crows. I've never liked crows. That crow hanging there on the fence got what he deserved. That's what I think.

Charlie is finding the hill up into the village hard going. I can see the church tower and below it the roof of the school. My mouth is dry with fear. I cling on tighter.

"First day's the worst, Tommo," Charlie's saying, breathing hard. "It's not so bad. Honest." Whenever Charlie says "honest", I know it's not true. "Anyway I'll look after you."

That I do believe, because he always has. He does look after me too, setting me down, and walking me through all the boisterous banter of the school yard, his hand on my shoulder, comforting me, protecting me.

The school bell rings and we line up in two silent rows, about twenty children in each. I recognise some of them from Sunday school. I look around and realise that Charlie is no longer beside me. He's in the other line, and he's winking at me. I blink back and he laughs. I can't wink with one eye, not yet. Charlie always thinks that's very funny. Then I see Mr Munnings standing on the school steps cracking his knuckles in the suddenly silent school yard. He has tufty cheeks and a big belly under his waistcoat. He has a gold watch open in his hand. It's his eyes that are frightening and I know they are searching me out.

"Aha!" he cries, pointing right at me. Everyone has turned to look. "A new boy, a new boy to add to my trials and tribulations. Was not one Peaceful enough? What have I done to deserve another one? First a Charlie Peaceful, and now a Thomas Peaceful. Is there no end to my woes? Understand this, Thomas Peaceful, that here I am your lord and master. You do what I say when I say it. You do not cheat, you do not lie, you do not blaspheme. You do not come to school in bare feet. And your hands will be clean. These are my commandments. Do I make myself absolutely clear?"

"Yes sir," I whisper, surprised I can find my voice at all.

We file in past him, hands behind our backs. Charlie smiles across at me as the two lines part: "Tiddlers" into my classroom, "Bigguns" into his. I'm the littlest of the Tiddlers. Most of the Bigguns are even bigger than Charlie, fourteen years old some of them. I watch him until the door closes behind him and he's gone. Until this moment I have never known what it is to feel truly alone.

My bootlaces are undone. I can't tie laces. Charlie can,

but he's not here. I hear Mr Munnings' thunderous voice next door calling the roll and I am so glad we have Miss McAllister. She may speak with a strange accent, but at least she smiles, and at least she's not Mr Munnings.

"Thomas," she tells me, "you will be sitting there, next to Molly. And your laces are undone."

Everyone seems to be tittering at me as I take my place. All I want to do is to escape, to run, but I don't dare do it. All I can do is cry. I hang my head so they can't see my tears coming.

"Crying won't do your laces up, you know," Miss McAllister says.

"I can't, Miss," I tell her.

"Can't is not a word we use in my class, Thomas Peaceful," she says. "We shall just have to teach you to tie your bootlaces. That's what we're all here for, Thomas, to learn. That's why we come to school, don't we? You show him, Molly. Molly's the oldest girl in my class, Thomas, and my best pupil. She'll help you."

So while she calls the roll Molly kneels down in front of me and does up my laces. She ties laces very differently from Charlie, delicately, more slowly, in a great loopy double knot. She doesn't look up at me while she's doing it, not once, and I wish she would. She has hair the same colour as Billyboy, Father's old horse – chestnut brown and shining – and I want to reach out and touch it. Then she looks up at me at last and smiles. It's all I need. Suddenly I no longer want to run home. I want to stay here with Molly. I know I have a friend.

In playtime, in the school yard, I want to go over and talk to her, but I can't because she's always surrounded by a gaggle of giggling girls. They keep looking at me over their shoulders and laughing. I look for Charlie, but Charlie's splitting conkers open with his friends, all of them Bigguns. I go to sit on an old tree stump. I undo my bootlaces and try to do them up again remembering how Molly did it. I try again and again. After only a short while I find I can do it. It's untidy, and it's loose, but I can do it. Best of all, from across the school yard Molly sees I can do it, and smiles at me.

At home we don't wear boots, except for church. Mother does of course, and Father always wore his great hobnail boots, the boots he died in. When the tree came down I was there in the wood with him, just the two of us. Before I ever went to school he'd often take me off to work with him, to keep me out of mischief, he said. I'd ride up behind him on Billyboy and hang on round his waist, my face pressed into his back. Whenever Billyboy broke into a gallop I'd love it. We galloped all the way that morning, up the hill, up through Ford's Cleave Wood. I was still giggling when he lifted me down.

"Off you go, you scallywag, you," he said. "Enjoy yourself."

I hardly needed to be told. There were badger holes and fox holes to peer into, deer prints to follow perhaps, flowers to pick, or butterflies to chase. But that morning I found a mouse, a dead mouse. I buried it under a pile of leaves. I was making a wooden cross for it. Father was chopping away rhythmically nearby, grunting and groaning at every stroke as he always did. It sounded at first as if Father was just groaning a bit louder. That's what I thought it was. But then, strangely, the sound seemed to be coming not from where he was, but from somewhere high up in the branches.

I looked up to see the great tree above me swaying when all the other trees were standing still. It was creaking while all the other trees were silent. Only slowly did I realise it was coming down, and that when it fell it would fall right on top of me, that I was going to die and there was nothing I could do about it. I stood and stared, mesmerised at the gradual fall of it, my legs frozen under me, quite incapable of movement.

I hear Father shouting: "Tommo! Tommo! Run, Tommo!" But I can't. I see Father running towards me through the trees, his shirt flailing. I feel him catch me up and toss me aside in one movement, like a wheat sheaf. There is a roaring thunder in my ears and then no more.

When I wake I see Father at once, see the soles of his boots with their worn nails. I crawl over to where he is lying, pinned to the ground under the leafy crown of the great tree. He is on his back, his face turned away from me as if he doesn't want me to see. One arm is outstretched towards me, his glove fallen off, his finger pointing at me. There is blood coming from his nose, dropping on the leaves. His eyes are open, but I know at once they are not seeing me. He is not breathing. When I shout at him, when I shake him, he does not wake up. I pick up his glove.

In the church we're sitting side by side in the front row, Mother, Big Joe, Charlie and me. We've never in our lives sat in the front row before. It's where the Colonel and his family always sit. The coffin rests on trestles, my father inside in his Sunday suit. A swallow swoops over our heads all through the prayers, all through the hymns, flitting from window to window, from the belfry to the altar, looking for some way out. And I know for certain it is Father trying to escape. I know it because he told us more than once that in his next life he'd like to be a bird, so he could fly free wherever he wanted.

Big Joe keeps pointing up at the swallow. Then without any warning he gets up and walks to the back of the church where he opens the door. When he gets back he explains to Mother what he's done in his loud voice, and Grandma Wolf, sitting beside us in her black bonnet, scowls at him, at all of us. I know then what I never understood before, that she is ashamed to be one of us. I didn't really understand why until later, until I was older.

The swallow sits perched on a rafter high above the coffin. It lifts off and swoops up and down the aisle until at last it finds the open door and is gone. And I know that Father is happy now in his next life. Big Joe laughs out loud and Mother takes his hand in hers. Charlie catches my eye. At that moment all four of us are thinking the very same thing.

The Colonel gets up into the pulpit to speak, his hand clutching the lapel of his jacket. He declares that James Peaceful was a good man, one of the best workers he has ever known, the salt of the earth, always cheerful as he went about his work, that the Peaceful family had been employed in one capacity or another, by his family, for five generations. In all his thirty years as a forester on the estate James Peaceful had never once been late for work and was a credit to his family and his village. All the while as the Colonel drones on I'm thinking of the rude things Father used to say about him – "silly old fart", "mad old duffer" and much worse – and how Mother had always told us that he might well be a "silly old fart" or "mad old duffer", but how it was the Colonel who paid Father's wages and owned the roof over our heads, how we children should show respect when we met him, smile and touch our forelocks, and we should look as if we meant it too, if we knew what was good for us.

Afterwards we all gather round the grave and Father's lowered down, and the vicar won't stop talking. I want

Father to hear the birds for the last time before the earth closes in on top of him and he has nothing left but silence. Father loves larks, loves watching them rising, rising so high you can only see their song. I look up hoping for a lark, and there is a blackbird singing from the yew tree. A blackbird will have to do... I hear Mother whispering to Big Joe that Father is not really in his coffin any more, but in heaven up there – she's pointing up into the sky beyond the church tower – and that he's happy, happy as the birds.

The earth thuds and thumps down on the coffin behind us as we drift away, leaving him. We walk home together along the deep lanes, Big Joe plucking at the foxgloves and the honeysuckle, filling Mother's hands with flowers, and none of us has any tears to cry or words to say. Me least of all. For I have inside me a secret so horrible, a secret I can never tell anyone, not even Charlie. Father needn't have died that morning in Ford's Cleave Wood. He was trying to save me. If only I had tried to save myself, if I had run, he would not now be lying dead in his coffin. As Mother smooths my hair and Big Joe offers her yet another foxglove, all I can think is that I have caused this.

I have killed my own father.

TWENTY TO ELEVEN

I don't want to eat. Stew, potatoes and biscuits. I usually like stew, but I've no appetite for it. I nibble at a biscuit, but I don't want that either. Not now. It's a good thing Grandma Wolf is not here. She always hated us leaving food on our plates. "Waste not, want not," she'd say. I'm wasting this, Wolfwoman, whether you like it or not.

Big Joe ate more than all the rest of us put together. Everything was his favourite – bread and butter pudding with raisins, potato pie, cheese and pickle, stew and dumplings – whatever Mother cooked, he'd stuff it in and scoff it down. Anything Charlie and I didn't like we'd shuffle on to his plate when Mother wasn't looking. Big Joe always loved the conspiracy of that, and he loved the extra food too. There was nothing he wouldn't eat. When we were little, before we knew better, Charlie once bet me an owl's skull I'd found that Big Joe would even eat rabbit droppings. I couldn't believe he would, because I thought Big Joe must know what they were. So I took the bet. Charlie put a handful of them in a paper bag and told him they were sweets. Big Joe took them out of the bag and popped them into his mouth, savouring every one of them. And when we laughed, he laughed too and offered us one each. But Charlie said they were especially for him, a present. I thought Big Joe might get ill after that, but he never did.

Mother told us when we were older that Big Joe had nearly died just a few days after he was born. Meningitis, they told her at the hospital. The doctor said Joe had brain damage, that he'd be no use to anyone, even if he lived. But Big Joe did live, and he did get better, though never completely. As we were growing up, all we knew was that he was different. It didn't matter to us that he couldn't speak very well, that he couldn't read or write at all, that he didn't think like we did, like other people did. To us he was just Big Joe. He did frighten us sometimes. He seemed to drift off to live in a dream world of his own, often a world of nightmares I thought because he could become very agitated and upset. But sooner or later he always came back to us and would be himself again, the Big Joe we all knew, the Big Joe who loved everything and everyone, especially animals and birds and flowers, totally trusting, always forgiving – even when he found out that his sweets were rabbit droppings.

Charlie and I got into real trouble over that. Big Joe would never have found out, not by himself. But, always generous, he went and offered one of the rabbit droppings to Mother. She was so angry with us I thought she'd burst. She put a finger in Big Joe's mouth, scooped out what was still in there and made him wash it out. Then she made Charlie and me eat one rabbit dropping each so that we'd know what it was like.

"Horrible, isn't it?" she said. "Horrible food for horrible children. Don't you treat Big Joe like that ever again."

We felt very ashamed of ourselves – for a while anyway. Ever since then someone has only had to mention rabbits, for Charlie and me to smile at one another and remember. It's making me smile again now, even just thinking of it. It shouldn't, but it does.

In a way our lives at home always revolved around Big Joe. How we thought about people depended largely on how they behaved with our big brother. It was quite simple really: if people didn't like him or were offhand or treated him as if he was stupid, then we didn't like them. Most people around us were used to him, but some would look the other way, or worse still, just pretend he wasn't there. We hated that more than anything. Big Joe never seemed to mind, but we did on his behalf – like the day we blew raspberries at the Colonel.

No one at home ever spoke well of the Colonel, except Grandma Wolf of course. Whenever she came for her visits she wouldn't hear a word against him. She and Father would have dreadful rows about him. We grew up thinking of him mostly as just a "silly old fart". But the first time I saw for myself what the Colonel was really like, was because of Big Joe.

One evening Charlie and Big Joe and I were coming back home up the lane. We'd been fishing for brown trout in the brook. Big Joe had caught three, tickled them to sleep in the shallows and then scooped them out on to the bank before they knew what had happened. He was clever like that. It was almost as if he knew what the fish were thinking. He never liked killing them though, and nor did I. Charlie had to do that.

Big Joe always said hello, loudly, to everyone. It's how he was. So when the Colonel rode by that evening, Big Joe called out hello, and proudly held up his trout to show him. The Colonel trotted by as if he hadn't even seen us. When he'd passed Charlie blew a noisy raspberry after him, and Big Joe did the same because he liked rude noises. But the trouble was that Big Joe was enjoying himself so much blowing raspberries that he didn't stop. The Colonel reined in his horse and gave us a very nasty look. For a moment I thought he was going to come after us. Luckily he didn't, but he did crack his whip. "I'll teach you, you young ruffians!" he roared. "I'll teach you!"

I've always thought that was the moment the Colonel began to hate us, that from then on he was always determined one way or another to get his own back. We ran for it all the way home. Whenever anyone farts or blows raspberries I always think of that meeting in the lane, of how Big Joe always laughs at rude noises, laughs like he'll never stop. I think too of the menacing look in the Colonel's eye and the crack of his whip, and how Big Joe blowing raspberries at him that evening may well have changed our lives for ever.

It was Big Joe, too, who got me into my first fight. There was a lot of fighting at school, but I was never much good at it and always seemed to end up getting a swollen lip or a bleeding ear. I learned soon enough that if you don't want to get hurt you keep your head down and you don't answer back, particularly if the other fellow is bigger. But one day I discovered that sometimes you've got to stand up for yourself and fight for what's right, even when you don't want to.

It was at playtime. Big Joe came up to school to see Charlie and me. He just stood and watched us from outside the school gate. He did that often when Charlie and I first went off to school together — I think he was finding it lonely at home without us. I ran over to him. He was breathless, bright-eyed with excitement. He had something to show me. He opened his cupped hands just enough for me to be able to see. There was a slowworm curled up inside. I knew where he'd got it from — the churchyard, his favourite hunting ground. Whenever we went up to put flowers on Father's grave, Big

Joe would go off on his own, hunting for more creatures to add to his collection; that's when he wasn't just standing there gazing up at the tower and singing *Oranges and Lemons* at the top of his voice and watching the swifts screaming around the church tower. Nothing seemed to make him happier than that.

I knew Big Joe would put his slowworm in with all his other creatures. He kept them in boxes at the back of the woodshed at home – lizards, hedgehogs, all sorts. I stroked his slowworm with my finger, and said it was lovely, which it was. Then he wandered off, walking down the lane humming his *Oranges and Lemons* as he went, gazing down in wonder at his beloved slowworm.

I am watching him go when someone taps me hard on my shoulder, hard enough to hurt. It is big Jimmy Parsons. Charlie has often warned me about him, told me to keep out of his way. "Who's got a loony for a brother?" says Jimmy Parsons, sneering at me.

I cannot believe what he's said, not at first. "What did you say?"

"Your brother's a loony, off his head, off his rocker, nuts, barmy."

I go for him then, fists flailing, screaming at him, but I don't manage to land a single punch. He hits me full in the face and sends me sprawling. I find myself suddenly sitting on the ground, wiping my bleeding nose and looking at the blood on the back of my hand. Then he puts the boot in, hard. I curl up in a ball like a hedgehog to protect myself, but it doesn't seem to do me much good. He just goes on kicking me on my back, on my legs, anywhere he can. When he finally stops I wonder why.

I look up to see Charlie grabbing him round the neck and pulling him to the ground. They're rolling over and over, punching each other and swearing. The whole school has gathered round to watch now, egging them on. That's when Mr Munnings comes running out of the school, roaring like a raging bull. He pulls them apart, takes them by their collars and drags them off inside the school. Luckily for me Mr Munnings never even notices me sitting there, bleeding. Charlie gets the cane, and so does Jimmy Parsons – six strokes each. So Charlie saves me twice that day. The rest of us stand there in the school yard in silence, listening to the strokes and counting them. Big Jimmy Parsons gets it first, and he keeps crying out: "Ow, sir! Ow, sir! Ow, sir!" But when it's Charlie's turn, all we hear are the whacks, and then the silences in between. I am so proud of him for that. I have the bravest brother in the world.

Molly comes over and, taking me by the hand, leads me towards the pump. She soaks her handkerchief under it and dabs my nose and my hands and my knee – the blood seems to be everywhere. The water is wonderfully cold and soothing, and her hands are soft. She doesn't say anything for a while. She's dabbing me very gently, very carefully so as not to hurt me. Then all of a sudden she says: "I like Big Joe. He's kind. I like people who are kind."

Molly likes Big Joe. Now I know for sure that I will love her till the day I die.

After a while Charlie came out into the school yard hitching up his trousers and grinning in the sunshine. Everyone was crowding around him.

"Did it hurt, Charlie?"

"Was it on the back of the knees, Charlie, or on your bum?"

Charlie never said a word to them. He just walked right through everyone, and came straight over to me and Molly. "He won't do it again, Tommo," he said. "I hit him where it hurts, in the goolies." He lifted my chin and peered at my nose. "Are you all right, Tommo?"

"Hurts a bit," I told him.

"So does my bum," said Charlie.

Molly laughed then, and so did I. So did Charlie, and so did the whole school.

From that moment on Molly became one of us. It was as if she had suddenly joined our family and become our sister. When Molly came home with us that afternoon Big Joe gave her some flowers he'd picked, and Mother treated her like the daughter she'd never had. After that, Molly came home with us almost every afternoon. She seemed to want to be with us all the time. We didn't discover the reason for this until a lot later. I remember Mother used to brush Molly's hair. She loved doing it and we loved watching.

Mother. I think of her so often. And when I think of her I think of high hedges and deep lanes and our walks down to the river together in the evenings. I think of meadowsweet and honeysuckle and vetch and foxgloves and red campion and dog roses. There wasn't a wild flower or a butterfly she couldn't name. I loved the sound of their names when she spoke them: red admiral, peacock, cabbage white, adonis blue. It's her voice I'm hearing in my head now. I don't know why, but I can hear her better than I can picture her. I suppose it was because of Big Joe that she was always talking, always explaining the world about us. She was his guide, his interpreter, his teacher.

They wouldn't have Big Joe at school. Mr Munnings said he was backward. He wasn't backward at all. He was different, "special" Mother used to call him, but he was not backward. He needed help, that's all, and Mother was his help. It was as if Big Joe was blind in some way. He could see perfectly well, but very often he didn't seem to understand what he was seeing. And he wanted to understand so badly. So Mother would be forever telling him how and why things were as they were. And she would sing to him often, too, because it always made him happy and soothed him whenever he had one of his turns and became anxious or troubled. She'd sing to Charlie and me as well, more out of habit, I think. But we loved it, loved the sound of her voice. Her voice was the music of our childhood.

After Father died the music stopped. There was a stillness and a quietness in Mother now, and a sadness about the house. I had my terrible secret, a secret I could scarcely ever put out of my mind. So in my guilt I kept more and more to myself. Even Big Joe hardly ever laughed. At meals the kitchen seemed especially empty without Father, without his bulk and his voice filling the room. His dirty work coat didn't hang in the porch any more, and the smell of his pipe lingered only faintly now. He was gone and we were all quietly mourning him in our way.

Mother still talked to Big Joe, but not as much as before. She had to talk to him, because she was the only one who truly understood the meaning of all the grunts and squawks Big Joe used for language. Charlie and I understood some of it, some of the time, but she seemed to understand all he wanted to say, sometimes even before he said it. There was a shadow hanging over her, Charlie and I could see that, and not only the shadow of Father's death. We were sure there was something else she wouldn't talk about, something she was hiding from us. We found out what it was only too soon.

We were back home after school having our tea – Molly was there too – when there was a knock on the door. Mother seemed at once to know who it was. She took time to gather herself, smoothing down her apron and arranging her hair before she opened the door. It was the Colonel. "I wanted a word, Mrs Peaceful," he said. "I think you know what I've come for."

Mother told us to finish our tea, closed the door and went out into the garden with him. Charlie and I left Molly and Big Joe at the table and dashed out of the back door. We hurdled the vegetables, ran along the hedge, crouched down behind the woodshed and listened. We were close enough to hear every word that was said.

"It may seem a little indelicate to broach the subject so soon after your late husband's sad and untimely death," the Colonel was saying. He wasn't looking at Mother as he spoke, but down at his top hat which he was smoothing with his sleeve. "But it's a question of the cottage. Strictly speaking, of course, Mrs Peaceful, you have no right to live here any more. You know well enough I think that this is a tied cottage, tied to your late husband's job on the estate. Now of course with him gone..."

"I know what you're saying, Colonel," Mother said. "You want us out."

"Well, I wouldn't put it quite like that. It's not that I want you out, Mrs Peaceful, not if we can come to some other arrangement."

"Arrangement? What arrangement?" Mother asked.

"Well," the Colonel went on, "as it happens there's a position up at the house that might suit you. My wife's lady's maid has just given notice. As you know my wife is not a well woman. These days she spends most of her life in a wheelchair. She needs constant care and attention seven days a week."

"But I have my children," Mother protested. "Who would look after my children?"

It was a while before the Colonel spoke. "The two boys are old enough now to fend for themselves, I should have thought. And as for the other one, there is the lunatic asylum in Exeter. I'm sure I could see to it that a place be found for—"

Mother interrupted, her fury only barely suppressed, her voice cold but still calm. "I could never do that, Colonel. Never. But if I want to keep a roof over our heads, then I have to find some way I can come to work for you as your wife's maid. That is what you're telling me, isn't it."

"I'd say you understand the position perfectly, Mrs Peaceful. I couldn't have put it better myself. I shall need your agreement within the week. Good day Mrs Peaceful. And once again my condolences."

We watched him go, leaving Mother standing there. I had never in my life seen her cry before, but she cried now. She fell on her knees in the long grass holding her face in her hands. That was when Big Joe and Molly came out of the cottage. When Big Joe saw Mother he ran and knelt down beside her, hugging and rocking her gently in his arms, singing *Oranges and Lemons* until she began to smile through her tears and join in. Then we were all singing together, and loudly in our defiance so that the Colonel could not help but hear us.

Later, after Molly had gone home, Charlie and I sat in silence in the orchard. I almost told him my secret then. I wanted to so badly. But I just couldn't bring myself to do it. I thought he might never speak to me again if I did. The moment passed. "I hate that man," said Charlie under his breath. "I'll do him, Tommo. One day I'll really do him."

Of course Mother had no choice. She had to take the job, and we only had one relative to turn to for help, Grandma Wolf. She moved in the next week to look after us. She wasn't our grandmother at all, not really – both our grandmothers were dead. She was Mother's aunt, but always insisted we called her "Grandma" because she thought Great Aunt made her sound old and crotchety, which she always was. We hadn't liked her before she moved in – as much on account of her moustache as anything else – and we liked her even less now that she had. We all knew her story; how she'd worked up at the Big House for the Colonel for years as housekeeper, and how, for some reason, the Colonel's wife couldn't stand her. They'd had a big falling out, and in the end she'd had to leave and go to live in the village. That was why she was free to come and look after us.

But between ourselves Charlie and I had never called her either Great Aunt or Grandma. We had our own name for her. When we were younger Mother had often read us *Little Red Riding Hood*. There was a picture in it Charlie and I knew well, of the wolf in bed pretending to be Little Red Riding Hood's grandma. She had a black bonnet on her head, like our "Grandma" always used to wear, and she had big teeth with gaps in between, just like our "Grandma" too. So ever since I could remember we had called her "Grandma Wolf" – never to her face, of course. Mother said it wasn't respectful, but secretly I think she always quite liked it.

Soon it wasn't only because of the book that we thought of her as Grandma Wolf. She very quickly showed us who was in charge now that Mother was not there. Everything had to be just so: hands washed, hair done, no talking with your mouth full, no leaving anything on your plate. Waste not, want not, she'd say. That wasn't so bad. We got used to it. But what we could not forgive was that she was nasty to Big Joe. She talked to him, and about him, as if he were stupid or mad. She'd treat him as if he were a baby. She was forever wiping his mouth for him, or telling him not to sing at the table. When Molly protested once, she smacked her and sent her home. She smacked Big Joe too, whenever he didn't do what she said, which was often. He would start to rock then and talk to himself, which is what he always did whenever he was upset. But now Mother wasn't there to sing to him, to calm him. Molly talked to him, and we tried too, but it was not the same.

From the day Grandma Wolf moved in, our whole world changed. Mother would go to work up at the Big House at dawn, before we went off to school, and she still wouldn't be back when we got home for our tea. Instead Grandma Wolf would be there, at the door of what seemed to us now to be her lair. And Big Joe, who she wouldn't allow to go off on his wanders as he'd always loved to do, would come rushing up to us as if he hadn't seen us in weeks. He'd do the same to Mother when she came home, but she was often so exhausted she could hardly talk to him. She could see what was going on but was powerless to do anything about it. It seemed to all of us as if we were losing her, as if she was being replaced and pushed aside.

It was Grandma Wolf who did all the talking now, even telling Mother what to do in her own house. She was forever saying how Mother hadn't brought us up properly, that our manners were terrible, that we didn't know right from wrong – and that Mother had married beneath her. "I told her then and I've told her since," she ranted on, "she could have done far better for herself. But did she listen? Oh no. She had to marry the first man to turn her head, and him nothing but a forester. She was meant for better things, a better class of person. We were shopkeepers – we ran a proper shop, I can tell you – made a tidy profit, too. In a big way of business, I'll have you know. But oh no, she wouldn't have it. Broke your grandfather's heart, she did. And now look what she's come to: a lady's maid, at her age. Trouble. Your mother's always been nothing but trouble from the day she was born."

We longed for Mother to stand up to her, but each time she just gave in meekly, too worn out to do anything else. To Charlie and me she seemed almost to have become a different person. There was no laughter in her voice, no light in her eyes. And all along I knew full well whose fault it was that this had all happened, that Father was dead, that Mother had to go to work up at the Big House, and that Grandma Wolf had moved in and taken her place.

At night we could sometimes hear Grandma Wolf snoring in bed, and Charlie and I would make up this story about the Colonel and Grandma Wolf; how one day we'd go up to the Big House and push the Colonel's wife into the lake and drown her, and then Mother could come home and be with us and Big Joe and Molly, and everything could be like it had been before. Then the Colonel and Grandma Wolf could marry one another and live unhappily ever after, and because they were so old they could have lots of little monster children born already old and wrinkly with gappy teeth: the girls with moustaches like Grandma Wolf, the boys with whiskers like the Colonel.

I remember I used to have nightmares filled with those monster children, but whatever my nightmare it would always end the same way. I would be out in the woods with Father and the tree would be falling, and I'd wake up screaming. Then Charlie would be there beside me, and everything would be all right again. Charlie always made things all right again.

NEARLY QUARTER PAST ELEVEN

There's a mouse in here with me. He's sitting there in the light of the lamp, looking up at me. He seems as surprised to see me as I am to see him. There he goes. I can hear him still, scurrying about somewhere under the hayrack. I think he's gone now. I hope he comes back. I miss him already.

Grandma Wolf hated mice. She had a deep fear of them that she could not hide. So Charlie and I had lots to smile about in the autumn when the rain and the cold came and the mice decided it was warmer inside and came to live with us in the cottage. Big Joe loved the mice – he'd even put out food for them. Grandma Wolf would shout at him for that and smack him. But Big Joe could never understand why he was being smacked, so he went on feeding the mice just as he had before. Grandma Wolf put traps down, but Charlie and I would find them and spring them. All that autumn she only ever managed to catch one.

That mouse had the best funeral any mouse ever had. Big Joe was chief mourner and he cried enough for all of us. Molly, Charlie and I dug the grave, and when we'd laid him to rest Molly piled the grave high with flowers and sang *What a friend we have in Jesus*. We did all this at the bottom of the orchard hidden behind the apple trees where Grandma Wolf could not see or hear us. Afterwards we sat in a circle round the grave and had a funeral feast of blackberries. Big Joe stopped crying to eat the blackberries, and then with blackened mouths we all sang *Oranges and Lemons* over the mouse's grave.

Grandma Wolf tried everything to get rid of the mice. She put poison down under the sink in the larder. We swept it up. She asked Bob James, the wart charmer from the village with the crooked nose, to come and charm the mice away. He tried, but it didn't work. So in the end, in desperation, she had to resort to chasing them out of the house with a broom. But they just kept coming back in again. All this made her nastier than ever towards us. But for Charlie and me, just to see her frightened silly and screeching like a witch was worth every smack she gave us.

In bed at night our Grandma Wolf story was changing every time we told it. Now the Colonel and Grandma Wolf didn't have human children at all. Instead she gave birth to giant mice-children, all of them with great long tails and twitchy whiskers. But after what she did next, we decided that even that horrible fate was too good for her.

Although Grandma Wolf did smack Molly from time to time, it soon became obvious that she liked her a great deal better than the rest of us. There were good reasons for this. Girls were nice, Grandma Wolf would often tell us, not coarse and vulgar like boys. Besides she was good friends with Molly's mother and father. They lived as we did in a cottage on the Colonel's estate – Molly's father was groom up at the Big House. They were *proper* people, Grandma Wolf told us; good, God-fearing people who had brought their child up well – which meant strictly. And from what Molly told us, they *were* strict too. She was forever being sent to her room, or strapped by her father for the least little thing. She was an only child of older parents and, as Molly often said, they wanted her to be perfect. Anyway, it was a good thing for us that Grandma approved of her family, otherwise I'm sure she would have forbidden Molly to come and see us. As it was, Grandma Wolf said Molly was a good influence, that she could teach us some manners, and make us a little less coarse and vulgar. So, thank goodness, Molly kept coming home with us for tea every day after school.

Not long after the mouse's funeral, it was Big Joe's birthday. Charlie and I had got him some humbugs from Mrs Bright's shop in the village – which he always loved – and Molly brought him a present in a little brown box with air holes in it and elastic bands round it. While we were in school she kept it hidden in the shrubs at the bottom of the school yard. It was only because we pestered her that she showed us what it was as we were walking home. It was a harvest mouse, the sweetest little mouse I ever saw, with oversized ears and bewildered eyes. She stroked him with the back of her finger and he sat up for her in the box and twitched his whiskers at us. She gave him to Big Joe after tea, down in the orchard out of sight of the cottage, well hidden from Grandma Wolf's ever watchful gaze. Big Joe hugged Molly as if he'd never let her go. He kept the birthday mouse in his own box and hid him away in a drawer in his bedroom cupboard – he said it would be too cold for him outside in the woodshed with all his other creatures. The mouse became his instant favourite. All of us tried to make Big Joe understand that he mustn't ever tell Grandma Wolf, that if she ever knew, she'd take his mouse away and kill it.

I don't know how she found out, but when we came home from school a few days later Big Joe was sitting on the floor of his room, sobbing his heart out, his drawer empty beside him. Grandma Wolf came storming in saying she wasn't going to have any nasty dirty animals in *her* house. Worse still, so that he'd never bring any of his other animals into the house, she'd got rid of them all: the slowworm, the two lizards, the hedgehog. Big Joe's family of animals were gone, and he was heartbroken. Molly screamed at her that she was a cruel, cruel woman and that she'd go to Hell when she was dead, and then ran off home in tears.

That night Charlie and I made up a story about how we'd put rat poison in Grandma Wolf's tea the next day and kill her. We did get rid of her in the end too, but thankfully without the use of rat poison. Instead, a miracle happened, a wonderful miracle.

First, the Colonel's wife died in her wheelchair, so we didn't have to push her into the lake after all. She choked on a scone at teatime, and despite everything Mother did to try to save her, she just stopped breathing. There was a big funeral which we all had to go to. She had a shining coffin with silver handles, piled high with flowers. The vicar said how loved she was in the parish, and how she'd devoted her life to caring for everyone on the estate – all of which was news to us.

Afterwards they opened up the church floor and lowered her into the family vault while we all sang *Abide with me*. And I was thinking that I'd rather be in Father's simple coffin and buried outside where the sun shines and the wind blows, not down in some gloomy hole with a crowd of dead relatives. Mother had to take Big Joe out in the middle of the hymn because he started singing *Oranges and Lemons* again very loudly and would not stop. Grandma Wolf bared her teeth at us – as wolves do – and furrowed her brow in disapproval. We didn't know it then, but very soon she would disappear almost totally from our lives, taking all her anger, all her threats and disapproval with her.

So suddenly, joy of joys, Mother was back home with us again, and we hoped it was only a question of time before

Grandma Wolf moved back up to the village. There was no job for Mother any more up at the Big House, no lady to be a maid to. She was home, and day by day she was becoming her old self again. There were wonderful blazing arguments between her and Grandma Wolf, mostly about how Grandma Wolf treated Big Joe. Mother said that now she was home she wouldn't stand for it any more. We listened to every word, and loved every moment of it. But there was one big shadow over all this new joy. We could see that with Mother out of work and no money coming in, things were becoming desperate. There was no money in the mug on the mantelpiece, and every day there was less food on the table. For a while we had little to eat but potatoes, and we all knew perfectly well that sooner or later the Colonel would put us out of the cottage. We were just waiting for the knock on the door. Meanwhile we were becoming very hungry.

It was Charlie's idea to go poaching: salmon, sea trout, rabbits, even deer if we were lucky, he said. Father had done a bit of poaching, so Charlie knew what to do. Molly and I would be on lookout. He could do the trapping or the fishing. So, at dusk, or dawn, whenever we could get away together, we went off poaching on the Colonel's land: in the Colonel's forests or in the Colonel's river where there were plenty of sea trout and plenty of salmon. We couldn't take Big Joe because he could start his singing at any time and give us away. Besides he'd tell Mother. He told Mother everything.

We did well. We brought back lots of rabbits, a few trout and, once, a fourteen-pound salmon. So now we had something to eat with our potatoes. We didn't tell Mother we'd been on the Colonel's land. She wouldn't have approved of that sort of thing at all, and we definitely didn't want Grandma Wolf knowing because she'd certainly have gone and reported us to the Colonel at once. "My friend, the Colonel," she called him. She was always full of his praises, so we knew we had to be careful. We said we'd caught our rabbits in the orchard and the fish from the village brook. The trout you could catch there were only small, but they didn't know that. Charlie told them that the salmon must have come up the brook to spawn, which they did do of course. Charlie always lied well, and they believed him. Thank God.

Molly and I would keep watch while Charlie set the traps or put out his nets. Lambert, the Colonel's bailiff, may have been old, but he was clever, and we knew he'd let his dog loose on us if he ever caught us at it. Late one evening, sitting by the bridge with Charlie busy at his nets downstream, Molly took my hand in hers and held it tight. "I don't like the dark," she whispered. I had never been so happy.

When the Colonel turned up at the house the next day, we thought it must be either because we'd been found out somehow or because he was going to evict us. It was neither. Grandma Wolf seemed to be expecting him, and that was strange. She went to the door and invited him in. He nodded at Mother and then frowned at us. Grandma Wolf waved us outside as she asked the Colonel to sit down. We tried eavesdropping but Big Joe was no good at keeping quiet, so we had to wait until later to hear the worst. As it turned out, the worst was not the worst at all, but the best.

After the Colonel had gone, Grandma Wolf called us in. I could see she was puffed up with self-importance, aglow with it. "Your mother will explain," she declared grandly, putting on her bonnet. "I have to get up to the Big House right away. I've work to do."

Mother waited until she'd gone and could not help smiling as she told us. "Well," she began, "you know some time ago your great aunt used to work as housekeeper up at the Big House?"

"And then she got kicked out by the Colonel's wife," said Charlie.

"She lost her job, yes," Mother went on. "Well, now the Colonel's wife has passed away it seems the Colonel wants her back as live-in housekeeper. She'll be moving up to the Big House as soon as possible."

I didn't cheer, but I certainly felt like it.

"What about the cottage?" Charlie asked. "Is the old duffer putting us out then?"

"No, dear. We're staying put," Mother replied. "He said his wife had liked me and made him promise to look after me if ever anything happened to her. So he's keeping that promise. Say what you like about the Colonel, he's a man of his word. I've agreed I'll do all his linen for him and his sewing work. Most of it I can bring home. So we'll have some money coming in. We'll manage. Well, are you happy? We're staying put!"

Then we did cheer and Big Joe cheered too, louder than any of us. So we stayed on in our cottage and Grandma Wolf moved out. We were liberated, and all was right with the world again. For a while at least.

Both of them being older than me, Molly by two years, Charlie by three, they always ran faster than I did. I seem to have spent much of my life watching them racing ahead of me, leaping the high meadow grass, Molly's plaits whirling about her head, their laughter mingling. When they got too far ahead I sometimes felt they wanted to be without me. I would whine at them then to let them know I was feeling all miserable and abandoned, and they'd wait for me to catch up. Best of all Molly would sometimes come running back and take my hand.

When we weren't poaching the Colonel's fish or scrumping his apples – more than anything we all loved the danger of it, I think – we would be roaming wild in the countryside. Molly could shin up a tree like a cat, faster than either of us. Sometimes we'd go down to the river bank and watch the kingfishers flash by, or we'd go swimming in Okement Pool hung all around by willows, where the water was dark and deep and mysterious, and where no one ever came.

I remember the day Molly dared Charlie to take off all his clothes, and to my amazement he did. Then she did, and they ran shrieking and bare-bottomed into the water. When they called me in after them, I wouldn't do it, not in front of Molly. So I sat and sulked on the bank and watched them splashing and giggling, and all the while I was wishing I had the courage to do what Charlie had done, wishing I was with them. Molly got dressed afterwards behind a bush and told us not to watch. But we did. That was the first time I ever saw a girl with no clothes on. She was very thin and white, and she wrung her plaits out like a wet cloth.

It was several days before they managed to entice me in. Molly stood waist-deep in the river and put her hands over her eyes. "Come on, Tommo," she cried. "I won't watch. Promise." And not wanting to be left out yet again, I stripped off and made a dash for the river, covering myself as I went just in case Molly was watching through her fingers. After I'd done it that first time, it never seemed to bother me again.

Sometimes when we tired of all the frolicking we'd lie and talk in the shallows, letting the river ripple over us. How we talked. Molly told us once that she wanted to die right there and then, that she never wanted tomorrow to come because no tomorrow could ever be as good as today. "I know," she said, and she sat up in the river then and collected a handful of small pebbles. "I'm going to tell our future. I've seen the gypsies do it." She shook the pebbles around in her cupped hands, closed her eyes and then scattered them out on to the muddy shore. Kneeling over them she spoke very seriously and slowly as if she were reading them. "They say we'll always be together, the three of us, for ever and ever. They say that as long as we stick together we'll be lucky and happy." Then she smiled at us. "And the stones never lie," she said. "So you're stuck with me."

For a year or two Molly's stones proved right. But then Molly got ill. She wasn't at school one day. It was the scarlet fever, Mr Munnings told us, and very serious. Charlie and I went up to her cottage that evening after tea with some sweetpeas Mother had picked for her – because they smell sweeter than any flower she knew, she said. We knew we wouldn't be allowed in to see her because scarlet fever was very catching, but Molly's mother did not look at all pleased to see us. She always looked grey and grim, but that day she was angry as well. She took the flowers with scarcely a glance at them, and told us it would be better if we didn't come again. Then Molly's father appeared from behind her, looking gruff and unkempt, and told us to be off, that we were disturbing Molly's sleep. As I walked away, all I could think of was how unhappy Molly must be living in that dingy little cottage with a mother and father like that, and how trees fall on the wrong fathers. We stopped at the end of the path and looked up at Molly's window, hoping she would come and wave at us. When she didn't we knew she must be really ill.

Charlie and I never said our prayers at all any more, not since Sunday school, but we did now. Kneeling side by side with Big Joe we prayed each night that Molly would not die. Joe sang *Oranges and Lemons* and we said *Amen* afterwards. We had our fingers crossed too, just for good measure.

TEN TO MIDNIGHT

I'm not sure I ever really believed in God, even in Sunday school. In church I'd gaze up at Jesus hanging on the cross in the stained-glass window, and feel sorry for him because I could see how cruel it was and how much it must be hurting him. I knew he was a good and kind man. But I never really understood why God, who was supposed to be his father, and almighty and powerful, would let them do that to him, would let him suffer so much. I believed then, as I believe now, that crossed fingers and Molly's stones are every bit as reliable or unreliable as praying to God. I shouldn't think like that because if there's no God, then there can be no heaven. Tonight I want very much to believe there's a heaven, that, as Father said, there is a new life after death, that death is not a full stop, and that we will all see one another again.

It was while Molly was ill in bed with the scarlet fever that Charlie and I discovered that although in one way Molly's stones had let us down, in another way they had indeed spoken the truth: with her, with the three of us together, we *were* lucky, and without her we weren't. Up until now, whenever the three of us had gone out together poaching the Colonel's fish, we had never been caught. We'd had a few close shaves with old Lambert and his dog, but our lookout system had always worked. Somehow we'd always heard them coming and managed to make ourselves scarce. But the very first time Charlie and I went out poaching without Molly, things went wrong, badly wrong, and it was my fault.

We had chosen a perfect poaching night, not a breath of wind so we could hear anyone coming. With Molly beside me on lookout I'd never felt sleepy, and we'd always heard old Lambert and his dog in plenty of time for Charlie to get out of the river, for us all to make good our escape. But on this particular night my concentration failed me. I'd made myself comfortable, probably too comfortable, in our usual place by the bridge with Charlie netting downstream. But after sitting there for a while I just fell asleep. I don't drop off all that easily, but when I do sleep I sleep deeply.

The first I knew of anything was a dog snuffling at my neck. Then he was barking in my face, and old Lambert was dragging me to my feet. And there was Charlie way out in the middle of the moonlit river hauling at the nets.

"Peaceful boys! You young rascals," Lambert growled. "Caught you red-handed. You're for it now, make no mistake."

Charlie could have left me there. He could have made a run for it and got clean away, but Charlie's not like that. He never has been.

At the point of a shotgun Lambert marched us back along the river and up to the Big House, his dog snarling at our heels from time to time just to remind us he was still there, and that he'd eat us alive if we made a run for it. Lambert locked us in the stables and left us. We waited in the darkness, the horses shifting and munching and snorting around us. All too soon we saw the approaching light of a lamp, and heard footsteps and voices. Then the Colonel was there in his slippers and his dressing gown, and he had Grandma Wolf with him in her nightcap looking every bit as fierce as Lambert's dog.

The Colonel looked from one to the other of us, shaking his head in disgust. But Grandma Wolf had the first word. "I've never in all my life been so ashamed," she said. "My own family. You're nothing but a downright disgrace. And after all the Colonel's done for us. Common thieves, that's what you are. Nothing but common thieves."

When she'd finished it was the Colonel's turn. "Only one way to deal with young ruffians like you," he said. "I could have you up before the magistrate, but since I'm the magistrate anyway there's no need to go to all that trouble, is there? I'll sentence you right now. You will come up here tomorrow morning at ten o'clock sharp, and I'll give each of you the hiding you so richly deserve. Then you can stay and clean out the hunt kennels till I say you can go. That should teach you not to come poaching on my land."

When we got home we had to tell Mother everything we'd done, everything the Colonel had said. Charlie did most of the talking. Mother sat listening in silence, her face stony. When she spoke, she spoke in little more than a whisper. "I can tell you one thing," she said. "There'll be no hiding. Over my dead body." Then she looked up at us, her eyes full of tears. "Why? You said you'd been fishing in the brook. You told me. Oh Charlie, Tommo." Big Joe stroked her hair. He was anxious and bewildered. She patted his arm. "It's all right, Joe. I'll go up there with them tomorrow. Cleaning out the kennels I don't mind – you deserve that. But it stops there. I won't let that man lay a finger on you, not one finger, no matter what."

Mother was as good as her word. How she did it and what was said we never knew, but the next day after Mother and the Colonel had had a meeting in his study, she made us stand in front of him and apologise. Then after a long lecture about trespassing on private property, the Colonel said that he'd changed his mind, that instead of the hiding we would be set to cleaning out the Colonel's kennels every Saturday and Sunday until Christmas.

As it turned out we didn't mind at all because, although the smell could be disgusting, the hounds were all around us as we worked, their tails high and waving and happy. So we often stopped work to pet them, after we'd made quite sure no one was looking. We had a particular favourite called Bertha. She was almost pure white with one brown foot and had the most beautiful eyes. She would always stand near us as we scraped and swept, gazing up at us in open adoration. Every time I looked into her eyes I thought of Molly. Like Bertha, she too had eyes the colour of heather honey.

We had to be careful, because Grandma Wolf, now more full of herself than ever, would frequently come out into the stable yard to make sure we were doing our work properly. She'd always have something nasty to say: "Serves you right," or "That'll teach you," or "You should be ashamed of yourselves," always delivered with a tut and a pained sigh. To finish there'd be some nasty quip about Mother. "Still, with a mother like that, I suppose you're not entirely to blame, are you?"

Then Christmas Eve came and our punishment was over at last. We said fond farewells to Bertha and ran off home down the Colonel's drive for the last time, blowing very loud raspberries as we went. Back in the cottage we found waiting for us the best Christmas present we could ever have hoped for. Molly was sitting there smiling at us as we came in through the door. She was pale, but she was back with us. We were together again. Her hair was cut shorter. The plaits were gone, and somehow that changed the whole look of her. She wasn't a girl any more. She had a different beauty now, a beauty that at once stirred in me a new and deeper love.

I think, without knowing it, I had always charted my own growing up by constant comparison to Molly and Charlie. Day by day I was becoming ever more painfully aware of how far behind them I was. I wasn't just smaller and slower than they were – I had never liked that, but I was used to it by now. The trouble was that it was becoming evident to me that the gap between us was more serious, and that it was widening. It really began when Molly was moved up into the Bigguns' class. I was stuck being a Tiddler and they were growing away from me. But whilst we were still at the village school together I didn't mind all that much because at least I was always near them. We walked to school together, ate our lunch together as we always had – up in the pantry in the vicarage, where the vicar's wife would bring us lemonade – and then we'd come home together.

I looked forward all day to that long walk home, the school day done, their other friends not with us, with the fearsome Mr Munnings out of sight and out of mind for another day. We'd hare down the hill to the brook, pull off our great heavy boots and release our aching feet and toes at long last. We'd sit there on the bank wiggling our toes in the blessed cool of the water. We'd lie amongst the grass and buttercups of the water meadows and look up at the clouds scudding across the sky, at the wind-whipped crows chasing a mewing buzzard. Then we'd follow the brook home, feet squelching in the mud, our toes oozing with it. Strange when I think of it now, but there was a time when I loved mud, the smell of it, the feel of it, the larking about in it. Not any more.

Then quite suddenly, just after my twelfth birthday, the last of the larking was all over. Charlie and Molly left school and I was alone. I was a Biggun, in Mr Munnings' class and hating him now even more than I feared him. I woke up dreading every day. Both Charlie and Molly had found work up in the Big House – almost everyone in the village worked up there or on the estate. Molly was under-parlour maid, and Charlie worked in the hunt kennels and in the stables looking after the dogs and the horses, which he loved. Molly didn't come round to see us nearly so often as before – like Charlie, she worked six days a week. So I hardly saw her.

Charlie would come home late in the evenings as Father had before him, and he'd hang his coat up on Father's peg and put his boots outside in the porch where Father's boots had always been. He warmed his feet in the bottom oven when he came in out of the cold of a winter's day, just as Father had done. That was the first time in my life I was ever really jealous of Charlie. I wanted to put *my* feet in the oven, and to come home from proper work, to earn money like

Charlie did, to have a voice that didn't pipe like the little children in Miss McAllister's class. Most of all though I wanted to be with Molly again. I wanted us to be a threesome again, for everything to be just as it had been. But nothing stays the same. I learnt that then. I know that now.

At nights as Charlie and I lay in bed together Charlie just slept. We never made up our stories any more. When I did see Molly, and it was only on Sundays now, she was as kind to me as she always had been, but too kind almost, too protective, more like a little mother to me than a friend. I could see that she and Charlie lived in another world now. They talked endlessly about the goings on and scandals up at the Big House, about the prowling Wolfwoman — it was around this time they dropped the "Grandma Wolf" altogether and began to call her "Wolfwoman". That was when I first heard the gossip about the Colonel and the Wolfwoman. Charlie said they'd had a thing going for years — common knowledge. That was why the late "Mrs Colonel" had kicked her out all those years before. And now they were like husband and wife up there, only she wore the trousers. There was talk of the Colonel's dark moods, how he'd shut himself up in his study all day sometimes, and of Cook's tantrums whenever things were not done just so. It was a world I could not be part of, a world I did not belong in.

I tried all I could to interest them in my life at school. I told them about how we'd all heard Miss McAllister and Mr

Munnings having a blazing argument because he refused to light the school stove, how she'd called him a wicked, wicked man. She was right too. Mr Munnings would never light the stove unless the puddles were iced over in the school yard, unless our fingers were so cold we couldn't write. He shouted back at her that he would light the stove when he thought fit, and that anyway suffering was part of life and good for a child's soul. Charlie and Molly made out they were interested, but I could tell they weren't. Then one day down by the brook, I turned and saw them walking away from me through the water meadows holding hands. We'd all held hands before, often, but then it had been the three of us. I knew at once that this was different. As I watched them I felt a sudden ache in my heart. I don't think it was anger or jealousy, more a pang of loss, of deep grief.

We did have some moments when we became a threesome again, but they were becoming all too few and far between. I remember the day of the yellow aeroplane. It was the first aeroplane any of us had ever seen. We'd heard about them, seen pictures of them, but until that day I don't think I ever really believed they were real, that they actually flew. You had to see one to believe it. Molly and Charlie and I were fishing down in the brook, just for tiddlers, or brown trout if we were lucky – we'd done no more salmon poaching, Mother had made us promise.

It was late on a summer evening and we were just about

to set off home when we heard the distant sound of an engine. At first we thought it was the Colonel's car – his Rolls Royce was the only car for miles around – but then we all realised at the same moment that this was a different kind of engine altogether. It was a sound of intermittent droning, like a thousand stuttering bees. What's more, it wasn't coming from the road at all; it was coming from high above us. There was a flurry of squawking and splashing further upstream as a flight of ducks took off in a panic. We ran out from under the trees to get a better look. An aeroplane! We watched, spellbound, as it circled above us like some ungainly yellow bird, its great wide wings wobbling precariously. We could see the goggled pilot looking down at us out of the cockpit. We waved frantically up at him and he waved back. Then he was coming in lower, lower. The cows in the water meadow scattered. The aeroplane was coming in to land, bouncing, then bumping along and coming to a stop some fifty yards away from us.

The pilot didn't get out, but beckoned us over. We didn't hesitate. "Better not switch off!" he shouted over the roar of the engine. He was laughing as he lifted up his goggles. "Might never get the damn thing started again. Listen, the truth is I reckon I'm a bit lost. That church up there on the hill, is that Lapford church?"

"No," Charlie shouted back. "That's Iddesleigh. St. James."

The pilot looked down at his map. "Iddesleigh? You sure?"

"Yes," we shouted.

"Whoops! Then I really was lost. Jolly good thing I stopped, wasn't it? Thanks for your help. Better be off." He lowered his goggles and smiled at us. "Here. You like humbugs?" And he reached out and handed Charlie a bag of sweets. "Cheerio then," he said. "Stand well back. Here we go."

And with that, off he went bouncing along towards the hedge, his engine spluttering. I thought he couldn't possibly lift off in time. He managed it, but only just, his wheels clipping the top of the hedge, before he was up and away. He did one steep turn, then flew straight at us. There was no time to run. All we could do was throw ourselves face down in the long grass. We felt the sudden blast of the wind as he passed above us. By the time we rolled over he was climbing up over the trees and away. We could see him laughing and waving. We watched him soaring over Iddesleigh church tower and then away into the distance. He was gone, leaving us lying there breathless in the silence he'd left behind.

For some time afterwards we lay there in the long grass watching a single skylark rising above us, and sucking on our humbugs. When Charlie came to share them out we had five each, and five for Big Joe, too.

"Was that real?" Molly breathed. "Did it really happen?"

"We've got our humbugs," said Charlie, "so it must have been real, mustn't it?"

"Every time I eat humbugs from now on," Molly said, "every time I look at skylarks, I'm going to think of that yellow aeroplane, and the three of us, and how we are right now."

"Me too," I said.

"Me too," said Charlie.

Most people in the village had seen the aeroplane, but only we three had been there when it landed, only we had talked to the pilot. I was so proud of that – too proud as it turned out. I told the story, several embellished versions of it, again and again at school, showing everyone my humbugs just to prove all I'd said was true. But someone must have snitched on me, because Mr Munnings came straight over to me in class and, for no reason at all, told me to empty out my pockets. I had three of my precious humbugs left and he confiscated them all. Then he took me by the ear to the front of the class where he gave me six strokes of the ruler in his own very special way, sharp edge down on to my knuckles. As he did it I looked him in the eye and stared him out. It didn't dull the pain, nor I'm sure did it make him feel bad about what he was doing, but my sullen defiance of him made me feel a lot better as I walked back to my desk.

As I lay in bed that night, my knuckles still throbbing, I was longing to tell Charlie about what had happened at school, but I knew that everything about school bored him now, so I said nothing. But the longer I lay there thinking about my knuckles and my humbugs the more I was bursting to talk to him. I could hear from his breathing that he was still awake. For just a moment it occurred to me this might be the time to tell him about Father, and how I'd killed him in the forest all those years before. That at least would interest him. I did try, but I still could not summon up the courage to tell him. In the end all I told him was that Mr Munnings had confiscated my humbugs. "I hate him," I said. "I hope he chokes on them." Even as I was speaking I could tell he wasn't listening.

"Tommo," he whispered, "I'm in trouble."

"What've you done?" I asked him.

"I'm in real trouble, but I had to do it. You remember Bertha, that whitey-looking foxhound up at the Big House, the one we liked?"

"Course," I said.

"Well, she's always been my favourite ever since. And then this afternoon the Colonel comes by the kennels and tells me... he tells me he's going to have to shoot Bertha. So I ask him why. Because she's getting a bit old, a bit slow, he says. Because whenever they go out hunting she's always going off on her own and getting herself lost. She's no use for hunting any more, he says, no use to anyone. I asked him not to, Tommo. I told him she was my favourite. 'Favourite!' he says, laughing at me. 'Favourite? How can you have a favourite? Lot of sentimental claptrap. She's just one of a pack of dumb beasts, boy, and don't you forget it.' I begged him, Tommo. I told him he shouldn't do it. That's when he got really angry. He said they're his foxhounds and he'd shoot them as and when he felt like it, and he didn't want any more lip from me about it. So you know what I did, Tommo? I stole her. I ran off with her after dark, through the trees so no one would see us."

"Where is she now?" I asked. "What've you done with her?"

"Remember that old forester's shack Father used, up in Ford's Cleave Wood? I've put her in there for the night. I gave her some food. Molly pinched some meat for me from the kitchen. She'll be all right up there. No one'll hear her, with a bit of luck anyway."

"But what'll you do with her tomorrow? What if the Colonel finds out?"

"I don't know, Tommo," Charlie said. "I don't know."

We hardly slept a wink that night. I lay there listening out for Bertha all the while. When I did drop off, I kept waking up suddenly thinking I had heard Bertha barking. But always it turned out to be a screeching fox. And once it was an owl hooting, right outside our window.

TWENTY-FOUR MINUTES PAST TWELVE

I haven't seen a fox while I've been out here. It's hardly surprising, I suppose. But I have heard owls. How any bird can survive in all this I'll never know. I've even seen larks over no-man's-land. I always found hope in that.

"He'll know," Charlie whispered to me in bed at dawn. "As soon as they find Bertha gone, the Colonel will know it was me. I won't tell him where she is. I don't care what he does, I won't tell him."

Charlie and I ate our breakfast in silence, hoping the inevitable storm wouldn't break, but knowing that sooner or later it must. Big Joe sensed something was wrong – he could always feel anxiety in the air. He was rocking back and forth and wouldn't touch his breakfast. So then Mother knew something was up as well. Once she was suspicious Mother was a difficult person to hide things from, and we weren't very good at it, not that morning.

"Is Molly coming over?" she asked, beginning to probe.

There was a loud and insistent knocking on the door. She could tell at once it wouldn't be Molly. It was too early for

Molly, and anyway she didn't knock like that. Besides, I think she could already see from our faces that Charlie and I were expecting an unwelcome visitor. As we feared, it was the Colonel.

Mother invited him in. He stood there glaring at us, thin-lipped and pale with fury. "I think you know why I've come, Mrs Peaceful," he began.

"No, Colonel, I don't," said Mother.

"So the young devil hasn't told you." He was shouting now, shaking his stick at Charlie. Big Joe began to whimper and clutched Mother's hand as the Colonel ranted on.

"That boy of yours is a despicable thief. First of all he steals the salmon out of my river. And now, in my employ, in a position of trust, he steals one of my foxhounds. Don't deny it, boy. I know it was you. Where is she? Is she here? Is she?"

Mother looked to Charlie for an explanation.

"He was going to shoot her, Mother," he said quickly. "I had to do it."

"You see!" roared the Colonel. "He admits it! He admits it!"

Big Joe was beginning to wail now and Mother was smoothing his hair, trying to reassure and comfort him as she spoke. "So you took her in order to save her, Charlie, is that right?"

"Yes, Mother."

"Well, you shouldn't have done that, Charlie, should you?"

"No, Mother."

"Will you tell the Colonel where you've hidden her?"

"No, Mother."

Mother thought for a moment or two. "I didn't think so," she said. She looked the Colonel full in the face. "Colonel, am I right in thinking that if you were going to shoot this dog, presumably it was because she's no use to you any more – as a foxhound I mean?"

"Yes," the Colonel replied, "but what I do with my own animals, or why I do it, is no business of yours, Mrs Peaceful. I don't have to explain myself to you."

"Of course not, Colonel," Mother spoke softly, sweetly almost, "but if you were going to shoot her anyway, then you wouldn't mind if I were to take her off your hands and look after her, would you?"

"You can do what you like with the damned dog," the Colonel snapped. "You can bloody well eat her for all I care. But your son stole her from me and I will not let that go unpunished."

Mother asked Big Joe to fetch the money mug from the mantelpiece. "Here, Colonel," she said, calmly offering him a coin from the money mug. "Sixpence. I'm buying the dog off you for sixpence, not a bad price for a useless dog. So now it's not stolen, is it?"

The Colonel was utterly dumbfounded. He looked from the coin in his hand to Mother, to Charlie. He was breathing hard. Then, regaining his composure, he pocketed the sixpence in his waistcoat and pointed his stick at Charlie. "Very well, but you can consider yourself no longer in my employ." With that he turned on his heel and went out, slamming the door behind him. We listened to his footsteps going down the path, heard the front gate squeaking.

Charlie and I went mad, mostly out of sheer relief, but also quite overwhelmed with gratitude and admiration. What a mother we had! We whooped and yahooed. Big Joe was happy again, and sang *Oranges and Lemons* as he gambolled wildly round the kitchen.

"I don't know what you've got to be so almightily pleased about," said Mother when we had all calmed down. "You do know you've just lost your job, Charlie?"

"I don't care," said Charlie. "He can stuff his stinking job. I'll find another. You put the silly old fart in his place good and proper. And we've got Bertha."

"Where is that dog anyway?" Mother asked.

"I'll show you," Charlie said.

We waited for Molly to come and then we all went off up to Ford's Cleave Wood together. As we neared the shack, we could hear Bertha yowling. Charlie ran on ahead and opened the door. Out she came, bounding up to us, squeaking with delight, her tail swiping at our legs. She jumped up at all of us, licking everything she could, but right away she seemed to attach herself particularly to Big

Joe. She followed him everywhere after that. She even slept on his bed at nights – Big Joe insisted on that no matter how much Mother protested. She'd sit under his apple tree howling up at him while he sang to her from high up in the branches. He only had to start singing and she'd join in, so from now on he never sang his *Oranges and Lemons* unaccompanied. He never did anything unaccompanied. They were always together. He fed her, brushed her and cleared up her frequent puddles (which were more like lakes). Big Joe had found a new friend and he was in seventh heaven.

After a few weeks going round all the farms in the parish looking for work, Charlie found a job as dairyman and shepherd at Farmer Cox's place on the other side of the village. He would go off before dawn on his bicycle to do the milking and was back home late, so I saw even less of him than before. He should have been much happier up there. He liked the cows and the sheep, though he said that the sheep were a bit stupid. Best of all, he said, he didn't have the Colonel or the Wolfwoman breathing down his neck all day.

But Charlie, like me, was very far from happy, because Molly had suddenly stopped coming. Mother said she was sure there could only be one reason. Someone must have put it about – and she thought it could only be the Colonel or the Wolfwoman or both – that Charlie Peaceful was a thieving rascal, and that therefore the Peaceful family were no longer considered fit folk for Molly to visit. She said Charlie should just let things cool down for a while, that Molly would be back. But Charlie wouldn't listen. Time after time he went to Molly's cottage. They wouldn't even answer the door. In the end, because he thought I'd have a better chance of getting to see Molly, he sent me over with a letter. Somehow, he said, I had to deliver it to her. I had to.

Molly's mother met me at the door with a face like thunder. "Go away," she yelled at me. "Just go away. Don't you understand? We don't want your kind here. We don't want you bothering our Molly. She doesn't want to see you." And with that she slammed the door in my face. I was walking away, Charlie's letter still in my pocket, when I happened to glance back and saw Molly waving at me frantically through her window. She was mouthing something I couldn't understand at all at first, gesticulating at me, pointing down the hill towards the brook. I knew then exactly what she meant me to do.

I ran down to the brook and waited under the trees where we'd always done our fishing together. I didn't have long to wait before she came. She took my hand without a word, and led me down under the bank where we couldn't possibly be seen. She was crying as she told me everything: how the Colonel had come to the cottage – she'd overheard it all – how he'd told her father that Charlie Peaceful was a thief; how he'd heard Charlie Peaceful had been seeing much more of Molly than was good for her, and that if he had any sense Molly's father should put a stop to it. "So my father won't let me see Charlie any more. He won't let me see any of you," Molly told me, brushing away her tears. "I'm so miserable without you, Tommo. I hate it up at the Big House without Charlie, and I hate it at home too. Father'll strap me if I see Charlie. And he said he'll take a gun to Charlie if he ever comes near me. I think he means it too."

"Why?" I asked. "Why's he like that?"

"He's always been like that," she said. "He says I'm wicked. Born in sin. Mother says he's only trying to save me from myself, so I won't go to Hell. He's always talking about Hell. I won't got to Hell, will I, Tommo?"

I did what I did next without thinking. I leant over and kissed her on the cheek. She threw her arms around my neck, sobbing as if her heart would break. "I so want to see Charlie," she cried. "I miss him so much." That was when I remembered to give her the letter. She tore it open and read it at once. It can't have been long because she read it so quickly. "Tell him yes. Yes, I will," she said, her eyes suddenly bright again.

"Just yes?" I asked, intrigued, puzzled and jealous all at the same time.

"Yes. Same time, same place, tomorrow. I'll write a letter back and you can give it to Charlie. All right?" She got up and pulled me to my feet. "I love you, Tommo. I love you both. And Big Joe, and Bertha." She kissed me quickly and was gone.

That was the first of dozens of letters I delivered from Charlie to Molly and from Molly to Charlie over the weeks and months that followed. All through my last year at school I was their go-between postman. I didn't mind that much, because it meant I got to see Molly often, which was all that really mattered to me. It was all done in great secrecy - Charlie insisted on that. He made me swear on the Holy Bible to tell no one, not even Mother. He made me cross my heart and hope to die.

Molly and I would meet most evenings and exchange letters in the same place, down by the brook, both of us having made quite sure we were not followed. We'd sit and talk there for a few precious minutes, often with the rain dripping through the trees, and once I remember with the wind roaring about us so violently that I thought the trees might come down on us. Fearing for our lives, we ran out across the meadow and burrowed our way into the bottom of a haystack and sat there shivering like a couple of frightened rabbits.

It was in the shelter of this haystack that I first heard news of the war. When Molly talked it was often, if not always, about Charlie – she'd forever be asking news of him. I never showed her I minded, but I did. So I was quite pleased that day when she started telling me about how all the talk up at the Big House these days was of war with Germany, how everyone now thought it would happen sooner rather than later. She'd read about it herself in the newspaper, so she knew it had to be true.

It was Molly's job every morning, she told me, to iron the Colonel's *Times* newspaper before she took it to him in his study. Apparently he insisted his newspaper should be crisp and dry, so that the ink should not come off on his fingers while he was reading it. She didn't really understand what the war was all about, she admitted, only that some archduke – whatever that was – had been shot in a place called Sarajevo – wherever that was – and Germany and France were very angry with each other about it. They were gathering their armies to fight with each other and, if they did, then we'd be in it soon because we'd have to fight on the French side against the Germans. She didn't know why. It made about as much sense to me as it did to her. She said the Colonel was in a terrible mood about it all, and that everyone up at the Big House was much more frightened of his moods than they were about the war.

But apparently the Colonel was gentle as a lamb compared to the Wolfwoman these days (everyone called her that now, not just us). It seemed that someone had put salt in her tea instead of sugar and she swore it was on purpose – which it probably was, Molly said. She'd been ranting and raving about it ever since, telling everyone how she'd find out who it was. Meanwhile she was treating all of them as if they were guilty.

"Was it you?" I asked Molly.

"Maybe," she said, smiling, "and maybe not." I wanted to kiss her again then, but I didn't dare. That has always been my trouble. I've never dared enough.

Mother had it all arranged before I left school. I was to go and work with Charlie up at Mr Cox's farm. Farmer Cox was getting on in years and, with no sons of his own, was in need of more help on the farm. He was a bit keen on the drink too, Charlie said. It was true. He was in the pub most evenings. He liked his beer and his skittles, and he liked to sing, too. He knew all the old songs. He kept them in his head, but he'd only sing if he'd had a couple of beers. So he never sang on the farm. He was always rather dour on the farm, but fair, always fair.

I went up there mostly to look after the horses at first. For me it couldn't have been better. I was with Charlie again, working alongside him on the farm. I'd put on a spurt and was almost as tall as him by now, but still not as fast, nor as strong. He was a bit bossy with me sometimes, but that didn't bother me – that was his job after all. Things were changing between us. Charlie didn't treat me like a boy any more, and I liked that, I liked that a lot.

The newspapers were full of the war that had now begun, but aside from the army coming to the village and buying up lots of the local farm horses for cavalry horses, it had hardly touched us at all. Not yet. I was still Charlie's postman, still Molly's postman. So I saw Molly often, though not as often as before. For some reason the letters between them seemed less frequent. But at least with me now working with Charlie for six days a week we were all three together again in a kind of way, linked by the letters. Then that link was cruelly broken, and what followed broke my heart, broke all our hearts.

I remember Charlie and I had been haymaking with Farmer Cox, young buzzards wheeling above us all day, swallows skimming the mown grass all about us as the shadows lengthened and the evening darkened. We arrived home later than usual, dusty and exhausted, and hungry, too. Inside we found Mother sitting upright in her chair doing her sewing and opposite her Molly and, to our surprise, her mother. Everyone in the room looked as grim-faced as Molly's mother, even Big Joe, even Molly whose eyes I could see were red from crying. Bertha was howling ominously from outside in the woodshed.

"Charlie," said Mother, setting her sewing aside. "Molly's mother has been waiting for you. She has something she wants to say to you."

"Yours, I believe," said Molly's mother, her voice as hard as stone. She handed Charlie a packet of letters tied up with a blue ribbon. "I found them. I've read them, every one of them. So has Molly's father. So we know, we know everything. Don't bother to deny it, Charlie Peaceful. The evidence is here, in these letters. Molly has been punished already, her father has seen to that. I've never read anything so wicked in all my life. Never. All that love talk. Disgusting. But you've been meeting as well, haven't you?"

Charlie looked across at Molly. The look between them said it all, and I knew then that I had been betrayed.

"Yes," said Charlie.

I couldn't believe what he was saying. They hadn't told me. They'd been meeting in secret and neither of them had told me.

"There. Didn't I tell you, Mrs Peaceful?" Molly's mother went on, her voice quivering with rage.

"I'm sorry," said Mother. "But you'll still have to tell me why it is they shouldn't be meeting. Charlie's seventeen now, and Molly sixteen. Old enough, I'd say. I'm sure we both had our little rendezvous here and there when we were their age."

"You speak for yourself, Mrs Peaceful," Molly's mother replied with a supercilious sneer. "Molly's father and I made it quite plain to both of them. We forbade them to have anything to do with each other. It's wickedness, Mrs Peaceful, pure wickedness. The Colonel has warned us, you know, about your son's wicked thieving ways. Oh yes, we know all about him."

"Really?" said Mother. "Tell me, do you always do what the Colonel says? Do you always think what the Colonel thinks? If he said the earth was flat, would you believe him? Or did he just threaten you? He's good at that."

Molly's mother stood up, full of righteous indignation. "I haven't come here to argue the toss. I have come to tell of your son's misdemeanours, to say that I won't have him leading our Molly into the ways of wickedness and sin. He must never see her again, do you hear? If he does, then the Colonel will know about it. I'm telling you the Colonel will know about it. I have no more to say. Come along, Molly." And taking Molly's hand firmly in hers she swept out, leaving us all looking at one another and listening to Bertha still howling.

"Well," said Mother after a while. "I'll get your supper, boys, shall I?"

That night I lay there beside Charlie not speaking. I was so filled with anger and resentment towards him that I never wanted to speak to him again, nor to Molly come to that. Then out of our silence he said: "All right, I should've told you, Tommo. Molly said I should tell you. But I didn't want to. I couldn't, that's all."

"Why not?" I asked. For several moments he did not reply.

"Because I know, and she does too. That's why she wouldn't tell you herself," Charlie said.

"Know what?"

"When it was just letters, it didn't seem to matter so much. But later, after we began seeing each other... we didn't want to hide it from you, Tommo, honest. But we didn't want to hurt you either. You love her, don't you?" I didn't answer. There was no need. "Well, so do I, Tommo. So you'll understand why I'm going to go on seeing her. I'll find a way no matter what that old cow says." He turned to me. "Still friends?" he said.

"Friends," I mumbled, but I did not mean it.

After that no more was ever said between us about Molly. I never asked because I didn't want to know. I didn't want even to think about it, but I did. I thought about nothing else.

No one could understand why, but shortly after this Bertha began to go missing from time to time. She hadn't wandered off at all until now; she'd always stuck close to Big Joe. Wherever Big Joe was, that's where you'd be sure to find Bertha. Big Joe was frantic with worry every time she went off. She'd come back home in the end of course, when she felt like it, either that or Mother and Joe would find her somewhere all muddied and wet and lost, and they'd bring her home. But the great worry was that she'd start chasing after sheep or cows, that some farmer or landowner would shoot her, as they'd shoot any dog they found trespassing on their land that could be molesting their animals. Fortunately

Bertha didn't seem to go chasing sheep, and anyway up until now she had never been gone that long, nor strayed too far.

We did our very best to keep her from wandering. Mother tried shutting her in the woodshed, but Big Joe couldn't stand her howling and would let her out. She tried tying her up, but Bertha would chew at the rope and whine incessantly so that in the end Big Joe would always take pity and go and untie her.

Then, one afternoon, Bertha went missing again. This time she did not come back. This time we could not find her. Charlie wasn't about. Mother and Big Joe went one way looking for her, down towards the river, and I went up into the woods, whistling for her, calling for her. There were deer to be found up in Ford's Cleave Wood, and badgers and foxes. It would be just the sort of place she'd go. I'd been an hour or more searching in the woods with not a sign of her. I was about to give up and go back – perhaps she'd gone home anyway by now, I thought – when I heard a shot ringing out across the valley. It came from somewhere higher in the woods. I ran up the track, ducking the low slung branches, leaping the badger holes, dreading, but already knowing what I would find.

As I came up the rise I could see ahead of me the chimney of Father's old shack, and then the shack itself at the side of the clearing. Outside lay Bertha, her tongue lolling, the grass beside her soaked with blood. The Colonel stood looking down at her, his shotgun in his hands. The door of the shack opened and Charlie and Molly were standing there frozen in disbelief and horror. Then Molly ran over to where Bertha lay and fell to her knees.

"Why?" she cried, looking up at the Colonel. "Why?"

NEARLY FIVE TO ONE

There's a sliver of a moon out there, a new moon. I wonder if they're looking at it back home. Bertha used to howl at the moon, I remember. If I had a coin in my pocket, I'd turn it over and make a wish. When I was young I really believed in all those old tales. I wish I still could believe in them.

But I mustn't think like that. It's no good wishing for the moon, no good wishing for the impossible. Don't wish, Tommo. Remember. Remembrances are real.

We buried Bertha the same day, where Big Joe always buried his creatures, where the mouse had been buried, at the bottom of the orchard. But this time we said no prayers. We laid no flowers. We sang no hymns. Somehow none of us had the heart for it. Perhaps we were all too angry to grieve. Walking back through the trees afterwards, Big Joe was pointing upwards and asking Mother if Bertha was up in Heaven now with Father. Mother said that she was. Then Big Joe asked if we all go up to Heaven after we die.

"Not the Colonel," Charlie muttered. "He'll go

downstairs where he belongs, where he'll burn." Mother darted a reproving glance at him for that.

"Yes, Joe," she went on, her arm around him. "Bertha's up in Heaven. She's happy now."

That evening Big Joe went missing. None of us was that worried, not at first, not while it was still light. Big Joe would often go wandering off on his own from time to time – he'd always done that – but never at night, because Big Joe was frightened of the dark. Our first thought was to look down in the orchard by Bertha's grave, but he wasn't there. We called, but he didn't come. So, as darkness fell and he still had not come home, we knew there was something wrong. Mother sent Charlie and me out in different directions. I went down the lane calling for him all the way. I went as far as the brook where I stood and listened for him, for his heavy stomping tread, for his singing. He sang differently when he was frightened, no tunes or songs, but instead a continuous wailing drone. But there was no drone to be heard, only the running of the brook, which always sounded louder at night. I knew Big Joe must be very frightened for it was by now quite dark. I made my way home, hoping against hope that either Charlie or Mother might have found him.

As I came into the house I could see neither of them had. They looked up hopefully at me as I came in. I shook my head. Out of the silence that followed Mother made up her mind what had to be done. We didn't have any choice, she said. All that mattered was finding Big Joe, and for that we needed more people. She would go up to the Big House right away to ask for the Colonel's help. She sent Charlie and me up to the village to raise the alarm. We knew the best place to go was the pub, that half the village would be in The Duke in the evening. They were singing when we got there, Farmer Cox in full voice. The hubbub and the singing took a while to die down as Charlie told them. By the time he had finished they were all listening in absolute silence. Afterwards, not one of them hesitated. They were putting on hats, shrugging on coats and heading homewards to search their farms, gardens and sheds. The vicar said he'd gather everyone he could in the village hall to organise a search around the village itself, and it was agreed the sounding of the church bell would be the signal that Big Joe had been found.

As everyone dispersed into the darkness outside The Duke, Molly came running up. She had just heard the news about Big Joe. It was her idea that he could be somewhere in the churchyard. I don't know why we hadn't thought of it before – it was always one of his favourite places. So the three of us made for the churchyard. We called for him. We looked behind every gravestone, up every tree. He was nowhere. All we heard was the wind sighing in the yew trees. All we saw were lights dancing through the village, down along the valley. Beyond, and as far as the dark horizon, the countryside was filled with pinpricks of moving lights. We knew then that Mother must have persuaded the Colonel to mobilise everyone on the estate to join in the search.

By dawn there was still no word of Big Joe, still no sign of him. The Colonel had called in the police, and as time passed everything was pointing towards the same dreadful conclusion. We saw the police searching the ponds and river banks with long poles – everyone knew Big Joe could not swim. That was when I first began to believe that the worst could really have happened. No one dared to voice this fear, but all of us were beginning to feel it, and we felt it in each other too. We were searching over ground we had already searched several times. All other explanations for Big Joe's disappearance were being discounted one by one. If he had fallen asleep somewhere, surely he must have woken up by now. If he'd gone and got himself lost, surely, with all the hundreds of people out looking, someone would have found him by now. Everyone I met was grey and grim-faced. All tried their best to raise a smile, but no one could look me in the eye. I could see it wasn't just fear any more. It was worse. There was desperation in those faces, a feeling of complete hopelessness that they could not disguise however hard they tried.

Round about noon, thinking it was just possible Big Joe might somehow have found his way home on his own, we went back to check. We found Mother sitting there alone, clutching the arms of her chair and staring ahead of her. Charlie and I tried to raise her spirits, tried to reassure her as best we could. I don't think we were at all convincing. Charlie made her a cup of tea but Mother would not touch it. Molly sat at her feet and laid her head in her lap. A ghost of a smile came to Mother's face then. Molly could give comfort where we could give none.

Charlie and I left them there together and went outside into the garden. Clinging to what little hope we had left we tried to go back in time, to work out what might have been in Big Joe's mind to make him go off like that. Perhaps it could help us to discover where he had gone if we understood why he had gone. Was he looking for something perhaps, something he'd lost? But what? Had he gone off to see someone? If so, who? There was little doubt in our minds that his sudden disappearance was in some way connected to Bertha's death. The day before, both Charlie and I had felt like going up to the Big House and killing the Colonel for what he had done. Maybe, we thought, maybe Big Joe was feeling the same. Perhaps he had gone out to avenge Bertha's death. Perhaps he was skulking up at the Big House, in the attics, in the cellars, just waiting for his opportunity to strike. But we realised, even as we voiced them, that all such ideas were nothing but ridiculous nonsense. Big Joe didn't have it in him even to think of doing such a thing. He had never in his life been angry at anyone, not even the Wolfwoman – and after all, she'd given him reason enough and plenty. He could be hurt very easily, but he was never angry, and certainly never violent. Time and again Charlie and I would come up with a new scenario, and a different reason for Big Joe's disappearance. But in the end we had to dismiss every one of them as fanciful.

Then we saw Molly come down the garden towards us. "I was just wondering," she said, "I was wondering where Big Joe would most want to be."

"What d'you mean?" Charlie asked.

"Well, I think he'd want to be wherever Bertha is. So he'd want to be in Heaven, wouldn't he? I mean, he thinks Bertha's up in Heaven, doesn't he? I heard your mother telling him. So if he wanted to be with Bertha, then he'd have to go up to Heaven, wouldn't he?"

I thought for one terrible moment that Molly was suggesting that Big Joe had killed himself so that he could go up to Heaven and be with Bertha. I didn't want to believe it, but it made a kind of dreadful sense. Then she explained.

"He told me once," Molly went on, "that your father was up in Heaven and could still see us easily from where he was. He was pointing upwards, I remember, and I didn't understand exactly what he was trying to tell me, not at first. I thought he was just pointing up at the sky in a general sort of a way, or at the birds maybe. But then he took my hand and made me point with him, to show me. We were pointing up at the church, at the top of the church tower. It sounds silly, but I think Big Joe believes that Heaven is at the top of the church tower. Has anyone looked up there?"

Even as she was speaking I remembered how Big Joe had pointed up the church tower the day we had buried Father, how he'd looked back up at it over his shoulder as he walked away.

"You coming, Tommo?" said Charlie. "Moll, will you stay with Mother? We'll ring the bell if it's good news." We ran down through the orchard, scrambled through a hole in the hedge and set off across the fields towards the brook – it would be the quickest way up to the village. We splashed through the brook and raced across the water meadows and up the hill towards the church. Trying to keep up with Charlie was difficult. I kept looking up at the church tower as I ran, all the while urging my legs to keep going, to take me faster, all the while praying that Big Joe would be up there in his heaven.

Charlie reached the village before I did and was haring up the church path ahead of me when he slipped on the cobbles and fell heavily. He sat there cursing and clutching his leg until I caught up with him. Then he called, and I called, "Joe! Joe! Are you up there?" There was no reply.

"You go, Tommo," said Charlie, grimacing in agony. "I

think I've done my ankle in." I opened the church door and walked into the silent dark of the church. I brushed past the bell ropes, and eased open the little belfry door. I could hear Charlie shouting, "Is he up there? Is he there?" I didn't answer. I began to climb the winding stairs. I'd been up into the belfry before, a while ago, when I was in Sunday school. I'd even sung up there in the choir one Ascension Day dawn, when I was little.

I dreaded those steps then and I hated them again now. The slit windows let in only occasional light. The walls were slimy about me, and the stairs uneven and slippery. The cold and the damp and the dark closed in on me and chilled me as I felt my way onwards and upwards. As I passed the silent hanging bells I hoped with all my heart that one of them would be ringing soon. Ninety-five steps I knew there were. With every step I was longing to reach the top, to breathe the bright air again, longing to find Big Joe.

The door to the tower was stiff and would not open. I pushed it hard, too hard, and it flew open, the wind catching it suddenly. I stepped out into the welcome warmth of day, dazzled by the light. At first glance I could see nothing. But then there he was. Big Joe was lying curled up under the shade of the parapet. He seemed fast asleep, his thumb in his mouth as usual. I didn't want to wake him too suddenly. When I touched his hand he did not wake. When I shook him gently by the shoulder he did not move. He was cold to my touch, and pale, deathly pale. I couldn't tell if he was breathing or not, and Charlie was calling up at me from below. I shook him again, hard this time, and screamed at him in my fear and panic. "Wake up, Joe. For God's sake, wake up!" I knew then that he wouldn't, that he'd come up here to die. He knew you had to die to go to Heaven, and Heaven was where he wanted to be, to be with Bertha again, with Father too.

When he stirred a moment later, I could hardly believe it. He opened his eyes. He smiled. "Ha, Tommo," he said. "Ungwee. Ungwee." They were the most beautiful words I'd ever heard. I sprang to my feet and leaned out over the parapet. Charlie was down there on the church path looking up at me.

"We've found him, Charlie," I called down. "We've got him. He's up here. He's all right."

Charlie punched the air and yahooed again and again. He yahooed even louder when he saw Big Joe standing beside me and waving. "Charie!" he cried. "Charie!"

Charlie hopped and limped into the church, and only moments later the great tenor bell rang out over the village, scattering the roosting pigeons from the tower, and sending them wheeling out over the houses, over the fields. Like the pigeons, Big Joe and I were shocked at the violence of the sound. It blasted our ears, sent a tremor through the tower that we felt through the soles of our feet. Alarmed at all this thunderous clanging, Big Joe looked suddenly anxious, his hands clapped over his ears. But when he saw me laughing, he did the same. Then he hugged me, hugged me so tight I thought he was squeezing me half to death. And when he began singing his *Oranges and Lemons*, I joined in, crying and singing at the same time.

I wanted him to come down with me, but Big Joe wanted to stay. He wanted to wave at everyone from the parapet. People were coming from all over: Mr Munnings, Miss McAllister and all the children were streaming out through the school yard and up towards the church. We saw the Colonel, coming down the road in his car, and could just make out the Wolfwoman's bonnet beside him. Best of all we saw Mother and Molly on bicycles racing up the hill, waving at us. Still Charlie rang the bell and I could hear him yahooing down below between each dong, and imagined him hanging on to the rope and riding with it up in the air. Still Big Joe sang his song. And the swifts soared and swooped and screamed all around us, in the sheer joy of being alive, and celebrating, it seemed to me, that Big Joe was alive too.

TWENTY-EIGHT MINUTES PAST ONE

I was once told in Sunday school that a church tower reaches up skywards because it is a promise of Heaven. Church towers are different in France. It was the first thing I noticed when I came here, when I changed my world of home for my world of war. In comparison the church towers at home seem almost squat, hiding themselves away in the folds of the fields. Here there are no folds in the fields, only wide open plains, scarcely a hill in sight. And instead of church towers they have spires that thrust themselves skywards like a child putting his hand up in class, longing to be noticed. But God, if there is one, notices nothing here. He has long since abandoned this place and all of us who live in it. There are not many steeples left now. I have seen the one in Albert, hanging down like a broken promise.

Now I come to think of it, it was a broken promise that brought me here, to France, and now to this barn. The mouse is back again. That's good.

There was a brief time just after we'd found Big Joe when all old hurts and grudges seemed suddenly to be forgiven and forgotten. Forgotten too was all talk of the war in France. No one spoke of anything that day except our search for Big Joe and its happy outcome. Even the Colonel and the Wolfwoman were celebrating with the rest of us up in The Duke. Molly's mother and father were there too, celebrating with everyone else, and smiling – though being strict chapel people, they didn't touch a drop of drink. I'd never seen Molly's mother smile before that. And then the Colonel announced that he was paying for all the drinks. It wasn't long – it only took a couple of pints – before Farmer Cox began singing. He was still singing when we left; some of the songs were getting a bit rude by then. I was there outside The Duke when Mother went up and thanked the Colonel for his help. He offered us all a lift home in his Rolls Royce! The Peacefuls in the back of the Colonel's car, and the Wolfwoman in the front, being friendly! We couldn't believe it, not after all the bad blood between us over the years.

The Colonel broke the spell on the way home, talking about the war, and how the army should be using more cavalry over in France.

"Horses and guns," he said, "in that order. That's how we beat the Boers in South Africa. That's what they should be doing. If I were younger, I'd go myself. They'll soon be needing every horse they can find, Mrs Peaceful, and every man, too. It's not going at all well out there."

Mother thanked him again as he helped us out of the car outside our gate. The Colonel touched his hat and smiled. "Don't you go running off again, young man," he said to Big Joe. "You gave us all a terrible fright." And even the Wolfwoman waved at us almost cheerily as they drove off.

That night Big Joe began coughing. He'd caught a chill and it had gone to his lungs. He was in bed with a fever for weeks afterwards, and Mother hardly left his side, she was so worried.

By the time he was better, the whole episode of his disappearance had been forgotten, overtaken by news in the papers of a great and terrible battle on the Marne, where our armies were fighting the Germans to a standstill, trying desperately to halt their advance through France.

One evening, Charlie and I arrived home from work a little late, having stopped on the way for a drink at The Duke as we often did. In those days, I remember, I had to pretend I liked the beer. The truth was I hated the stuff, but I loved the company. Charlie might have bossed me about on the farm, but after work, up at The Duke, he never treated me like the fifteen-year-old I was, though some of the others did. I couldn't have them knowing that I hated beer. So I'd force down a couple of pints with Charlie, and often left The Duke a little befuddled in the head. That was why I was woozy when we came home that evening. When I opened the door and saw Molly, sitting there on the floor with her head on Mother's lap, it seemed I was suddenly back to the day Big Joe had gone missing. Molly looked up at us, and I could see that she had been crying, and that this time it was Mother doing the comforting.

"What is it?" Charlie asked. "What's happened?"

"You may well ask, Charlie Peaceful," Mother said. She didn't sound at all pleased to see us. I wondered at first if she had seen we'd been drinking. Then I noticed a leather suitcase under the windowsill, and Molly's coat over the back of Father's fireside chair.

"Molly's come to stay," Mother went on. "They've thrown her out, Charlie. Her mother and father have thrown her out, and it's your fault."

"No!" Molly cried. "Don't say that. It isn't his fault. It's no one's fault." She ran over to Charlie and threw herself into his arms.

"What's happened, Moll?" asked Charlie. "What's going on?"

Molly was shaking her head as she wept uncontrollably now on his shoulder. He looked at Mother.

"What's going on, Charlie, is that she's going to have your baby," she said. "They packed her case, put her out of the door and told her never to come back. They never want to see her again. She had nowhere else to go, Charlie. I said she was family, that she belongs with us now, that she can stay as long as she likes."

It seemed an age before Charlie said anything. I saw his face go through all manner of emotions: incomprehension, bewilderment, outrage, through all these at once, and then at last to resolve. He held Molly away from him now and brushed away her tears with his thumb as he looked steadily into her eyes. When he spoke at last, it wasn't to Molly, but to Mother. "You shouldn't have said that to Moll, Mother," he spoke slowly, almost sternly. Then he began to smile. "That was for me to say. It's our baby, my baby, and Moll's my girl. So I should have said it. But I'm glad you said it all the same."

After that Molly became even more one of us than she had been before. I was both overjoyed and miserable at the same time. Molly and Charlie knew how I must have felt, I think, but they never spoke of it and neither did I.

They were married up in the church a short time later. It was a very empty church. There was no one there except the vicar and the four of us, and the vicar's wife sitting at the back. Everyone knew about Molly's baby by now, and because of that the vicar had agreed to marry them only on certain conditions: that no bells were to be rung and no hymns to be sung. He rushed through the marriage service as if he wanted to be somewhere else. There was no wedding feast afterwards, only a cup of tea and some fruit cake when we got home.

Shortly afterwards, Mother received a letter from the Wolfwoman saying it had been a marriage of shame; how she had thought of dismissing Molly and only decided against it because, whilst Molly was clearly a weak and immoral girl, she felt she could not in all conscience punish Molly for something that she was sure was much more Charlie's fault than hers, and that anyway Molly had already been punished enough for her wickedness. Mother read the letter out loud to all of us, then scrunched it up and threw it into the fire – where it belonged, she said.

I moved into Big Joe's room and slept with him in his bed, which wasn't easy because he was big and the bed very narrow. He muttered to himself loudly in his dreams, and tossed and turned almost constantly. But, as I lay awake at nights, that was not what troubled me most. In the next room slept the two people I most loved in all the world who, in finding each other, had deserted me. Sometimes, in the dead of night, I thought of them lying in each other's arms and I wanted to hate them. But I couldn't. All I knew was that I had no place at home any more, that I would be better off away, and away from them in particular.

I tried never to be alone with Molly for I did not know what to say to her any more. I didn't stop to drink with Charlie any more at The Duke, for the same reason. On the farm, I took every opportunity that came my way to work on my own, so as to be nowhere near him. I volunteered for any fetching and carrying that had to be done away from the farm. Farmer Cox seemed more than happy for me to do that. He was always sending me off with the horse and cart on some errand or other: bringing back feed from the merchants maybe, fetching the seed potatoes, or perhaps taking a pig to market to sell for him. Whatever it was, I took my time about it and Farmer Cox never seemed to notice. But Charlie did. He said I was skiving off work, but he knew that all I was doing was avoiding him. We knew each other so well. We never argued, not really; perhaps it was because neither of us wanted to hurt the other. We both knew enough hurt had been done already, that more would only widen the rift between us and neither of us wanted that.

It was while I was off "skiving" in Hatherleigh market one morning that I came face to face with the war for the first time, a war that until now had seemed unreal and distant to all of us, a war only in newspapers and on posters. I'd just sold Farmer Cox's two old rams, and got a good price for them too, when I heard the sound of a band coming down the High Street, drums pounding, bugles blaring. Everyone in the market went running, and so did I.

As I came round the corner I saw them. Behind the band there must have been a couple of dozen soldiers, splendid in their scarlet uniforms. They marched past me, arms swinging in perfect time, buttons and boots shining, the sun glinting on their bayonets. They were singing along with the band: *It's a long way to Tipperary, it's a long way to go.* And I remember thinking it was a good thing Big Joe wasn't there, because he'd have been bound to join in with his *Oranges and Lemons*. Children were stomping alongside them, some in paper hats, some with wooden sticks over their shoulders. And there were women throwing flowers, roses mostly, that were falling at the soldiers' feet. But one of them landed on a soldier's tunic and somehow stuck there. I saw him smile at that.

Like everyone else, I followed them round the town and up into the square. The band played *God Save the King* and then, with the Union Jack fluttering behind him, the first sergeant major I'd ever set eyes on got up on to the steps of the cross, slipped his stick smartly under his arm, and spoke to us, his voice unlike any voice I'd heard before: rasping, commanding.

"I shan't beat about the bush, ladies and gentlemen," he began. "I shan't tell you it's all tickety-boo out there in France – there's been too much of that nonsense already in my view. I've been there. I've seen it for myself. So I'll tell you straight. It's no picnic. It's hard slog, that's what it is, hard slog. Only one question to ask yourself about this war. Who would you rather see marching through your streets? Us lot or the Hun? Make up your minds. Because, mark my words, ladies and gentlemen, if we don't stop them out in France the Germans will be here, right here in Hatherleigh, right here on your doorstep."

I could feel the silence all around.

"They'll come marching through here burning your houses, killing your children, and yes, violating your women. They've beaten brave little Belgium, swallowed her up in one gulp. And now they've taken a fair slice of France too. I'm here to tell you that unless we beat them at their own game, they'll gobble us up as well." His eyes raked over us. "Well? Do you want the Hun here? Do you?"

"No!" came the shout, and I was shouting along with them.

"Shall we knock the stuffing out of them then?"

"Yes!" we roared in unison.

The sergeant major nodded. "Good. Very good. Then we shall need you." He was pointing his stick now into the crowd, picking out the men. "You, and you and you." He was looking straight at me now, into my eyes. "And you too, my lad!"

Until that very moment it had honestly never occurred to me that what he was saying had anything to do with me. I had been an onlooker. No longer.

"Your king needs you. Your country needs you. And all the brave lads out in France need you too." His face broke into a smile as he fingered his immaculate moustache. "And remember one thing, lads – and I can vouch for this – all the girls love a soldier."

The ladies in the crowd all laughed and giggled at that. Then the sergeant major returned the stick under his arm.

"So, who'll be the first brave lad to come up and take the king's shilling?"

No one moved. No one spoke up. "Who'll lead the way? Come along now. Don't let me down, lads. I'm looking for boys with hearts of oak, lads who love their King and their country, brave boys who hate the lousy Hun."

That was the moment the first one stepped forward, flourishing his hat as he pushed his way through the cheering crowd. I knew him at once from school. It was big Jimmy Parsons. I hadn't seen him for a while, not since his family had moved away from the village. He was even bigger than I remembered, fuller in the face and neck, and redder too. He was showing off now just like he always had done in the school yard. Egged on by the crowd, others soon followed.

Suddenly someone prodded me hard in the small of my back. It was a toothless old lady pointing at me with her crooked finger. "Go on, son," she croaked. "You go and fight. It's every man's duty to fight when his country calls, that's what I say. Go on. Y'ain't a coward, are you?"

Everyone seemed to be looking at me then, urging me on, their eyes accusing me as I hesitated. The toothless old lady jabbed me again, and then she was pushing me forward. "Y'ain't a coward, are you? Y'ain't a coward?" I didn't run, not at first. I sidled away from her slowly, and then backed out of the crowd hoping no one would notice me. But she did. "Chicken!" she screamed after me. "Chicken!" Then I did run. I ran helter-skelter down the deserted High Street, her words still ringing in my ears.

As I drove the cart out of the market, I heard the band strike up again in the square, heard the echoing thump thump of the big bass drum calling me back to the flag. Filled with shame, I kept on going. All the way back to the farm I thought about the toothless old lady, about what she had said, what the sergeant major had said. I thought about how fine and manly the men looked in their bright uniforms, how Molly would admire me, might even love me, if I joined up and came home in my scarlet uniform, how proud Mother would be, and Big Joe. By the time I was unhitching the horse back at the farm, I was quite determined that I would do it. I would be a soldier. I would go to France and, like the sergeant major said, kick the stuffing out of the lousy Germans. I made up my mind I would break the news to everyone at supper. I couldn't wait to tell them, to see the look on their faces.

We'd barely sat down before I began. "I was in Hatherleigh this morning," I said. "Mr Cox sent me to market."

"Skiving as usual," Charlie muttered into his soup.

I ignored him and went on. "The army was there, Mother. Recruiting, they were. Jimmy Parsons joined up. Lots of others too."

"More fool them," Charlie said. "I'm not going, not ever. I'll shoot a rat because it might bite me. I'll shoot a rabbit because I can eat it. Why would I ever want to shoot a German? Never even met a German."

Mother picked up my spoon and handed it to me. "Eat," she said, and she patted my arm. "And don't worry about it, Tommo, they can't make you go. You're too young anyway."

"I'm nearly sixteen," I said.

"You've got to be seventeen," said Charlie. "They won't let you join unless you are. They don't want boys."

So I ate my soup and said no more about it. I was disappointed at first that I hadn't had my big moment, but as I lay in bed that night I was secretly more than a little relieved that I wouldn't be going off to the war, and that by the time I was seventeen it would all be over anyway, as like as not.

A few weeks later the Colonel paid Mother a surprise visit, whilst Charlie and I were out at work. We didn't hear about it until we got home in the evening and Molly told us. I thought something strange was going on as Mother was unusually preoccupied and quiet at supper. She wouldn't even answer Big Joe's questions. Then when Molly got up saying she felt like a walk, and suggested both Charlie and I came with her, I knew for sure something was up. It was a very long time since we'd been out together, just the three of us. If Charlie had asked me, I'd have said no for sure.

But it was always more difficult for me to refuse Molly.

We went down to the brook, just like we'd done in the old days whenever we'd wanted to be alone together, where Molly and I had met up so often when I'd been their go-between postman. Molly didn't tell us until we were sitting either side of her on the river bank, until she had taken each of us by the hand.

"I'm breaking a promise I made to your mother," she began. "I so much don't want to tell you this, but I must. You have to know what's going on. It's the Colonel. He came in and told her this morning. He said he was only doing what he called his 'patriotic duty'. He told us that the war was going badly for us, that the country was crying out for men. So he's decided that now is the time for every able-bodied man who lives or works on his estate, everyone who can be spared, to volunteer, to go off to the war and do his bit for King and country. The estate will just have to manage without them for a while." I felt Molly's grip tighten on my hand, and a tremor come into her voice. "He said you've got to go, Charlie, or else he won't let us stay on in the cottage. Your mother protested all she could, but he wouldn't listen. He just lost his temper. He'll put us out, Charlie, and he won't go on employing your mother or me unless you go."

"He wouldn't do that, Moll. It's just a threat," Charlie said. "He can't do it. He just can't."

"He would," Molly replied, "and he can. You know he

can. And when the Colonel gets it into his head to do something, and he's in the mood to do it, he will. Look what he did to Bertha. He means it, Charlie."

"But the Colonel promised," I said. "And his wife did too before she died. She said she wanted Mother looked after. And the Colonel said we could stay on in the cottage. Mother told us."

"Your mother reminded him of that," Molly replied. "And d'you know what he said? He said it had never been a promise as such, only his wife's wish, and that anyway the war had changed everything. He was making no exceptions. Charlie has to join up or we'll be out of the cottage at the end of the month."

We sat there holding hands, Molly's head on Charlie's shoulder, as evening fell around us. Molly was sobbing quietly from time to time but none of us spoke. We didn't need to. We all knew there was no way out of this, that the war was breaking us apart, and that all our lives would be changed for ever. But at that moment, I treasured Molly's hand in mine, treasured this last time together.

Suddenly, Charlie broke the silence. "I'll be honest, Moll," he said. "It's been bothering me a lot just lately. Don't get me wrong. I don't want to go. But I've seen the lists in the papers – y'know, all the killed and the wounded. Poor beggars. Pages of them. It hardly seems right, does it, me being here, enjoying life, while they're over there. It's not all bad, Moll. I saw Benny Copplestone yesterday. He was sporting his uniform up at the pub. He's back on leave. He's been a year or more out in Belgium. He says it's all right. 'Cushy,' he called it. He says we've got the Germans on the run now. One big push, he reckons, and they'll all be running back to Berlin with their tails between their legs, and then all our boys can come home."

He paused, and kissed Molly on her forehead. "Anyway, it looks like I haven't got much choice, have I, Moll?"

"Oh Charlie," Molly whispered. "I don't want you to go."

"Don't worry, girl," Charlie said. "With a bit of luck I'll be back to wet the baby's head. And Tommo will look after you. He'll be the man about the place, won't you, Tommo? And if that silly old fart of a Colonel sticks his lousy head in our front door again when I'm gone, shoot the bastard, Tommo, like he shot Bertha." And I knew he was only half-joking, too.

I don't believe I even thought about what I said next. "I'm not staying," I told them. "I'm coming with you, Charlie."

They both tried all they could to dissuade me. They argued, they bullied, but I would not be put off, not this time. I was too young, Charlie said. I said I was sixteen in a couple of weeks and as tall as he was, that all I had to do was shave and talk deeper and I could easily be taken for seventeen. Mother wouldn't let me go, Molly said. I said I'd run away, that she couldn't lock me up.

"And who'll be there to look after us if you both go?" Molly was pleading with me now.

"Who would you rather I look after, Molly," I replied. "All of you at home who can perfectly well look after yourselves? Or Charlie, who's always getting himself into nasty scrapes, even at home?" When they had no answer to this, they knew I'd won, and I knew it too. I was going to fight in the war with Charlie. Nothing and no one could stop me now.

I've had two long years to think on why I decided like that, on the spur of the moment, to go with Charlie. In the end I suppose it was because I couldn't bear the thought of being apart from him. We'd lived our lives always together, shared everything, even our love for Molly. Maybe I just didn't want him to have this adventure without me. And then there was that spark in me newly kindled by those scarlet soldiers marching bravely up the High Street in Hatherleigh, the steady march of their feet, the drums and bugles resounding through the town, the sergeant major's stirring call to arms. Perhaps he had awoken in me feelings I never realised I'd had before, and that I had certainly never talked about. It was true that I did love all that was familiar to me. I loved what I knew, and what I knew was my family, and Molly, and the countryside I'd grown up in. I did not want any enemy soldier ever setting foot on our soil, on my place. I would do all I could to stop him and to protect the people I loved. And I would be doing it with Charlie. Deep down though, I knew that, more than Charlie, more than my country or the band or the sergeant major, it was that toothless old woman taunting me in the square. "Y'ain't a coward, are you? Y'ain't a coward?"

The truth was that I wasn't sure I wasn't, and I needed to find out.

I had to prove myself. I had to prove myself to myself.

Two days later, two days of parrying Mother's many attempts to keep me from going, we all went off together to Eggesford Junction Station where Charlie and I were to catch the train to Exeter. Big Joe had not been told anything about us going off to war. We were going away for a while, and we'd be back soon. We didn't tell him the truth, but we told him no lies either. Mother and Molly tried not to cry because of him. So did we.

"Look after Charlie for me, Tommo," Molly said. "And look after yourself too." I could feel the swell of her belly against me as we hugged.

Mother told me to promise to keep clean, to be good, to write home and to come home. Then Charlie and I were on the train – the first train we'd ever been on in our lives, and we were leaning out of the window and waving, only pulling back spluttering and coughing when we were engulfed suddenly in a cloud of sooty smoke. When it cleared and we looked out again, the station was already out of sight. We sat down opposite each other.

"Thanks, Tommo," said Charlie.

"For what?" I said.

"You know," he replied, and we both looked out of the window. There was no more to say about it. A heron lifted off the river and accompanied us for a while before veering away from us and landing high in the trees. A startled herd of Ruby Red cows scattered as we passed by, tails high as they ran. Then we were in a tunnel, a long dark tunnel filled with din and smoke and blackness. It seems like I've been in that tunnel every day since. So Charlie and I went rattling off to war. It all seems a very long time ago now, a lifetime.

FOURTEEN MINUTES PAST TWO

I keep checking the time. I promised myself I wouldn't, but I can't seem to help myself. Each time I do it, I put the watch to my ear and listen for the tick. It's still there, softly slicing away the seconds, then the minutes, then the hours. It tells me there are three hours and forty-six minutes left. Charlie told me once this watch would never stop, never let me down, unless I forgot to wind it. The best watch in the world, he said, a wonderful watch. But it isn't. If it was such a wonderful watch it would do more than simply keep the time – any old watch can do that. A truly wonderful watch would *make* the time. Then, if it stopped, time itself would have to stand still, then this night would never have to end and morning could never come. Charlie often told me we were living on borrowed time out here. I don't want to borrow any more time. I want time to stop so that tomorrow never comes, so that dawn will never happen.

I listen to my watch again, to Charlie's watch. Still ticking. Don't listen, Tommo. Don't look. Don't think. Only remember.

"Stand still! Look to your front, Peaceful, you horrible little man!" ... "Stomach in, chest out, Peaceful." ... "Down in that mud, Peaceful, where you belong, you nasty little worm. Down!" ... "God, Peaceful, is that the best they can send us these days? Vermin, that's what you are. Lousy vermin, and I've got to make a soldier of you."

Of all the names Sergeant "Horrible" Hanley bellowed out across the parade ground at Etaples when we first came to France, Peaceful was by far the most frequent. There were two Peacefuls in the company of course, and that made a difference, but it wasn't the main reason. Right from the very start Sergeant Hanley had it in for Charlie. And that was because Charlie just wouldn't jump through hoops like the rest of us, and that was because Charlie wasn't frightened of him, like the rest of us were.

Before we ever came to Etaples, all of us, including Charlie and me, had had an easy ride, a gentle enough baptism into the life of soldiering. In fact we'd had several weeks of little else but larks and laughter. On the train to Exeter, Charlie said we could easily pass for twins, that I'd have to watch my step, drop my voice, and behave like a seventeen-year-old from now on. When the time came, in front of the recruiting sergeant at the regimental depot, I stood as tall as I could and Charlie spoke up for me, so my voice wouldn't betray me. "I'm Charlie Peaceful, and he's Thomas Peaceful. We're twins and we're volunteering."

"Date of birth?"

"5th October," said Charlie.

"Both of you?" asked the recruiting sergeant, eyeing me a little I thought.

"Course," Charlie replied, lying easily, "only I'm older than him by one hour." And that was that. Easy. We were in.

The boots they gave us were stiff and far too big – they hadn't got any smaller sizes. So Charlie and I and the others clomped about like clowns, clowns in tin hats and khaki. The uniforms didn't fit either, so we swapped about until they did. There were some faces from home we recognised in amongst the hundreds of strangers. Nipper Martin, a little fellow with sticking-out ears, who grew turnips on his father's farm in Dolton, and who played a wicked game of skittles up at The Duke. There was Pete Bovey, thatcher and cider drinker from Dolton too, red-faced and with hands like spades, who we'd often seen around the village in Iddesleigh, thumping away at the thatch, high up on someone's roof. With us too was little Les James from school, son of Bob James, village rat catcher and wart charmer. He had inherited his father's gifts with rats and warts and he always claimed to be able to know whether it was going to rain or not the next day. He was usually right too. He always had a nervous tick in one eye that I could never stop looking at when we were in class together.

At training camp on Salisbury Plain, living cheek by jowl,

we all got to know each other fast, though not necessarily to like one another – that came later. And we got to know our parts, too, how to make believe we were soldiers. We learnt how to wear our khaki costumes – I never did get to wear the scarlet uniform I'd been hoping for – how to iron creases in and iron wrinkles out, how to patch and mend our socks, how to polish our buttons and badges and boots. We learnt how to march up and down in time, how to about-turn without bumping into one another, how to flick our heads right and salute whenever we saw an officer. Whatever we did, we did together, in time – all except for little Les James who could never swing his arms in time with the rest of us, no matter how much the sergeants and corporals bellowed at him. His legs and arms stepped and swung in time with each other, and with no one else, and that was all there was to it. He didn't seem to mind how often they shouted at him that he had two left feet. It gave us all something to laugh about. We did a lot of laughing in those early days.

They gave us rifles and packs and trenching shovels. We learnt to run up hills with heavy packs, and how to shoot straight. Charlie didn't have to be taught. On the rifle range he proved to be far and away the best shot in the company. When they gave him his red marksman's badge I was so proud of him. He was pretty pleased himself, too. Even with the bayonets it was still a game of make-believe. We'd have to charge forward screaming whatever obscenities we knew

– and I didn't know many, not then – at the straw-filled dummies. We'd plunge our bayonets in up to the hilt, swearing and cursing the filthy Hun as we stabbed him, twisting the blade and pulling it out as we'd been taught. "Go for the stomach, Peaceful. Nothing to get hung up on in there. Jab. Twist. Out."

Everything in the army had to be done in lines or rows. We slept in long lines of tents, sat on privies in rows. Not even the privy was private, I learnt that very quickly. In fact nowhere was private any more. We lived every moment of every day together, and usually in lines. We lined up together for shaves, for food, for inspections. Even when we dug trenches, they had to be in lines, straight trenches with straight edges, and we had to dig fast, too, one company in competition with another. We poured sweat, our backs ached, our hands were permanently raw with blisters. "Faster!" the corporals shouted. "Deeper! You want to get your head blowed off, Peaceful?"

"No, Corporal."

"You want to get your arse blowed off, Peaceful?"

"No, Corporal."

"You want to get your nuts blowed off, Peaceful?"

"No, Corporal."

"Then dig, you lazy beggars, dig, 'cos when you get out there, that's all you've got to hide in, God's good earth. And when they whizzbangs come over I'm telling you you'll always wish you'd dug deeper. The deeper you dig the longer you'll live. I know, I've been there."

No matter what the officers and NCOs told us of the hardships and dangers of trench warfare, we still all believed we were simply in some kind of rehearsal, actors in costume. We had to play our part, dress our part, but in the end it would only be a play. That was what we tried to believe – if ever we spoke about it, that is. But the truth was that we didn't speak of it much. I think we didn't dare because deep down we all knew and we all trembled, and were trying to deny it or disguise it or both.

I remember we were on exercise in the hills, lying there on our backs in the sunshine one morning when Pete sat up suddenly. "Hear that?" he said. "It's guns, from over in France, real guns." We sat up and listened. We heard it. Some said it was distant thunder. But we heard it all right. We saw the sudden fear in each other's eyes and knew it for what it was.

But that same afternoon we were back to play-acting, war games in full pack, attacking some distant "enemy" copse. When the whistles blew we climbed out of our trenches and walked forward, bayonets fixed. Then on a bellowed command we threw ourselves face down and crawled on through the long grass. The ground under us was still warm with summer, and there were buttercups. I thought of Molly then and Charlie and the buttercups in the water meadows back home. A bee, heavy with pollen and still greedy for more, clover-hopped in front of me as I crawled. I remember I spoke to him. "We're much alike, bee, you and me," I said. "You may carry your pack underneath you and your rifle may stick out of your bottom. But you and me, bee, are much alike." The bee must have taken offence at this, because he took off and flew away. I lay where I was, propped up on my elbows, and watched him go, until my thoughts were rudely interrupted by the corporal.

"What d'you think you're on, Peaceful, a bloody picnic? On your feet!"

In those first few weeks in uniform I hardly had time to miss anyone, not even Molly, though I thought of her often, and Mother and Big Joe. But they were only ever fleeting thoughts. Charlie and I rarely talked of home – we were hardly ever alone together anyway. We'd even stopped cursing the Colonel by now. There didn't seem any point, not any more. It was a hateful thing he'd done, but it was a done thing. We were soldiers now, and it wasn't bad, so far. In fact, despite all the lining up and the bellowing, it was turning out to be a lark, a real lark. Charlie and I wrote cheery letters home – most of his were to Molly, all of mine to Mother and Big Joe. We read them aloud to each other, those bits we wanted to share anyway. We weren't allowed to say where we were or anything about the training, but we always found plenty to tell them, plenty to brag about, plenty to ask about. We told them the truth, that we were having a good time – eating well and being good – mostly. But the moment we got on the ship for France the good times ended. Little Les James said he smelled a storm in the air, and as usual he was right.

There wasn't a man on board that ship that didn't want to die before he ever got to France. Most of us, Charlie and me included, had never seen the sea before, much less the heaving grey waves of the English Channel, and we lurched about the deck like drunken ghosts longing only to be released from our agony. Charlie and I were vomiting over the side when a seaman came up to us, clapped us heartily on the back and told us that if we were going to die we'd feel much better doing it down below in the hold with the horses. So Charlie and I staggered down the gangways until we found ourselves deep in the bowels of the ship and in amongst the terrified horses, who seemed happy to have someone for company as we crawled in and curled up in their straw, too close to their hooves for safety, but feeling too ill to care. The seaman was right. Down here the ship seemed to roll much less, and despite the stifling stench of oil and horse dung we began to feel better almost at once.

When at long last the engines finally stopped we went up on deck and looked out at France for the first time. The

French gull that hovered overhead eyeing me with deep suspicion looked much like every gull I'd seen following the plough back at home. Every voice I heard on the quayside below was English. Every uniform and every helmet was like our own. Then, as we came down the gangplank into the fresh morning air, we saw them, the lines of walking wounded shuffling along the quay towards us, some with their eyes bandaged, holding on to the shoulder of the one in front. Others lay on stretchers. One of them, puffing on a cigarette between pale parched lips, looked up at me out of sunken yellow eyes. "G'luck lads," he cried as we passed. "Give 'em what for." The rest stayed silent and their staring silence spoke to each of us as we formed up and marched out of town. We all knew then that the larking and the play-acting were over. From that moment none of us doubted the seriousness of what this would be about. It was our lives we would be acting out over here, and for many of us, our deaths.

If any of us had any last lingering delusions then they were very soon dispelled by our first sight of the vast training camp at Etaples. The camp stretched away as far as the eye could see, a tented city, and everywhere I looked there were soldiers drilling – marching, doubling, crawling, wheeling, saluting, presenting arms. I had never in my life seen such a bustle of people, never heard such a racket of humanity. The air echoed with the din of barked orders and shrieked obscenities. That was when we first came across

Sergeant Horrible Hanley, our chief scourge and tormentor over the coming weeks, who was to do his utmost to make all our lives a misery.

From the moment we saw him most of us lived in dread of him. He was not a big man, but he had eyes of steel that bore into us, and a lashing snarl in his voice that terrified us. We just buckled under and did what he wanted us to. It was the only way to survive. However much he doubled us up hills with stones in our packs, however much he made us throw ourselves down in the freezing mud and crawl through it, we did it, and with a will, too. We knew that anything less – to protest, to complain, to talk back, even to look him in the eye – would be to draw down upon us even more fury, even more pain, even more punishment. We knew because we saw what happened to Charlie. Charlie wouldn't even go along with his little jokes. It was this that got him into trouble in the first place.

It was a Sunday morning and we were being inspected before a church parade when Sergeant Hanley found fault with Charlie's cap badge. He said it was crooked. Nose to nose, Hanley bellowed into Charlie's face. I was in the rank behind Charlie, but even there I could feel the spray from Hanley's spittle. "You know what you are? You're a blot on Creation, Peaceful. What are you?"

Charlie thought for a moment and then replied in a clear, firm voice, and utterly without fear: "Happy to be here, Sergeant."

Hanley looked taken aback. We all knew the answer Hanley was looking for. He asked again. "You're a blot on Creation. What are you?"

"Like I said, Sergeant, happy to be here." Charlie just would not give Hanley the satisfaction of playing his game, no matter how often Hanley asked, nor how loud he shouted. For that Charlie was put on extra sentry duty, so that night after night Charlie hardly got any sleep. Hanley never let up after that, never missed an opportunity to pick on Charlie and punish him.

There were some in the company who didn't at all like what Charlie was doing, Pete amongst them. He said Charlie was stirring Hanley up unnecessarily, and was making things difficult for the rest of us. I've got to say I half agreed with them – though I didn't tell them that, and I certainly didn't tell Charlie. It was quite true that Hanley was giving our company in particular a lot of grief, and it was obvious this was because he had a vendetta against Charlie. Charlie was swiping at the wasp, and the wasp wasn't just stinging him, he was stinging all of us. Charlie was beginning to be thought of as a bit of a liability in the company, a bit of a Jonah. No one said as much to him – they all liked and respected Charlie too much – but Pete and Little Les and Nipper Martin did come to me on the quiet, and asked me to talk to him. I tried as best I could to warn Charlie. "He's like Mr Munnings back at school, Charlie. Our lord and master, remember? Hanley's our lord and master out here. You can't fight him."

"But that doesn't mean I have to lie down and let him walk all over me," he said. "I'll be all right, you'll see. You look after yourself. You watch your back. He's got his eye on you, Tommo, I've seen him." That was typical Charlie. I was trying to warn him, and he just turned the whole thing around and ended up warning me.

It was a little enough thing that sparked it off, a dirty rifle barrel. Thinking back now I know for sure Hanley must have done it quite deliberately, to provoke Charlie. Everyone knew by now that I was Charlie's younger brother, and a year too young to enlist. We'd long ago given up the pretence of being twins. After we'd first met up with Pete and Little Les and Nipper from home, we'd had to come clean about it, and by then it didn't much matter. There were dozens of others underage in the regiment and everyone knew it. After all, they needed all the men they could get. The other lads teased me about it, about having a chin like a baby's bottom and about my not needing to shave, which wasn't true, and about my squeaky voice, too. But they all knew that Charlie was looking out for me. If ever the teasing got a bit out of hand, Charlie would give them a little look and it would stop. He never nannied me, but everyone knew he'd stick by me no matter what.

Hanley was nasty but he wasn't stupid. He must have sensed it too, and that was why he began picking on me as well. I'd had plenty of practice at putting up with this kind of thing back at school with Mr Munnings, but Horrible Hanley was a tormentor in a class of his own. He found excuse after excuse to pick on me and punish me. Worn down by extra drills and sentry duty, I was very soon exhausted. The more exhausted I became the more mistakes I made, and the more mistakes I made, the more Hanley punished me.

We'd been drilling one morning, and were stood to attention in three ranks, when he grabbed my rifle. Looking down the barrel, Hanley pronounced it "dirty". I knew the punishment, we all did: five times doubling around the parade ground holding your rifle above your head. After only two circuits I just could not keep my rifle up there any more. My arms buckled at the elbows, and Hanley bellowed at me: "Every time you let that rifle fall, Peaceful, you begin the punishment again. Five more, Peaceful."

My head was swimming. I was staggering now, not running, and barely able to keep upright. My back was on fire with pain. I simply hadn't the strength to lift the rifle above my head at all. I remember hearing a shout, knowing it was Charlie, and wondering why he was shouting. Then I passed out. When I woke in my tent they told me what had happened. Charlie had broken ranks and run at Hanley, screaming at him. He hadn't actually hit him, but he had stood there nose to nose with Hanley telling him exactly what he thought of him. They said it was magnificent, that everyone cheered when he'd finished. But Charlie had been marched off to the guardroom under arrest.

The next day, in heavy rain, the whole battalion was paraded to witness Charlie's punishment. He was brought out and lashed to a gun wheel. Field Punishment Number One, they called it. The brigadier in command sat high on his horse and said that this should be a warning to all of us, that Private Peaceful had got off lightly, that insubordination in time of war could be seen as mutiny and that mutiny was punishable by death, by the firing squad. All day long Charlie was lashed there in the rain, legs apart, arms spread-eagled. As we marched past him, Charlie smiled at me. I tried to smile back, but no smile came, only tears. He seemed to me like Jesus hanging on the cross in the church back home in Iddesleigh. And I thought then of the hymn we used to sing in Sunday school, *What a friend we have in Jesus*, and sang it to myself only to banish my tears as I marched. I remembered Molly singing it down in the orchard when we buried Big Joe's mouse, and as I remembered I found myself involuntarily changing the words, changing Jesus into Charlie. I sang it to myself under my breath as we were marched away. "What a friend I have in Charlie."

A MINUTE PAST THREE

I dropped off to sleep. I've lost precious minutes – I don't know how many, but they are minutes I can never have back. I should be able by now to fight off sleep. I've done it often enough on lookout in the trenches, but then I had cold or fear or both as my wakeful companions. I long for that moment of surrender to sleep, just to drift away into the warmth of nothingness. Resist it, Tommo, resist it. After this night is over, then you can drift away, then you can sleep for ever, for nothing will ever matter again. Sing *Oranges and Lemons*. Go on. Sing it. Sing it like Big Joe does, over and over again. That'll keep you awake.

> *Oranges and Lemons, say the bells of St. Clements,*
> *You owe me five farthings, say the bells of St. Martins.*
> *When will you pay me? say the bells of Old Bailey.*
> *When I grow rich, say the bells of Shoreditch.*
> *When will that be? say the bells of Stepney.*
> *I'm sure I don't know, says the great bell at Bow.*
> *Here comes a candle to light you to bed,*
> *And here comes a chopper to chop off your head.*

They tell us we're going up to the front, and we're all relieved. We are leaving Etaples and Sergeant Hanley for ever, we hope. We're leaving France and marching into Belgium, singing as we go. Captain Wilkes likes us to sing. Good for morale, he says, and he's right too. The more we sing the more cheery we become, and that's in spite of all we see – the shell-shattered villages we march through, the field hospitals we pass, the empty coffins waiting. The captain was a choirmaster and a teacher back home in Salisbury, so he knows what he's doing. We hope he'll know what he's doing when we get to the trenches. It's difficult to believe he and Sergeant Horrible Hanley are in the same army, on the same side. We have never come across anyone who treats us with such kindness and consideration. As Charlie says, "he treats us right". So we treat him right too, except that is for Nipper Martin who ribs him whenever he can. Nipper can be like that, a bit mean sometimes. He's the only one who still keeps on about my squeaky voice.

"Are we downhearted? No! Then let your voices ring and altogether sing: are we downhearted? No." We sing out and march with a new spring in our step. And when that finishes and there's just the sound of marching feet Charlie starts up with *Oranges and Lemons*, which makes us all laugh, the captain too. I join in and soon they're all singing along. No one knows why we sing it of course. It's a secret between Charlie and me, and I know as we sing that he's thinking of Big Joe and home as I am.

The captain has told us we're going to a sector that's been quiet for a while now, that things shouldn't be too bad. We're happy about that of course, but we honestly don't care that much. Nothing could be worse than what we've just left. We pass a battery of heavy guns, the gunners sitting round a table playing cards. The guns are silent now, their barrels gaping at the enemy. I look where they point but can see no enemy. All I have seen of our enemy so far is a huddle of ragged prisoners sheltering from the rain under a tree as we marched past, their grey uniforms caked in mud. Some of them were smiling. One of them even waved and called out: "Hello, Tommy."

"He's talking to you," said Charlie laughing. So I waved back. They seemed much like us, only dirtier.

Two aeroplanes circle like buzzards in the distance. As they come closer I see they are not circling at all, but chasing one another. They are still too far away for us to see which of them is ours. We make up our minds it is the smaller one and cheer for him madly, and I'm wondering suddenly if the pilot from the yellow plane that landed in the water meadows that day might be up there in our plane. I can almost taste the humbugs he gave us as I watch them. I lose them in the sun, and then the smaller one spirals earthwards and our cheering is instantly silenced.

At rest camp they give us our first letters. Charlie and I lie in our tent and read them over and over again, till we know them almost by heart. We've both had letters from Mother and Molly, and Big Joe's put his mark at the bottom of each one, his smudged thumbprint in ink with "Joe" written large beside it in heavily indented pencil. That makes us smile. I can see him writing it, nose to the paper, tongue between his teeth. Mother writes that they're turning most of the Big House into a hospital for officers, and the Wolfwoman rules the roost up there more than ever. Molly says the Wolfwoman now wears a lady's wide-brimmed straw hat with a big white ostrich feather instead of her old black bonnet, and that she smiles all the time "like Lady Muck". Molly writes, too, that she's missing me, and that she is well, except that she feels a little sick sometimes. She hopes the war will be over quickly and then we can all be together again. I can't read the rest, or her name, because Joe's finger has blotted everything else out.

They let us out of camp for an evening and we go into the nearest village, Poperinghe, "Pop" everyone seems to call it. Captain Wilkes tells us there's an *estaminet* there – that's a sort of pub he says, where you can drink the best beer outside England and eat the best egg and chips in the entire world. He's right. Pete, and Nipper, Little Les, Charlie and me stuff ourselves on egg and chips and beer. We're like camels filling up at an oasis that we've discovered by accident and may never find again.

There's a girl in the restaurant who smiles at me when she

clears the plates away. She's the daughter of the owner who is always very smartly dressed and very round and very merry, like a Father Christmas without the beard. It's difficult to believe she's his daughter, for in every way she's the opposite, wonderfully elf-like and delicate. Nipper notices her smiling at me and makes something dirty of it. She knows it and moves away. But I don't forget her smile, nor the egg and chips and the beer. Charlie and me drink to the Colonel and the Wolfwoman again and again, wishing them all the misfortune and misery and all the little monster children they so richly deserve, and then we stagger back to camp. I'm properly drunk for the first time in my life, and feel very proud of myself, until I lie down and my head swirls and threatens to drag me down into some black abyss where I fear to go. I struggle to think straight, to picture the girl in the *estaminet* in Pop. But the more I think of her the more I see Molly.

The big guns bring me to my senses. We crawl out of our tent into the night. The sky is lit up all along the horizon. Whoever is underneath all that, friend or foe, is taking a terrible pounding. "That's Ypres," says the captain beside me in the darkness.

"Poor beggars," says someone else. "Glad we're not in Wipers tonight."

We go back to our tent, huddle under our blankets and thank God it's not us, but every one of us knows our time must come, and soon.

The next evening we go up into the line. There are no big guns tonight, but rifle fire and machine-gun fire crackle and rattle ahead of us, and flares go up, intermittently lighting the darkness. We know we are close now. It seems as if the road is taking us down into the earth itself, until it is a road no more but rather a tunnel without a roof, a communications trench. We have to be silent now. Not a whisper, not a word. If the German machine gunners or mortars spot us, and there are places they can, then we're done for. So we stifle our curses as we slither and slide in the mud, holding on to one another to stop ourselves falling. A line of soldiers passes us coming the other way, dark-eyed men, sullen and weary. No need for questions. No need for answers. The haunted, hunted look in their eyes tells it all.

We find our dugout at last, every one of us yearning only for sleep now. It has been a long, cold march. A mug of hot sweet tea and to lie down, it's all I want. But with Charlie, I'm posted to sentry duty. For the first time I look out through the wire over no-man's-land and towards the enemy trenches, less than two hundred yards from our front line, they tell us, but we can't see them, only the wire. The night is still now. A machine gun stutters and instantly I duck down. I needn't have bothered. It's one of ours. I'm overwhelmed by fear, numbed by it, and for the moment that fear banishes the wretched discomfort of my wet feet and frozen hands. I feel Charlie there beside me. "Fine night for poaching, Tommo," he whispers. I can see his smile in the dark and my fear is gone at once.

It's just as the captain said it would be, quiet. Every day I wait for the Germans to shell us, and they don't. It seems they're too busy shelling Wipers further up the line to bother about us, and I can't say I'm sorry. I even begin to hope that they might have run out of shells. Every time I look through the periscope I expect to see the grey hordes coming at us across no-man's-land, but no one comes. I am almost disappointed. We hear occasional sniper fire, so there is no smoking in the trenches at night, "unless you want your head shot off," the captain says. Our artillery lobs a shell or two over into their trenches once in a while, and they do the same. Each one, theirs or ours – and ours sometimes drop short – comes as a surprise and terrifies me at first, terrifies all of us, but in time we become used to it and pay less attention.

Our trench and our dugouts have been left in a mess by the previous occupants, a company of Jocks from the Seaforths, so when we're not on stand-to at dawn, brewing up or sleeping, we're set to clearing up their mess. Captain Wilkes – or "Wilkie" as we call him now – is meticulous about tidiness and cleanliness, "because of the rats," he says. We find out soon enough he's right again. I am the first to find them. I am detailed to begin shoring up a dilapidated trench wall. I plunge my shovel in and open up an entire nest of them. They come pouring out, skittering away over my boots. I recoil in horror for a moment and then set about stamping them to death in the mud. I don't kill a single one, and we see them everywhere after that. Fortunately we have Little Les, our own professional rat-catcher, who is now called upon whenever a rat is spotted, whatever the time, day or night, he doesn't mind. He jokes that it makes him feel at home. He knows the ways of rats, and kills with a will each time, tossing their corpses up into no-man's-land with a flourish of triumph. After a while the rats seem to know they have met their match in Little Les and leave us be.

But our other daily curse, lice, we all have to deal with ourselves. Each of us has to burn off his own with a lighted cigarette end. They inhabit us wherever they can, the folds of our skin, the creases of our clothes. We long for a bath to drown the lot of them, but above all we long to be warm again and dry.

Our greatest scourge is neither rats nor fleas but the unending drenching rain, which runs like a stream along the bottom of our trench, turning it into nothing but a mud-filled ditch, a stinking gooey mud that seems to want to hold us and then suck us down and drown us. I have not had dry feet since I got here. I go to sleep wet. I wake up wet, and the cold soaks through my sodden clothes and into my aching bones. Only sleep brings any real relief, sleep and food. God, how we long for both. Wilkie moves among us at dawn on the firestep, a word here, a smile there. He keeps us going, keeps us up to the mark. If he has fear he never shows it, and if that is courage then we're beginning to catch it.

But we couldn't do without Charlie either. It's Charlie who keeps us together, breaks up our squabbles (which are many and frequent now that we are so closely confined together) and jollies each of us along when we get downhearted. He's become like a big brother to everyone. After Sergeant Hanley and the field punishment, and the way Charlie managed to smile through it all, there isn't a man in the company who doesn't look up to him. Being his real brother I could feel I live in his shadow, but I never have and I do not now. I live in his glow.

We have a few more miserable days in the line, all of us longing for the comforts of rest camp. But when we get there they keep us endlessly busy. We clean our kit, march up and down, turn out for inspections again and again, do our gas mask drill again, and then there are always more ditches and drains to dig to take away the incessant rain. But we do have letters from home, from Molly and Mother, and they have knitted woollen scarves and gloves and socks for us both. We have communal baths in great steaming vats in a barn down the road and, best of all, eggs and chips and beer at the *estaminet* in Pop. The beautiful girl with the doe eyes is there, but she does not always notice me, and when she doesn't I drink even more, to drown my sorrows.

The first snow of winter sees us back in the trenches. It freezes as it falls, hardening the mud – and that certainly is a blessing. Providing there is no wind we are no colder than we were before and can at least keep our feet dry. The guns have stayed relatively silent in our sector and we have had few casualties so far: one wounded by a sniper, two in hospital with pneumonia, and one with chronic trench foot – which affects us all. From what we hear and read we are in just about the luckiest sector we could be.

Word has come down from Headquarters, Wilkie says, that we must send out patrols to find out what regiments have come into the line opposite us and in what strength – though why we have to do that we do not know. There are spotter planes doing that almost every day. So most nights now, four or five of us are picked, and a patrol goes out into no-man's-land to find out what they can. More often than not they find out nothing. No one likes going, of course, but nobody's been hurt so far, and you get a double rum ration before you go and everyone wants that.

My turn soon comes up as it was bound to. I'm not particularly worried. Charlie's going with me, and Nipper Martin, Little Les and Pete – "the whole skittle team", Charlie calls us. Wilkie's heading the patrol and we're glad of that. He tells us we have to achieve what the other patrols have not. We have to bring back one prisoner for questioning. They give us each a double rum ration, and

I'm warmed instantly to the roots of my hair, to the toes of my feet.

"Stay close, Tommo," Charlie whispers, and then we are climbing out over the top, crawling on our bellies through the wire. We snake our way forward. We slither into a shell hole and lie doggo there for a while in case we've been heard. We can hear Fritz talking now, and laughing. There's the sound of a gramophone playing – I've heard all this before on lookout, but distantly. We're close now, very close, and I should be scared witless. Strangely, I find I'm not so much frightened as excited. Maybe it's the rum. I'm out poaching again, that's what it feels like. I'm tensed for danger. I'm ready for it, but not frightened.

It takes an eternity to cross no-man's-land. I begin to wonder if we'll ever find their trenches at all. Then we see their wire up ahead. We wriggle through a gap, and still undetected we drop down into their trench. It looks deserted, but we know it can't be. We can still hear the voices and the music. I notice the trench is much deeper than ours, wider too and altogether more solidly constructed. I grip my rifle tighter and follow Charlie along the trench, bent double like everyone else. We're trying not to, but we're making too much noise. I can't understand why no one has heard us. Where are their sentries, for God's sake? Up ahead I can see Wilkie waving us on with his revolver. There is a flickering of light now coming from a dugout ahead, where the voices are, where the music is. From the sound of it there could be half a dozen men in there at least. We only need one prisoner. How are we going to manage half a dozen of them?

At that moment the light floods into the trench as the dugout curtain opens. A soldier comes out shrugging on his coat, the curtain closing behind him. He is alone, just what we are after. He doesn't seem to see us right away. Then he does. For a split second the Hun does nothing and neither do we. We just stand and look at one another. He could so easily have done what he should have done, just put up his hands and come with us. Instead he lets out a shriek and turns, blundering through the curtain back into the dugout. I don't know who threw the grenade in after him, but there is a blast that throws me back against the trench wall. I sit there stunned. There is screaming and firing from inside the dugout, then silence. The music has stopped.

By the time I get in there Little Les is lying on his side shot through the head, his eyes staring at me. He looks so surprised. Several Germans are sprawled across their dugout, all still, all dead – except one. He stands there naked, blood spattered and shaking. I too am shaking. He has his hands in the air and is whimpering. Wilkie throws a coat over him and Pete bundles him out of the dugout. Frantic now to get back we scrabble our way up out of the trench, the Hun still whimpering. He is beside himself with terror. Pete is shouting at him to stop, but he's only making it worse. We follow the captain through the German wire and run.

For a while I think we have got away with it, but then a flare goes up and we are caught suddenly in broad daylight. I hurl myself to the ground and bury my face in the snow. Their flares last so much longer than ours, shine so much brighter. I know we're for it. I press myself into the ground, eyes closed. I'm praying and thinking of Molly. If I'm going to die I want her to be my last thought. But she's not. Instead I'm saying sorry to Father for what I did, that I didn't mean to do it. A machine gun opens up behind us and then rifles fire. There is nowhere to hide, so we pretend to be dead. We wait till the light dies and the night is suddenly black again. Wilkie gets us to our feet and we go on, running, stumbling, until more lights go up, and the machine gunners start up again. We dive into a crater and roll down crashing through the ice into the watery bottom. Then the shelling starts. It seems as if we have woken up the entire German army. I cower in the stinking water with the German and Charlie, the three of us clinging together, heads buried in one another as the shells fall all about us. Our own guns are answering now but it is little comfort to us. Charlie and I drag the Hun prisoner out of the water. Either he is talking to himself or he's saying a prayer, it's difficult to tell.

Then we see Wilkie lying higher up the slope, too close to the lip of the crater. When Charlie calls out to him he doesn't reply. Charlie goes to him and turns him over. "It's my legs," I hear the captain whisper. "I can't seem to move my legs." He's too exposed up there, so Charlie drags him back down as gently as he can. We try to make him comfortable. The Hun keeps praying out loud. I'm quite sure he's praying now. "*Du lieber Gott*," I hear. They call God by the same name. Pete and Nipper are crawling over towards us from the far side of the crater. We are together at least. The ground shudders, and with every impact we are bombarded by showers of mud and stone and snow. But the sound I hate and fear most is not the sound of the explosion – by then it's done and over with, and you're either dead or not. No, it's the whistle and whine and shriek of the shells as they come over. It's the not knowing where they will land, whether this one is for you.

Then, as suddenly as the barrage begins, it stops. There is silence. Darkness hides us again. Smoke drifts over us and down into our hole, filling our nostrils with the stench of cordite. We stifle our coughing. The Hun has stopped his praying, and is lying curled up in his overcoat, his hands over his ears. He's rocking like a child, like Big Joe.

"I won't make it," Wilkie says to Charlie. "I'm leaving it to you to get them all back, Peaceful, and the prisoner. Go on now."

"No sir," Charlie replies. "If one goes we all go. Isn't that right, lads?"

That's how it happened. Under cover of an early-morning mist we made it back to our trenches, Charlie carrying Wilkie on his back the whole way, until the stretcher bearers came for him in the trench. As they lifted him, Wilkie caught Charlie by the hand and held it. "Come and see me in hospital, Peaceful," he said. "That's an order." And Charlie promised he would.

We had a brew up with our prisoner in the dugout before they came for him. He smoked a cigarette Pete had given him. He'd stopped shaking now, but his eyes still held their fear. We had nothing to say to one another until the moment he got up to leave. "*Danke*," he said. "*Danke sehr.*"

"Funny that," Nipper said when he'd gone. "Seeing him standing there with not a stitch on. Take off our uniforms and you can hardly tell the difference, can you? Not a bad bloke, for a Fritz that is."

That night I didn't think, as I should have done, of Little Les lying out there in the German dugout, with a hole in his head. I thought of the Hun prisoner we'd brought back. I didn't even know his name, yet, after that night cowering in the shell hole with him, I felt somehow I knew him better than I'd ever known Little Les.

We are back at last at rest camp, most of us anyway. We soon find out which hospital Wilkie is in, and we go to see him as Charlie had promised. It's a big chateau of a place, with ambulances coming and going, and crisp-looking nurses bustling everywhere. "Who are you?" asks the orderly at the desk.

"Peaceful," says Charlie smiling – he loves playing this joke. "Both of us are Peaceful."

The orderly does not look amused, but he seems to have been expecting us. "Which of you is Charlie Peaceful?"

"I am," says Charlie.

"Captain Wilkes said you would come." The orderly is reaching into the desk drawer. He takes out a watch. "He left this for you," he says, and Charlie takes the watch.

"Where is he?" Charlie asks. "Can we see him?"

"Back in Blighty by now. Left yesterday. In a bad way. Nothing more we could do for him here, I'm afraid."

As we walk down the steps of the hospital Charlie is putting the watch on his wrist.

"Does it work?" I ask.

"Course it does," he says. He shows it to me on his wrist. "What d'you think?"

"Nice," I reply.

"It's not just nice, Tommo," Charlie says. "It's wonderful, that's what it is. Ruddy wonderful. Tell you what – if anything happens to me it's yours, all right?"

TWENTY-FIVE PAST THREE

The mouse is here again. He keeps stopping and looking up at me. He's wondering if he should run away, whether I'm friend or foe. "*Wee, sleekit, caw'rin tim'rous beastie.*" I don't know what half the words mean, but I still know the poem. Back at school Miss McAllister made us stand up and recite it on Burns Day. She said it was good for us to have at least one great Scottish poem in our heads for ever. This wee beastie is tim'rous all right, but he's not Scottish, he's a Belgian mouse. I recite the poem to him all the same. He seems to understand because he listens politely. I do it in Miss McAllister's Scottish accent. I'm almost word perfect. I think Miss McAllister would have been proud of me. But the moment I finish he's gone, and I'm alone once more.

Earlier they came and asked if I wanted someone to stay with me through the night, and I said no. I even sent the padre away. They asked if there was anything I wanted, anything they could do to help, and I said there was nothing. Now I long to have them all here, the padre too. We could have had singsongs. They could have brought me egg and chips. We could have drunk ourselves silly and I could be numb with it by now. But all I've had for company is a mouse, a vanishing Belgian mouse.

The next time they sent us up into the line it wasn't back to our "quiet" sector, it was into the Wipers salient itself. For months now Fritz had been pounding away at Wipers, trying everything he could to batter it into submission. Time and again he'd almost broken through into the town and had only been driven back at the last moment. But the salient around the town was shrinking all the time. From the talk in the *estaminet* in Pop and from the almost constant bombardment a few miles to the east of us we all knew how bad it must be in there. Everyone knew they had us surrounded and overlooked on three sides, so that they could chuck all they wanted into our trenches and there was nothing much we could do about it, except grin and bear it.

Our new company commander, Lieutenant Buckland, told us how things were, how if we gave way then Wipers would be lost, and that Wipers must not be lost. He didn't say why it mustn't be lost, but then he wasn't Wilkie. We all felt the loss of Wilkie very keenly. Without him we were like sheep without a shepherd. Lieutenant Buckland was doing his best, but he was straight out from England. He might have been very properly spoken, but he knew even less about fighting this war than we did. Nipper said he was just a young pipsqueak, and that he belonged back at school. And it was true, he seemed younger than any of us, even me.

As we marched through Wipers that evening I wondered why it was worth fighting for at all. So far as I could see there was no town left, nothing you could call a town anyway. Rubble and ruin, that's all the place was, more dogs and cats than townspeople. We saw two horses lying dead and mangled in the street, as we passed by what was left of the town hall; and everywhere there were soldiers and guns and ambulances on the move, and hurrying. They were not shelling the town as we came through, but I was as terrified then as I ever had been. I could not get those horses and their terrible wounds out of my head. The sight of them haunted me, haunted all of us, I think. None of us sang. None of us talked. I longed only to reach the sanctuary of our new trenches, to crawl into the deepest dugout I could find and hide.

But when we got there the trenches were a bitter disappointment to us. Wilkie would have been appalled at the state of them. In places they were little more than shallow dilapidated ditches affording us precious little protection, and the mud here was even deeper than before. There was a sickly-sweet stench about the place that had to be more than stagnant mud and water. I knew well enough what it was, we all did, but no one dared speak of it. Word came back that from now on we should keep our heads down because here was where we could be most easily spotted by their snipers. But there was at least some consolation when we reached the dugout. It was the best we'd ever had, deep and warm and dry. I could not sleep though. I lay there that night, knowing how a hunted fox must feel lying low in his lair with the hounds waiting for him outside.

I am on stand-to the next morning, locked inside my gas mask in a world of my own, listening to myself breathing. The mist rises over no-man's-land. I see in front of me a blasted wasteland. No vestige of fields or trees here, not a blade of grass – simply a land of mud and craters. I see unnatural humps scattered over there beyond our wire. They are the unburied, some in field-grey uniforms and some in khaki. There is one lying in the wire with his arm stretched heavenwards, his hand pointing. He is one of ours, or was. I look up where he is pointing. There are birds up there, and they are singing. I see a beady-eyed blackbird singing to the world from his barbed-wire perch. He has no tree to sing from.

The pipsqueak of a lieutenant says, "Keep your eyes peeled, lads. Keep your wits about you." He's always doing that, always telling us to do things we're already doing. But nothing moves out there in no-man's-land but the crows. It is a dead man's land.

We're back down in the dugout after stand-to, brewing up when the bombardment starts. It doesn't stop for two whole days. They are the longest two days of my life. I cower there, we all do, each of us alone in our own private misery. We cannot talk for the din. There can be little sleep. When I do sleep I see the hand pointing skywards, and it is Father's hand, and I wake shaking. Nipper Martin has got the shakes, too, and Pete tries to calm him but he can't. I cry like a baby sometimes and not even Charlie can comfort me. We want nothing more than for it to stop, for the earth to be still again, for there to be quiet. I know that when it's over they'll be coming for us, that I'll have to be ready for them, for the gas maybe, or the flame-thrower, or the grenades, or the bayonets. But I don't mind how they come. Let them come. I just want this to stop. I just want it to be over.

When at last it does we are ordered out on to the firestep, gas masks on, bayonets fixed, eyes straining through the smoke that drifts across in front of us. Then out of the smoke we see them come, their bayonets glinting, one or two at first, but then hundreds, thousands. Charlie's there beside me.

"You'll be all right, Tommo," he says. "You'll be fine."

He knows my thoughts. He sees my terror. He knows I want to run.

"Just do what I do, right? And stay by me."

I stay and I do not run, only because of Charlie. The firing starts all along the line, machine guns and rifle fire, shelling, and I'm firing too. I'm not aiming, just firing, firing, loading and firing again. And still they do not stop. For a few moments it seems as if bullets do not touch them. They come on towards us unscathed, an army of invincible grey ghosts. Only when they begin to crumple and cry out and fall do I begin to believe they are mortal. And they are brave, too. They do not falter. No matter how many are cut down, those that are left keep coming. I can see their wild eyes as they reach our wire. It is the wire that stops them. Somehow enough of it has survived the bombardment. Only a few of them find the gaps, and they are shot down before they ever reach our trenches. Those that are left, and there are not many now, have turned and are stumbling back, some throwing away their rifles. I feel a surge of triumph welling inside me, not because we have won, but because I have stood with the others. I have not run.

"*Y'ain't a coward, are you?*"

No, old woman, I am not, I am not.

Then the whistle goes, and I am up with the others and after them. We pour through the gap in the wire. They lie here so thick on the ground it is hard not to step on them. I have no pity for them, but no hatred either. They came to kill us, and we killed them. I look up. They are running from us as we go forward. We fire at will now, picking them off. We are across no-man's-land before we know it. We find a way through their wire and leap down into their frontline trenches. I am a hunter seeking out my quarry, a quarry I will kill, but my quarry has gone. The trench is deserted.

Lieutenant Buckland is up on the parapet above us, screaming at us to follow him, that we've got them on the run. I follow. We all follow. He is not so much of a pipsqueak as we all thought. Everywhere I look, to my right, to my left, as far as I can see, we are advancing and I am a part of it and I feel suddenly exhilarated. But in front of us the enemy seems to have vanished. I am unsure what to do now. I look all around for Charlie, and cannot see him anywhere. That's when the first shell comes screaming over. I throw myself down, flatten myself into the mud, as it explodes close behind me, deafening me instantly. After a while I force myself to lift up my head and look. Ahead of me I see us advancing still, and everywhere in front of us the flash of rifle fire, the spitting flame of machine guns. For a moment I think I am dead already. All is soundless, all is unreal. A silent storm of shelling rages about me. Before my eyes we are scythed down, blown apart, obliterated. I see men crying out but I hear nothing. It is as if I am not there, as if this horror cannot touch me.

They are stumbling back towards me now. I can't see Charlie among them. The lieutenant grabs me and hauls me to my feet. He's shouting at me, then turning me and pushing me back towards our trenches. I am trying to run with the others, trying to keep with them. But my legs are leaden and will not let me run. The lieutenant stays with me, urging me on, urging us all on. He is a good man. He's right there alongside me when he's hit. He drops to his knees and dies looking up at me. I see the light fade in his eyes. I watch him fall forward on his face. I do not know how I manage to get back after that, but I do. I find myself curled up in the dugout, and the dugout is half-empty. Charlie is not there. He has not come back.

At least I can hear again now, even if it is mostly the ringing in my head. Pete has news of Charlie. He says he's sure he saw him on the way back from the German trenches, hobbling, using his rifle as a stick, but all right. That gives me some fragile hope, but it is hope that ebbs away as the hours pass. As I lie there I relive each and every horror. I see the puzzled look on the lieutenant's face as he kneels there, trying to speak to me. I see a thousand silent screams. To drive these visions away I tell myself all manner of reassuring tales about Charlie: how Charlie must be out there in some crater, only waiting for the clouds to cover the moon before he crawls back; how he's got himself lost and has landed up somewhere down the line with another regiment and will find his way back to us in the morning – it happens all the time. My mind races and will not let me rest. There is no shelling to interrupt my thoughts. Outside the world has fallen silent. Both armies lie exhausted in their trenches and bleeding to death.

By stand-to the next morning I knew for sure that Charlie would not be coming back, that all my stories had been just that, stories. Pete and Nipper and the others had tried to convince me that he might still be alive. But I knew he was not. I was not grieving. I was numb inside, as void of all feeling as the hands that clutched my rifle. I looked out over no-man's-land where Charlie had died. They lay as if they'd been heaped against the wire by the wind, and Charlie, I knew, was one of them. I wondered what I would write to Molly and Mother. I could hear Mother's voice in my head, hear her telling Big Joe how Charlie would not be coming back, how he had gone to Heaven to be with Father and Bertha. Big Joe would be sad. He would rock. He would hum *Oranges and Lemons* mournfully up his tree. But after a few days his faith would comfort him. He would believe absolutely that Charlie was up there in the blue of Heaven, high above the church tower somewhere. I envied him that. I could no longer even pretend to myself that I believed in a merciful god, nor in a heaven, not any more, not after I had seen what men could do to one another. I could believe only in the hell I was living in, a hell on earth, and it was man-made, not God-made.

That night, like a man sleepwalking, I got up to take my turn on sentry duty. The sky was filled with stars. Molly knew the stars well – the Plough, the Milky Way, the Pole Star – she'd often tried to teach me them all when we were out poaching. I tried to remember, tried to identify them in amongst the millions, and failed. As I was looking up in wonder at the immensity and beauty of it all, I found myself almost believing in Heaven again. I picked one bright star in the west to be Charlie and another next to him. That was Father. They were together looking down on me. I wished then I had told Charlie about how Father had died, for there would be no secrets between us now. I shouldn't have kept it from him. So, unspeaking, I told him then, saw him glisten and wink at me, and knew he had understood and did not blame me. Then I heard Charlie's voice in my head. "Don't go all dreamy on lookout, Tommo," he was saying. "You'll fall asleep. You can get shot for that." I widened my eyes, blinked them hard, and took in a deep gulp of cold air to wake me up.

Only moments later I saw something move out beyond the wire. I listened. There was still a ringing in my ears, so I couldn't be sure of it, but I thought I could hear someone, a voice, and a voice that was not inside my head. It was a whisper. "Hey! Anyone there? It's me, Charlie Peaceful. D Company. I'm coming in. Don't shoot." Perhaps I was already asleep and deep in a wonderful dream I wanted to be true. But the voice came again, louder this time. "What's the matter with you lot? Are you all fast asleep or what? It's Charlie, Charlie Peaceful."

From under the wire a dark shape shifted and moved towards me. Not a dream, not one of my make-believe stories. It was Charlie. I could see his face now and he could see mine. "Tommo, you dozy beggar, you. Give us a hand, will you?" I grabbed him and tumbled him down into the trench. "Am I glad to see you!" he said. We hugged one another then. I don't think we ever had before. I cried, and tried unsuccessfully to hide it, until I felt him crying too.

"What happened?" I asked.

"They shot me in the foot, can you believe it? Shot right through my boot. I bled like a pig. I was on my way back and I passed out in some shell hole. Then by the time I woke up all you lot had gone off and left me. I had to stay put till nightfall. Seems like I've been crawling all bloody night."

"Does it hurt?"

"I can't feel a thing," Charlie said. "But then, I can't feel the other foot either – I'm frozen stiff. Don't you worry, Tommo. I'll be right as rain."

They stretchered him to hospital that night, and I did not see him again until they pulled us out of the line a few days later. Pete and I went to see him as soon as we could. He was sitting up in his bed and grinning all over his face. "It's good in here," he said. "You want to try it sometime. Three decent meals a day, nurses, no mud, and a nice long way from Mister Fritz."

"How's the foot?" I asked him.

"Foot? What foot?" He patted his leg. "That's not a foot, Tommo. That's my ticket home. Some nice, kind Mister Fritz gave me the best present he could, a ticket home to Blighty.

They're sending me to a hospital back home. It's a bit infected. Lots of bones broken, they said. It'll mend, but it'll take an operation, and then I've got to rest it up. So they're packing me off tomorrow."

I knew I should be pleased for him, and I wanted to be, but I just could not bring myself to think that way. All I could think was that we'd come to this war together. We'd stuck together through thick and thin, and now he was breaking the bond between us, and deserting me. Worst of all he was going home without me, and he was so unashamedly happy about it.

"I'll give them your best, Tommo," he said. "Pete'll keep an eye on you for me. You'll look after him, won't you Pete?"

"I don't need looking after," I snapped.

But Charlie either hadn't heard me or he ignored me. "And you make sure he behaves, Pete. That girl in the *estaminet* in Pop, she's got her eye on him. She'll eat him alive." They laughed at my embarrassment, and I could not disguise my hurt and discomfort. "Hey, Tommo." Charlie put his hand on my arm. "I'll be back before you know it." And he was serious now, for the first time. "Promise," he said.

"You'll be seeing Molly, then, and Mother?" I asked.

"Just let them try and stop me," he said. "I'll wangle a bit of leave. Or maybe they'll come and see me in hospital. With a bit of luck I could get to see the baby. Less than a month to go now, Tommo, and I'll be a father. You'll be an uncle too. Think of that."

But the evening after Charlie had left for Blighty I wasn't thinking of that at all. I was in the *estaminet* in Pop drowning my anger in beer. And it *was* anger I was drowning, not just sorrows: anger at Charlie for abandoning me, anger that he was to see Molly and home, and that I was not. In my befuddled state I even thought of deserting, of going after him. I'd make my way to the Channel and find a boat. I'd get home somehow.

I looked around me. There must have been a hundred or more soldiers in the place that evening, Pete and Nipper Martin, and some of the others among them, but I felt completely alone. They were laughing and I could not laugh. They were singing and I could not sing. I couldn't even eat my egg and chips. It was stiflingly hot in there and the air was thick with cigarette smoke. I could hardly breathe. I went outside to get some air. That brought me very quickly to my senses, and I gave up at once all idea of deserting. I would go back to camp instead. It was the easier choice – you can get shot for desertion.

"Tommy?"

It was her, the girl from the *estaminet*. She was carrying out a crate of wine bottles.

"You are ill?" she asked me.

Tongue-tied, I shook my head. We stood for some moments

listening to the thunder of the guns as a heavy barrage opened up over Wipers, the sky lit up over the town like an angry sunset. Flares rose and hovered and fell over the front line.

"It is beautiful," she said. "How can it be beautiful?"

I wanted to speak, but I did not trust myself to do so. I felt suddenly overwhelmed by tears, by longing for home and for Molly.

"How old?" she asked.

"Sixteen," I muttered.

"Like me," she said. I found her looking at me more closely. "I have seen you before, I think?" I nodded. "I will see you again perhaps?"

"Yes," I said. Then she was gone and I was alone again in the night. I was calmer now, more at peace with myself and stronger, too. Walking back to camp I made up my mind. We were being sent away for training the next day, but as soon as I came back, I would go straight to Pop, to the *estaminet*, and when the girl brought me my egg and chips I would be brave – I would ask her her name.

Two weeks later I was back, and that's just what I did. "Anna," she told me. And she tinkled with laughter when I told her my name was Tommo. "It's true then," she said. "Every English soldier is called Tommy."

"I'm not Tommy, I'm Tommo," I replied.

"It's the same," she laughed. "But you are different, different from the others, I think."

When she heard I had worked on a farm, and with horses, she took me into the stable and showed me her father's carthorse. He was massive and magnificent. Our hands met as we patted him. She kissed me then, brushed my cheek with her lips. I left her and walked back along the gusty road to camp under the high riding moon, singing *Oranges and Lemons* at the top of my voice.

Pete greeted me in the tent with a scowl. "You won't be so ruddy happy, Tommo, when you hear what I've got to tell you."

"What?" I asked.

"Our new sergeant. It's only Horrible-bleeding-Hanley from Etaples."

From then on, every waking hour of every day, Hanley was at us. We'd been mollycoddled, he said. We were sloppy soldiers and he was going to lick us back into shape. And we weren't allowed out of camp until he was satisfied. And of course he was never satisfied. So I couldn't get out of camp to see Anna again. By the time we went back up into the line, Hanley snapping at our heels, his voice had become a vicious bark inside each of our heads. Every one of us hated him like poison, a great deal more than we had ever hated Fritz.

NEARLY FOUR O'CLOCK

There is the beginning of day in the night sky, not yet the pale light of dawn, but night is certainly losing its darkness. A cockerel sounds his morning call, and tells me what I already know but do not want to believe, that morning will break and soon.

Morning at home used to be walking with Charlie to school, wading through piles of autumn leaves and stamping the ice in the puddles, or the three of us coming up through the woods after a night's poaching on the Colonel's river, and crouching down to watch a badger that didn't know we were there. Morning here has always been to wake with the same dread in the pit of my stomach, knowing that I will have to look death in the face again, that up to now it may have been someone else's death, but that today it could be mine, that this may be my last sunrise, my last day on earth.

All that is different about this morning is that I know whose death it will be and how it will happen.

Looking at it that way it seems not so bad. Look at it that way, Tommo. Look at it that way.

I always imagined I'd be lost without Charlie at my side, and the truth is that I might have been had it not been for the new batch of recruits that joined us straight from home. And how we needed them. Almost half of us were missing by this time, killed or wounded or sick. Those of us that were left were to them battle-hardened soldiers, old lags who had seen it all, and therefore to be admired, respected, and even a little feared, it seemed. Young though I still felt, I don't think I looked it, not any more. Pete and Nipper Martin and I were old soldiers now, and we behaved like it, alternately reassuring the new recruits or terrifying them with our stories, befriending them or teasing them. I think we rather played up to the role they gave us and we revelled in it, too, particularly Pete, who was more inventive with his stories than Nipper and me. All this gave me less time to dwell on my own fears. I was far too busy pretending I was someone else.

For some time, life was about as quiet as it could get in the front line. We and Fritz did little more than irritate each other with occasional whizzbangs and night patrols, and in the close confinement of the dugout and the trenches even Sergeant Hanley could do little to make our lives any more of a misery than they already were, though he still did his very best, with an endless succession of inspections and consequent punishments. But for days on end the guns stayed silent, the spring sun shone, warming our backs and drying out the mud. And best of all, we went to bed dry – a rare treat, a miraculous treat. Yes, the rats were still there and the lice loved us as much as ever, but this was a picnic compared to all we'd been through before.

By now I think the new recruits were all beginning to think that we old lags had been exaggerating with some of our harsher tales of trench warfare. Boredom and Sergeant Hanley seemed to them to be the worst they had had to endure so far. And it was certainly true, particularly in Pete's case, that we had laid it on a bit thick. But Pete, like the rest of us, had, for the most part anyway, told them stories that had at least some connection with the truth. None of us, not even Pete, could have imagined or invented what would happen to us on the quietest of May mornings, when we were least expecting it.

Stand-to on the firestep at dawn had been normal, by now a mere routine, and an annoying one too. Attacks came mostly at dawn, we knew that, but after all this time we expected nothing to happen, and nothing had happened, not for a long while now. We were lulled by the blue skies perhaps, or by sheer boredom. Fritz seemed to have gone to sleep on us and as far as we were concerned that suited us fine. We thought we could go to sleep too. The awakening came suddenly. I was in the dugout, and I was just beginning a letter home.

•

I am writing to Mother – I haven't written for a while and am feeling guilty about it. My pencil keeps breaking and I am sharpening it again. Everyone else is lying asleep in the sun or is sitting about smoking and chatting. Nipper Martin is cleaning his rifle again. He's always very particular about that.

"Gas! Gas!"

The cry goes up and is echoed all along the trench. For a moment we are frozen with panic. We have trained for this time and again, but nonetheless we fumble clumsily, feverishly with our gas masks.

"Fix bayonets!" Hanley's yelling while we're still trying frantically to pull on our gas masks. We grab our rifles and fix bayonets. We're on the firestep looking out into no-man's-land, and we see it rolling towards us, this dreaded killer cloud we have heard so much about but have never seen for ourselves until now. Its deadly tendrils are searching ahead, feeling their way forward in long yellow wisps, scenting me, searching for me. Then finding me out, the gas turns and drifts straight for me. I'm shouting inside my gas mask. "Christ! Christ!" Still the gas comes on, wafting over our wire, through our wire, swallowing everything in its path.

I hear again in my head the instructor's voice, see him shouting at me through his mask when we went out on our last exercise. "You're panicking in there, Peaceful. A gas mask is like God, son. It'll work bloody miracles for you, but you've got to believe in it." But I don't believe in it! I don't believe in miracles.

The gas is only feet away now. In a moment it will be on me, around me, in me. I crouch down hiding my face between my knees, hands over my helmet, praying it will float over my head, over the top of the trench and seek out someone else. But it does not. It's all around me. I tell myself I will not breathe, I must not breathe. Through a yellow mist I see the trench filling up with it. It drifts into the dugouts, snaking into every nook and cranny, looking for me. It wants to seek us all out, to kill us all, every one of us. Still I do not breathe. I see men running, staggering, falling. I hear Pete shouting out for me. Then he's grabbing me and we run. I have to breathe now. I can't run without breathing. Half-blinded by my mask I trip and fall, crashing my head against the trench wall, knocking myself half-senseless. My gas mask has come off. I pull it down, but I have breathed in and know already it's too late. My eyes are stinging. My lungs are burning. I am coughing, retching, choking. I don't care where I'm running so long as it is away from the gas. At last I'm in the reserve trench and it is clear of gas. I'm out of it. I wrench off my mask, gasping for good air. Then I am on my hands and knees, vomiting violently. When at last the worst is over I look up through blurred and weeping eyes. A Hun in a gas mask is standing over me, his rifle aimed at my head. I have no rifle. It is the end. I brace myself, but he does not fire. He lowers his rifle slowly. "Go boy," he says, waving me away with his rifle. "Go. Tommy, go."

So by the whim of some kind and unknown Fritz I survived and escaped. Later, back at our field hospital I heard that we had counterattacked, and had driven the Germans back and retaken our frontline trenches but, from what I could see all around me, it was at a terrible cost. I lined up with the rest of the walking wounded to see the doctor. He washed out my eyes, examined them, and listened to my chest. Despite all my coughing he pronounced me fit. "You're lucky. You can only have got a whiff of it," he said.

As I walked away I passed the others, those that had not been as lucky. They were lying stretched out in the sun, many of them faces I knew, and would never see again; friends I had lived with, joked with, played cards with, fought with. I looked for Pete amongst them. He was not there. But Nipper Martin was, the last body I came to. He lay so still. There was a green grasshopper on his trousers. When I got back to rest camp that evening I found Pete alone in the tent. He looked up at me, wide-eyed, as if he had seen a ghost. When I told him about Nipper Martin he was as near to tears as I'd ever seen him. We exchanged our escape stories over a mug of hot sweet tea.

When the gas attack came, Pete had run like me, like most of us, but with some of the others he had then regrouped in the reserve trench, had been part of the counterattack. "We're still here, Tommo, we're alive," he said. "And that's all that matters I suppose. Unfortunately, so is Horrible-bloody-Hanley. But at least I've got some good news for you." He waved a couple of letters at me. "You've got two of them, you lucky devil. No one back home writes to me. Hardly surprising I suppose, because they can't write, can they? Well, my sister can, but we don't speak, not any more. Tell you what, Tommo, you can read yours out to me and then I can pretend they're written to me as well, can't I? Go on, Tommo. I'm listening." He lay back, put his hands under his head and closed his eyes. He didn't leave me much choice.

I have them with me now, my very last letters from home. I tried to keep all the others, but some got lost and others were so often soaked through that they became unreadable and I threw them away. But these I've looked after with the greatest of care because everyone I love is in them. I keep them in waxed paper in my pocket, close to my heart. I've read them over and over again, and each time I can hear their voices in the words, see their faces in the writing. I'll read them aloud again now, just as I read them to Pete that first time in the tent. I'll read Mother's letter first because I read it first then.

My dear Son,

    I hope this letter finds you in good health. I have such good news to tell you. Last Monday, in the early morning, Molly gave birth to a little boy. As you can imagine we are all delighted at the happy event. You can imagine also our surprise and joy when I answered a knock on the door less than a week later to find your brother Charlie standing in the porch. He looks thinner than I remember him and much older too. I do not think he has been eating enough and have told him he must do so in future. He says that in spite of everything we read in the papers here you have been having a fine time together over in Belgium. Everyone I meet in the village asks how you are, even your great-aunt. She was the first to come to see the baby. She said that although he was handsome she thought he had rather pointed ears, which is untrue of course, and upset Molly greatly. Why does she always say such hurtful things? As for the Colonel, if we are to believe all he says, he could win this war all by himself. Your father was so right about him.

    Much has changed in the village, and none of it for the better. More of our young men go to join up all the time. There are scarcely enough men left to work the land. Hedges go untrimmed and many fields lie fallow. Sad to say Fred and Margaret Parsons had news only last month that Jimmy will not be coming home. It seems he died of his wounds in France.

> *But Charlie's short visit and the birth of the baby have cheered us all. Charlie tells us that very soon there will be another big push and then the war will be won and over with. We pray he is right. Dear Son, even with Charlie home, with Big Joe and Molly and the new baby, this little house seems empty because you are not with us. Come home safe and soon.*
>
> *Your loving mother.*

And Big Joe's inky thumbprint was smeared along the bottom of the page as usual, with his name beside it in huge spidery lettering.

"So that's what we're having, is it?" said Pete suddenly and angrily. "A fine time. Why does he tell them that? Why doesn't he say what it's really like out here, what a hopeless bloody mess it all is, how there's good men, thousands of them, dying for nothing – for nothing! I'll tell them. Give me half a chance and I'll tell them. Saying things like that, Charlie should be ashamed of himself. Those men who died today, were they having a fine time? Were they?" I'd never seen Pete this angry before. He was always the joker, the wag, always playing the fool. He rolled over on his side with his back to me and didn't speak again.

So I read the next letter to myself. It was from Charlie, mostly anyway. Unlike Mother he'd made lots of mistakes and crossings out, so his letter was much harder to read.

Dear Private Peaceful,

I am home again as you can see, Tommo. Better late than never as they say. I am the proud father, and you are the proud uncle, of the finest looking little fellow you ever saw. I wish you could see him. But you will, and soon I hope. Molly tells me he is even more handsome than his father, which I'm very sure is not true. Big Joe sits over him while he sleeps, like he used to do with Bertha. He worries I shall go off again soon, which of course I shall. He does not understand — how could he? — where we have been or what we have been doing. And I'd rather not tell him. I'd rather not tell anyone.

After I came out of hospital I managed to wangle only three days' leave, of which I now have only one day left. I shall make the best use of it. Lastly, you should know that we have all decided the little fellow will be called Tommo. Each time we say his name it makes me think you are here with us, as we all wish you were. Molly has said that she wants to write a few words also, so I shall end now. Chin up.

Your brother Charlie, or the other Private Peaceful.

Dear Tommo,

I write to say that I have told little Tommo all about his brave uncle, about how one day when this dreadful war is over, we shall all be together again. He has your blue eyes, Charlie's dark hair and Big Joe's great grin. Because of all this I love him more than I can say.

Your Molly.

These two letters I kept by me and read and re-read till I knew them almost by heart. They kept me going during the days ahead. I took from them the hope of Charlie's return, and the strength I needed to stop myself from going mad.

We might have thought, we certainly hoped, that Sergeant Hanley would let up on us now and let us rest before going back up into the line. But we were to discover what we should have known already, that this wasn't in his nature. He said we had shamed the regiment, that we had behaved like a bunch of cowards when the gas attack came, that if it was the last thing he did he would put backbone into us. So Hanley kept us at it morning, noon and night, day in, day out. Inspections, training, drilling, exercising, more inspections. He drove us mercilessly, drove us all to despair and exhaustion. Caught sleeping one night at his post, Ben Guy, the innkeeper's son from Exbourne, one of the new recruits, was subjected, as Charlie had been before him, to Field Punishment Number One. For day after day he was strapped there on the gun wheel in all weathers. As with Charlie at Etaples, we were forbidden even to speak to him or take him water.

These were the darkest days we had ever lived through. Sergeant Hanley had done what all the bloody attrition in the trenches had never done. He had taken away our spirit, and drained the last of our strength, destroyed our hope. More than once as I lay there in my tent at night I thought of deserting, or running to Anna in Pop and asking her to hide me, to help me find a way back to England. But when morning came, even my courage to be a coward had evaporated. I stayed each time because I was too cowardly to go, because I couldn't abandon Pete and the others, and not be there when Charlie got back. And I stayed, too, because Molly had said I was brave and had named little Tommo after me. I couldn't shame her. I couldn't shame him.

Much to our surprise we were granted one night of freedom before we were to be sent off up into the line again, and we all headed straight into Pop, to the *estaminet*. Most of us were going for the beer and food, and I longed for all that as well, but as we walked into town I realised I had Anna on my mind a lot more than eggs and chips. But Anna did not bring us our beers. Another girl did, a girl none of us had seen before. I looked around me, but I could not see Anna serving at any of the other tables either. When the girl brought us our egg and chips I asked her where Anna was. She just shrugged as if she didn't understand, but there was something about her that told me she did understand, that she did know but would not tell me. Thanks to Pete and Charlie, my liking for Anna had not been a secret in the company for some time now, and now everyone was teasing me mercilessly as I looked around for her. Tiring of it, I left their mocking laughter behind me and went outside to look for her.

I looked first in the stable, where she'd taken me before, but it was empty. I walked down the darkening farm track past the henhouses to see if the horse might be out in the field, and Anna there with him. There were a couple of bleating tethered goats, but I could see no horse, and no Anna. Only then did I think of going back and knocking on the back door. I screwed my courage up. I had to knock loudly to be heard because of all the noise coming from the *estaminet*. The door opened slowly, and there was her father, not dapper and smiling as I'd always known him, but in his braces and shirt, unshaven and dishevelled. He had a bottle in his hand and his face was heavy with drink. He was not pleased to see me.

"Anna?" I said. "Is Anna in?"

"No," he replied. "Anna isn't in. Anna will never be in again. Anna is dead. You hear this, Tommy? You come here and you fight your war in my place. Why? Tell me this. Why?"

"What happened?" I asked him.

"What happened? I tell you what happened. Two days ago I send Anna to fetch the eggs. She is driving the cart home along the road and a shell comes, a big Boche shell. Only one, but one is enough. I bury her today. So if you want to see my Anna, Tommy, then go to the graveyard. Then you can go to Hell all of you, British, German, French, you think I care? And you can take your war to Hell with you, they will like it there. Leave me alone, Tommy, leave me alone."

The door was slammed shut in my face.

There were several recently dug graves in the churchyard, but I found only one that was freshly dug and covered with fresh flowers. I had known Anna only from a few laughing words, from the light in her eyes, a touch of hands and a fleeting kiss, but I felt an ache inside me such as I had not felt since I was a child, since my father's death. I looked up at the church steeple, a dark arrow pointing at the moon and beyond, and tried with all my heart and mind to believe she was up there somewhere in that vast expanse of infinity, up there in Sunday-school Heaven, in Big Joe's happy Heaven. I couldn't bring myself to think it. I knew she was lying in the cold earth at my feet. I knelt down and kissed the earth, then left her there. The moon sailed above me, following behind me, through the trees, lighting my way back to camp. By the time I got there I had no more tears left to cry.

The next night we were marching up into the trenches

again along with hundreds of others, to stiffen the line they told us. That could only mean one thing: an attack was expected and we would be in for a packet of trouble. As it turned out, Fritz was to give us a couple of days' grace – no attack came, not yet.

Charlie came instead, just strolled into our dugout as if he'd been gone five minutes. "Afternoon, Tommo. Afternoon, all," he said, grinning from ear to ear. His arrival gave us all new heart. With Sergeant Hanley still on our backs, always on the prowl, we had our champion back, the only one of us who had ever faced him down. As for me, I had my guardian back, my brother and my best friend. Like everyone else I felt suddenly safer.

I was there when Sergeant Hanley and Charlie came face to face in the trench. "What a nice surprise, Sergeant," Charlie chirped. "I heard you'd joined us."

"And I heard you'd been malingering, Peaceful," Hanley snarled. "I don't like malingerers. I've got my eye on you, Peaceful. You're a troublemaker, always have been. I'm warning you, one step out of line..."

"Don't you worry yourself, Sergeant," said Charlie. "I'll be good as gold. Cross my heart and hope to die."

The sergeant looked first nonplussed, then explosive.

"Nice weather we're having, Sergeant," Charlie went on. "It's raining in Blighty, you know. Cats and dogs." Hanley pushed past him, muttering to himself as he went. It was a little enough victory, but it cheered all of us who witnessed it to the bottom of our hearts.

That evening Charlie and I sat drinking our tea over a guttering lamp and talked quietly together for the first time. I was full of questions about everyone at home, but he seemed unwilling to say much about them. I was taken aback by this, hurt even, until he saw I was and explained why.

"It's like we're living two separate lives in two separate worlds, Tommo, and I want to keep it that way. I never want the one to touch on the other. I didn't want to bring horrible Hanley and whizzbangs back home, did I? And for me it's the same the other way round. Home's home. Here's here. It's difficult to explain, but little Tommo and Molly, Mother and Big Joe, they don't belong in this hell hole of a place, do they? By talking about them I bring them here, and I don't want to do that. You understand, Tommo?"

And I did.

We hear the shell coming and know from the shriek of it that it will be close, and it is. The blast of it throws us all to the ground, putting out lamps and plunging us into pungent darkness. It is the first shell of thousands. Our guns answer almost at once, and from then on the titanic duel is almost constant as the world above us erupts, the roar and thunder pounding us remorselessly all day, all night. When the guns do let up it is all the more cruel, for it gives us some fragile hope it might at last be over, only to snatch that hope away again minutes later.

To begin with we huddle together in the dugout and try to pretend to ourselves it isn't happening, and even if it is, that our dugout is deep enough to see us through. We all know in our heart of hearts that a direct hit will be the end of all of us. We know it and accept it. We just prefer not to think about it, and certainly not to talk about it. We drink our tea, smoke our Woodbines, eat when food comes – which isn't often – and go on living as best we can, as normally as we can.

It doesn't seem possible, but on the second day the bombardment intensifies. Every heavy gun the Germans have seems to be aimed at our sector. There is a moment when the last fragile vestiges of controlled fear give way to terror, a terror that can be hidden no longer. I find myself curled into a ball on the ground and screaming for it to stop. Then I feel Charlie lying beside me, folding himself around me to protect me, to comfort me. He begins to sing *Oranges and Lemons* softly in my ear, and soon I am singing with him, and loudly too, singing instead of screaming. Before we know it the whole dugout is singing along with us. But the barrage goes on and on and on, until in the end neither Charlie nor *Oranges and Lemons* can drive away the terror that is engulfing me and invading me, destroying any last glimmer of courage and composure I may have left. All I have now is my fear.

When their attack comes, in the pearly light of dawn, it falters before it even gets near our wire. Our machine gunners see to that, knocking them down like thousands of grey skittles, never to rise again. My hands are shaking so much I can hardly reload my rifle. When they recoil and turn and run we wait for the whistle and then go out over the top. I go because the others go, moving forward as if in a trance, as if outside myself altogether. I find myself suddenly on my knees and I don't know why. There is blood pouring down my face, and my head is wracked with a sudden burning pain so terrible that I feel it must burst. I feel myself falling out of my dream down into a world of swirling darkness. I am being beckoned into a world I have never been to before where it is warm and comforting and all-enveloping. I know I am dying my own death, and I welcome it.

FIVE TO FIVE

Sixty-five minutes to go. How shall I live them? Shall I try to sleep? It would be useless to try. Should I eat a hearty breakfast? I don't want it. Shall I scream and shout? What would be the point? Shall I pray? Why? What for? Who to?

No. They will do what they will do. Field Marshal Haig is God out here, and Haig has signed. Haig has confirmed the sentence. He has decreed that Private Peaceful will die, will be shot for cowardice in the face of the enemy at six o'clock on the morning of the twenty-fifth of June 1916.

The firing squad will be having their breakfast by now, sipping their tea, hating what they will have to do. No one has told me where exactly it will happen. I don't want it to be in some dark prison yard with grey walls all around. I want it to be where there is sky and clouds and trees, and birds. It will be easier if there are birds. And let it be quickly over. Please let it be quickly over.

I wake to the muffled sound of machine-gun fire, to the distant shriek of the shells. The earth quivers and trembles about me, but I am strangely relieved, for all this must mean that I'm not dead. Nor am I all that alarmed at first when I find that all I can see is darkness, because I remember at once that I have been wounded – I can still feel the throbbing in my head. It must be night and I am lying wounded somewhere in no-man's-land, looking up into the black of the sky. But then I try to move my head a little and the blackness begins to crumble and fall in on me, filling my mouth, my eyes, my ears. It is not the sky I am looking at, but earth. I feel the weight of it now, pressing down on my chest. My legs cannot move, nor my arms. Only my fingers. How slowly I come to know and understand that I am buried, buried alive, but then how fast I panic. They must have thought I was dead, and buried me, but I am not. I am not! I scream then, and the earth fills my mouth and at once chokes off my breathing. My fingers scrabble, clawing frantically at the earth, but I am suffocating and they cannot help me. I try to think, to calm my raging panic, to try to lie still, to force myself to try to breathe through my nose. But there is no air to breathe. I think of Molly then and commit myself to holding her in my head until the moment I die.

I feel a hand on my leg. One foot is gripped, then the other. From far away I think I hear a voice, and I know it is Charlie's voice. He is calling for me to hang on. They are digging for me, pulling at me, dragging me out into blessed daylight, out into blessed air. I gulp the air like water, choking on it, coughing on it, and then at last I can breathe it in.

The next thing I know I am sitting deep down in what looks like the remains of a concrete dugout, full of exhausted men, all faces I know. Pete is coming down the steps. He is gasping for breath like me. Charlie is still pouring the last dribbles from his water bottle on to my face, trying to clean me up. "Thought we'd lost you, Tommo," Charlie is saying. "The same shell that buried you killed half a dozen of us. You were lucky. Your head's a bit of a mess. You lie still, Tommo. You've lost a lot of blood." I'm shaking now. I'm cold all over and weak as a kitten.

Pete is crouching beside us now, his forehead pressed against his rifle. "All hell's broken loose out there," he says. "We're going down like flies, Charlie. They've got us pinned down, machine guns on three sides. Stick your head out of there and you're a dead man."

"Where are we?" I ask.

"Middle of bloody no-man's-land, that's where, some old German dugout," Pete replies. "Can't go forward, can't go back."

"Then we'd best stay put for a while, hadn't we?" Charlie says.

I look up and see Sergeant Hanley standing over us, rifle in hand and shouting at us. "Stay put? Stay put? You listen to me, Peaceful. I give the orders round here. When I say we go, we go. Do I make myself clear?"

Charlie looks him straight in the eye in open defiance and does not look away, just as he used to do with Mr Munnings at school when he was being ticked off.

"Soon as I give the word," the sergeant goes on, to everyone in the dugout now, "we make a dash for it, and I mean all of us. No stragglers, no malingerers – that means you, Peaceful. Our orders are to press home the attack and then hold our ground. Only fifty yards or so to the German trenches. We'll get there easy."

I wait till the sergeant moves away, until he can't hear. "Charlie," I whisper, "I don't think I can make it. I don't think I can stand up."

"It's all right," he says, and his face breaks into a sudden smile. "You look a right mess, Tommo. All blood and mud, with a couple of little white eyes looking out. Don't you worry, we'll stay together, no matter what. We always have, haven't we?"

The sergeant waits a minute or two by the opening of the dugout until there is a lull in the firing outside. "Right," he says. "This is it. We're going out. Make sure you've all got a full magazine and one up the spout. Everyone ready? On your feet. Let's go." No one moves. The men are looking at one another, hesitating. "What in Hell's name is the matter with you? On your feet, damn you! On your feet!"

Then Charlie speaks up, very quietly. "I think they're thinking what I'm thinking, Sergeant. You take us out there now and their machine guns'll just mow us down. They've seen us go in here, and they'll be waiting for us to come out. They're not stupid. Maybe we should stay here and then go back after dark. No point in going out there and getting ourselves killed for nothing, is there, Sergeant?"

"Are you disobeying my order, Peaceful?" The sergeant is ranting like a man demented now.

"No, I'm just letting you know what I think," Charlie replies. "What we all think."

"And I'm telling you, Peaceful, that if you don't come with us when we go, it won't just be field punishment again. It'll be a court martial for you. It'll be the firing squad. Do you hear me, Peaceful? Do you hear me?"

"Yes, Sergeant," says Charlie. "I hear you. But the thing is, Sergeant, even if I wanted to, I can't go with you because I'd have to leave Tommo behind, and I can't do that. As you can see, Sergeant, he's been wounded. He can hardly walk, let alone run. I'm not leaving him. I'll be staying with him. Don't you worry about us, Sergeant, we'll make our way back later when it gets dark. We'll be all right."

"You miserable little worm, Peaceful." The sergeant is threatening Charlie with his rifle now, the bayonet inches from Charlie's nose and trembling with fury. "I should shoot you right where you are and save the firing squad the trouble." For just a moment it looks as if the sergeant really will do it, but then he remembers himself, and turns away. "You lot, on your feet. On my word, I want you men out there. Make no mistake, it's a court martial for anyone who stays."

One by one the men get unwillingly to their feet, each one preparing himself in his own way, a last drag on a cigarette, a silent prayer, eyes closed.

"Go! Go! Go!" The sergeant is screaming, and they do go, leaping up the steps of the dugout and dashing out into the open. I hear the German machine guns opening up again. Pete is the last to leave the dugout. He pauses on the step and looks back down at us. "You should come, Charlie," he says. "He means it. The bastard means what he says, I promise you."

"I know he does," says Charlie. "So do I. G'luck, Pete. Keep your head down."

Then Pete is gone and we're alone together in the dugout. We don't need to imagine what is going on out there. We can hear it, the screams cut short, the death rattle of machine guns, the staccato of rifle fire picking them off one by one. Then it goes quiet and we wait. I look across at Charlie. I see there are tears in his eyes. "Poor beggars," he says. "Poor beggars." And then: "I think I've cooked my goose good and proper this time, Tommo."

"Maybe the sergeant won't come back," I tell him.

"Let's hope," says Charlie. "Let's hope."

I must have drifted in and out of consciousness after that. Each time I woke I saw that another one or two had made it back to the dugout, but still no Sergeant Hanley. Still I hoped. Then I woke to find myself lying with Charlie's arm around me, my head resting on his shoulder.

"Tommo? Tommo?" he said. "You awake?"

"Yes," I said.

"Listen Tommo, I've been thinking. If the worst happens—"

"It's not going to happen," I interrupted.

"Just listen, Tommo, will you? I want you to promise me you'll look after things for me. You understand what I'm saying? You promise?"

"Yes," I said.

Then after a long silence he went on: "You still love her, don't you? You still love Moll?" My silence was enough. He knew already. "Good," said Charlie. "And there's something else I want you to look after too." He lifted his arm away from behind me, took off his watch, and strapped it on my wrist. "There you are, Tommo. It's a wonderful watch, this. Never stopped, not once. Don't lose it." I didn't know what to say. "Now you can go back to sleep again," he said.

And in my sleep I dreamt again my childhood nightmare, Father's finger pointing at me, and I promised myself even as I dreamt that when I woke this time I would at last tell Charlie what I did in that forest all those years ago.

I opened my eyes. Sergeant Hanley was sitting across the dugout from us, looking at us darkly from under his helmet. As we waited for any others to come in and for darkness to fall, the sergeant sat there not saying another word to Charlie or to anyone, just glaring unwaveringly at Charlie. There was cold hate in his eyes.

By nightfall there was still no sign of Pete, nor of a dozen others who'd gone out with the sergeant to join that futile charge. The sergeant decided it was time to go. So in the dark of the night, by twos and threes, the remnants of the company crawled back to our trenches across no-man's-land, Charlie half dragging me, half lifting me all the way. From my stretcher in the bottom of the trench I looked up and saw Charlie being taken away under close arrest. It all happened so fast after that. There was no time for goodbyes. Only when he'd gone did I remember again my dream and the promise I'd made in it, and had not kept.

They did not let me see him again for another six weeks, and by then the court martial was all over, the death sentence passed and then confirmed. That was all I knew, all anyone knew. I knew nothing whatever of how it had all happened until yesterday, when at last I was allowed to see him. They were holding him at Walker Camp. The guard outside said he was sorry, but I had only twenty minutes. Orders, he said.

It is a stable – and it still smells like it – with a table and two chairs, a bucket in the corner, and a bed along one wall. Charlie is lying on his back, hands under his head, legs crossed. He sits up as soon as he sees me, and smiles broadly. "I hoped you'd come, Tommo," he says. "I didn't think they'd let you. How's your head? All mended?"

"Good as new," I tell him, trying to respond in kind to his cheeriness. And then we're standing there hugging one another, and I can't help myself.

"I want no tears, Tommo," he whispers in my ear. "This is going to be difficult enough without tears." He holds me at arm's length. "Understand?"

I can do no more than nod.

He has had a letter from home, from Molly, which he must read out to me, he says, because it makes him laugh and he needs to laugh. It's mostly about little Tommo. Molly writes that he's already learning to blow raspberries and they're every bit as loud and rude as ours when we were young. And she says Big Joe sings him to sleep at night, *Oranges and Lemons* of course. She ends by sending her love and hoping we're both well.

"Doesn't she know?" I ask.

"No," Charlie says. "And they won't know, not until afterwards. They'll send them a telegram. They didn't let me write home until today." As we sit down at the table he lowers his voice and we talk in half-whispers now. "You'll tell them how it really was, won't you, Tommo? It's all I care about now. I don't want them thinking I was a coward. I don't want that. I want them to know the truth."

"Didn't you tell the court martial?" I ask him.

"Course I did. I tried, I tried my very best, but there's none so deaf as them that don't want to hear. They had their one witness, Sergeant Hanley, and he was all they needed. It wasn't a trial, Tommo. They'd made up their minds I was guilty before they even sat down. I had three of them, a brigadier and two captains looking down their noses at me as if I was some sort of dirt. I told them everything, Tommo, just like it happened. I had nothing to be ashamed of, did I? I wasn't going to hide anything. So I told them that, yes, I did disobey the sergeant's order because the order was stupid, suicidal – we all knew it was – and that anyway I had to stay behind to look after you. They knew a dozen or more got wiped out in the attack, that no one even got as far as the German wire. They knew I was right, but it made no difference."

"What about witnesses?" I ask him. "You should have had witnesses. I could have said. I could have told them."

"I asked for you, Tommo, but they wouldn't accept you because you were my brother. I asked for Pete, but then they told me that Pete was missing. And as for the rest of the company, I was told they'd been moved into another sector, and were up in the line and not available. So they heard it all from Sergeant Hanley, and they swallowed everything he told them, like it was gospel truth. I think there's a big push coming, and they wanted to make an example of someone, Tommo. And I was the Charlie." He laughed at that. "A right Charlie. Then of course there was my record as a troublemaker, 'a mutinous troublemaker' Hanley called me. Remember Etaples? Had up on a charge of gross insubordination? Field Punishment Number One? It was all there on my record. So was my foot."

"Your foot?"

"That time I was shot in the foot. All foot wounds are suspicious, they said. It could have been self-inflicted – it goes on all the time, they said. I could have done it myself just to get myself out of the trenches and back to Blighty."

"But it wasn't like that," I say.

"Course it wasn't. They believed what they wanted to believe."

"Didn't you have anyone to speak up for you?" I ask him. "Like an officer or someone?"

"I didn't think I needed one," Charlie tells me. "Just tell them the truth, Charlie, and you'll be all right. That's what I thought. How wrong could I be? I thought maybe a letter of good character from Wilkie would help. I was sure they'd listen to him, him being an officer and one of them. I told them where I thought he was. The last I'd heard he was up in a hospital in Scotland somewhere. They told me they'd written to the hospital, but that he'd died of his wounds six months before. The whole court martial took less than an hour, Tommo. That's all they gave me. An hour for a man's life. Not a lot, is it? And do you know what the brigadier said, Tommo? He said I was a worthless man. Worthless. I've been called a lot of things in my life, Tommo, but none of them ever upset me, except that one. I didn't show it, mind. I wouldn't have given them the satisfaction. And then he passed sentence. I was expecting it by then. Didn't upset me nearly as much as I thought it would."

I hang my head, because I cannot stop my eyes filling.

"Tommo," he says, lifting my chin. "Look on the bright side. It's no more than we were facing every day in the trenches. It'll be over very quick. And the boys are looking after me all right here. They don't like it any more than I do. Three hot meals a day. A man can't grumble. It's all over and done with, or it will be soon anyway. You want some tea, Tommo? They brought me some just before you came."

So we sit either side of the table and share a mug of sweet strong tea, and speak of everything Charlie wants to talk about: home, bread and butter pudding with the raisins in and the crunchy crust on top, moonlit nights fishing for sea trout on the Colonel's river, Bertha, beer at The Duke, the yellow aeroplane and the humbugs.

"We won't talk of Big Joe or Mother or Moll," Charlie says, "because I'll cry if I do, and I promised myself I wouldn't." He leans forward suddenly in great earnest, clutching my hand. "Talking of promises, that promise you made me back in the dugout, Tommo. You won't forget it, will you? You will look after them?"

"I promise," I tell him, and I've never meant anything so much in all my life.

"You've still got the watch then," he says, pulling back my sleeve. "Keep it ticking for me, and then when the time comes, give it to Little Tommo, so he'll have something from me. I'd like that. You'll make him a good father, like Father was to us."

It is the moment. I have to do it now. It is my last chance. I tell him about how Father had died, about how it had happened, what I had done, how I should have told him years ago, but had never dared to. He smiles. "I always knew that, Tommo. So did Mother. You'd talk in your sleep. Always having nightmares, always keeping me awake about it, you were. All nonsense. Not your fault. It was the tree that killed Father, Tommo, not you."

"You sure?" I ask him.

"I'm sure," he says. "Quite sure."

We look at one another and know that time is getting short now. I see a flicker of panic in his eyes. He pulls some letters out of his pocket and pushes them across the table. "You'll see they get these, Tommo?"

We grip hands across the table, put our foreheads together and close our eyes. I manage to say what I've been wanting to say.

"You're not worthless, Charlie. They're the worthless bastards. You're the best friend I've ever had, the best person I've ever known."

I hear Charlie starting to hum softly. It is *Oranges and Lemons*, slightly out of tune. I hum with him, our hands clasping tighter, our humming stronger now. Then we are singing, singing it out loud so that the whole world can hear us, and we are laughing as we sing. And there are tears, but it does not matter because these are not tears of sadness, they are tears of celebration. When we've finished, Charlie says: "It's what I'll be singing in the morning. It won't be God Save the ruddy King or All Things bleeding Bright and Beautiful. It'll be *Oranges and Lemons* for Big Joe, for all of us."

The guard comes in and tells us our time is up. We shake hands then as strangers do. There are no words left to say. I hold our last look and want to hold it forever. Then I turn away and leave him.

When I got back to camp yesterday afternoon I expected the sympathy and the long faces and all those averted eyes I'd been used to for days before. Instead I was greeted by smiles and with the news that Sergeant Hanley was dead. He had been killed, they told me, in a freak accident, blown up by a grenade out on the ranges. So there was some justice, of a sort, but it had come too late for Charlie. I hoped someone at Walker Camp had heard about it and would tell Charlie. It would be small consolation for him, but it would be something. Any jubilation I felt, or any of us felt, turned very soon to grim satisfaction, and then evaporated completely. It seemed as if the entire regiment was subdued, like me quite unable to think of anything else but Charlie, of the injustice he was suffering, and the inevitability of what must happen to him in the morning.

We have been billeted this last week or so around an empty farmhouse, less than a mile down the road from where they're keeping Charlie at Walker Camp. We've been waiting to go up into the trenches further down the line on the Somme. We live in bell tents, and the officers are billeted in the house. The others have been doing their very best to make it as easy as they can for me. I know from their every look how much they feel for me, NCOs and officers too. But kind though they are I do not want or need their sympathy or their help. I do not even want the distraction of their company. I want simply to be alone. Late in the evening I take a lamp with me and move out of the tent into this barn, or what is left of it. They bring me blankets and food, and then leave me to myself. They understand. The padre comes to do what he can. He can do nothing. I send him away. So here I am now with the night gone so fast and the clock ticking towards six o'clock. When the time comes, I will go outside, and I will look up at the sky because I know Charlie will be doing the same as they take him out. We'll be seeing the same clouds, feeling the same breeze on our faces. At least that way we'll be together.

ONE MINUTE TO SIX

I try to close my mind to what is happening this minute to Charlie. I try just to think of Charlie as he was at home, as we all were. But all I can see in my mind are the soldiers leading Charlie out into the field. He is not stumbling. He is not struggling. He is not crying out. He is walking with his head held high, just as he was after Mr Munnings caned him at school that day. Maybe there's a lark rising, or a great crow wheeling into the wind above him. The firing squad stands at ease, waiting. Six men, their rifles loaded and ready, each one wanting only to get it over with. They will be shooting one of their own and it feels to them like murder. They try not to look at Charlie's face.

Charlie is tied to the post. The padre says a prayer, makes the sign of the cross on his forehead and moves away. It is cold now but Charlie does not shiver. The officer, his revolver drawn, is looking at his watch. They try to put a hood over Charlie's head, but he will not have it. He looks up to the sky and sends his last living thoughts back home.

"Present! Ready! Aim!"

He closes his eyes and as he waits he sings softly. "*Oranges and Lemons, say the bells of St. Clements.*" Under my breath I sing it with him. I hear the echoing volley. It is done. It is over. With that volley a part of me has died with him. I turn back to go to the solitude of my hay barn, and I find I am far from alone in my grieving. All over the camp I see them standing to attention outside their tents. And the birds are singing.

I am not alone that afternoon either when I go to Walker Camp to collect his belongings, and to see where they have buried him. He would like the place. He looks out over a water meadow down to where a brook runs softly under the trees. They tell me he walked out with a smile on his face as if he were going for an early-morning stroll. They tell me that he refused the hood, and that they thought he was singing when he died. Six of us who were in the dugout that day stand vigil over his grave until sundown. Each of us says the same thing when we leave.

"Bye Charlie."

The next day the regiment is marching up the road towards the Somme. It is late June, and they say there's soon going to be an almighty push and we're going to be part of it. We'll push them all the way to Berlin. I've heard that before. All I know is that I must survive. I have promises to keep.

POSTSCRIPT

In the First World War, between 1914 and 1918, over 290 soldiers of the British and Commonwealth armies were executed by firing squad, some for desertion and cowardice, two for simply sleeping at their posts.

Many of these men we now know were traumatised by shell shock. Court martials were brief, the accused often unrepresented.

To this day the injustice they suffered has never been officially recognised. The British Government continues to refuse to grant posthumous pardons.

By Michael Morpurgo

The Amazing Story of Adolphus Tips
Private Peaceful
Cool!
The Dancing Bear
Farm Boy
Dear Olly
Billy the Kid
Toro! Toro!
The Butterfly Lion

For Younger Readers

Mr Skip
Jigger's Day Off
Albertine, Goose Queen
And Pigs Might Fly
Martians at Mudpuddle Farm
Mossop's Last Chance
Mum's the Word

Picture Books

The Gentle Giant
Wombat Goes Walkabout

Audio

The Amazing Story of Adolphus Tips (read by Jenny Agutter
and Michael Morpurgo)
Private Peaceful (read by Jamie Glover)
Kensuke's Kingdom (read by Derek Jacobi)
Dear Olly (read by Paul McGann)
Out of the Ashes (read by Sophie Aldred)
The Butterfly Lion (read by Virginia McKenna
and Michael Morpurgo)
Billy the Kid (read by Richard Attenborough)
Farm Boy (read by Derek Jacobi and Michael Morpurgo)

Billy THE Kid

I was faster than all the kids twice my age.
And somehow I could always make a football do
whatever I wanted it to. It just came easy to me,
I don't know why, but it did.

The only thing Billy ever wanted to do was to play for Chelsea.
His dream came true when he was picked for the team – but that
was 1939, and the Second World War began, and then Billy's
life, like everyone else's, was changed for ever.

Billy's no kid now – he's eighty today. But he's got
memories, such memories...

"... told with all the author's open-hearted clarity,
and richly illustrated by Michael Foreman." *Philip Pullman*

HarperCollins *Children's Books*

Dear Olly,

Matt wouldn't look at her as he spoke.
"I'm going to be a clown, Olly, I mean a real clown.
And now I know where I'm going to do it.
I'm going where my swallows go. I'm going to Africa."

As Olly waits for her brother's letters, she watches the swallows preparing to leave for the winter. Hero the swallow starts his long journey to Africa, not knowing the terrible dangers he will meet on the way. And when Matt sees the children in the African orphanage – sick, injured and lonely – he knows he's made the right decisions, but he never could have dreamt of what was going to happen to him there…

"My daughter got to Michael Morpurgo's *Dear Olly* before me. 'This is excellent,' she informed me gravely. And it is… we both cried buckets." *The Times*

HarperCollins *Children's Books*

The Butterfly Lion

Bertie rescues an orphaned white lion cub from the African veld. They are inseparable until Bertie is sent to boarding school far away in England and the lion is sold to a circus. Bertie swears that one day they will see one another again, but it is the butterfly lion which ensures that their friendship will never be forgotten.

Winner of the Smarties Prize and the Writers' Guild Award.

A novel for 8-12 year olds

HarperCollins *Children's Books*

THE BUTTERFLY LION

"*The Butterfly Lion* tells of loneliness and love in a way that is wholly appropriate for young readers."
>Julia Eccleshare, chair of adult judging panel,
>Smarties Prize 1996

"A magical, mysterious story with the power to draw readers back again and again."
>Jenny Morris, adult judging panel,
>Smarties Prize 1996

"This beautiful story of love and war has everything – even a great twist."
>*Young Telegraph*

"This sensitive, highly visual story deserves to be recognized as a masterpiece."
>*Junior Education*

"The most beautifully crafted story I've read for a long time."
>Wendy Cooling, *Treasure Islands*, BBC Radio 4

"Morpurgo writes with a fine mixture of clarity, depth and feeling."
>*Sunday Times*

First published in Great Britain by HarperCollins *Children's Books* 1996

40

HarperCollins *Children's Books* is a division of HarperCollins*Publishers* Ltd,
77–85 Fulham Palace Road, Hammersmith, London W6 8JB

The HarperCollins *Children's Books* website address is:
www.harpercollinschildrensbooks.co.uk

Copyright © Michael Morpurgo 1996
Illustrations copyright © Christian Birmingham 1996

ISBN-13   978 0 00 67503 8
ISBN-10   0 00 675103 2

The author and illustrator assert the moral right to be
identified as the author and illustrator of this work.

A CIP record for this title is available from the British Library.

Set in Palatino 14/21pt

Printed and bound in England by
Clays Ltd, S. Ives plc

Conditions of Sale
This book is sold subject to the condition that it shall not by
way of trade or otherwise be lent, re-sold, hired out or
otherwise circulated without the publisher's prior consent in any
form, binding or cover other than that in which it is published
and without a similar condition including this condition being
imposed on the subsequent purchaser

This book is proudly printed on paper which contains wood
from well managed forests, certified in accordance with
the rules of the Forest Stewardship Council.
For more information about FSC,
please visit www.fsc-uk.org

Mixed Sources
Product group from well-managed
forests and other controlled sources
www.fsc.org Cert no. SW-COC-1806
FSC © 1996 Forest Stewardship Council

michael morpurgo

THE
BUTTERFLY
LION

Illustrated by

CHRISTIAN BIRMINGHAM

HarperCollins *Children's Books*

For Virginia McKenna

The Butterfly Lion

The Butterfly Lion grew from several magical roots: the memories of a small boy who tried to run away from school a long time ago; a book about a pride of white lions discovered by Chris McBride; a chance meeting in a lift with Virginia McKenna, actress and champion of lions and all creatures born free; a true story of a soldier of the First World War who rescued some circus animals in France from certain death; and the sighting from a train of a white horse carved out on a chalky hillside near Westbury in Wiltshire.

To Chris McBride, to Virginia McKenna and to Gina Pollinger – many, many thanks. And to you the reader – enjoy it!

Michael Morpurgo
February 1996

Chilblains and Semolina Pudding

Butterflies live only short lives. They flower and flutter for just a few glorious weeks, and then they die. To see them, you have to be in the right place at the right time. And that's how it was when I saw the butterfly lion – I happened to be in just the right place, at just the right time. I didn't dream him. I didn't dream any of it. I saw him, blue and shimmering in the sun, one afternoon in June when I was young. A long time ago. But I don't forget. I mustn't forget. I promised them I wouldn't.

I was ten, and away at boarding school in deepest Wiltshire. I was far from home and I didn't want to be. It was a diet of Latin and stew and rugby and detentions and cross-country runs and chilblains and marks and squeaky beds and semolina pudding. And then there was Basher Beaumont who terrorised and tormented me, so that I lived every waking moment of my life in dread of him. I had often thought of running away, but only once ever plucked up the courage to do it.

I was homesick after a letter from my mother. Basher Beaumont had cornered me in the bootroom and smeared black shoe-polish in my hair. I had done badly in a spelling test, and Mr Carter had stood me in the corner with a book on my head all through the lesson – his favourite torture. I was more miserable than I had ever been before. I picked at the plaster in the wall, and determined there and then that I would run away.

I took off the next Sunday afternoon. With any luck I wouldn't be missed till supper, and by that time I'd be home, home and free. I climbed the fence at the bottom of the school park, behind the trees where I couldn't be seen. Then I ran for it. I ran as if bloodhounds were after me, not stopping till I was through Innocents Breach and out onto the road beyond. I had my escape all planned. I would walk to the station – it was only five miles or so – and catch the train to London. Then I'd take the underground home. I'd just walk in and tell them that I was never, ever going back.

There wasn't much traffic, but all the same I turned up the collar of my raincoat so that no one could catch a glimpse of my uniform. It was beginning to rain now, those heavy hard drops that mean there's more of the same on the way. I crossed the road, and ran along the wide grass verge under the shelter of the trees. Beyond the grass verge was a high brick wall, much of it covered in ivy. It stretched away into the distance, continuous as far as the eye could see, except for a massive arched gateway at the bend of the road. A great stone lion bestrode the gateway. As I came closer I could see he was roaring in the rain, his lip curled, his teeth bared.

I stopped and stared up at him for a moment. That was when I heard a car slowing down behind me. I did not think twice. I pushed open the iron gate, darted through, and flattened myself behind the stone pillar. I watched the car until it disappeared round the bend.

To be caught would mean a caning, four strokes, maybe six, across the back of the knees. Worse, I would be back at school, back to detentions, back to Basher Beaumont. To go along the road was dangerous, too dangerous. I would try to cut across country to the station. It would be longer that way, but far safer.

Strange Meeting

I was still deciding which direction to take when I heard a voice from behind me.

"Who are you? What do you want?"

I turned.

"Who are you?" she asked again. The old lady who stood before me was no bigger than I was. She scrutinised me from under the shadow of her dripping straw hat. She had piercing dark eyes that I did not want to look into.

"I didn't think it would rain," she said, her voice gentler. "Lost, are you?"

I said nothing. She had a dog on a leash at her side, a big dog. There was an ominous growl in his throat, and his hackles were up all along his back.

She smiled. "The dog says you're on private property," she went on, pointing her stick at me accusingly. She edged aside my raincoat with the end of her stick. "Run away from that school, did you? Well, if it's anything like it used to be, I can't say I blame you. But we can't just stand here in the rain, can we? You'd better come inside. We'll give him some tea, shall we, Jack? Don't you worry about Jack. He's all bark and no bite." Looking at Jack, I found that hard to believe.

I don't know why, but I never for one moment thought of running off. I often wondered later why I went with her so readily. I think it was because she expected me to, willed me to somehow. I followed the old lady and her dog up to the house, which was huge, as huge as my school. It looked as if it had grown out of the ground.

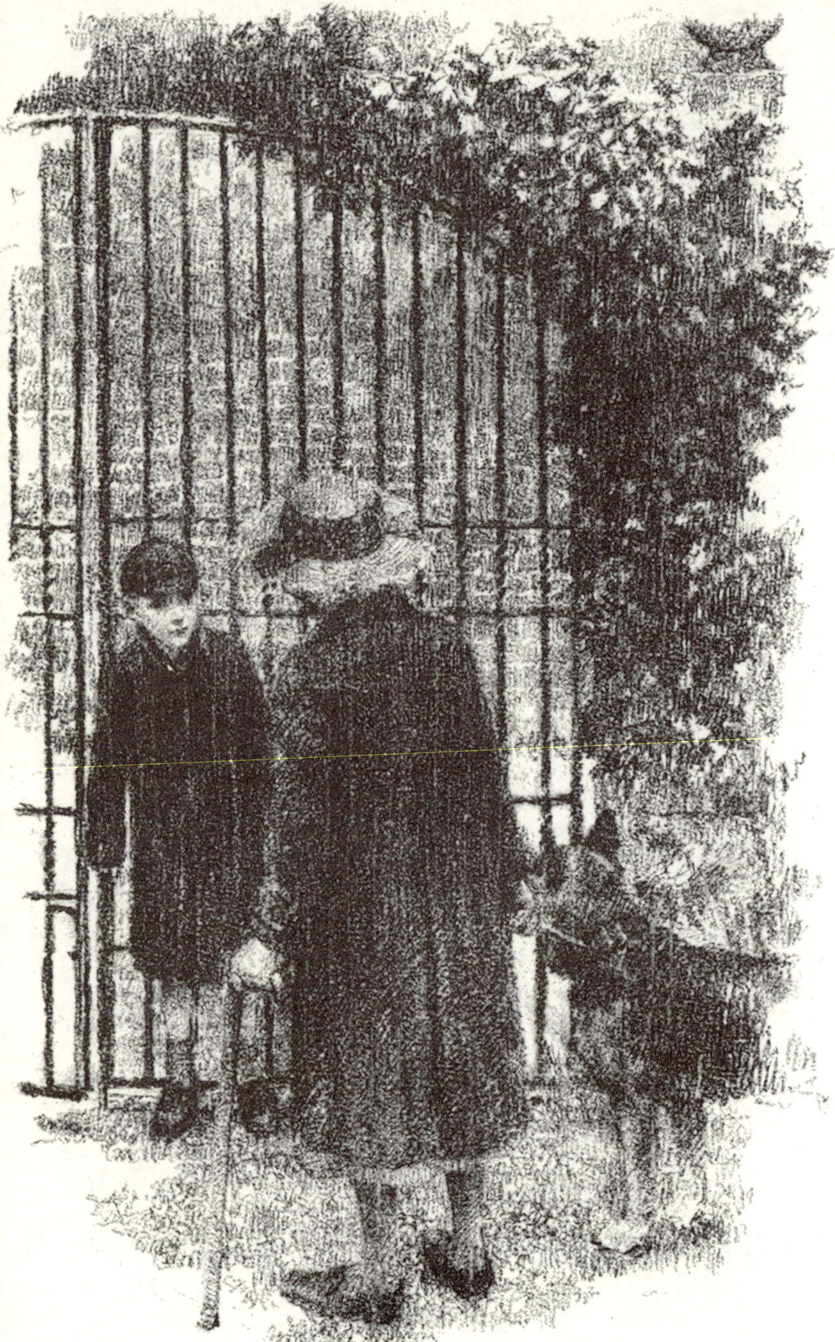

There was hardly a brick or a stone or a tile to be seen. The entire building was smothered in red creeper, and there were a dozen ivy-clad chimneys sprouting skywards from the roof.

We sat down close to the stove in a vast vaulted kitchen. "The kitchen's always the warmest place," she said, opening the oven door. "We'll have you dry in no time. Scones?" she went on, bending down with some difficulty and reaching inside. "I always have scones on a Sunday. And tea to wash it down. All right for you?" She went on chatting away as she busied herself with the kettle and the teapot. The dog eyed me all the while from his basket, unblinking. "I was just thinking," she said. "You'll be the first young man I've had inside this house since Bertie." She was silent for a while.

The smell of the scones wafted through the kitchen. I ate three before I even touched my tea. They were sweet and crumbly, and succulent with melting butter. She talked on merrily again, to me, to the dog – I wasn't sure which. I wasn't really listening. I was looking out of the window behind her. The sun was bursting through the clouds and lighting the hillside. A perfect rainbow arched through the sky. But miraculous though it was, it wasn't the rainbow that fascinated me. Somehow, the clouds were casting a strange shadow over the hillside, a

shadow the shape of a lion, roa[...]
the one over the archway.

"Sun's come out," said the old[...]
offering me another scone. I took it
eagerly. "Always does, you know. It may
be difficult to remember sometimes, but
there's always sun behind the clouds, and
the clouds do go in the end. Honestly."

She watched me eat, a smile on her face
that warmed me to the bone.

"Don't think I want you to go, because
I don't. Nice to see a boy eat so well, nice
to have the company; but all the same,
I'd better get you back to school after
you've had your tea, hadn't I? You'll only
be in trouble otherwise. Mustn't run off,
you know. You've got to stick it out, see
things through, do what's got to be done,
no matter what." She was looking out of
the window as she spoke. "My Bertie
taught me that, bless him, or maybe I
taught him. I can't remember now." And

e went on talking and talking, but my mind was elsewhere again.

The lion on the hillside was still there, but now he was blue and shimmering in the sunlight. It was as if he were breathing, as if he were alive. It wasn't a shadow any more. No shadow is blue.

"No, you're not seeing things," the old lady whispered. "It's not magic. He's real enough. He's our lion, Bertie's and mine. He's our butterfly lion."

"What d'you mean?" I asked.

She looked at me long and hard. "I'll tell you if you like," she said. "Would you like to know? Would you really like to know?"

I nodded.

"Have another scone first and another cup of tea. Then I'll take you to Africa where our lion came from, where my Bertie came from too. Bit of a story, I can tell you. You ever been to Africa?"

"No," I replied.

"Well, you're going," she said. "We're both going."

Suddenly I wasn't hungry any more. All I wanted now was to hear her story. She sat back in her chair, gazing out of the window. She told it slowly, thinking before each sentence; and all the while she never took her eyes off the butterfly lion. And neither did I.

Timbavati

Bertie was born in South Africa, in a remote farmhouse near a place called Timbavati. It was shortly after Bertie first started to walk that his mother and father decided a fence must be put around the farmhouse to make a compound where Bertie could play in safety. It wouldn't keep the snakes out – nothing could do that – but at least Bertie would be safe now from the leopards, and the lions and the spotted hyenas. Enclosed within the compound were the lawn and gardens at the front of the house, and the stables and barns at the back – all the room a child would need or want, you might think. But not Bertie.

The farm stretched as far as the eye could see in all directions, twenty thousand acres of veld. Bertie's father farmed cattle, but times were hard. The rains had failed too often, and many of the rivers and waterholes had all but dried up. With fewer wildebeest and impala to prey on, the lions and leopards would sneak up on the cattle whenever they could. So Bertie's father was more often than not away from home with his men, guarding the cattle. Every time he left, he'd say the same thing: "Don't you ever open that gate, Bertie, you hear me? There's lions out there, leopards, elephants, hyenas. You stay put, you hear?" Bertie would stand at the fence and watch him ride out, and he would be left behind with his mother, who was also his teacher. There were no schools for a hundred miles. And his mother too was always warning him to stay inside the fence. "Look what happened in *Peter and the Wolf*," she would say.

His mother was often sick with malaria, and even when she wasn't sick she would be listless and sad. There were good days, days when she would play the piano for him and play hide-and-seek around the compound. Or he'd sit on her lap on the sofa out on the veranda and she'd just talk and talk, all about her home in England, about how much she hated the wildness and the loneliness of Africa, and about how Bertie was everything to her.

But they were rare days. Every morning he'd climb into her bed and snuggle up to her, hoping against hope that today she'd be well and happy; but so often she wasn't, and Bertie would be left on his own again, to his own devices.

There was a waterhole downhill from the farmhouse, and some distance away. That waterhole, when there was water in it, became Bertie's whole world. He would spend hours in the dusty compound, his hands gripping the fence, looking out at the wonders of the veld, at the giraffes drinking, spread-legged, at the waterhole; at the browsing impala, tails twitching, alert; at the warthogs snorting and snuffling under the shade of the shingayi trees; at the baboons, the zebras, the wildebeests, and the elephants bathing in the mud. But the moment Bertie always longed for was when a pride of lions came padding out of the veld. The impala were the first to spring away, then the zebra would panic and gallop off. Within seconds the lions would have the waterhole to themselves, and they would crouch to drink.

From the safe haven of the compound Bertie looked and learned as he grew up. By now, he could climb the tree by the farmhouse, and sit high in its branches. He could see better from up there. He would wait for his lions for hours on end. He got to know the life of the waterhole so well that he could feel the lions were out there, even before he saw them.

Bertie had no friends to play with, but he always said he was never lonely as a child. At night he loved reading his books and losing himself in the stories, and by day his heart was out in the veld with the animals. That was where he yearned to be. Whenever his mother was well enough, he would beg her to take him outside the compound, but her answer was always the same.

"I can't, Bertie. Your father has forbidden it," she'd say. And that was that.

The men would come home with their stories of the veld, of the family of cheetahs sitting like sentinels on their kopje, of the leopard they had spotted high in his tree larder watching over his kill, of the hyenas they had driven off, of the herd of elephants which had stampeded the cattle. And Bertie would listen wide-eyed, agog. Again and again he asked his father if he could go with him to help guard the cattle. His father just laughed, patted his head, and said it was man's work. He did teach Bertie how to ride, and how to shoot too, but always within the confines of the compound.

Week in, week out, Bertie had to stay behind his fence. He made up his mind though, that if no one would take him out into the veld, then one day he would go by himself. But something always held him back. Perhaps it was one of those tales he'd been told of black mamba snakes whose bite would kill you within ten minutes, of hyenas whose jaws would crunch you to bits, of vultures who would finish off anything that was left so that no one would ever find even the bits. For the time being he stayed behind the fence. But the more he grew up, the more his compound became a prison to him.

One evening – Bertie must have been about six years old by now – he was sitting high up in the branches of his tree, hoping against hope the lions might come down for their sunset drink as they often did. He was thinking of giving up, for it would soon be too dark to see much now, when he saw a solitary lioness come down to the waterhole. Then he saw that she was not alone. Behind her, and on unsteady legs, came what looked like a lion cub – but it was white, glowing white in the gathering gloom of dusk.

While the lioness drank, the cub played at catching her tail; and then, when she had had her fill, the two of them slipped away into the long grass and were gone.

Bertie ran inside, screaming with excitement. He had to tell someone, anyone. He found his father working at his desk.

"Impossible," said his father. "You're seeing things that aren't there, or you're telling fibs – one of the two."

"I saw him. I promise," Bertie insisted. But his father would have none of it, and sent him to his room for arguing.

His mother came to see him later. "Anyone can make a mistake, Bertie dear," she said. "It must have been the sunset. It plays tricks with your eyes sometimes. There's no such thing as a white lion."

The next evening Bertie watched again at the fence, but the white lion cub and the lioness did not come, nor did they the next evening, nor the next. Bertie began to think he must have been dreaming it.

A week or more passed, and there had been only a few zebras and wildebeest down at the waterhole. Bertie was already upstairs in his bed when he heard his father riding into the compound, and then the stamp of his heavy boots on the veranda.

"We got her! We got her!" he was saying. "Huge lioness, massive she was.

She's taken half a dozen of my best cattle in the last two weeks. Well, she won't be taking any more."

Bertie's heart stopped. In that one terrible moment he knew which lioness his father was talking about. There could be no doubt about it. His white lion cub had been orphaned.

"But what if," Bertie's mother was saying, "what if she had young ones to feed? Perhaps they were starving."

"So would we be if we let it go on. We had to shoot her," his father retorted.

Bertie lay there all night listening to the plaintive roaring echoing through the veld, as if every lion in Africa was sounding a lament. He turned his face into his pillow and could think of nothing but the orphaned white cub, and he promised himself there and then that if ever the cub came down to the waterhole looking for his dead mother, then he would do what he had never dared to do, he would open the gate and go out and bring him home. He would not let him die out there all alone. But no lion cub came to his waterhole. All day, every day, he waited for him to come, but he never came.

Bertie and the Lion

One morning, a week or so later, Bertie was woken by a chorus of urgent neighing. He jumped out of his bed and ran to the window. A herd of zebras was scattering away from the waterhole, chased by a couple of hyenas. Then he saw more hyenas, three of them, standing stock still, noses pointing, eyes fixed on the waterhole. It was only now that Bertie saw the lion cub. But this one wasn't white at all. He was covered in mud, with his back to the waterhole, and he was waving a pathetic paw at the hyenas who were beginning to circle. The lion cub had nowhere to run to, and the hyenas were sidling ever closer.

Bertie was downstairs in a flash, leaping off the veranda and racing barefoot across the compound, shouting at the top of his voice. He threw open the gate and charged down the hill towards the waterhole, yelling and screaming and waving his arms like a wild thing. Startled at this sudden intrusion, the hyenas turned tail and ran, but not far. Once within range Bertie hurled a broadside of pebbles at them, and they ran off again, but again not far. Then he was at the waterhole and between the lion cub and the hyenas, shouting at them to go away. They didn't. They stood and watched, uncertain for a while. Then they began to circle again, closer, closer…

That was when the shot rang out. The hyenas bolted into the long grass, and were gone. When Bertie turned round he saw his mother in her nightgown, rifle in hand, running towards him down the hill.

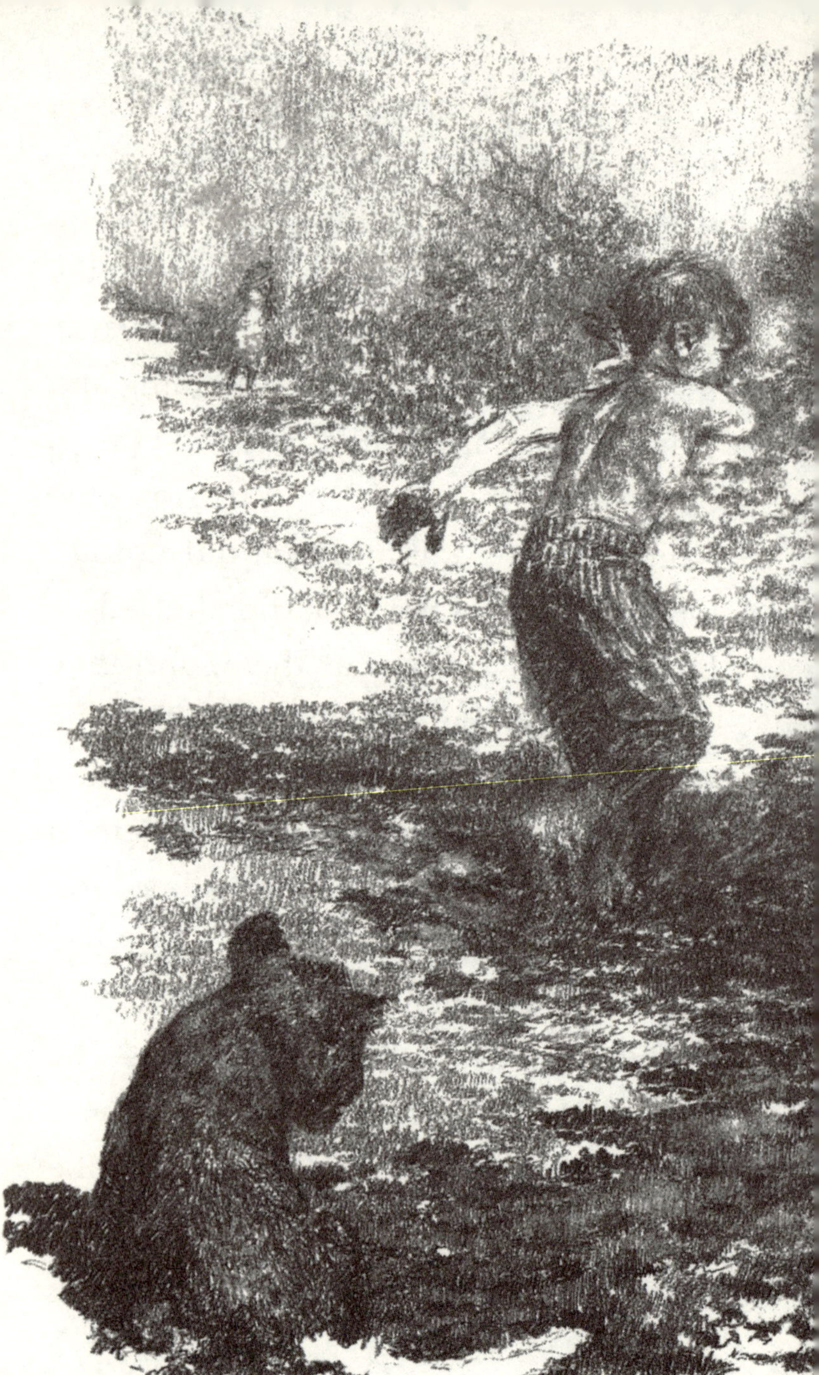

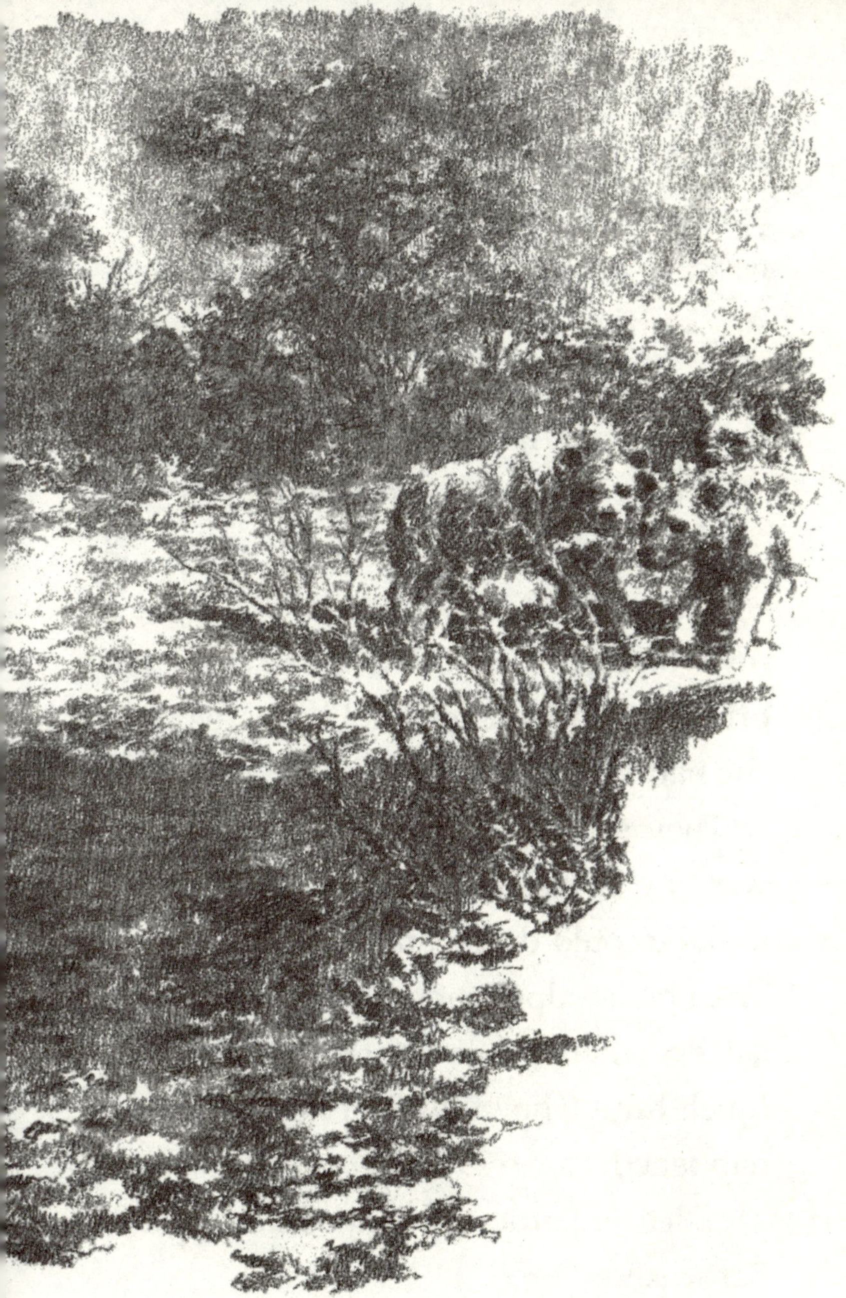

He had never seen her run before. Between them they gathered up the mud-matted cub and brought him home. He was too weak to struggle, though he tried. As soon as they had given him some warm milk, they dunked him in the bath to wash him. As the first of the mud came off, Bertie saw he was white underneath.

"You see!" he cried triumphantly. "He *is* white! He *is*. I told you, didn't I? He's my white lion!" His mother still could not bring herself to believe it. Five baths later, she had to.

They sat him down by the stove in a washing basket and fed him again, all the milk he could drink, and he drank the lot. Then he lay down and slept. He was still asleep when Bertie's father got back at lunch time. They told him how it had all happened.

"Please, Father. I want to keep him," Bertie said.

"And so do I," said his mother. "We both do." And she spoke as Bertie had never heard her speak before, her voice strong, determined.

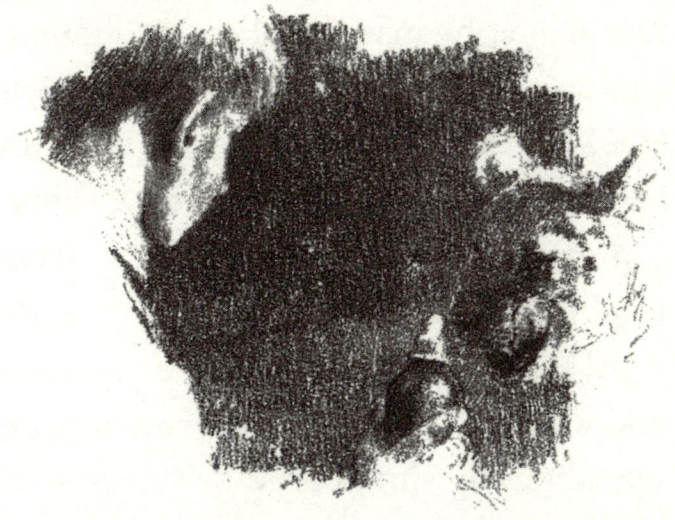

Bertie's father didn't seem to know quite how to reply. He just said: "We'll talk about it later," and then he walked out.

They did talk about it later when Bertie was supposed to be in bed. He wasn't, though. He heard them arguing. He was outside the sitting-room door, watching, listening. His father was pacing up and down.

"He'll grow up, you know," he was saying. "You can't keep a grown lion, you know that."

"And *you* know we can't just throw him to the hyenas," replied his mother. "He needs us, and maybe we need him. He'll be someone for Bertie to play with for a while." And then she added sadly: "After all, it's not as if he's going to have any brothers and sisters, is it?"

At this, Bertie's father went over to her and kissed her gently on the forehead. It was the only time Bertie had ever seen him kiss her.

"All right then," he said. "All right. You can keep your lion."

So the white lion cub came to live amongst them in the farmhouse. He slept at the end of Bertie's bed. Wherever Bertie went, the lion cub went too – even to the bathroom, where he would watch Bertie have his bath and lick his legs dry afterwards. They were never apart. It was Bertie who saw to the feeding – milk four times a day from one of his father's beer bottles – until later on when the lion cub lapped from a soup bowl. There was impala meat whenever he wanted it, and as he grew – and he grew fast – he wanted more and more of it.

For the first time in his life Bertie was totally happy. The lion cub was all the brothers and sisters he could ever want, all the friends he could ever need. The two of them would sit side by side on the sofa out on the veranda and watch the great red sun go down over Africa, and Bertie would read him *Peter and the Wolf*, and at the end he would always promise him that he would never let him go off to a zoo and live behind bars like the wolf in the story. And the lion cub would look up at Bertie with his trusting amber eyes.

"Why don't you give him a name?" his mother asked one day.

"Because he doesn't need one," replied Bertie. "He's a lion, not a person. Lions don't need names."

Bertie's mother was always wonderfully patient with the lion, no matter how much mess he made, how many cushions he pounced on and ripped apart, no matter how much crockery he smashed. None of it seemed to upset her. And strangely, she was hardly ever ill these days. There was a spring to her step, and her laughter pealed around the house. His father was less happy about it. "Lions," he'd mutter on, "should not live in houses. You should keep him outside in the compound." But they never did. For both mother and son, the lion had brought new life to their days, life and laughter.

Running Free

It was the best year of Bertie's young life. But when it ended, it ended more painfully than he could ever have imagined. He'd always known that one day when he was older he would have to go away to school, but he had thought and hoped it would not be for a long time yet. He'd simply put it out of his mind.

His father had just returned home from Johannesburg after his yearly business trip. He broke the news at supper that first evening. Bertie knew there was something in the wind. His mother had been sad again in recent days, not sick, just strangely sad. She wouldn't look him in the eye and she winced whenever she tried to smile at him. The lion had just lain down beside him, his head warm on Bertie's feet, when his father cleared his throat and began. It was going to be a lecture. Bertie had had them before often enough, about manners, about being truthful, about the dangers of leaving the compound.

"You'll soon be eight, Bertie," he said. "And your mother and I have been doing some thinking. A boy needs a proper education, a good school. Well, we've found just the right place for you, a school near Salisbury in England. Your Uncle George and Aunt Melanie live nearby and have promised to look after you in the holidays, and to visit you from time to time. They'll be father and mother to you for a while. You'll get on with them well enough, I'm sure you will. They are fine, good people. So you'll be off on the ship to England in

July. Your mother will accompany you. She will spend the summer with you in Salisbury, and after she has taken you to your school in September, she'll then return here to the farm. It's all arranged."

As his heart filled with a terrible dread, all Bertie could think of was his white lion. "But the lion," he cried, "what about the lion?"

"I'm afraid there's something else I have to tell you," his father said. Looking across at Bertie's mother, he took a deep breath. And then he told him. He told him he had met a man whilst he was in Johannesburg, a Frenchman, a circus owner from France. He was over in Africa looking for lions and elephants to buy for his circus. He liked them young, very young, a year or less, so that he could train them up without too much trouble. Besides, they were easier and cheaper to transport when they were young. He would be coming out to the farm in a few days' time to see the white lion for himself. If he liked what he saw, he would pay good money and take him away.

It was the only time in his life Bertie had ever shouted at his father. "No! No, you can't!" It was rage that wrung the hot tears from him, but they soon gave way to silent tears of sadness and loss. There was no comforting him, but his mother tried all the same.

"We can't keep him here for ever, Bertie," she said. "We always knew that, didn't we? And you've seen how he stands by the fence gazing out into the veld. You've seen him pacing up and down. But we can't just let him out. He'd be all on his own, no mother to protect him. He couldn't cope. He'd be dead in weeks. You know he would."

"But you can't send him to a circus! You can't!" said Bertie. "He'll be shut up behind bars. I promised him he never would be. And they'll point at him. They'll laugh at him. He'd rather die. Any animal would." But he knew as he looked across the table at them that it was hopeless, that their minds were quite made up.

For Bertie the betrayal was total. That night he made up his mind what had to be done. He waited until he heard his father's deep breathing next door. Then, with his white lion at his heels, he crept downstairs in his pyjamas, took down his father's rifle from the rack and stepped out into the night. The compound gate yawned open noisily when he pushed it, but then they were out, out and running free. Bertie had no thought of the dangers around him, only that he must get as far from home as he could before he did it.

The lion padded along beside him, stopping every now and again to sniff the air. A clump of trees became a herd of elephants wandering towards them out of the dawn. Bertie ran for it. He knew how elephants hated lions. He ran and ran till his legs could run no more. As the sun came up over the veld he climbed to the top of a kopje and sat down, his arm round the lion's neck. The time had come.

"Be wild now," he whispered. "You've got to be wild. Don't come home. Don't ever come home. They'll put you behind bars. You hear what I'm saying? All my life I'll think of you, I promise I will. I won't ever forget you." And he buried his head in the lion's neck and heard the greeting groan from deep inside him. He stood up. "I'm going now," he said. "Don't follow me. Please don't follow me." And Bertie clambered down off the kopje and walked away.

When he looked back, the lion was still sitting there watching him; but then he stood up, yawned, stretched, licked his lips and sprang down after him. Bertie shouted at him, but he kept coming. He threw sticks. He threw stones. Nothing worked. The lion would stop, but then as soon as Bertie walked on, he simply followed at a safe distance.

"Go back!" Bertie yelled, "you stupid, stupid lion! I hate you! I hate you! Go back!" But the lion kept loping after him whatever he did, whatever he said.

There was only one thing for it. He didn't want to do it, but he had to. With tears filling his eyes and his mouth, he lifted the rifle to his shoulder and fired over the lion's head. At once the lion turned tail and scampered away through the veld. Bertie fired again. He watched till he could see him no more, and then turned for home. He knew he'd have to face what was coming to him. Maybe his father would strap him – he'd threatened it often enough – but Bertie didn't mind. His lion would have his chance for freedom, maybe not much of one. Anything was better than the bars and whips of a circus.

The Frenchman

They were there waiting on the veranda, his mother in her nightgown, his father in his hat, his horse saddled, ready to come after him. "I've set him free," Bertie cried. "I've set him free, so he won't ever have to live behind bars." He was sent to his room at once, where he threw himself on his bed and buried his face in his pillow.

Day after day his father went out looking for the white lion, but each evening he came back empty-handed and blazing with fury.

"What'll I tell the Frenchman when he comes, eh? Did you for one minute think of that, Bertie? Did you? I should strap you. Any father worth his salt would strap you." But he didn't.

Bertie spent all day and every day at the fence, or up his tree in the compound, or at his bedroom window, his eyes scanning the veld for anything white moving through the grass. He prayed at his bedside every night until his knees were numb, prayed that his white lion would learn how to kill, would somehow find enough to eat, would avoid the hyenas, and other lions too, come to that. Above all, he prayed he would not come back, at least not until the Frenchman from the circus had come and gone.

The day the Frenchman came, it rained, the first rain for months, it seemed. Bertie watched him as he stood there, dripping on the veranda, his thumb hooked into his waistcoat pocket, as Bertie's father broke the news that there was no white lion to collect, that he had escaped. That was the moment when Bertie's mother put her hand to her throat, cried out and pointed. The white lion was wandering through the open compound gate, yowling pitifully. Bertie ran to him and fell on his knees and held him. The lion was soaked to the skin and trembling. He was panting with hunger and so thin that you could see his rib cage. They all helped to rub him down, and then looked on as he ate ravenously.

"*Incroyable*! *Magnifique*!" said the Frenchman. "And white, just as you said, white like the snow, and tame too. He will be the star of my circus. I shall call him *'Le Prince Blanc'*, 'The White Prince'. He will have all he needs, all he wants, fresh meat every day, fresh straw every night. I love my animals, you know. They are my family, and this lion of yours, he will be my favourite son. Have no fear, young man, I promise you that he will never be hungry again." He put his hand on his heart. "As God is my witness, I promise it."

Bertie looked up into the Frenchman's face. It was a kind face, not smiling, yet earnest and trustworthy. But even so, it did not make Bertie feel any better.

"There, you see," said Bertie's mother. "He'll be happy, and that's all that matters, Bertie, isn't it?"

Bertie knew that there was no point in begging. He knew now that the lion could never survive on his own in the wild, that he would have to go with the Frenchman. There was nothing else for it.

That night as they lay in the dark together side by side, Bertie made him a last promise. "I will find you," he whispered. "Always remember that I will find you. I promise I will."

The next morning the Frenchman shook hands with Bertie on the veranda and said goodbye. "He'll be fine, don't you worry. And one day you must come to France and see my circus, *Le Cirque Merlot*. It is the best circus in all of France." Then they left, the white lion in a wooden crate rocking from side to side in the back of the Frenchman's wagon. Bertie watched until the wagon disappeared from view.

A few months later, Bertie found himself on a ship steaming out of Cape Town, bound for England and school and a new life. As the last of Table Mountain vanished in a heat haze, he said goodbye to Africa and was not at all unhappy. He had his mother with him, for the time being at least. And after all, England was nearer France than Africa was, much nearer.

Strawbridge

The old lady drank her tea and wrinkled her nose in disgust. "I'm always doing that," she said. "I'm always letting my tea go cold." The dog scratched his ear, groaning with the pleasure of it, but eyeing me all the time.

"Is that the end then?" I asked.

She laughed and put down her cup. "I should say not," she said. And then she went on, picking a tea leaf off the tip of her tongue. "Up till now it's been just Bertie's story. He told it to me so often that I almost feel I was there when it happened. But from now on it's my story too."

"What about the white lion?" I had to know. "Did he find the white lion? Did he keep his promise?"

The old lady seemed suddenly clouded with sadness. "You must remember," she said, putting a bony hand on mine, "that true stories do not always end just as we would wish them to. Would you like to hear the truth of what happened, or shall I make something up for you just to keep you happy?"

"I want to know what really happened," I replied.

"Then you shall," she said. She turned from me and looked out of the window again at the butterfly lion, still blue and shimmering on the hillside.

****

Whilst Bertie was growing up on his farm in Africa with his fence all around, I was growing up here at Strawbridge in this echoing cold cavern of a house with its deer park and its high wall all around. And I grew up, for the most part, alone. I too was an only child. My mother had died giving birth to me, and Father was rarely at home. Maybe that was why the two of us, Bertie and I, got on so well from the first moment we met. We had so much in common from the very start.

Like Bertie, I scarcely ever left the confines of my home, so I had few friends.

I didn't go to school either, not to start with. I had a governess instead, Miss Tulips – everyone called her "Nolips" because she was so thin-lipped and severe. She moved around the house like a cold shadow. She lived on the top floor, like Cook, and like Nanny. Nanny Mason – bless her heart – brought me up and taught me all the do's and don'ts of life like all good nannies should. But she was more than just a nanny to me, she was a mother to me, and a wonderful one too, the best I could have had, the best anyone could have had.

My mornings were always spent at my studies with Nolips, but all the while I was looking forward to my afternoons out walking with Nanny Mason – except on Sundays, when I was allowed to be on my own all day, if Father wasn't home for the weekend, which he usually wasn't. Then I could fly my kites when it was fine, and read my books when it wasn't. I loved my books – *Black Beauty, Little Women, Heidi* – I loved them all, because they took me outside the park walls, they took me all over the world. I met the best friends I ever had in those books – until I met Bertie, that is.

I remember it was just after my tenth birthday. It was Sunday and I was out flying my kites. But there wasn't much wind, and no matter how hard I ran, I just couldn't get even my best box kite to catch the wind and fly. I climbed all the way up Wood Hill, looking for wind. And there at the top I found it at last, enough to send my kite soaring. But then the wind gusted and my kite swirled away crazily towards the trees. I couldn't haul it in in time. It caught on a branch and stuck fast in a high elm tree in amongst the rookery. The rooks flew out cawing in protest whilst I tugged at my line, crying in my fury and frustration. I gave up, sat down and howled. That was when I noticed a boy emerging from the shadow of the trees.

"I'll get it down for you," he said, and began to climb the tree. Easy as you like, he crawled along the branch, reached out and released my kite. It floated down and landed at my feet. My best kite was torn and battered, but at least I had it back. Then he was down the tree and standing there in front of me.

"Who are you? What do you want?" I asked.

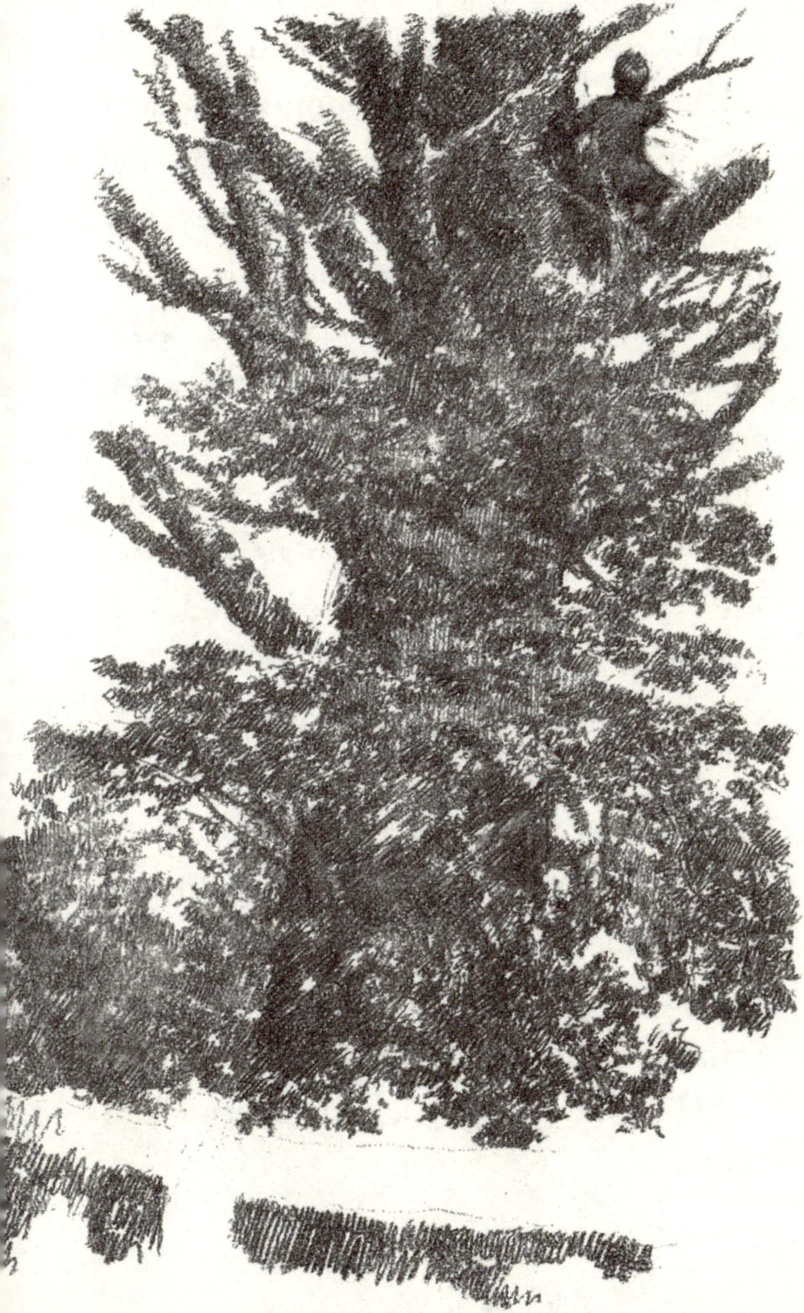

"I can mend it, if you like," he said.

"Who are you?" I asked again.

"Bertie Andrews," he replied. He was wearing a grey school uniform, and one I recognised at once. From the lion gateway I had often watched them on their walks, two by two, blue school caps, blue socks.

"You're from the school up the road, aren't you?" I said.

"You won't tell on me, will you?" His eyes were wide with sudden alarm. I saw then that his legs were scratched and bleeding.

"Been in the wars, have you?" I said.

"I've run away," he went on. "And I'm not going back, not ever."

"Where are you going?" I asked him.

He shook his head. "I don't know. In the holidays I live at my Auntie's in Salisbury, but I don't like it there."

"Haven't you got a proper home?" I said.

" 'Course I have," he replied. "Everyone has. But it's in Africa."

That whole afternoon we sat together on Wood Hill and he told me all about Africa, about his farm, about his waterhole, about his white lion and how he was somewhere in France now, in a circus and how he couldn't bear to think about him. "But I'll find him," he said fiercely. "I'll find him somehow."

To be honest, I wasn't sure how much I really believed all this about a white lion. I just didn't think lions could be white.

"But the trouble is," he went on, "even when I do find him, I won't be able to take him home to Africa like I always wanted to."

"Why not?" I asked.

"Because my mother died." He looked down and pulled at the grass beside him. "She had malaria, but I think she really died of a broken heart." When he looked up his eyes were swimming with tears. "You can, you know. Then my father sold the farm and married someone else. I never want to go back. I never want to see him again, never."

I wanted to say how sorry I was about his mother, but I couldn't find the right words to say it.

"You really live here, do you?" he said. "In that big place? It's as big as my school."

I told him then what little there was to know of me, all about Father being away in London so much, about Nolips and Nanny Mason. He sucked at the purple clover as I talked; and when neither of us had anything more to say we lay back in the sun and watched a pair of mewing buzzards wheeling overhead. I was wondering what would happen to him if he got caught.

"What are you going to do?" I said at last. "Won't you get into trouble?"

"Only if they catch me."

"But they will, they're bound to, in the end," I said. "You've got to go back, before they miss you."

After a while he propped himself up on his elbow and looked down at me.

"Maybe you're right," he said. "Maybe they won't have missed me yet. Maybe it's not too late. But if I go back, could I come again? I can face it if I can come again. Would you let me? I'll mend your kite, really I will." And he gave me a smile so melting that I couldn't refuse him.

So it was arranged. He would meet me under the big wych elm on Wood Hill every Sunday afternoon at three, or as close to three as he could. He would have to come through the woods so that he could never be seen from the house. I knew full well that if Nolips ever found out, there'd be merry hell to pay – for both of us, probably. Bertie shrugged, and said that if he got caught, all they could do at school was beat him, and that once more wouldn't make much difference anyway. And if they expelled him, well then, that would suit him fine.

And All's Well

Bertie came every Sunday after that. Sometimes it couldn't be for long because he had detention back at school, or maybe I'd have to send him away because Father was down for the weekend, shooting pheasants in the park with his friends. We had to be careful. He *did* mend my best box kite, but after a while we forgot all about flying kites, and we just talked and walked.

Bertie and I lived for our Sundays. In those next two years we became, first, good companions, and then best of friends. We never told each other we were, because we didn't need to. The more I got to know him, the more I believed everything about Africa, and about "The White Prince" in the circus somewhere in France. I believed him too when he told me again and again how somehow, someday he would find his white lion, and make sure that he'd never have to live behind bars again.

The school holidays always dragged interminably because Bertie wasn't there on Sundays. But at least there were no lessons to endure with Nolips. She always went off in the holidays to stay with her sister by the sea in Margate. Instead of her lessons though, Nanny Mason would take me on endless nature walks – "walks on the wild side", she called them.

I grumbled and stamped my feet. "But it's so boring," I'd tell her. "If we had zebras and water buffaloes and elephants and baboons and giraffes and wildebeests and spotted hyenas and black mamba snakes and vultures and lions, I wouldn't mind. But a few deer, a fox's hole, and maybe a badger's set? A dozen rabbit droppings, one robin's nest and some cuckoo pint?" Once, before I could stop myself, I said: "And do you know, Nanny, there's white lions in Africa, real white lions?"

"Fancy that," she laughed. "You and your fairy tales, Millie. You read too many books."

Bertie and I didn't dare write letters to each other in case someone found them and read them. But school term came round again and he'd be there under the wych elm on the first Sunday at three o'clock without fail. What we found to talk about all the time I cannot honestly remember. He sometimes said how he could never look at a circus poster without thinking of "The White Prince". But as time passed, he talked less and less of the white lion, and then not at all. I thought that maybe he had forgotten all about him.

We both grew up too quickly. We had one last summer term together, before I was to be sent off to a convent school by the sea in Sussex, and he was to go away to a college under the shadow of Canterbury Cathedral. We treasured each meeting, knowing how few we had left. We were silent in our sadness. The love between us stayed unspoken. We knew it when our eyes met, when our hands touched. We were just so sure of each other. Before he left me that last Sunday he gave me a kite he had made in carpentry lessons at school and told me I had to think of him every time I flew it.

Then he went his way to his college and I went mine to my convent, and we didn't see each other again. I was always very careful where I flew the kite he'd given me, just in case I lost it up a tree and couldn't get it back again. I thought that if I lost the kite it would be like losing Bertie for ever. I kept it on top of my cupboard in my bedroom. It's still up there to this day.

Now we did write because we were away from home and it was safe to do so. We wrote letters that talked to each other just as we had done all those years on Wood Hill. My letters were long and rambling, about tittle-tattle at school, about how much happier it was at home now that Nolips had left. His were always short and his handwriting so tiny you could hardly read it. He was no happier shut inside the walls of his cathedral precinct than he had been before. There were bells, he wrote, always bells – bells to wake you up, bells for meals, bells for lessons, bells, bells, bells cutting his days into thin slices. How we both hated bells. The last thing he heard at night was the nightwatchman walking the city walls outside his dormitory window, ringing his bell and calling out: "Twelve o'clock. A fine night. And all's well." But he knew, as I knew, as everyone knew, that all was not well, that a great war was coming. His letters, and mine, were full of the dread of it.

Then the storm of war broke. Like many storms, it rumbled only distantly at first, and we all hoped it would somehow pass us by. But it was not to be like that. Father looked so grand in his khaki uniform and shiny brown boots. He said goodbye to Nanny Mason and me on the front steps, climbed into his car and was driven away. We never saw him again. I can't pretend I grieved much when the news came that he had been killed. I know a daughter should grieve for a dead father, and I tried to. I was sad of course, but it is difficult to grieve for someone you never really knew, and my father had always been a stranger to me. Worse, so much worse for me, was the thought that the same thing might one day happen to Bertie.

I just hoped and prayed that the war would end whilst he was still safe at college in Canterbury. Nanny Mason kept saying it would all be over by Christmas. But Christmas came each year and it never was over.

I remember Bertie's last letter from college by heart.

Dearest Millie,

I am old enough now to join up, so I shall. I have had all I can take of fences and walls and bells. I want to fly free, and this seems to be the only way I can do it. Besides, they need men. I can see you smiling at that. All you remember is a boy. I am over six foot now, and I shave twice a week. Honestly! I may not write again for some time, but whatever happens I shall be thinking of you always.

Your

Bertie

And that was the last I was to hear of him
– for a while, at least.

A Lot of Old Codswallop

The dog was whining at the kitchen door. "Let Jack out for me, will you?" said the old lady. "There's a dear. I'll tell you what, I'll fetch down the kite Bertie made for me, shall I? You'd like to see it, wouldn't you?" And she went out.

I was only too happy to let the dog out and shut the door on him.

She was back sooner than I expected. "There," she said, setting the kite down on the table in front of me. "What do you think of it then?" It was huge, much bigger than I had expected, and covered in dust. It was made of brown canvas stretched over a wooden frame. All the kites I had seen had been more colourful, more flamboyant. I think the disappointment must have shown in my face.

"She still flies, you know," she said, blowing the dust off. "You should see how she goes. You should see her." She sat down in her chair and I waited for her to begin again. "Now then, where was I?" she asked. "I'm so forgetful these days."

"Bertie's last letter," I said. "He was just going off to the war. But what about the white lion, 'The White Prince'? What happened to him?" I could hear the dog barking wildly outside. She smiled at me. "Everything comes to he who waits," she said. "Why don't you have a look out of the window?"

I looked. The lion on the hillside was blue no more. It was white now, and the dog was bounding across the hillside, chasing away a cloud of blue butterflies that rose all around him. "He chases everything that moves," she said. "But don't worry. He won't catch a single one. He never catches anything."

"Not *that* lion," I said. "I meant the lion in the story. What happened to him?"

"Don't you see? They're the same. The lion out there on the hillside and the lion in the story. They're the same."

"I don't understand," I said.

"You soon will," she replied. "You soon will." She took a deep breath before she began again.

****

For many years Bertie never spoke about the fighting in the trenches. He always said it was a nightmare best forgotten, best kept to himself. But later on when he'd had time to reflect, when time had done its healing perhaps, then he told me something of how it had been.

At seventeen, he'd found himself marching with his regiment along the straight roads of northern France up to the front line, heads and hearts high with hope and expectation. Within a few months he was sitting huddled at the bottom of a muddy trench, hands over his head, head between his knees, curling himself into himself as tight as he would go, sick with terror as the shells and whizzbangs blew the world apart around him. Then the whistle would blow and they'd be out and over the top into No Man's Land, bayonets fixed and walking towards the German trenches into the ratatat of machine-gun fire. To the left of him and to the right of him his friends would fall, and he would walk on, waiting for the bullet with his name on which he knew could cut him down at any moment.

At dawn they always had to come out of their dugouts and "stand to" in the trenches, just in case there was an attack. The Germans often attacked at dawn. That's how it was on the morning of his twentieth birthday. They came swarming over No Man's Land out of the early morning sun, but they were soon spotted and mown down like so much ripe corn. Then they were turning and running. The whistle went, and Bertie led his men over the top to counter-attack. But as always the Germans were expecting them, and the usual slaughter began. Bertie was hit in the leg and fell into a shellhole. He thought of waiting there all day and then crawling back under cover of darkness, but his wound was bleeding badly and he could not staunch it. He decided he had to try to crawl back to the trenches whilst he still had the strength to do it.

Hugging the ground, he was almost at the wire, almost back to safety, when he heard someone crying out in No Man's Land. It was a cry he could not ignore. He found two of his men lying side by side, and so badly wounded that they could not move. One of them was already unconscious. He hoisted him onto his shoulders and made for the trenches, the bullets whipping and whining around him. The man was heavy and Bertie fell several times under his weight, but he got himself to his feet again and staggered on,

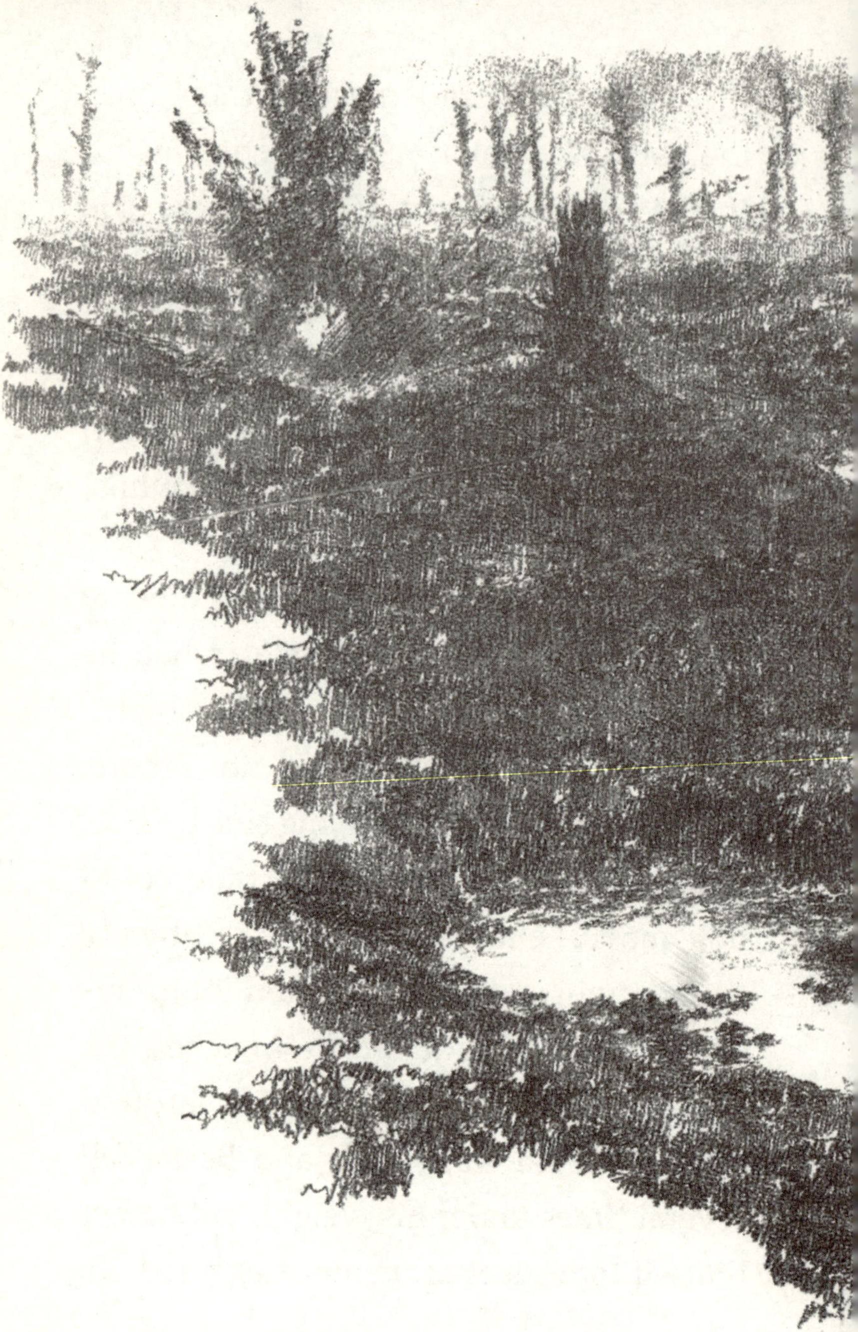

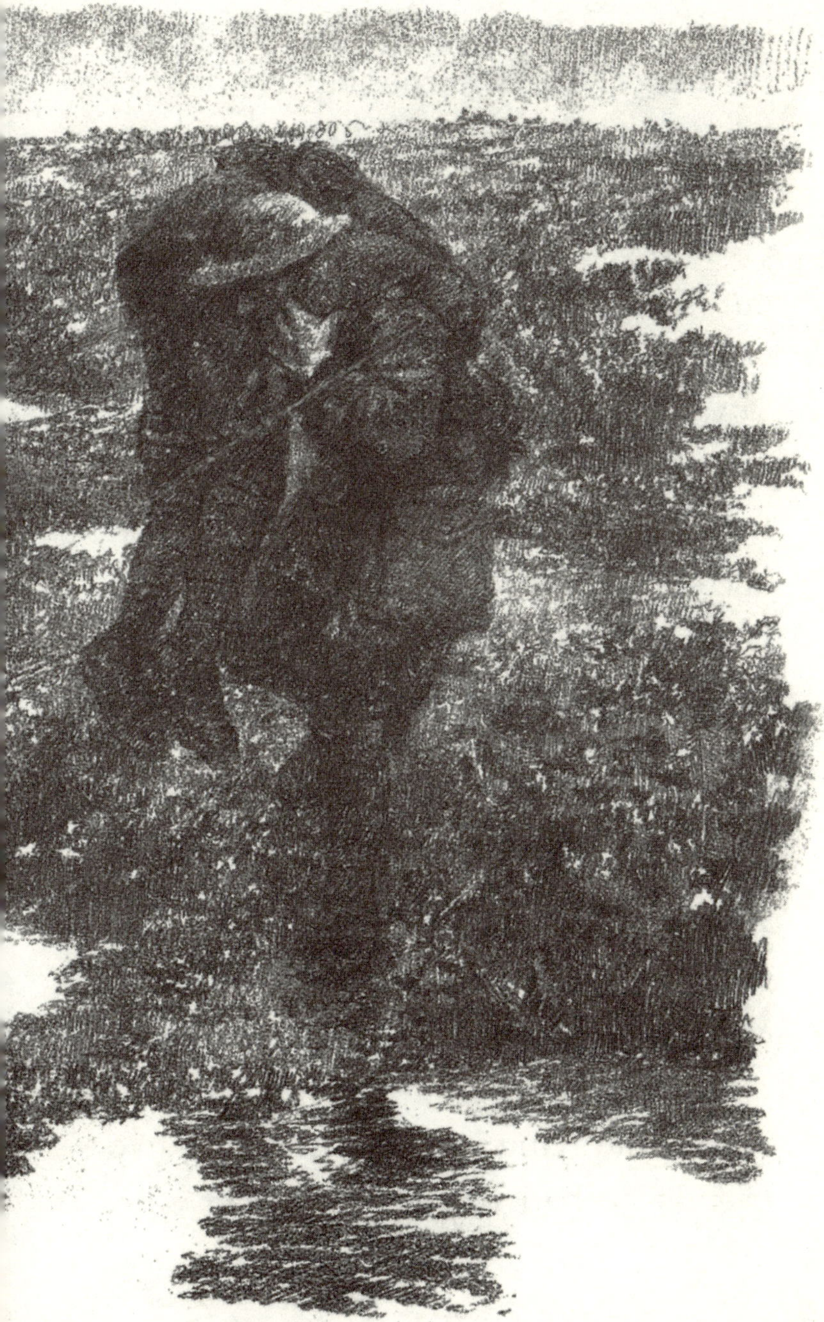

until they tumbled together down into the trench. The stretcher-bearers tried to take Bertie away. He'd bleed to death, they said. But he would not listen. One of his own men was still lying wounded out there in No Man's Land, and he was going to bring him in, no matter what.

Waving his hands above his head, Bertie climbed out of the trench and walked forward. The firing stopped almost at once. He was so weak himself by now that he could scarcely walk, but he managed to reach the wounded man and drag him back. They say that in the end both sides, German and British, were up on the parapets and cheering him on as he stumbled back towards his lines. Then other men were running out to help him and after that he didn't know any more.

When he woke up he found himself in hospital lying in a bed, with the two friends he had rescued on either side.

He was still there some weeks later when he was told that he was to be awarded the Victoria Cross for his bravery under fire. He was the hero of the hour, the pride of his regiment.

Afterwards Bertie always called it a "lot of old codswallop". To be really brave, he said, you have to overcome fear. You have to be frightened in the first place, and he hadn't been. There wasn't time to be frightened. He did what he did without thinking, just as he had saved the white lion cub all those years before when he was a boy in Africa. Of course, they made a great fuss of him in the hospital, and he loved all that, but his leg did not heal as well as it should have. He was still there in the hospital when I found him.

It was not entirely by accident that I found him. For over three years now there had been no letter, no word from him at all. He had warned me, I know, but the long silence was hard to bear. Every time the postman came, I hoped, and the pang of disappointment was sharper each time there was no letter from him. I told all to Nanny Mason who dried my tears and told me to pray, and that she would too. She was sure there'd be a letter soon.

Without Nanny I don't know how I would have gone on living. I was so miserable. I had seen the wounded men coming back from France, blinded, gassed, crippled, and always dreaded seeing

Bertie's face amongst them. I had seen the long lists in the newspapers of all the men who had been killed or who were "missing". I looked each day for his name and thanked God every time I did not find it. But still he never wrote, and I had to know why. I thought maybe he had been so badly wounded that he could not write, that he was lying in some hospital alone and unloved. So I determined I would become a nurse. I would go to France, and heal and comfort as best I could, and just hope that somehow I might find him. But I soon discovered that amongst so many men in uniform it would be hopeless to go looking for him. I did not even know his regiment, nor his rank. I had no idea where to begin.

I was sent to a hospital some fifty miles behind the lines, not too far from Amiens. The hospital was a converted chateau with turrets and great wide staircases, and chandeliers in the wards. But it was so cold in winter that many of the men died as much from the cold as from their wounds. We did all we could for them, but we were short of doctors and short of medicines. There were always so many men coming in, and their wounds were terrible, so terrible. Each time we saved one it was such a joy to us. In the midst of the suffering all around us, we needed some joy, believe me.

I was at breakfast one morning – it was June of 1918. I was reading a magazine, the *Illustrated London News*, I remember, when I turned the page and saw a face I knew at once. He was older, thinner in the face and unsmiling, but I was sure it was Bertie. His eyes were deepset and gentle, just as I remembered them. And there was his name: "Captain Albert Andrews VC". There was a whole article underneath about what he had done, and how he was still recovering from his wounds in a hospital, a hospital that turned out to be little more than ten miles away. Wild horses would not have kept me from him. The next Sunday I cycled over.

He was sleeping when I saw him first, propped up on his pillows, one hand behind his head. "Hello," I said.

He opened his eyes and frowned at me. It was a moment or two before he knew me.

"Been in the wars, have you?" I said.

"Something like that," he replied.

The White Prince

They said I could take him out in his wheelchair every Sunday so long as I didn't tire him, so long as he was back by supper. As Bertie said, it was just like our Sundays had been when we were little. There was only one place we could go to, a small village only a mile away. There wasn't much left of the village, a few streets of battered houses, a church with its steeple broken off halfway up, and a café in the square, thankfully still intact. I would push him in his chair some of the way and he would hobble along with his stick when he felt strong enough. Mostly we would sit in the café and talk, or walk along the river and talk. We had so many years to catch up on.

He hadn't written, he told me, because he'd thought that each day at the front might be his last, that he might be dead by sunset. So many of his friends were dead. Sooner or later, it had to be his turn. He wanted me to forget him, so that I wouldn't know when he was killed, so that I wouldn't be hurt. What you don't know, you don't grieve over, he said. He had never imagined that he would survive, that he would ever see me again.

It was on one of our Sunday outings that I noticed the poster across the street on the wall of what was left of the post office. The colours were faded and the bottom half had been torn away, but at the top the print was quite clear. It was in French. *Cirque Merlot*, it read, and underneath: *Le Prince Blanc* – The White

Prince! And just discernible, a picture of a lion roaring, a white lion. Bertie had seen it too.

"It's him!" he breathed. "It has to be him!" With no help from me, he was out of his wheelchair, stick in hand, limping across the street towards the café.

The café owner was wiping down the tables outside on the pavement. "The circus," Bertie began, pointing back at the poster. He didn't speak much French, so he shouted in English instead. "You know, lions, elephants, clowns!"

The man looked at him blankly and shrugged. So Bertie started roaring like a lion and clawing the air. I could see alarmed faces at the window of the café, and the man was backing away shaking his head. I ripped the poster off the wall and brought it over. My French was a little better than Bertie's. The café owner understood at once.

"Ah," he said, smiling with relief. "Monsieur Merlot. *Le cirque. C'est triste, très triste.*" And he went on in broken English: "The circus. He is finished. Sad, very sad. The soldiers, you understand, they want beer and wine, and girls maybe.

They do not want the circus. No one comes, and so Monsieur Merlot, he have to close the circus. But what can he do with all the animals? He keep them. He feed them.

But the shells come, more and more they come, and his house – how you say it? – it is bombarded. Many animals are dead. But Monsieur Merlot, he stay. He keep only the elephants, the monkeys, and the lion, 'The White Prince'. Everyone love The White Prince. The army, they take all the hay for the horses. There is no food for the animals. So Monsieur Merlot, he take his gun and he have to shoot them. No more circus. Finish. *Triste, très triste.*"

"All of them?" cried Bertie. "He shot all of them?"

"No," said the man. "Not all. He keep The White Prince. He could not shoot The White Prince, never. Monsieur Merlot, he bring him from Africa many years ago. Most famous lion in all of France. He love the lion like a son. That lion, he make Monsieur Merlot a rich man. But he is not rich no more. He lose everything. Now he have nothing, just The White

Prince. It is true. I think they die together. Maybe they die already. Who knows?"

"This Monsieur Merlot," Bertie said, "where does he live? Where can I find him?"

The man pointed out of the village. "Seven, maybe eight kilometres," he said. "It is an old house by the river. Over the bridge and on the left. Not too far. But maybe Monsieur Merlot he is not there no more. Maybe the house is not there no more. Who knows?" And with a last shrug he turned and went indoors.

There were always army lorries rumbling through the village, so it was not at all difficult to hitch a ride. We left the wheelchair behind in the café. Bertie said it would only get in the way, that he could manage well enough with his stick. We found the house, a mill house, just over the bridge where the café owner had said it would be. There wasn't much left of it. The barns all around were shell-blasted, the ruins blackened by fire. Only the main house still had a roof, but it too had not gone unscathed. One corner of the building had been holed and was partially covered by canvas that flapped in the wind. There was no sign of life.

Bertie knocked on the door several times, but there was no answer. The place frightened me. I wanted to leave at once, but Bertie would not hear of it. When he pushed gently at the door, it opened. Everything was dark inside. I did not want to go in, but Bertie took me firmly by the hand.

"He's in here," he whispered. "I can smell him."

And it was true. There was a smell in the air, pungent and rank, and to me quite unfamiliar.

"*Qui est là?*" said a voice from the darkness of the room. "*Qu'est-ce que vous voulez?*" He spoke so quietly you could hardly hear him over the rush of the river outside. I could just make out a large bed under the window at the far end of the room. A man was lying there, propped up on a pile of cushions.

"Monsieur Merlot?" Bertie asked.

"*Oui?*"

As we walked forward together, Bertie went on: "I am Bertie Andrews. Many years ago you came to my farm in Africa, and you bought a white lion cub. Do you still have him?"

As if in answer the white blanket at the end of the bed became a lion, rose from the bed, sprang down and was padding towards us, a terrible rumble in his throat. I froze where I was as the lion came right up to us.

"It's all right, Millie. He won't hurt us," said Bertie, putting an arm round me. "We're old friends." Moaning and yowling, the lion rubbed himself up against Bertie so hard that we had to hold on to each other to stop ourselves from falling over.

A Miracle, A Miracle!

The lion eyed Bertie for a few moments. The yowling stopped, and he began to grunt and groan with pleasure as Bertie smoothed his mane and scratched him between the eyes. "Remember me?" he said to the lion. "Remember Africa?"

"You are the one? I am not dreaming this?" said Monsieur Merlot. "You are the boy in Africa, the one who tried to set him free?"

"I've grown a bit," said Bertie, "but it's me." Bertie and Monsieur Merlot shook hands warmly, while the lion turned his attention on me, licking my hand with his rough warm tongue. I just gritted my teeth and hoped he wouldn't eat it.

"I did all I could," Monsieur Merlot said, shaking his head. "But look at him now. Just skins and bones like me. All my animals they are gone, except *Le Prince Blanc*. He is all I have left. I had to shoot my elephants, you know that? I had to. What else could I do? There was no food to feed them. I could not let them starve, could I?"

Bertie sat down on the bed, put his arms around the lion's neck and buried his head in his mane. The lion rubbed up against him, but he kept looking at me. I kept my distance, I can tell you. I just could not get it out of my head that lions do *eat* people, particularly if they are hungry lions. And this lion was very hungry indeed. You could see his ribs, and his hip bones too.

"Don't worry, *monsieur*," said Bertie. "I will find you food. I will find food enough for both of you. I promise."

The driver of the ambulance I waved down thought at first that he was just giving a nurse a lift back to the village. He was, as you can imagine, a little more reluctant when he saw the old man, and then Bertie, and still more when he saw a huge white lion.

The driver swallowed a lot, said nothing all the way, and just nodded when Bertie asked him to let us out in the village square. And so there we were half an hour or so later, the four of us sitting outside the café in the sun, the lion at our feet gnawing a huge bone the butcher was only too pleased to sell us. Monsieur Merlot ate a plate of fried potatoes in complete silence and washed it down with a bottle of red wine. Around us gathered an astonished crowd of villagers, of French soldiers, of British soldiers – at a safe distance. All the while Bertie scratched the lion's head right between his eyes.

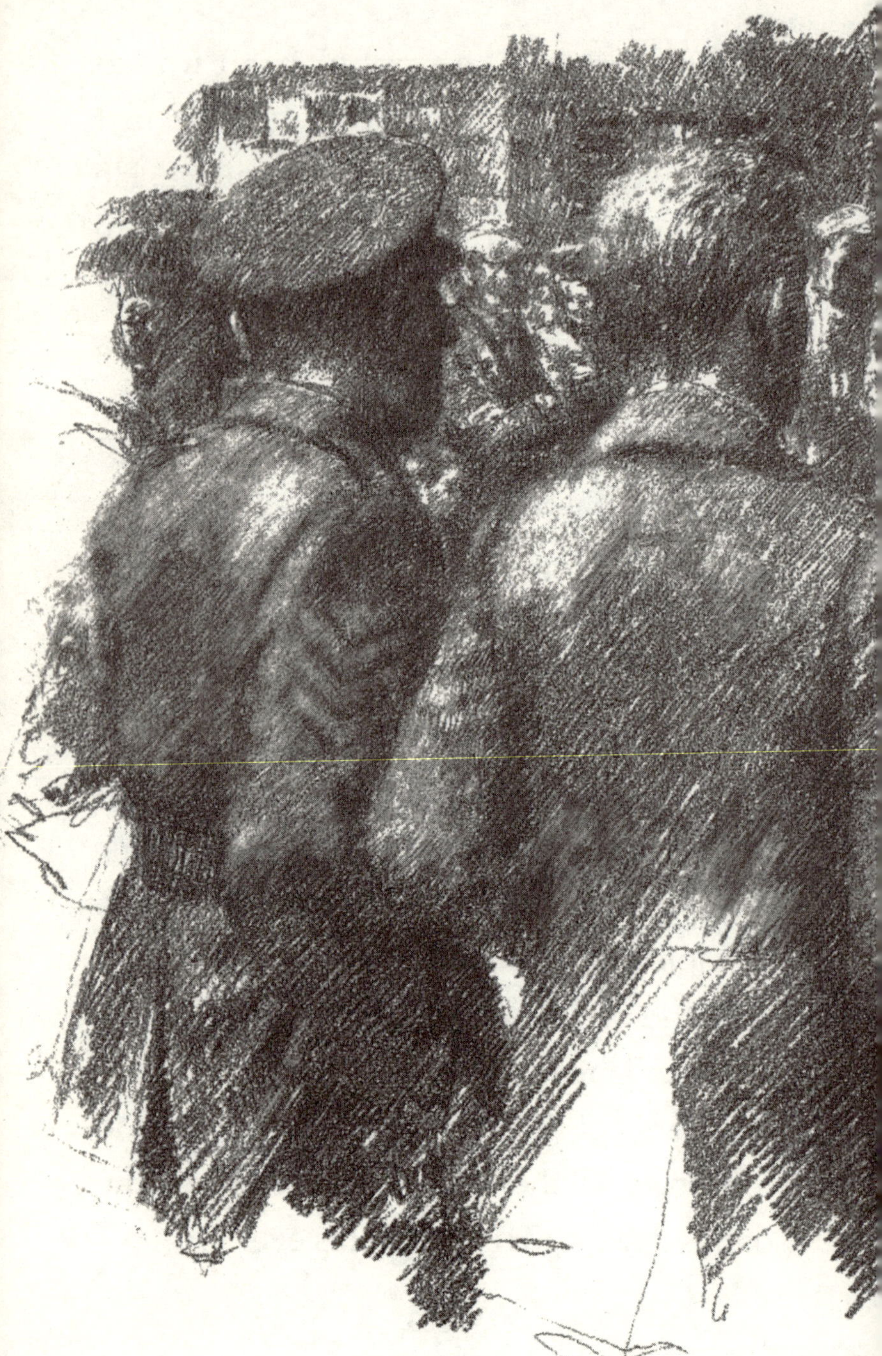

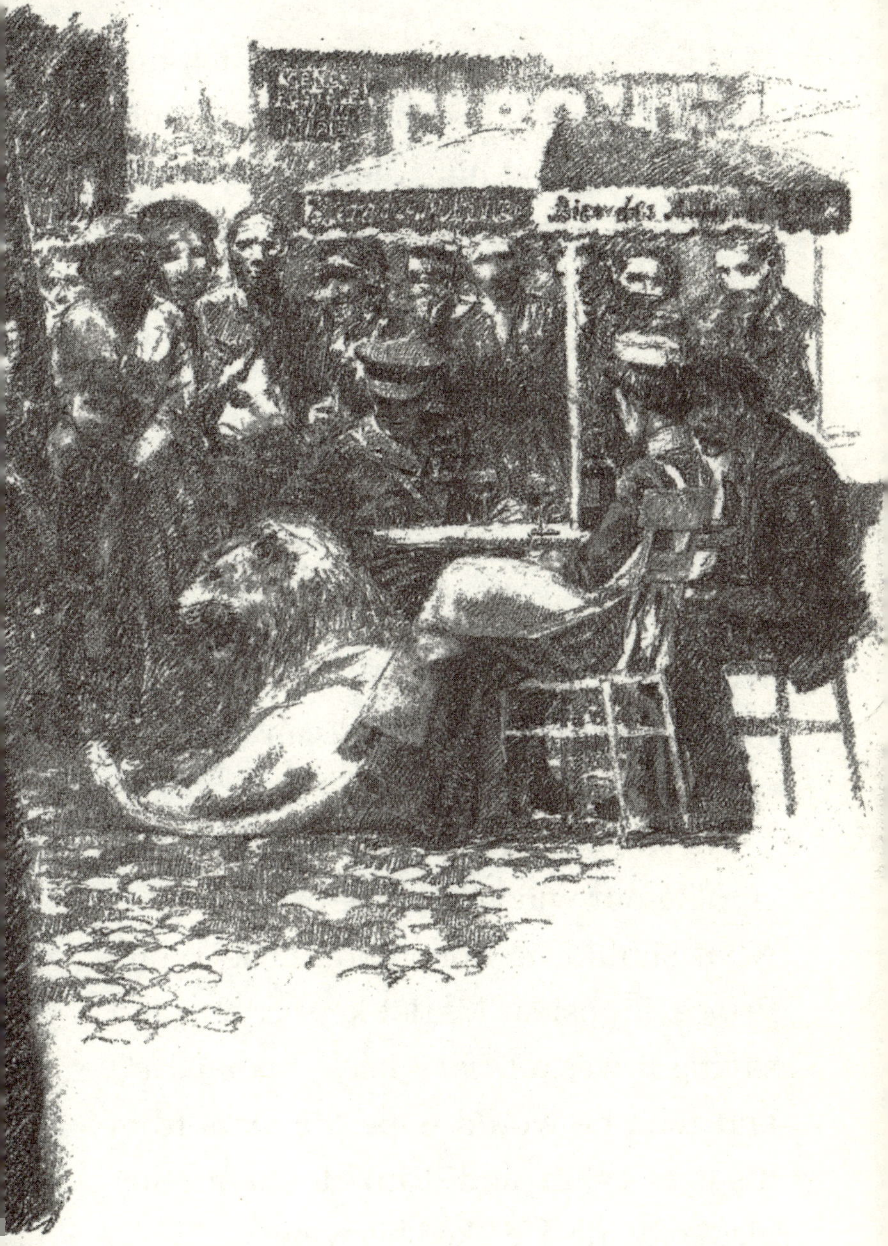

"He always liked a good scratch just there," Bertie said, smiling at me. "I told you I would find him, didn't I?" he went on. "I was never sure you really believed me."

"Well, I did," I replied, and then I added: "After a while, anyway." It was the truth. I suppose that may explain why I took all that happened that morning so much in my stride. It was amazing, surreal almost, but it was no surprise. A prophecy come true, like a wish come true – and this was both – can never be entirely surprising.

As we sat there outside the café sipping our wine, the three of us decided what should be done about The White Prince. Monsieur Merlot kept crying and saying it was all "*un miracle, un miracle*"; and then he would wipe the tears from his eyes again, and drink down another glass of wine. He liked his wine.

The whole plan was entirely Bertie's idea. To be honest, I didn't see how it could possibly be done. I should have known better. I should have known that once Bertie had set his heart on something, he would see it through.

As we walked the lion down the village street, Bertie leaning on the lion, me pushing Monsieur Merlot in the wheelchair, the crowd parted in front of us and backed away. Then they began to follow us, at a discreet distance, of course, up the road towards Bertie's hospital. Someone must have gone on ahead to warn them, because we could now see a huddle of doctors and nurses gathered on the front steps, and there were people peering out of every window. As we came up to the hospital, an officer stepped forward, a colonel it was.

Bertie saluted. "Sir," he began, "Monsieur Merlot here is a very old friend of mine. He will need a bed in the hospital.

He's in need of rest, sir, and a lot of good food. The same goes for the lion. So I wondered, sir, if you'd mind if we used the walled garden behind the hospital. There's a shed in there where the lion could sleep. He'd be quite safe, and so would we. I know him. He doesn't eat people. Monsieur Merlot here has said that if I can feed the lion and take care of him, then I can take him back to England with me."

"The brass cheek of it!" the colonel spluttered as he came down the steps. "Who the devil do you think you are anyway?" he said. And that was when he recognised Bertie. "You're the fellow that won the VC, aren't you?" he said, suddenly a lot more polite. "Andrews, isn't it?"

"Yes, sir, and I want to take the lion back to England when I go. We've got somewhere in mind for him to live," and he turned to me. "Haven't we?" he said.

"Yes," I said.

It wasn't at all easy persuading the colonel to agree. He began to soften only when we told him that if we didn't look after the white lion, no one else would, and then he would have to be taken away and shot. A lion, the symbol of Britain, shot! Not at all good for morale, Bertie argued. And the colonel listened.

It wasn't any easier persuading the powers that be in England to allow the lion to come back home when the war was over, but somehow Bertie managed it. He just wouldn't take no for an answer. Bertie always said afterwards that it was the medal that did it, that without the prestige of the Victoria Cross behind him he'd never have got away with it, and The White Prince would never have come home.

When we docked at Dover, the band was playing and the bunting was out, and there were photographers and newspaper reporters everywhere. The White Prince walked off the ship at Bertie's side to a hero's welcome. "The British Lion Comes Home" roared the newspapers the next day.

So we came back here to Strawbridge, Bertie, The White Prince and me. I married Bertie in the village church. I remember, Bertie had a bit of a disagreement with the vicar because he wouldn't allow the lion inside the church for the wedding. I was very glad he didn't – but I never told Bertie that. Nanny Mason adored both Bertie and The White Prince, but she insisted on washing him often, because he smelt – the lion, not Bertie. Nanny Mason stayed on with the three of us – "her three children", she called us – until she retired to the seaside in Devon.

The Butterfly Lion

We never had children of our own – just The White Prince – and I can tell you, he was enough of a family for anyone. He roamed free in the park just as we had planned he would, and chased the deer and the rabbits whenever he felt like it; but he never did learn how to kill for himself. You can't teach old lions new tricks. He lived well, on venison mostly, and slept on a sofa on the landing – I wouldn't have him inside our bedroom, no matter how often Bertie asked. You have to draw the line somewhere.

Bertie's leg never recovered completely. When it was bad, he often needed a stick, or me, or the lion to lean on. It pained him a lot, particularly when the weather was cold and damp, and he never slept well. On Sundays the three of us would wander the park together, and he would sit on the top of Wood Hill with his arm around his old friend's neck and I would fly kites. As you know, I've always loved kites; and so, it turned out, did the lion, who pounced on several of them as they landed, savaged them and ripped them to pieces.

The lion never showed any interest in escaping, and even if he'd wanted to, the park wall was too high for an old lion to jump. Wherever Bertie went he wanted to go too. And if ever Bertie went out in the car, then he'd sit by me near the stove in the kitchen, and watch me with those great amber eyes, listening all the while for the sound of Bertie's car coming up the gravel to the front of the house.

The old lion lived on into a ripe old age. But he became stiff in his legs and could see very little towards the end. He spent his last days stretched out asleep at Bertie's feet, right where you're sitting now. When he died, we buried him at the bottom of the hill out there. Bertie wanted it that way so he could always see the spot from the kitchen window. I suggested we plant a tree in case we forgot where he was. "I'll never forget," he said fiercely. "Never. And besides, he deserves a lot more than a tree."

Bertie grieved on for weeks, months after the lion died. There was nothing I could do to cheer him or even console him. He would sit for hours in his room, or go off on long walks all on his own. He seemed so shut away inside himself, so distant. Try as I did, I could not reach him.

Then one day I was in the kitchen here, when I saw him hurrying down the hill, waving his stick and shouting for me.

"I've got it," he cried, as he came in, "I've got it at last." He showed me the end of his stick. It was white. "See that, Millie? Chalk! It's chalk underneath, isn't it?"

"So?" I said.

"You know the famous White Horse on the hillside at Uffington, the one they carved out of the chalk a thousand years ago? That horse never died, did it? It's still alive, isn't it? Well, that's what we're going to do, so he'll never be forgotten.

We'll carve The White Prince out on the hillside – he'll be there for ever, and he'll be white for ever too."

"It'll take a bit of time, won't it?" I said.

"We've got plenty, haven't we?" he replied, with the same smile he had smiled at me when he was a ten-year-old boy asking me if he could come back and mend my kite for me.

It took the next twenty years to do it. Every spare hour we had, we were up there scraping away with spades and trowels; and we had buckets and wheelbarrows to carry away the turf and the earth. It was hard, back-breaking work, but it was a labour of love. We did it, Bertie and I, we did it together – paws, claws, tail, mane, until he was whole and perfect in every detail.

It was just after we'd finished that the butterflies first came. We noticed that when the sun comes out after the rain in the summer, the butterflies – Adonis Blues, they are, I looked them up – come out to drink on the chalk face. Then The White Prince becomes a butterfly lion, and breathes again like a living creature.

So now you know how Bertie's white lion became The White Prince and how The White Prince became our butterfly lion.

And the Lion Shall Lie Down with the Lamb

The old lady turned to me and smiled. "There," she said. "That's my story."

"And what about Bertie?" I knew as I asked that I shouldn't have. But I had to know.

"He's dead, dear," the old lady replied. "It's what happens when you get old. It's nothing to worry about. It's lonely, though. That's why I've got Jack. And Bertie, like his lion, lived on to a good age. He's buried out there under the hill beside The White Prince." She looked back at the hill for a moment. "And that's where I belong too," she said.

She tapped the table with her fingers. "Come on. Time to go. Back to school with you before they miss you and you get yourself into trouble. We wouldn't want that, would we?" She laughed. "Do you know, that's just what I told Bertie all those years ago when he ran away from school. You remember?" She was on her feet now. "Come on, I'll drive you. And don't look so worried. I'll make sure no one sees you. It'll be like you've never been gone."

"Can I come again?" I asked.

" 'Course you can," she said. "I may not always be easy to find, but I'll be here. I'll just tidy away the tea things, and then we'll go, shall we?"

It was a very old-fashioned car, black and upright and dignified, with a leathery smell and a whiny engine.

She dropped me at the bottom of the school park, by the fence.

"Take care, dear," she said. "And be sure you come again soon, won't you? I'll be expecting you."

"I will," I replied. I climbed the fence before I turned to wave; but by that time the car had gone.

To my huge relief no one had missed me. And best of all, Basher Beaumont was in the sickroom. He'd gone down with measles. I just hoped his measles would last a long time, a very long time.

All through supper I could think of nothing but Bertie Andrews and his white lion. Stew and dumplings and then semolina pudding with raspberry jam – again! It was as I was picking my way through my slimy semolina that I remembered Bertie Andrews had been at this school. Maybe, I thought, maybe he'd had to sit here and eat slimy semolina just as we did now.

I looked up at the honours boards around the dining hall, at the names of all the boys who had won scholarships over the years. I looked for Bertie Andrews. He wasn't there. But then, I thought, why should he be? Maybe, like me, he wasn't brilliant at his school work. Not everyone wins scholarships.

Cookie – Mr Cook, my history teacher – was sitting beside me at the end of my table. "Who were you looking for, Morpurgo?" he asked suddenly.

"Andrews, sir," I said. "Bertie Andrews."

"Andrews? Andrews? There's an Albert Andrews who won the Victoria Cross in the First World War. You mean him?" Cookie scraped his bowl clean and licked the back of his spoon. "I love raspberry jam. You'll find his name in the chapel, under the East Window, under the War memorial. But he wasn't killed in the war, you know. He lived down at Strawbridge, that place with the lion on the gateway, just across the main road. He died, maybe ten, twelve years ago, soon after I came to teach here. The only old boy ever to win the VC. That's why they put up a memorial plaque to him in the chapel after he died. I remember the day his wife came to unveil it – his widow, I should say. Poor dear, just herself and her dog in that great big place. She died only a few months later. Broken heart, they say. You can, you know. You can die of a broken heart.

That house has been empty ever since. No family to take it on. No one wants it. Too big, you see. Shame."

I said I wanted to be excused, to go to the toilet. I hurtled down the passage, out across the courtyard and into the chapel. The small brass plaque was exactly where Cookie had said it was, but hidden by a vase of flowers. I moved the vase to one side. The plaque read:

> ALBERT ANDREWS VC
> BORN 1897. DIED 1968.
> AN OLD BOY OF THIS SCHOOL.
> AND THE LION SHALL LIE DOWN
> WITH THE LAMB.

All night long I tried to puzzle it out. Cookie was wrong. He just had to be. I never slept a wink.

Adonis Blues

The next afternoon after games were over, I went over the fence at the bottom of the park, hared up through Innocents Breach, across the road, along the wall and slipped through the iron gateway with the stone lion roaring above me. It was raining a light summer rain.

I tried knocking at the front door. No one came. No dog barked. I went round to the back and peered in through the kitchen window. The box kite was still there on the kitchen table, but there was no sign of the old lady anywhere. I rattled the kitchen door, and knocked louder, again and again. I called out: "Hello!

Hello!" There was no reply. I banged on the window. "Are you there? Are you there?"

"We all are," came a voice from behind me. I turned. There was no one there. I was alone, alone with the white lion on the hillside. I had imagined it.

I climbed the hill and went to sit in the grass above the white of the lion's mane. I looked down at the great house beneath me. Jackdaws cawed overhead. There was bracken and grass growing out of the gutters and around the chimney pots. Some of the windows were boarded up. Drainpipes hung loose and rusting. The place was empty, quite empty.

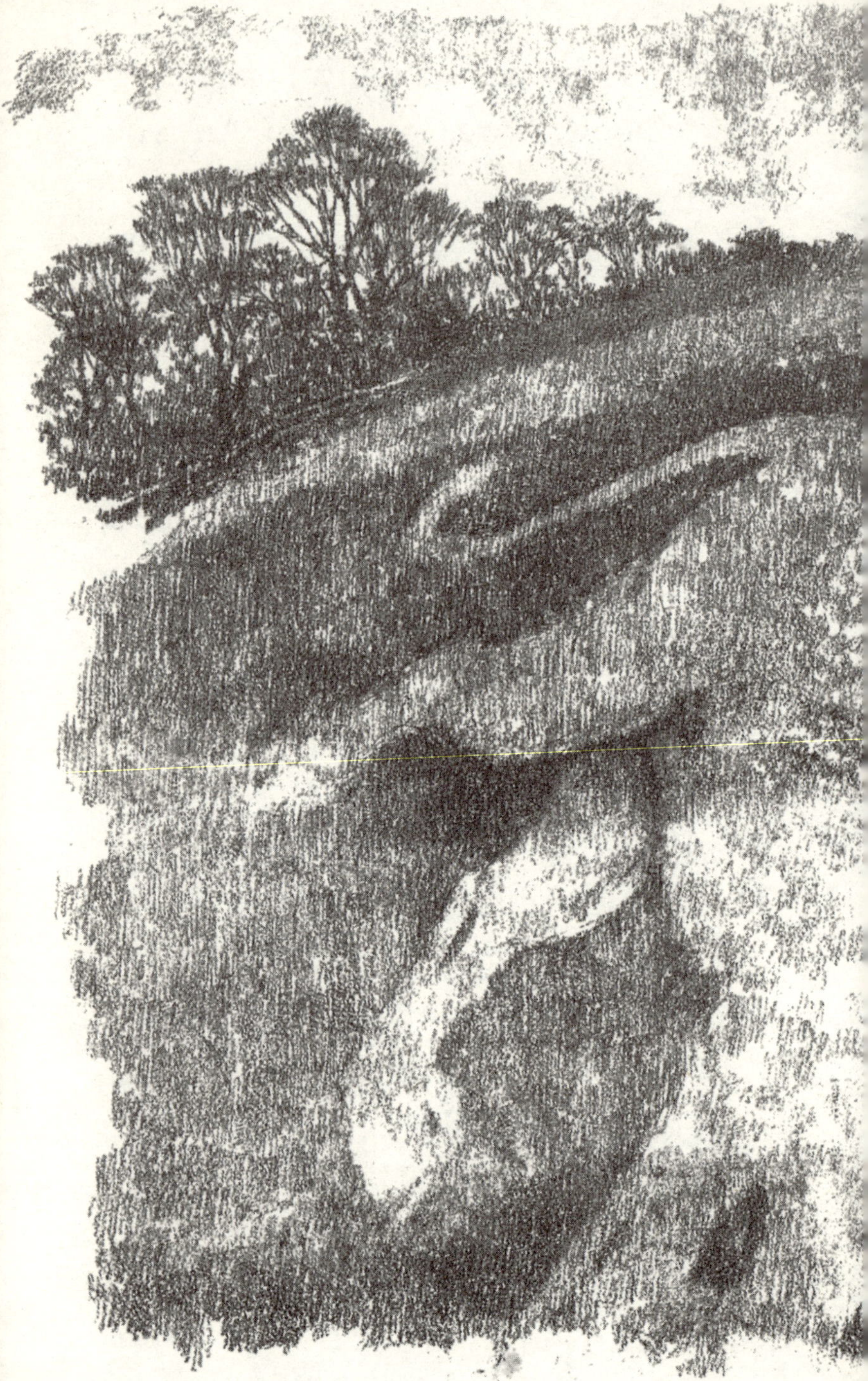

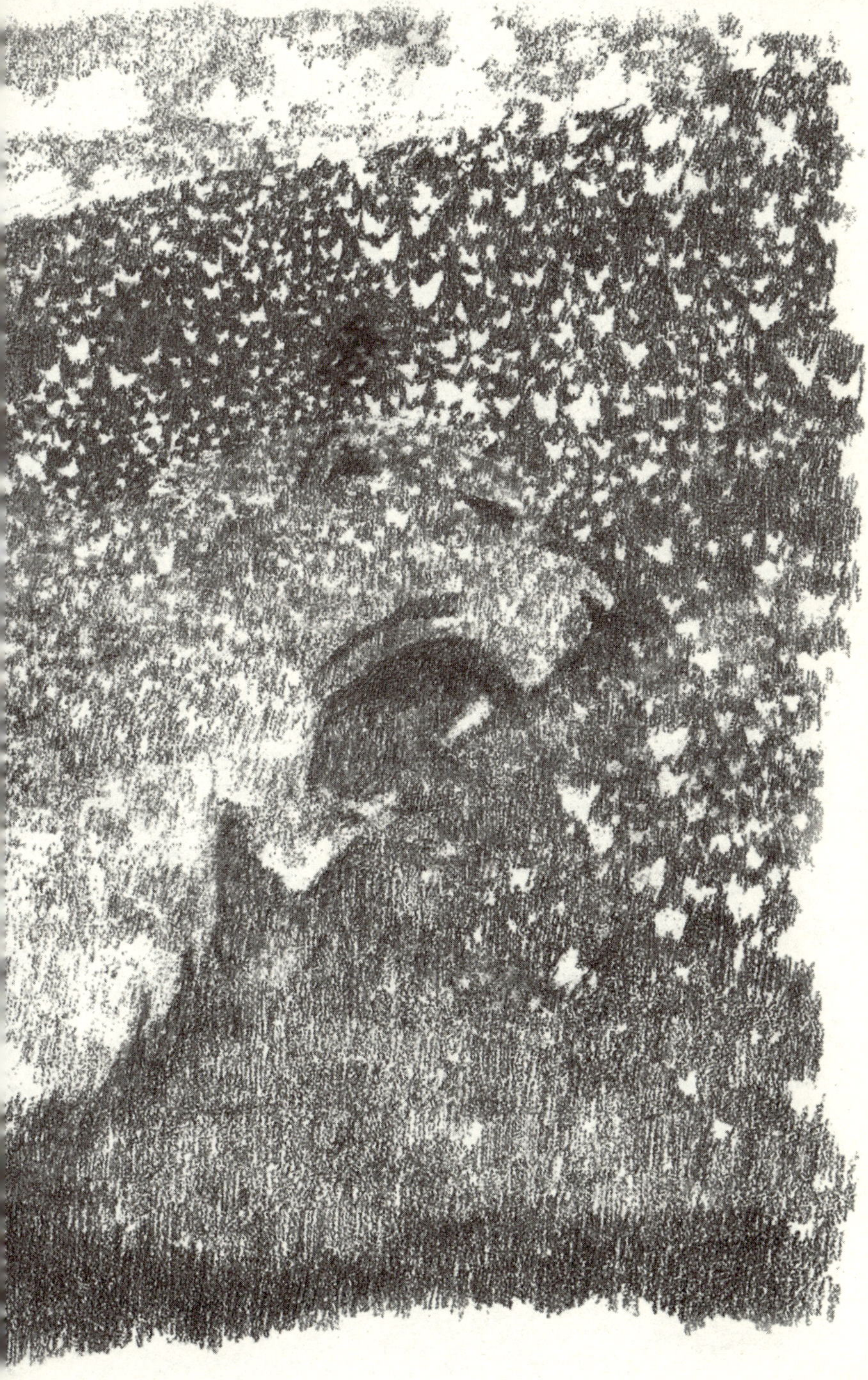

The rain suddenly stopped and the sun warmed the back of my neck. The first butterfly landed on my arm. It was blue. "Adonis Blues, Adonis Blues," came the voice again, like an echo in my head. Then the sky around me was filled with butterflies, and they were settling to drink on the chalk.

"Adonis Blues, remember?" The same voice, a real voice, her voice. And this time I knew it was not in my head. "Keep him white for us, there's a dear. We don't want him forgotten, you see. And think of us sometimes, won't you?"

"I will," I cried. "I will."

And I swear I felt the earth tremble beneath me with the roar of a distant lion.

The Amazing Story of
Adolphus Tips

Praise for
The Amazing Story of Adolphus Tips

"This is a succinctly engaging tear-jerker, it is also full of happiness and affection and has a joyful ending." *Sunday Times,* Children's Book of the Week

"A heartwarming tale of courage, set during the Second World War, about a cat who survives against the odds." *Independent*

"It's an unshowy yet artfully crafted tale." *Telegraph*

"As always, Morpurgo writes with solid confidence in a voice that's gentle yet spellbinding." *Evening Standard*

"Deceptively simple in tone, Lily's diary reveals the complexities faced by ordinary people caught up in momentous events. This is a story within a story, one that crosses generations to remind us that the events of the past resonate through the years, giving pause for reflection and offering room for hope." *Guardian,* Critic's Choice

"Michael Morpurgo's use of language is impeccable, and the conclusion – both heartbreaking and strange – could not be more satisfying." *Carousel*

michael morpurgo

The Amazing Story of Adolphus Tips

Illustrated by Michael Foreman

HarperCollins *Children's Books*

Although the evacuation of the South Hams and the practices for D-day actually took place, this novel is a work of fiction. Any reference to real people (living or dead), actual locales and historical events are used solely to lend the fiction an appropriate cultural and historical setting. All other names, characters, places and incidents portrayed in this book are the product of the author's imagination, and any resemblance to actual persons, living or dead, is entirely coincidental.

First published in Great Britain by HarperCollins *Children's Books* 2005
HarperCollins *Children's Books* is a division of HarperCollins*Publishers* Ltd
77-85 Fulham Palace Road, Hammersmith, London W6 8JB

The HarperCollins *Children's Books* website address is
www.harpercollinschildrensbooks.co.uk

14

Text copyright © Michael Morpurgo 2005

ISBN-13   978 0 00 718246 6
ISBN-10   0 00 718246 5

The author asserts the moral right to be
identified as the author of the work.

Printed and bound in England by Clays Ltd, St Ives plc

Conditions of Sale
This book is sold subject to the condition that it shall not, by way of trade or otherwise, be lent, re-sold, hired out or otherwise circulated without the publisher's prior consent in any form, binding or cover other than that in which it is published and without a similar condition including this condition being imposed on the subsequent purchaser.

Mixed Sources
Product group from well-managed forests and other controlled sources
www.fsc.org   Cert no. SW-COC-1806
© 1996 Forest Stewardship Council

For Ann and Jim Simpson, who brought us to Slapton,
and for their family too, especially Atlanta, Harriet and Effie.

Acknowledgement:
Some of the detail for this story was gleaned from a local history
of Slapton, entitled *The Land Changed its Face* by Grace Bradbeer
(Harbour Books, 1984)

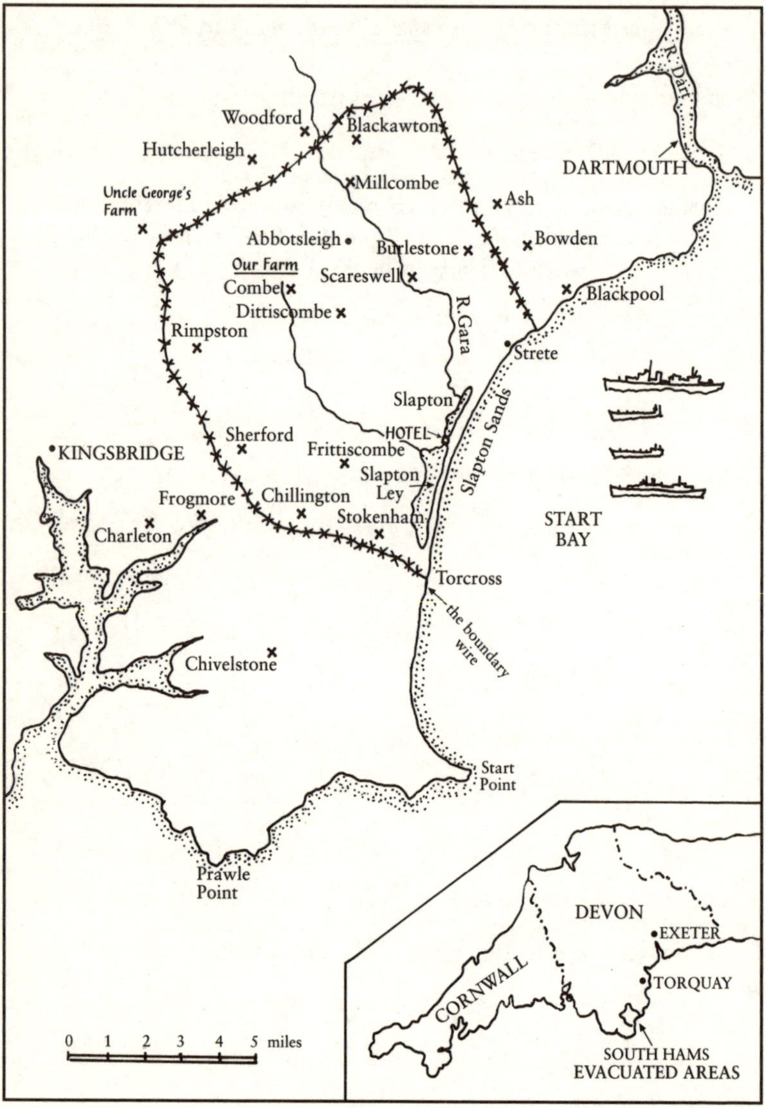
R. Dart
Woodford
Blackawton
Hutcherleigh
DARTMOUTH
Millcombe
Uncle George's Farm
Ash
Abbotsleigh
Burlestone
Bowden
Our Farm
Combe
Scareswell
Blackpool
R. Gara
Dittiscombe
Rimpston
Strete
Slapton
Slapton Sands
HOTEL
Sherford
KINGSBRIDGE
Frittiscombe
Slapton Ley
Frogmore
Chillington
Charleton
Stokenham
START BAY
Torcross
the boundary wire
Chivelstone
Start Point
Prawle Point
DEVON
EXETER
CORNWALL
TORQUAY
SOUTH HAMS EVACUATED AREAS
0 1 2 3 4 5 miles

I first read Grandma's letter over ten years ago, when I was twelve. It was the kind of letter you don't forget. I remember I read it over and over again to be sure I'd understood it right. Soon everyone else at home had read it too.

"Well, I'm gobsmacked," my father said.

"She's unbelievable," said my mother.

Grandma rang up later that evening. "Boowie? Is that you, dear? It's Grandma here."

It was Grandma who had first called me Boowie. Apparently Boowie was the first "word" she ever heard me speak. My real name is Michael, but she's never called me that.

"You've read it then?" she went on.

"Yes, Grandma. Is it true – all of it?"

"Of course it is," she said, with a distant echoing chuckle. "Blame it on the cat if you like, Boowie. But remember one thing, dear: only dead fish swim with the flow, and I'm not a dead fish yet, not by a long chalk."

So it was true, all of it. She'd really gone and done it. I

felt like whooping and cheering, like jumping up and down for joy. But everyone else still looked as if they were in a state of shock. All day, aunties and uncles and cousins had been turning up and there'd been lots of tutting and shaking of heads and mutterings.

"What does she think she's doing?"

"And at her age!"

"Grandpa's only been dead a few months."

"Barely cold in his grave."

And, to be fair, Grandpa *had* only been dead a few months: five months and two weeks to be precise.

It had rained cats and dogs all through the funeral service, so loud you could hardly hear the organ sometimes. I remember some baby began crying and had to be taken out. I sat next to Grandma in the front pew, right beside the coffin. Grandma's hand was trembling, and when I looked up at her she smiled and squeezed my arm to tell me she was all right. But I knew she wasn't, so I held her hand. Afterwards we walked down the aisle together behind the coffin, holding on tightly to one another.

Then we were standing under her umbrella by the

graveside and watching them lower the coffin, the vicar's words whipped away by the wind before they could ever be heard. I remember I tried hard to feel sad, but I couldn't, and not because I didn't love Grandpa. I did. But he had been ill with multiple sclerosis for ten years or more, and that was most of my life. So I'd never felt I'd known him that well. When I was little he'd sit by my bed and read stories to me. Later I did the same for him. Sometimes it was all he could do to smile. In the end, when he was really bad, Grandma had to do almost everything for him. She even had to interpret what he was trying to say to me because I couldn't understand any more. In the last few holidays I spent down at Slapton I could see the suffering in his eyes. He hated being the way he was, and he hated me seeing the way he was too. So when I heard he'd died I was sad for Grandma, of course – they'd been married for over forty years. But in a way I was glad it was finished, for her and for him.

After the burial was over we walked back together along the lane to the pub for the wake, Grandma still clutching my hand. I didn't feel I should say anything to her in case I disturbed her thoughts. So I left her alone.

We were walking under the bridge, the pub already in sight, when she spoke at last. "He's out of it now, Boowie," she said, "and out of that wheelchair too. God, how he hated that wheelchair. He'll be happy again now. You should've seen him before, Boowie. You should have known him like I knew him. Strapping great fellow he was, and gentle too, always kind. He tried to stay kind, right to the end. We used to laugh in the early days – how we used to laugh. That was the worst of it in a way; he just stopped laughing a long time ago, when he first got ill. That's why I always loved having you to stay, Boowie. You reminded me of how he had been when he was young. You were always laughing, just like he used to in the old days, and that made me feel good. It made Grandpa feel good too. I know it did."

This wasn't like Grandma at all. Normally with Grandma I was the one who did the talking. She never said much, she just listened. I'd confided in her all my life. I don't know why, but I found I could always talk to her easily, much more easily than with anyone at home. Back home, people were always busy. Whenever I talked to them I'd feel I was interrupting something. With Grandma

I knew I had her total attention. She made me feel I was the only person in the world who mattered to her.

Ever since I could remember I'd been coming down to Slapton for my holidays, mostly on my own. Grandma's bungalow was more of a home to me than anywhere, because we'd moved house often – too often for my liking. I'd just get used to things, settle down, make a new set of friends and then we'd be off, on the move again. Slapton summers with Grandma were regular and reliable and I loved the sameness of them, and Harley in particular.

Grandma used to take me out in secret on Grandpa's beloved motorbike, his pride and joy, an old Harley-Davidson. We called it Harley. Before Grandpa became ill they would go out on Harley whenever they could, which wasn't often. She told me once those were the happiest times they'd had together. Now that he was too ill to take her out on Harley, she'd take me instead. We'd tell Grandpa all about it, of course, and he liked to hear exactly where we'd been, what field we'd stopped in for our picnic and how fast we'd gone. I'd relive it for him and he loved that. But we never told my family. It was to be our secret, Grandma said, because if anyone back home ever got to know she took me out on Harley they'd never let me come to stay again. She was right too. I had the impression that neither my father (her own son) nor my mother really saw eye to eye with Grandma. They always thought she was a bit stubborn, eccentric, irresponsible even. They'd be sure to think that my going out on Harley with her was far too dangerous. But it wasn't. I never felt unsafe on Harley, no matter how fast we went. The faster the better. When we got back, breathless with excitement, our faces numb from the wind, she'd always say the same thing: "Supreme, Boowie! Wasn't that just supreme?"

When we weren't out on Harley, we'd go on long walks down to the beach and fly kites, and on the way back we'd watch the moorhens and coots and herons on Slapton Ley. We saw a bittern once. "Isn't that supreme?" Grandma whispered in my ear. Supreme was always her favourite word for anything she loved: for motorbikes or birds or lavender. The house always smelt of lavender. Grandma adored the smell of it, the colour of it. Her soap was always lavender, and there was a sachet in every wardrobe and chest of drawers – to keep moths away, she said.

Best of all, even better than clinging on to Grandma as

we whizzed down the deep lanes on Harley, were the wild and windy days when the two of us would stomp noisily along the pebble beach of Slapton Sands, clutching on to one another so we didn't get blown away. We could never be gone for long though, because of Grandpa. He was happy enough to be left on his own for a while, but only if there was sport on the television. So we would generally go off for our ride on Harley or on one of our walks when there was a cricket match on, or rugby. He liked rugby best. He had been good at it himself when he was younger, very good, Grandma said proudly. He'd even played for Devon from time to time – whenever he could get away from the farm, that is.

Grandma had told me a little about the busy life they'd had before I was born, up on the farm – she'd taken me up there to show me. So I knew how they'd milked a herd of sixty South Devon cows and that Grandpa had gone on working as long as he could. In the end, as his illness took hold and he couldn't go up and down stairs any more, they'd had to sell up the farm and the animals and move into the bungalow down in Slapton village. Mostly, though, she'd want to talk about me, ask about me, and she really wanted to know, too. Maybe it was because I was her only grandson. She never seemed to judge me either. So there was nothing I didn't tell her about my life at home or my friends or my worries. She never gave advice, she just listened.

Once, I remember, she told me that whenever I came to stay it made her feel younger. "The older I get," she said, "the more I want to be young. That's why I love going out on Harley. And I'm going to go on being young till I drop, no matter what."

I understood well enough what she meant by "no matter what". Each time I'd gone down in the last couple of years before Grandpa died she had looked more grey and weary. I would often hear my father pleading with her to have Grandpa put into a nursing home, that she couldn't go on looking after him on her own any longer. Sometimes the pleading sounded more like bullying to me, and I wished he'd stop. Anyway, Grandma wouldn't hear of it. She did have a nurse who came in to bath Grandpa each day now, but Grandma had to do the rest all by herself, and she was becoming exhausted. More and more of my walks along the beach were alone nowadays. We couldn't go out on Harley at all. She couldn't leave Grandpa even for ten minutes without him fretting, without her worrying about him. But after Grandpa was in bed we would either play Scrabble, which she would let me win sometimes, or we'd talk on late into the night – or rather I would talk and she would listen. Over the years I reckon I must have given Grandma a running commentary on just about my entire life, from the first moment I could speak, all the way through my childhood.

But now, after Grandpa's funeral, as we walked

together down the road to the pub with everyone following behind us, it was her turn to do the talking, and she was talking about herself, talking nineteen to the dozen, as she'd never talked before. Suddenly I was the listener.

The wake in the pub was crowded, and of course everyone wanted to speak to Grandma, so we didn't get a chance to talk again that day, not alone. I was playing waiter with the tea and coffee, and plates of quiches and cakes. When we left for home that evening Grandma hugged me especially tight, and afterwards she touched my cheek as she'd always done when she was saying good night to me before she switched off the light. She wasn't crying, not quite. She whispered to me as she held me. "Don't you worry about me, Boowie dear," she said. "There's times it's good to be on your own. I'll go for rides on Harley – Harley will help me feel better. I'll be fine." So we drove away and left her with the silence of her empty house all around her.

A few weeks later she came to us for Christmas, but she seemed very distant, almost as if she were lost inside herself: there, but not there somehow. I thought she must still be grieving and I knew that was private, so I left her alone and we didn't talk much. Yet, strangely, she didn't seem too sad. In fact she looked serene, very calm and still, a dreamy smile on her face, as if she was happy enough to be there, just so long as she didn't have to join in too much. I'd often find her sitting and gazing into space, remembering a Christmas with Grandpa perhaps, I thought, or maybe a Christmas down on the farm when she was growing up.

On Christmas Day itself, after lunch, she said she wanted to go for a walk. So we went off to the park, just the two of us. We were sitting watching the ducks on the pond when she told me. "I'm going away, Boowie," she said. "It'll be in the New Year, just for a while."

"Where to?" I asked her.

"I'll tell you when I get there," she replied. "Promise. I'll send you a letter."

She wouldn't tell me any more no matter how much I badgered her. We took her to the station a couple of days later and waved her off. Then there was silence. No letter, no postcard, no phone call. A week went by. A fortnight. No one else seemed to be that concerned about her, but I was. We all knew she'd gone travelling, she'd made no secret of it, although she'd told no one where she was going. But she had promised to write to me and nothing had come. Grandma never broke her promises. Never. Something had gone wrong, I was sure of it.

Then one Saturday morning I picked up the post from the front door mat. There was one for me. I recognised her handwriting at once. The envelope was quite heavy too. Everyone else was soon busy reading their own post, but I wanted to open Grandma's envelope in private. So I ran upstairs to my room, sat on the bed and opened it. I pulled out what looked more like a manuscript than a letter, about thirty or forty pages long at least, closely typed. On the cover page she had sellotaped a black and white photograph (more brown and white really) of a small girl who looked a lot like me, smiling toothily into the camera and cradling a large black and white cat in her arms. There was a title: *The Amazing Story of Adolphus Tips*, with her name underneath, Lily Tregenza. Attached to the manuscript by a large multicoloured paperclip was this letter.

Dearest Boowie,

This is the only way I could think of to explain to you properly why I've done what I've done. I'll have told you some of this already over the years, but now I want you to know the whole story. Some people will think I'm mad, perhaps most people — I don't mind that. But you won't think I'm mad, not when you've read this. You'll understand, I know you will. That's why I particularly wanted you to read it first. You can show it to everyone else afterwards. I'll phone soon... when you're over the surprise.

When I was about your age — and by the way that's me on the front cover with Tips — I used to keep a diary. I was an only child, so I'd talk to myself in my diary. It was company for me, almost like a friend. So what you'll be reading is the story of my life as it happened, beginning in the autumn of 1943, during the Second World War, when I was growing up on the family farm. I'll be honest with you, I've done quite a lot of editing. I've left bits out here and there because some of it was too private or too boring or too long. I used to write pages and pages sometimes, just talking to myself, rambling on.

The surprise comes right at the very end. So don't cheat, Boowie. Don't look at the end. Let it be a surprise for you — as it still is for me.

Lots of love,

Grandma

PS Harley must be feeling very lonely all on his own in the garage. We'll go for a ride as soon as I get back; as soon as you come to visit. Promise.

THE AMAZING STORY OF ADOLPHUS TIPS

Lily Tregenza

Friday, September 10th 1943

I've been back at school a whole week now. When Miss McAllister left at the end of last term I was cock-a-hoop (I like that word), we all were. She was a witch, I'm sure she was. I thought everything would be tickety-boo (I like that word too) just perfect, and I was so much looking forward to school without her. And who do we get as a head teacher instead? Mrs "Bloomers" Blumfeld. She's all smiles on the outside, but underneath she's an even worser witch than Miss McAllister. I know I'm not supposed to say worser but it sounds worser than worse, so I'm using it. So there. We call her Bloomers because of her name of course, and also because she came into class once with her skirt hitched up by mistake in her navy-blue bloomers.

Today Bloomers gave me a detention just because my hands were dirty again. "Lily Tregenza, I think you are one of the most untidiest girls I have ever known." She can't even say her words properly. She says zink instead of think and de instead of the. She can't even speak English properly and she's supposed to be our teacher. So I said it wasn't fair, and she gave me another detention. I hate her accent; she could be German. Maybe she's a spy! She looks like a spy. I hate her, I really do. And what's more, she favours the townies, the evacuees. That's because she's come down from London like they have. She told us so.

We've got three more townies in my class this term, all from London like the others. There's so many of them now there's hardly enough room to play in the playground. There's almost as many of them as there are of us. They're always fighting too. Most of them are all right, I suppose, except that they talk funny. I can't understand half of what they say. And they stick together too much. They look at us sometimes like we've got measles or mumps or something, like they think we're all stupid country bumpkins, which we're not.

One of the new ones – Barry Turner he's called – is living in Mrs Morwhenna's house, next to the shop. He's got red hair everywhere, even red eyebrows. And he picks his nose which is disgusting. He gets lots more spellings wrong than me, but Bloomers never gives *him* a detention. I know why too. It's because Barry's dad was killed in the airforce at Dunkirk. My dad's away in the army, and he's alive. So just because he's not dead, I get a detention. Is that fair? Barry told Maisie, who sits next to me in class now and who's my best friend sometimes, that she could kiss him if she wanted to. He's only been at our school a week. Cheeky monkey. Maisie said she let him because he's young – he's only ten – and because she was sorry for him, on account of his dad, and also because she wanted to find out if townies were any good at it. She said it was a bit sticky but all right. I don't do kissing. I don't see the point of it, not if it's sticky.

Tips is going to have her kittens any day now. She's all saggy baggy underneath. Last time she had them on my bed. She's the best cat (and the biggest) in the whole wide world and I love her more than anyone or anything. But she keeps having kittens, and I wish she wouldn't because we can't ever keep them. No one wants them because everyone's got cats of their own already, and they all have kittens too.

It was all because of Tips and her kittens that I had my row with Dad, the biggest row of my life, when he was last home on leave from the army. He did it when I was at school, without even telling me. As soon as they were born he took all her kittens out and drowned them just like that. When I found out I said terrible things to him, like I would never ever speak to him again and how I hoped the Germans would kill him. I was horrible to him. I never made it up with him either. I wrote him a letter saying I was sorry, but he hasn't replied and I wish he would. He probably hates me now, and I wouldn't blame him. If anything happened to him I couldn't bear it, not after what I said.

Mum keeps telling me I shouldn't let my tongue do my thinking for me, and I'm not quite sure what that means. She's just come in to say good night and blow out my lamp. She says I spend too much time writing my diary. She thinks I can't write in the dark, but I can. My writing may look a bit wonky in the morning, but I don't care.

Sunday, September 12th 1943

We saw some American soldiers in Slapton today; it's the first time I've ever seen them. Everyone calls them Yanks, I don't know why. Grandfather doesn't like them, but I do. I think they've got smarter uniforms than ours and they look bigger somehow. They smiled a lot and waved – particularly at Mum, but that was just because she's pretty, I could tell. When they whistled she went very red, but she liked it. They don't say "hello", they say "hi" instead, and one of them said "howdy". He was the one who gave me a sweet, only he called it "candy". I'm sucking it now as I'm writing. It's nice, but not as nice as lemon sherberts or peppermint humbugs with the stripes and chewy centres. Humbugs are my best favourites, but I'm only allowed two a week now because of rationing. Mum says we're really lucky living on the farm because we can grow our own vegetables, make our own milk and butter and cream and eat our own chickens. So when I complain about sweet rationing, which I do, she always gives me a little lecture on how lucky we are. Barry says they've got rationing for everything in London, so maybe Mum is right. Maybe we are lucky. But I still don't see how me having less peppermint humbugs is going to help us win the war.

Thursday, September 16th 1943

Mum got a letter from Dad today. Whenever she gets a letter she's very happy and sad at the same time. She says he's out in the desert in Africa with the Eighth Army and he's making sure the lorries and the tanks work – he's very good at engines, my dad. It's very hot in the daytime, he says, but at night it's cold enough to freeze your toes off. Mum let me read the letter after she had. He didn't say anything about Tips and the kittens or the row we had. Maybe he's forgotten all about it. I hope so.

I feel bad about writing this, but I must write what I really feel. What's the point in writing at all otherwise? The truth is, I don't really miss Dad like I know I should, like I know Mum does. When I'm actually reading his letters I miss him lots, but then later on I forget all about him unless someone talks about him, unless I see his photo maybe. Perhaps it's because I'm still cross with him about the kittens. But it's not just because of the kittens that I'm cross with him. The thing is, he didn't need to go to fight in the war; he could have stayed with us and helped Grandfather and Mum on the farm. Other farmers were allowed to stay. *He* could have. But he didn't. He tried to explain it to me before he joined up. He said he wouldn't feel right about staying home when there were so many men going off to the war, men the same age as he was. I told him he should think of Grandfather and Mum and me, but he wouldn't listen. They've got to do all the work on their own now, all the milking and the muck spreading, all the haymaking and the lambing. Dad was the only one who could fix his Fordson tractor and the thresher, and now he's not here to do it. I help out a bit, but I'm not much use. I'm only twelve (almost anyway) and I'm off to school most days. He should be here with us, that's what I think. I'm fed up with him being away. I'm fed up with this war. We're not allowed down on the beach any more to fly our kites. There's barbed wire all around it to keep us off, and there's mines buried all over it. They've put horrible signs up everywhere warning us off. That wasn't much use to Farmer Jeffrey's smelly old one-eyed sheepdog that lifted his leg on everything he passed (including my leg once). He wandered on to the beach under the wire yesterday and blew himself up. Poor old thing.

I had this idea at school (probably because Bloomers was reading us the King Arthur stories). I think we should dress Churchill and Hitler up in armour like King Arthur's knights, stick them on horses, give them a lance each and let them sort it out between them. Whoever is knocked off loses, and the war would be over and we could all go back to being normal again. Churchill would win of course, because Hitler looks too weak and feeble even to sit on a horse, let alone hold a lance. So we would win. No more rationing. All the humbugs I want. Dad could come home and everything would be like it was before. Everything would be tickety-boo.

Friday, September 17th 1943

I saw a fox this morning running across south field with a hen in his mouth. When I shouted at him, he stopped and looked at me for a moment as if he was telling me to mind my own business. Then he just trotted off, cool as you like, without a care in the world. Mum says it wasn't one of her hens, but she was someone's hen, wasn't she? Someone should tell that fox about rationing. That's what I think.

There's lots of daddy-longlegs crawling up my window, and a butterfly. I'll just let them out...

It's still light outside. I love light evenings. It was a red admiral butterfly. Beautiful. Supreme.

Mum and Grandfather are having an argument downstairs, I can hear them. Grandfather is going on about the American soldiers again, "ruddy Yanks" he calls them. He says they're all over the place, hundreds of them, and walking about as if they own the place, smoking cigars, chewing gum. Like an invasion, he says. Mum speaks more quietly than Grandfather, so it's difficult to hear what she's saying.

They've stopped arguing now. They've got the radio on instead. I don't know why they bother. The news of the war is always bad, and it only makes them feel miserable. It's hardly ever off, that radio.

Monday, September 20th 1943

Two big surprises. One good, one bad. We were all sent home from school today. That was the good one. It was all because of Mr Adolf Ruddy Hitler, as Grandfather calls him. So thanks for the holiday, Mr Adolf Ruddy Hitler. We were sitting doing arithmetic with Bloomers – long division which I can't understand no matter how hard I try – when we heard the roaring and rumbling of an aeroplane overhead, getting louder and louder, and the classroom windows started to rattle. Then there was this huge explosion and the whole school shook. We all got down on the floor and crawled under the desks like we have to do in air-raid practice, except this was very much more exciting because it was real. By the time Bloomers had got us out into the playground the German bomber was already far out over the sea. We could see the black crosses on its wings. Barry pretended he was firing an ack-ack gun and tried to shoot it

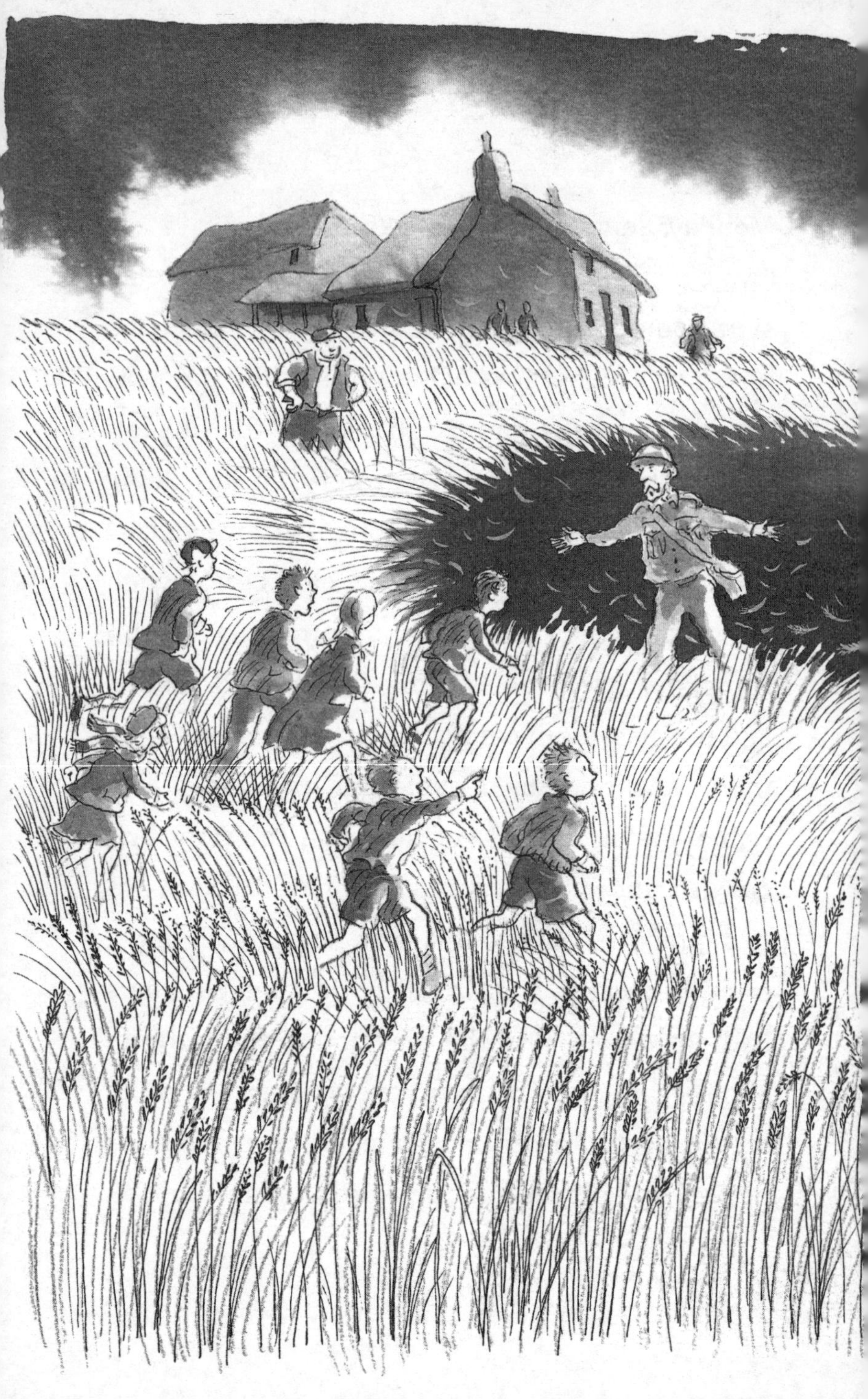

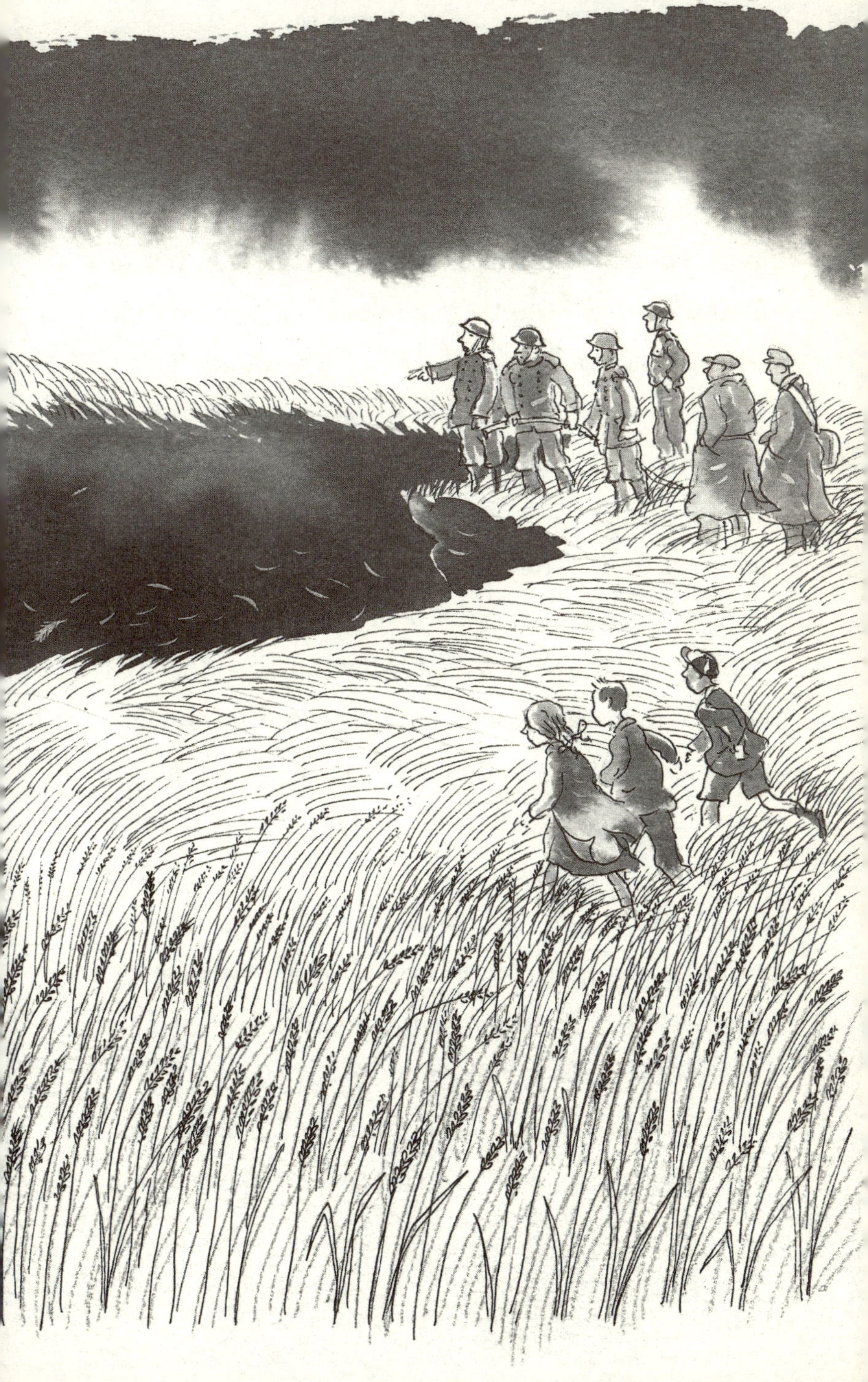

down. Most of the boys joined in, making their silly machine-gun noises – dadadadadada.

Bloomers sent us home just in case there were more bombers on the way. But we didn't go home. Instead we all went off to see if we could find where the bomb had landed. We found it too. There was a massive hole in Mr Berry's cornfield just outside the village. The Home Guard was there already, Uncle George in his uniform telling them all what to do. They were making sure no one fell in, I suppose. No one had been hurt, except a poor old pigeon who was probably having a good feed of corn when the bomb fell. His feathers were everywhere. Then one of the townies got all hoity-toity about it and said he'd seen much bigger holes than this one back home, in London. Big Ned Simmons told him just where he could go and just what he thought of him and all the snotty-nosed townies, and it all got a bit nasty after that, us against them. So I walked away.

I was on my way home afterwards when I saw this jeep coming down the lane towards me. There was one soldier in it. He had an American helmet on. He screeched to a stop and said, "Hi there!" He was a black man. I've never in my life seen a black person before, only in pictures in books, so I didn't quite know what to say. I kept trying not to stare, but I couldn't help myself. He had to ask me twice if he was on the right road to Torpoint before I even managed a nod. "You know something? You got pigtails just like my littlest sister." Then he said, "See ya!" and off he went, splashing through the puddles. I was a bit disappointed not to get any candy.

When I got home I had my other surprise, my bad one. I told them about the bomb and about Uncle George and the Home Guard being there, and I told them about the black soldier I'd met in the lane. They didn't seem very interested in any of it. I thought that was strange. And it was strange too that neither of them seemed to want to talk to me much or even to look at me. We were all having tea in the kitchen when Tips came in. She rubbed herself against my leg and then went off mewing under the table, under the dresser, into the pantry. But she wasn't mewing like she does when she's after food or love, or when she brings in a mouse. She was calling, and when I picked her up she felt different. Still saggy baggy underneath, but definitely different. She wasn't full and fat any more. I knew what they'd done at once.

"We had to do it, Lily," Mum said. "It's better straight away, before she gets too fond of them. Sometimes you have to be cruel to be kind."

I screamed at them: "Murderers! Murderers!" Then I brought Tips up to my room. I'm still up here with her now. I've been crying ever since, and really loudly too so they can hear me, so they'll feel really bad, as bad as I do.

Tips is lying in my lap and washing herself just like nothing's happened. She's even purring. Maybe she doesn't know yet. Or maybe she does and she's forgiven us already. Now she's stopped licking herself. She's looking at me as if she knows. I don't think she has forgiven us. I don't think she'll ever forgive us. Why should she?

Tuesday, October 5th 1943

My birthday. I was born twelve years ago today at ten o'clock in the morning. I've been calling myself twelve for a long time, and now I really am. All I want to be now is thirteen. And even thirteen isn't old enough. I so much want to be much older than I am, but not old like Grandfather so that I walk bent and my hands are all hard and wrinkly and veiny. I don't want a drippy nose and hairs growing out of my ears. But I do want the years to hurry on by until I'm about seventeen, so school and Bloomers and long division are over and done with, so that no one can take my kittens away and drown them. It'll be so good when I'm seventeen, because the war will be over by then, that's for sure. Grandfather says that we're already winning and so it can't be long till it's finished. Then I can go up to London on the train – I've never been on a train – and I can see the shops and ride on those big red buses and go on the underground. Barry

Turner's told me all about it. He says there's lights in the streets, millions of people everywhere, and cinemas and dance halls. His dad used to work in a cinema before the war, before he was killed. He told me that one day. That was the first thing he's ever told me about his dad.

Which reminds me: I still haven't had a letter from *my* dad. I think he's still cross with me after what I said. I wish, I wish I hadn't said it. I had a dream about him the other night. I don't usually remember my dreams at all, but I remember this one, some of it anyway. He was back at home milking cows again, but he was in uniform with his tin helmet on. It was scary because, when I came into the milking parlour, I spoke to him and he never looked up. I shouted but he still never looked at me. It was like one of us wasn't there, but we were. We both were.

Monday, November 1st 1943

"Pinch, punch, first day of the month. Slap and a kick for being so quick. Punch in the eye for being so sly." Barry kept saying it to me every time he saw me. It was really annoying. In the end I shouted at him and hurt his feelings. I know I shouldn't have, he was only trying to be friendly. He didn't cry but he nearly did.

But tonight I feel worse about something else, something much worse. Ever since Bloomers came I've been giving her a hard time, we all have, but me most of all. I'm really good at giving people a hard time when I want to. I cheeked her when she first came because I didn't like her and she got ratty and punished me. So I cheeked her again and she punished me again and on it went, and after that I could never get on with her at all. I've been mean to her ever since I've known her, and now this has happened.

The vicar came into school today and told us

he'd be teaching us for the morning because Mrs Blumfeld wasn't feeling very well. She wasn't ill so much as sad, he said, sad because she had just heard the news that her husband, who is in the merchant navy, had been lost at sea in the Atlantic. His ship had been torpedoed. They'd picked up a few survivors, but Mrs Blumfeld's husband wasn't one of them. The vicar told us that when she came back into school we had to be very good and kind, so as not to upset her. Then he said we should close our eyes and hold our hands together and pray for her. I did pray for her too, but I also prayed for myself, because I don't want God to have his own back on me for all the horrible things I've said and thought about her. I prayed for my dad too, that God wouldn't make him die in the desert just because I'd been mean to Mrs Blumfeld, that I hadn't meant it when I'd said I wanted him to die because he drowned the kittens. I've never prayed so hard in my life. Usually my mind wanders when I'm supposed to be praying, but it didn't today.

After lunch Mrs Blumfeld came into school. She had no lipstick on. She looked so pale and cold. She was trembling a little too. We left a letter for her on her desk which we had all signed, to say how sorry we all were about her husband. She looked very calm, as if she was in a daze. She wasn't crying or anything, not until she read our letter. Then she tried to smile at us through her tears and said it was very thoughtful of us, which it wasn't because it was the vicar's idea, but we didn't tell her that. We all went around whispering and being extra good and quiet all day. I feel so bad for her now because she's all alone. I won't call her Bloomers ever again. I don't think anyone will.

Monday, November 8th 1943

Ever since Mrs Blumfeld's husband was killed, I've been worrying a lot about Dad. I didn't before, but I am now, all the time. I keep thinking of him lying dead in the sand of Africa. I try not to, but the picture of him lying there keeps coming into my head. And it's silly, I know it is, because I got a letter from him only yesterday, at last, and he's fine. (His letters take for ever to come. This one was dated two months ago.) He never said anything about me being cross. In fact he sent his love to Tips. Dad says it's so hot out in the desert he could almost fry an egg on the bonnet of his jeep. He says he longs for a few days of good old Devon drizzle, and mud. He really misses mud. How can you miss mud? We're all sick of mud. It's been raining here for days now: mizzly, drizzly, horrible rain. Today it was blowing in from the sea, so I was wet through by the time I got home from school.

Grandfather came in later. He'd been drinking a

bit, but then he always drinks a bit when he goes to market, just to keep the cold out, he says. He sat down in front of the stove and put his feet in the bottom oven to warm up. Mum hates him doing it but he does it all the same. He's got holes in his socks too. He always has.

"There's hundreds of gum-chewing Yanks everywhere in town," he said. "Like flies on a ruddy cow clap." I like it when Grandfather talks like that. He got a dirty look from Mum, but he didn't mind. He just gave me a big wink and a wicked grin and went on talking. He said he was sure something's going on: there are fuel dumps everywhere you look, tents going up all over the place, tanks and lorries parked everywhere. "It's something big," he said. "I'm telling you."

Still raining out there. It's lashing the windowpanes as I'm writing, and the whole house is creaking and shaking, almost as if it's getting ready to take off and fly out over the sea. I can hear the cows lowing in the barn. They're scared. Tips is frightened silly too. She wants to hide. She keeps jogging my writing. She's trying to push her head deeper and deeper into my armpit. *I'm* not frightened, I like storms. I like it when the sea comes thundering in and the wind blows so hard that it takes your breath away.

Mrs Blumfeld said something this morning that took my breath away too. That Daisy Simmons, Ned's little sister, is always asking questions when she shouldn't and today she put her hand up and asked Mrs Blumfeld if she was a mummy, just like that! Mrs Blumfeld didn't seem to mind at all. She thought for a bit, then she said that she would never have any children of her own because she didn't need them; she had all of us instead. We were her family now. And she had her cats, which she loved. I didn't know she had cats. I was watching her when she said it and you could see she really did love them. I was so wrong about her. She likes cats so she must be nice. I'm going to sleep now and I'm not going to think of Dad lying out in the desert. I'm going to think of Mrs Blumfeld at home with her cats instead.

I just went to shut the window, and I saw a barn owl flying across the farmyard, white and silent in the darkness. There one moment, gone the next. A ghost owl. He's screeching now. They screech, they don't toowit-toowoo. That word looks really funny when you write it down, but owls don't have to write it down, do they? They just have to hoot it, or toowit-toowoo it.

Saturday, November 13th 1943

Today was a day that will change my life for ever.

Grandfather was right when he said something was up. And it is something big too, something very big – I have to keep pinching myself to believe it's true, that it's really going to happen. Yesterday was just like any other day. Rain. School. Long division. Spelling test. Barry picking his nose. Barry smiling at me from across the classroom with his big round eyes. I just wish he wouldn't smile at me so. He's always so smiley.

Then today it happened. I knew all day there was going to be some kind of meeting in the church in the evening, that someone from every house had to go and it was important. I knew that, because Mum and Grandfather were arguing about it over breakfast before I went off to school. Grandfather was being a grumpy old goat. He's been getting crotchety a lot just lately. (Mum says it's because of his rheumatism – it gets worse in damp weather.) He kept saying he had too much to do on the farm to be bothered with meetings and such. And besides, he said, women were better at talking because they did more of it. Of course that made Mum really mad, so they had a fair old ding-dong about it. Anyway in the end Mum gave in and said she'd go, and she asked me to go along with her for company. I didn't want to go but now I'm glad I did, really glad.

The place was packed out. There was standing room only by the time we got there. Then this bigwig, Lord Somethingorother, got up and started talking. I didn't pay much attention at first because he had this droning-on hoity-toity (I like that word) sort of voice that almost put me to sleep. But suddenly I felt a strange stillness and silence all around me. It was almost as if everyone had stopped breathing. Everyone was listening, so I listened too. I can't remember his exact words, but I think it went something like this.

"I know it's asking a lot of you," the bigwig was saying, "but I promise we wouldn't be asking you if we didn't have to, if it wasn't absolutely necessary. They'll be needing the beach at Slapton Sands and the whole area behind it, including this village. They need it because they have to practise landings from the sea for the invasion of France when it comes. That's all I can tell you. Everything else is top secret. No point in asking me anything about it, because I don't know any more than you do. What I do know is that you have seven weeks from today to move out, lock, stock and barrel – and I mean that. You have to take everything with you: furniture, food, coal, all your animals, farm machinery, fuel, and all fodder and crops that can

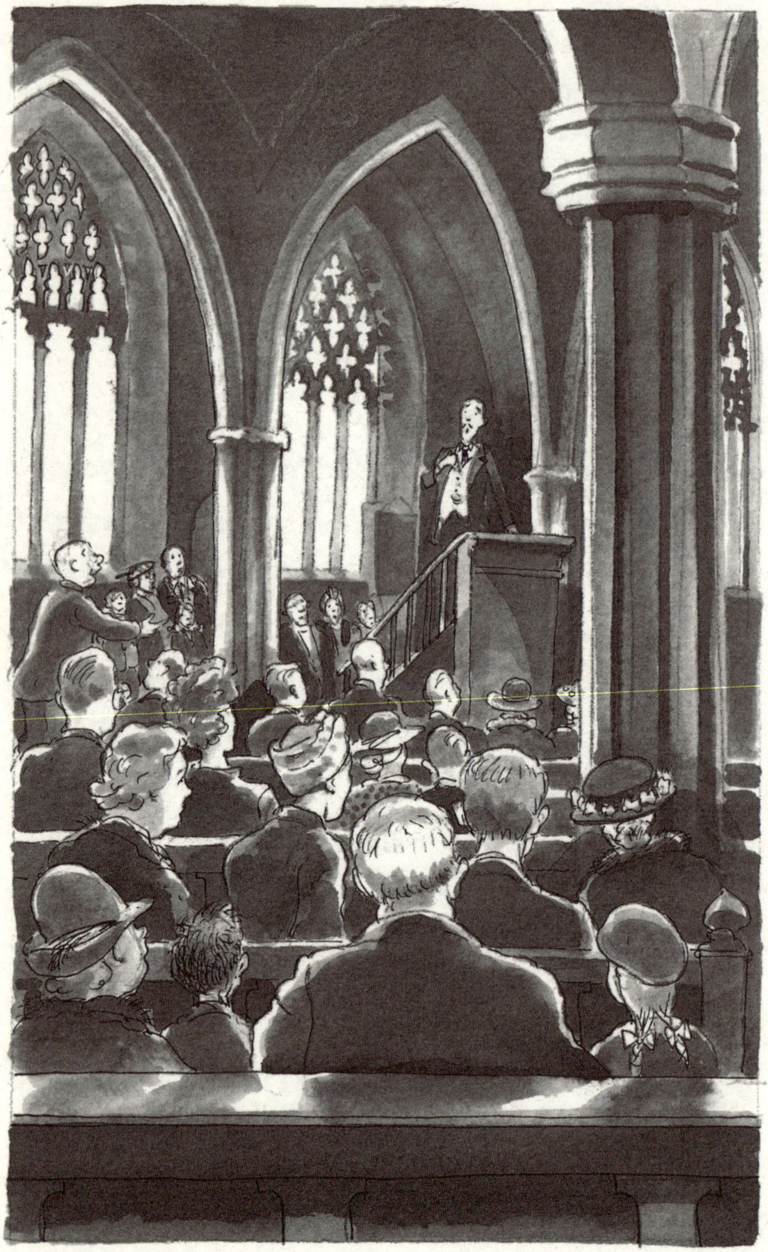

be carried. Nothing you value must be left behind. After the seven weeks is up, no one will be allowed back – and I mean no one. There'll be a barbed-wire perimeter fence and guards everywhere to keep you out. Besides which, it will be dangerous. There'll be live firing going on: real shells, real bullets. I know it's hard, but don't imagine it's just Slapton, that you're the only ones. Torcross, East Allington, Stokenham, Sherford, Chillington, Strete, Blackawton: 3000 people have got to move out; 750 families, 30,000 acres of land have got to be cleared in seven weeks."

Some people tried to stand up and ask questions, but it was no use. He just waved them down.

"I've told you. It's no good asking me the whys and wherefores. All I know is what I've told you. They need it for the war effort, for training purposes. That's all you need to know."

"Yes, but for how long?" asked the vicar from the back of the hall.

"About six months, nine months, maybe longer.

We can't be sure. And don't worry. We'll make sure everyone has a place to live, and of course there'll be proper compensation paid to everyone, to all the farms and businesses for any loss or damage. And I have to be honest with you here, I have to warn you that there will be damage, lots of it."

You could have heard a pin drop. I was expecting lots of protests and questions, but everyone seemed to be struck dumb. I looked up at Mum. She was staring ahead of her, her mouth half open, her face pale. All the way home in the dark, I kept asking her questions, but she never said a word till we reached the farmyard.

"It'll kill him," she whispered. "Your grandfather. It'll kill him."

Once back home she came straight out with it. Grandfather was in his chair warming his toes in the oven as usual. "We've got to clear out," she said, and she told him the whole thing. Grandfather was silent for a moment or two. Then he just said, "They'll have to carry me out first. I was born here and I'll die here. I'm not moving, not for they ruddy Yanks, not for no one." Mum's still downstairs with him, trying to persuade him. But he won't listen. I know he won't. Grandfather doesn't say all that much, but what he says he means. What he says, he sticks to. Tips has jumped up on my bed and walked all over my diary with her muddy paws! She's lucky I love her as much as I do.

Tuesday, November 16th 1943

At school, in the village, no matter where you go or whoever you meet, it's all anyone talks about: the evacuation. It's like a sudden curse has come down on us all. No one smiles. No one's the same. There's been a thick fog ever since we were told. It hangs all around us, tries to come in at the windows. It makes me wonder if it'll ever go away, if we'll ever see the sun again.

I've changed my mind completely about Barry. That skunkhead Bob Bolan came up to me at playtime and started on about Grandfather, just because he's the only one in the village refusing to go. He said he was a stupid old duffer. He said he should be sent away to a lunatic asylum and locked up. Maisie was there with me and *she* never stood up for me, and I thought she was supposed to be my best friend. Well she's not, not any more. No one stood up for me, so I had to stand up for myself. I pushed Skunkhead (I won't call him Bob any more because Skunkhead suits him better) and Skunkhead pushed me, and I fell over and grazed my elbow. I was sitting there, picking the grit out of my skin and trying not to let them see I was crying, when Barry came up. The next thing I know he's got Skunkhead on the ground and he's punching him. Mrs Blumfeld had to pull him off, but not before Skunkhead got a bleeding nose, which served him right. As she took them both back into school Barry looked over his shoulder and smiled. I never got a chance to say thank you, but I will. If only he'd stop picking his nose and smiling at me I think I could really like him a lot. But I'm not doing kissing with him.

Tuesday, November 30th 1943

Some people have started moving their things out already. This morning I saw Maisie's dad going up the road with a cartload of beds and chairs, cupboards, tea chests and all sorts. Maisie was sitting on the top and waving at me. She's my friend again, but not my best friend. I think Barry's my best friend now because I know I can really trust him. Then I saw Miss Langley driving off in a car with lots of cases and trunks strapped on top. She had Jimbo on her lap, her horrible Jack Russell dog who chases Tips up trees whenever he sees her. Mum told me that Miss Langley is off to stay with a cousin up in Scotland, hundreds of miles away. I've just told Tips and suddenly she's purring very happily. It's a "good riddance" purr, I think.

A lot of people are going to stay with relatives, and we could too except that Grandfather won't hear of it. Uncle George farms only a couple of miles away, just beyond where the wire fence will be. They're beginning to put it up already. He said that family's family, and he'd be only too happy to help us out. I heard him telling Grandfather. We could take our milking cows up to his place, all our sheep, all the farm machinery, Dad's Fordson tractor, everything. It'll be a tight squeeze, Uncle George said, but we could manage. Grandfather won't listen. He won't leave, and that's that.

Wednesday, December 1ˢᵗ 1943

At playtime I found Barry sitting on his own on the dustbins behind the bike shed. He was all red around the eyes. He'd been crying, but he was trying not to show it. He wouldn't tell me why at first, but after a while I got it out of him. It's because there won't be room for him any more with Mrs Morwhenna when she moves into Kingsbridge next week. He likes her a lot and now he has nowhere to go. So, to make him feel better, and because of what he had done for me the other day with Skunkhead, I said he could come home with me and play after school, so long as he didn't pick his nose. He perked up after that, and he was even chirpier when he saw the cows and the sheep. And when he saw Dad's Fordson tractor he went loopy. It was like he'd been given a new toy of his own to play with. I couldn't get him off it. Grandfather took him off around the farm, letting him steer the tractor – which wasn't fair because he's never let me do that. By the time they came back they were both of them as happy as larks. I haven't heard Grandfather laugh so much in ages.

Barry tucked into Mum's cream sponge cake, slice after slice of it, and all the time he never stopped talking about the tractor and the farm (and no one told him not to talk with his mouth full, which wasn't fair either because Mum's always ticking me off for that). He'd have scoffed the lot if Mum hadn't taken it away. He still smiles at me, but I don't mind so much now. In fact I quite like it really.

Afterwards, when we were walking together down the lane to the farm gate, he seemed suddenly down in the dumps. He hardly said a word all the way. Then suddenly he just blurted it out. "I could come and stay," he said. "I wouldn't be a nuisance, honest. I wouldn't pick my nose, honest." I couldn't say no, but I didn't want to say yes, not exactly. I mean, it would be like having a brother in the house. I'd never had a brother and I wasn't sure I wanted one, even if Barry was my best friend now, sort of. So I said maybe. I said I'd ask. And I did, at supper time. Grandfather didn't even have to think about it. "The lad needs a home, doesn't he?" he said. "We've got a home. He needs feeding. We've got food. We should have had one of those evacuee children before, but I never liked townies much till now. This one's all right though. He's a good lad. Besides, it'll be good to have a boy about the place. Be like the old days, when your father was a boy. You tell him he can come."

He never asked me what I thought, never asked Mum. He just said yes. It took me so much by surprise that I wasn't ready for it, and neither was Mum. So it looks as if I'm going to have a sort of brother living with us, whether I like it or not. Mum came in a minute ago and sat on my bed. "Do you mind about Barry?" she asked me.

"He's all right, I suppose," I told her. And he is too, except when he's picking his nose of course.

"One thing's for sure, it'll make Grandfather happier," Mum said. "And if he's happier, then maybe it'll be easier to talk him into leaving, into moving to Uncle George's place. They're going to move us out, you know, Lily. One way or another, they're going to do it." She gave me a good long cuddle tonight. She hasn't done that for ages. I think she thinks I'm too old for it or something, but I'm not.

I haven't had my nightmare about Dad for a long time now, which is good. But I haven't thought much about him either, which is not so good.

Wednesday, December 15th 1943

Barry moved in this afternoon. He walked home with me from school carrying his suitcase. He skipped most of the way. He's sleeping in the room at the end of the passage. Grandfather says that's where Dad always used to sleep when he was a boy. Straight after tea Grandfather took him out to feed the cows. From the look on Barry's face when he came back I'm sure he thinks he's in heaven. Like he says, there's no tractors in London, no cows, no sheep, no pigs. He's already decided he likes the sheep best. And he likes mud too, and he likes rolling down hills and getting his coat covered in sheep poo. He told Mum that brown's his favourite colour because he likes mud, and sausages. I learnt a little bit more about him today – he tells Mum more than he tells me. But I listen. He didn't say much about his dad of course, but his mum works on the buses in London, a "clippy", he says – that's someone who sells the tickets. That's about all I know about him so far, except that he twiddles his hair when he's upset and he doesn't like cats because they smile at him. He's a good one to talk. He's always smiling at me. If he's living with us, he'd better be nice to Tips, that's all I can say. He twiddles his hair a lot at school. I've noticed it in class, especially when he's doing his writing. He can't do his handwriting very well. Mrs Blumfeld tries to help him with his letters and his spelling but he still keeps getting everything back to front. (I think he's frightened of them – of letters, I mean.) He's good with numbers though. He doesn't have to use his fingers at all. He does it all in his head, which I can't do.

Grandfather's still telling everyone he's not going to be moved out. Lots of people have had a go at persuading him, the vicar, Doctor Morrison, even Major Tucker came to see us from the Manor House. But Grandfather won't budge. He just carries on as if nothing is happening. Half the village has moved out now, including Farmer Gent next door. I saw the last of his machinery being taken away yesterday. All his animals have gone already. They went to market last week. His farmhouse is empty. Usually I can see a light or two on in there from my window, but not any more. It's dark now, pitch black. It's like the house has gone too.

We see more and more American soldiers and lorries coming into the village every day. Grandfather's turning a blind eye to all of it. Barry's out with him now. They've gone milking. I saw them go off together a while ago, stomping across the yard in their wellies. Barry looked like he'd been doing it all his life, as if he'd always lived here, as if he was Grandfather's grandson. To tell the truth I feel a little jealous. No, that's not really true. I feel a *lot* jealous. I've often thought Grandfather wanted me to be a boy. Now I'm sure of it.

Thursday, December 16th 1943

When school ends tomorrow it'll be the end of term and that's four days earlier than we thought. We've got four days' extra holiday. Hooray! Yippee! That's because they've got to move out all the desks, the blackboard, the bookshelves, everything, down to the last piece of chalk. Mrs Blumfeld told us the American soldiers will be coming tomorrow to help us move out. We'll be going to school in Kingsbridge after Christmas. There'll be a bus to take us in because it's too far to walk. And Mrs Blumfeld said today that she'll go on being our teacher there. We all cheered and we meant it too. She's the best teacher I've ever had, only sometimes I still don't exactly understand her because of how she speaks. Because she's from Holland we've got lots of pictures of Amsterdam on the wall. They've got canals instead of roads there. She's put up two big paintings, both by Dutchmen, one of an old lady in a hat by a painter called Rembrandt (that's funny spelling, but it's right), and one of colourful ships on a beach by someone else. I can't remember his name, I think it's Van something or other. I was looking at that one today while we were practising carols. We were singing *I Saw Three Ships Come Sailing In*, and there they were up on the wall, all these ships. Funny that. I don't really understand that carol. What's three ships sailing in got to do with the birth of Jesus? I like the tune though. I'm humming it now as I write.

We all think she's very brave to go on teaching us like she has after her husband was drowned. Everyone else in the village likes her now. She's always out cycling in her blue headscarf, ringing her bell and waving whenever she sees us. I hope she doesn't remember how mean I was to her when she first came. I don't think she can do because she chose me to sing a solo in the carol concert, the first verse of *In the Bleak Midwinter*. I practise all the time: on the way home, out in the fields, in the bath. Barry says it sounds really good, which is nice of him. And he doesn't pick his nose at all any more, nor smile at me all the time. Maybe he knows he doesn't need to smile at me – maybe he knows I like him. My singing sounds really good in the bath, I know it does. But I can't take the bath into church, can I?

Saturday, December 18th 1943

I love Christmas carols, especially *In the Bleak Midwinter*. I wish we didn't only sing them at Christmas time. We had our carol concert this afternoon in the church and I had to sing my verse in front of everyone. I wobbled a bit on one or two notes, but that's because I was trembling all over, like a leaf, just before I did it. Barry told me it sounded perfect, but I knew he said that just to make me happy. And it did, but then I thought about it. The thing is that Barry can sing only on one note, so he wouldn't really know if it sounded good or bad, would he?

There's only a fortnight to go now before we're supposed to leave. Barry keeps asking me what will happen to Grandfather if he doesn't move out. He's frightened they'll take him off to prison. That's because we had a visit yesterday from the army and the police telling Grandfather he had to pack up and go, or he'd be in real trouble. Grandfather saw them off good and proper, but they said they'll be back. I just wish Barry wouldn't keep asking me about what's going to happen, because I don't know, do I? No one does. Maybe they will put him in prison. Maybe they'll put us all in prison. It makes me very frightened every time I think about it. So I'll try not to. If I do think about it, then I'll just have to make myself worry about something else.

This evening Barry and me were sitting at the top of the staircase in our dressing gowns listening to Mum and Grandfather arguing about it again down in the kitchen. Grandfather sounded more angry than I've ever heard him. He said he'd rather shoot himself than be moved off the farm. He kept on about how he doesn't hold with this war anyhow, and never did, how he went through the last one in the trenches and that was horror enough for one lifetime. "If people only knew what it was really like," he said, and he sounded as if he was almost crying he was so angry. "If they knew, if they'd seen what I've seen, they'd never send young men off to fight again. Never." He just wanted to be left alone in peace to do his farming.

Again and again Mum tried to reason with him, tried to tell him that everyone in the village was leaving, not just us; that no one wanted to go but we had to, so that the Americans could practise their landings, go over to France, and finish the war quickly. Then we'd all be back home soon enough and Dad would be back with us and the war would be over and done with. It would only be for a short time, she said. They'd promised. But Grandfather wouldn't believe her and he wouldn't believe them. He said the Yanks were just saying that so they could get him out.

In the end he slammed out of the house and left her. We heard Mum crying, so we went downstairs. Barry made her a cup of tea, and I held her hands and told her it would be all right, that I was sure Grandfather would give in and go in the end. But I was just saying it. He won't go, not of his own accord anyway, not in a million years. They'll have to carry him out, and, like Mum said, when they do it will break his heart.

Thursday, December 23rd 1943

Letter from Dad to all of us, wishing us a happy Christmas. He says he's in Italy now, and it's nothing but rain and mud and you go up one hill and there's always another one ahead of you, but that at least each hill brings him nearer home. We'd just finished reading it at breakfast when there was a knock on the door. It was Mrs Blumfeld. She was bringing her Christmas card, she said. Mum asked her in. She was all red in the face and breathless from her cycling. It seemed so strange having her here in the house. She didn't seem like our teacher at all, more like a visiting aunt. Tips was up on her lap as soon as she'd sat down. She sipped her tea and said how nice Tips was, even when she was sharpening her claws on her knees.

Then suddenly she looked across at Grandfather. I don't remember everything she said, but it was something like this. "You and me, Mr Tregenza," she said, "I think we have so much – how do you say it in English? – in common." Grandfather looked a bit flummoxed (good word that). "They tell me you are the only one in the village who won't leave. I would be just like you, I think. I loved our home in Holland, in Amsterdam. It is where I grew up. All I loved was in our home. But we had to leave; we could do nothing else. There was no choice for us because the Germans were coming. They were invading our country. We did what we could to stop them but it was no good. There were too many tanks and planes. They were too strong for us. My husband, Jacobus, was a Jew, Mr Tregenza. I am a Jew. We knew what they wanted to do with Jews. They wanted to kill us all, like rats, get rid of us. We knew this. So we had to leave our home. We came to England, Mr Tregenza, where we could be safe. Jacobus, he joined the merchant navy. He was a sea captain in Holland. We Dutch are good sailors, like you English. He was a good man and a very kind man, as you are – Barry has told me this and Lily too. They may have killed him, Mr Tregenza, but they have not killed me, not yet.

They would if they could. If they come here they will."

Grandfather's eyes never left her face all the time she was talking. "That is why I ask you to leave your home, as I did, so that the American soldiers can come. They will borrow your house and your fields for a few months to do their practising. Then they can go across the sea and liberate my people and my country, and many other countries too. This way the Germans will never come here, never march in your streets. This way my people will not suffer any longer. I know it is hard, Mr Tregenza, but I ask you to do this for me, for my husband, for my country – for your country too. I think you will, because I know you have a good heart."

I could see Grandfather's eyes were full of tears. He got up, shrugged on his coat and pulled on his hat without ever saying a word. At the door he stopped and turned around. Then all he said was, "I'll say one thing, missus. I wish I'd had a teacher like you when I was a little 'un." Then he went out and Barry ran out after him, and we were left there looking at one another in silence.

Mrs Blumfeld didn't stay long after that, and we didn't see Grandfather and Barry again until they came back for lunch. Grandfather was washing his hands in the sink when he suddenly said that he'd been thinking it over and that we could all start packing up after lunch, that he'd begin moving the sheep over to Uncle George's right away, and he'd be needing both Barry and me to give him a hand. Then very quietly he said: "Just so long as we can come back afterwards."

"We will, I promise," Mum told him, and she went over to hug him. He cried then. That was the first time I've ever seen Grandfather cry.

Saturday, December 25th 1943

Christmas Day. There's no point in pretending this was a happy Christmas. We tried to make the best of it. We had decorations everywhere as usual and a nice Christmas tree. We had our stockings all together in Grandfather's bed. But Dad wasn't there. Mum missed him a lot and so did I. Barry was homesick too and Grandfather was really down in the dumps all day and grumpy about moving. We had roast chicken for lunch, which did make everyone feel a little happier. I found a silver threepenny bit in the Christmas pudding and Barry found one too, so that made him forget he was homesick, for a while anyway. We all gave Grandfather a hand with the evening milking to cheer him up, and it worked, but not for long. There's only a week to go now before we have to have everything out of here. It's all Grandfather can think about. The house is piled high with tea chests and boxes. The curtains and lamp shades are all down, most of the crockery is already packed. We may have the Christmas decorations up, but it doesn't feel at all like Christmas.

For my present I got a pair of red woolly gloves that Mum had knitted specially and secretly, and Barry had a navy blue scarf which he wears all the time, even at meal times. Mum didn't knit that, she didn't have time. We all went off to church this evening. It's the last time we'll be doing that for a long while. They're going to empty it of all its precious things – stained glass windows, candlesticks, benches – in case they get damaged. The American soldiers are coming to take it all away. They'll be putting sandbags around everything that's too heavy to move, so that everything will be protected as much as possible. That's what the vicar told us – he also said they'll be needing all the help they can get. They're starting to empty the church tomorrow. Mum says we've all got to be there to lend a hand.

I gave Tips some cold chicken this evening for her Christmas supper. She licked the plate until it was shiny clean. She's a bit upset, I think. She knows something's up. She can see it for herself and she can feel it too. I think she's unhappy because she knows we're unhappy.

I'm getting a bit fed up with Uncle George already, and we haven't even moved in with him yet. All he talks about is the war: the Germans this and the Russians that. He sits there with his ear practically glued to the radio, tutting and huffing at the news. Even today, on Christmas Day, he has to go on and on about how we should "bomb Germany to smithereens, because of all they've done to us"! Then once he got talking about it, everyone was talking about it, arguing about it. So I came up to bed and left them to it. It's supposed to be a day of peace and goodwill towards all men. And all they can talk about is the war. It makes me so sad, and I shouldn't be sad on Christmas Day. But now I am. Happy Christmas, Dad.

PS Just after I finished my diary I heard Barry crying in his room, so I went to see him. He didn't want to tell me at first. Then he said he was just a bit homesick, missing his mum, he said. And his dad – mostly his dad. What could I say? My dad is alive and I'm living in my own home, going to my own school. Then I had an idea. "Shall we say Happy Christmas to the cows?" I said. He cheered up at once. So we crept downstairs in our dressing gowns and slippers, and ran out to the barn. They were all lying down in the straw grunting and chewing the cud, their calves curled up asleep beside them. Barry crouched down and stroked one

of them, who sucked his finger until he giggled and pulled it out. We were walking back across the yard when he told me. "I hate the radio," he said suddenly. "It's always about the war, and the bombing raids, and that's when I think of Mum most and miss her most. I don't want her to die. I don't want to be an orphan."

I held his hand and squeezed it. I was too upset to say anything.

Sunday, December 26th 1943

I've had the strangest day and the happiest day for a long time. I met someone who's the most different person I've ever met. He's different in every way. He looks different, he sounds different, he is different. And, best of all, he's my friend.

We were supposed to be helping to move things out of the church, but mostly we were just watching, because the Yanks were doing it all for us. Grandfather's right: they do chew gum a lot. But they're very happy-looking, always laughing and joking around. Some of them were carrying sandbags into the church, whilst others were carrying out the pews and chairs, hymn books and kneelers.

Suddenly I recognised one of them. He was the same black soldier I had seen in the jeep a while ago. And he recognised me too. "Hi there! How you doing?" he said. I never saw anyone smile like he did. His whole face lit up with it. He looked too young to be a soldier. He seemed so pleased to see me there, someone he recognised. He bent down so that his face was very close to mine. "I got three little sisters back home in Atlanta – that's in Georgia and that's in the United States of America, way across the sea," he said. "And they's all pretty, just like you."

Then another soldier came along – I think he was a sergeant or something because he had lots of stripes on his arm, upside-down ones, not like our soldiers' stripes at all. The sergeant told him he should be carrying sandbags, not chatting to kids. So he said, "Yessir." Then he went off, smiling back at me over his shoulder. The next time I saw him he was coming past me with a sandbag under each arm. He stopped right by me and looked down at me from very high up. "What do you call yourself, girl?" he asked me. So I told him. Then he said, "I'm Adolphus T. Madison. (That's T for Thomas.) Private First Class, US Army. My friends call me Adie. I'm mighty pleased to make your acquaintance, Lily. A ray of Atlanta sunshine, that's what you are, a ray of Atlanta sunshine."

No one has ever talked to me like that before. He looked me full in the eye as he spoke, so I knew he meant every word he said. But the sergeant shouted at him again and he had to go.

Then Barry came along, and for the rest of the morning we stood at the back of the church watching the soldiers coming and going, all of them fetching and carrying sandbags now, and Adie would give me a great big grin every time he went by. The vicar was fussing about them like an old hen, telling the Yank soldiers they had to be more careful, particularly when they were sandbagging the font. "That font's very precious, you know," said the vicar. I could see they didn't like being pestered, but they were all too polite and respectful to say anything. The vicar kept on and on nagging at them. "It's the most precious thing in the church. It's Norman, you know, very old." A couple of Yanks were just coming past us with more sandbags a few moments later when one of them said, "Who is this old Norman guy, anyway?"

After that Barry and me couldn't stop ourselves giggling. The vicar told us we shouldn't be giggling in church, so we went outside and giggled in the graveyard instead.

We told Grandfather and Mum about that when

we got back this evening and they laughed so much they nearly cried. It's been a happy, happy day. I hope Adie doesn't get killed in the war. He's so nice. I'm going to pray for him tonight, and for Dad too.

Tips has just brought in a dead mouse and dropped it at my feet. She knows how much I hate mice, dead or alive. I really wish she wouldn't do it. She's sitting there, licking her lips and looking so pleased with herself. Sometimes I think I understand why Barry doesn't like cats.

Monday, December 27th 1943

It's my very last night in my own bedroom. Until now I don't think I thought it would ever really happen, not to us, not to me. It was happening to everyone else. Everyone else was moving out, but somehow I just didn't imagine that the day would ever come when we'd have to do the same. But tomorrow is the final day and tomorrow will come. This time tomorrow my room will be empty – the whole house will be empty. I've never slept anywhere else in my whole life except in this room. For the first time I think I understand why Grandfather refused to leave for so long. It wasn't just because he was being stubborn and difficult and grumpy. He loves this place, and so do I. I look around this room and it's a part of me. I belong here. I'll start to cry if I write any more, so I'll stop.

Tuesday, December 28th 1943

Our first night at Uncle George's and it's cold. But there's something worse than that, much worse. Tips has gone missing. We haven't got her with us.

We moved up here today. We were the last ones in the whole village to move out. Grandfather is very proud of that. We had lots of help. Mrs Blumfeld came and so did Adie, along with half a dozen other Yanks. We couldn't have managed without them. Everything is here, all the tea chests, all the furniture. Most of it is stored in Uncle George's granary under an old tarpaulin. But the cows are still back home on the farm. We'll go back for them tomorrow, Grandfather said, and drive them up the lane.

Uncle George has made room here for all of us. He's very kind, I suppose, but he talks to himself too much and he grunts and wheezes a lot, and when he blows his nose it sounds like a foghorn.

He's very dirty and scruffy and untidy, which Mum doesn't like, and I think he's a bit proud too. I was only trying to be polite, because Mum said I should be, when I asked him which chair was his before I sat down. Uncle George said: "They'm all my chairs Lil." (I wish he wouldn't call me Lil, only Mum and Dad call me that.) He was laughing as he said it, but he meant it, I know he did. I think it's because he's Mum's eldest brother that he's a bit bossy with us. He keeps saying Dad shouldn't have gone off to the war and left her on her own. That's what I think too, but I don't like it when Uncle George says it. Anyway, she's not on her own. She's got Grandfather and she's got me.

Mum says I have to be very patient with him because he's a bachelor, which means that he's lived on his own all his life which is why he's untidy and doesn't know how to get on with people very well. I'll try, but it's not going to be easy. And what's more, he looks like a scarecrow, except when he's in his Home Guard uniform.

When he's in his uniform he looks very pleased with himself. Grandfather says he doesn't do much in the Home Guard, that he just sits up in the lookout post on top of the hill. They're supposed to be looking for enemy ships and planes, but Grandfather says they just have a good natter and a smoke.

I miss my room at home already. My bedroom here is not just cold, it's very small, a bit like a cupboard – a cupboard I have to share with Mum. Barry's in with Grandfather. It was the only way to fit us all in. Mum and me have to share a bed too, but I don't mind that. We'll cuddle up. She'll keep me warm! I haven't got a table, so I'm writing this sitting up in bed with my diary on my knees.

I wish Tips was here. I miss her and I'm really worried about her. She ran off when everyone came to the house to carry the furniture out. I called and called, but she didn't come. I'm trying my best not to be worried. Mum says she's just gone off on her wanders somewhere, that she'll come back when the house is quiet again. She's sure she'll be there when we go to fetch the animals tomorrow. She keeps saying there are still three days to go before they close the farm off, but I can't stop thinking that after that we won't be allowed back for six months or even more. What if Tips isn't there tomorrow? What if we can't find her?

Barry's happier than ever, because he's got two farmers to work with now, and two tractors. But what's more surprising is that Grandfather is happy too. I thought he was going to be very sad when we left home. I was there when he locked the door and slipped the key into his waistcoat pocket. He stood looking up at the house for some moments. He even tried to smile. But he never said anything. He just took my hand and Barry's, and we all walked off without looking back. He made himself at home in Uncle George's kitchen right away. He's got his feet in the oven already, which you can see Uncle George doesn't like. But Grandfather's much older than he is, so Uncle George will just have to put up with it, won't he?

Oh yes, I forgot. This afternoon Adie introduced me to his friend Harry, while they were carrying out our kitchen table. He's from Atlanta too, and he's black like Adie is. They're both quite difficult to understand sometimes because they speak English differently from us. Adie does most of the talking. "Harry's like my brother, Lily, not my brother brother, if you get my meaning, just my friend. Like twins, ain't we, Harry? Always on the lookout for one another. Harry and me, we growed up together, same street, same town. We was born on the same day too – 25th November. Both of us is eighteen, but I'm the oldest by six hours – that's what our mamas told us, and they should know I reckon. Ain't that right Harry?" Harry just smiled at me and nodded. "Harry don't say much," Adie said, "but he thinks real deep." The two of them worked together all day, fetching and carrying. They must be very strong too. They picked up Grandfather's dresser all by themselves. No huffing, no puffing.

They just picked it up as if it was light as a feather.

I keep thinking I hear Tips outside, but every time I look it's Uncle George's ginger tomcat mewing round the yard. I just hope Tips gets on with Uncle George's cat. Tips doesn't much like other cats. But if I've got to be polite to Uncle George, then she'll have to be polite to Uncle George's cat, won't she? This time tomorrow Tips will be here and everything will be just tickety-boo! That word always makes me smile, even when I'm sad. So I'll write it again: tickety-boo, tickety-boo. The lamp's just gone out so I suppose I'll have to finish now.

Thursday, December 30th 1943

I still can't find Tips. I've been looking for her all day today – and all yesterday too. I looked in every barn, every shed. Grandfather opened up the house again for me and I went into every room, up into the attic too. I looked in all the cupboards, just in case she'd got herself shut in by mistake. Grandfather even climbed up a ladder to look in the roof valleys. I wandered the fields, tapping her bowl with a spoon, calling and calling, then listening for her. All I could hear were cawing crows and the sound of the wind in the trees and the rumble of a tractor engine in the distance. Once they'd driven the cows and sheep up the lane to Uncle George's everyone came back to help me. Mrs Blumfeld went off to search the village on her bike, with Barry on the back. They didn't find Tips, but they did find lots of Yanks. They were all over the place, they said, in lorries and jeeps and some of them in tanks.

Mum still says I'm not to worry. Grandfather says that cats have nine lives, that Tips will turn up as she always does, and it's true she always has. But I do worry. I can't think about anything else now except Tips. She's out there somewhere in the night, cold and wet, hungry and lost, and I've only got one more day to find her before they close off the farm. I'm going to get up early tomorrow; Barry says he'll come with me. We're going to look and look until we find her, he says. I'm not coming back to Uncle George's until I do.

Our farm looked strange when I went back today, so empty and silent: a phantom farm, a house full of ghosts.

Be there tomorrow, Tips. Please be there. It's your last chance.

Friday, December 31st 1943

I never want to live another day like this. I think I knew right from the start we wouldn't find her. There were too many people out looking – I knew they would only frighten her away, and they did. If it had just been Barry and me and Mum and Grandfather, maybe we'd have found her. Tips knows us.

It wasn't her fault. Mrs Blumfeld was only trying to be helpful, but she'd gone and told everyone how Tips was lost and she brought practically the whole village along with her. She was there at dawn organising the search. The Yanks came too, dozens of them, Adie and Harry telling them all the places they had to look. They combed the whole farm: every barn, every feed bin, every corner of every field, all along the stream. They went searching down in the bluebell wood, down in the disused quarry, and I went with them, trying to tell them all the time to go more quietly, just to look, not call out. But it was no use. I could hear them all over the farm, banging tins, trying to call her, trying to sweeten Tips in.

All morning long it drizzled and in the afternoon a sea mist came rolling in over the fields and covered the whole farm in thick fog, so you couldn't see further than a few feet in front of you. There was no point in even looking any more. We listened instead, but there was nothing to hear. Even the crows were silent. I think I've been crying off and on all day, as the hours passed and hope faded. Barry kept on and on telling me he was sure we'd find her sooner or later and in the end I got cross and shouted at him, which I shouldn't have done. He was only trying to cheer me up, trying to be nice. That's the trouble with him, he's always trying to be nice. Uncle George just said that a cat's a cat, that there're other cats I can have, which didn't exactly help.

It was nearly dark when one of the Yanks with upside-down stripes on his arm said he was sorry but they had orders to close the place off now, so we had to leave. Adie came up and gave me some chocolate. "Hershey bar," he said. "It'll make you feel better. And don't you worry none, Lily. I ain't making no promises, but if that old cat's still living out there, we're gonna find her, one way or the other. You can be real sure of that. So don't you worry none, Lily, y'hear."

They closed the barbed wire behind us then, cutting us off from our home and from Tips. I promised myself as I watched them that I would go back and find her, and I will too. I will. I gave

Barry half my Hershey Bar to make up for being so mean to him, and we ate it before we got back to Uncle George's. Adie was right. It did make me feel better, but I think that was more because I gave half of it to Barry.

I'm coughing a lot and I'm feeling hot and sweaty all over. I have been ever since we got back. Mum says I've caught a chill and that I have to stay in bed tomorrow else it'll get on my chest. I hated today, every horrible minute of it – except for Adie and the Hershey bar. The only hope I've got left is that maybe, just maybe, Adie and Harry might still find Tips. I've got this feeling they might. I don't know why. One thing's for sure though: if they don't find her then I'm going to crawl in under the wire and find her for myself, no matter what they say. They can put up all the barbed wire they like. They can shoot all the shells they want. Nothing's going to keep me out. I'm never ever going to give up on Tips. Never.

Wednesday, January 12th 1944

This is the first time I've felt like writing in my diary for days. Mum was right, I did catch a chill that day when we all went out looking for Tips, and it did go to my chest. Mum told me I had a temperature of 104 for nearly a week and the doctor had to be called because I became delirious. That sounds like it means I was just happy – I certainly was not. It meant I was out of my head. And I must have been because I remember very little. I only remember bits of the last few days. I remember Barry coming in after school and telling me what the new school in Kingsbridge was like and giving me get-well cards from Mrs Blumfeld and the class. I remember waking up to see Grandfather and Mum sitting in the chair watching me, or just sitting there sleeping. And from time to time I could hear the murmur of voices downstairs and Uncle George blowing his nose like a foghorn.

I'm much better now, but Mum says I've got to

stay inside for at least another week. Doctor's orders, she says, but I think they're just *her* orders. She always gets very fierce and strict with me when I'm ill. She's been feeding me soup and then sitting and watching me, just to make sure I finish it. She makes me eat stewed apple every day and I have to drink lots of warm milk with honey in it. She knows I hate milk. But now she's got the perfect excuse to make me drink it. "It'll build up your strength, Lily," she says. "Drink it." And she always stays until I do.

As for Tips, there's still no sign of her. No one has been back to look for her, of course. But I haven't given up. I still keep hoping she's all right, that one day she'll come and find us. She's a good hunter, she can take care of herself. She knows warm places to go. I try to hope and believe Adie will find her somehow. But then when I think about it again I know he won't. I keep thinking of her lying dead in some ditch. I try not to think like that. I try so hard. Soon as I'm better, I'm going to go looking for her. I promised myself I would, and I will.

Mum came up today and read me a letter from Dad. It's such a long time since I saw him I find it difficult to see his face in my head any more. I tried to hear his voice as she was reading the letter, but I couldn't. He says they had corned beef and tinned potatoes for Christmas lunch, and they wore paper hats made out of newspaper, sang Christmas carols and thought of home. He sounded so sad and far away. When Mum finished reading she was sad too. I could tell she wanted to cry but she wouldn't let herself.

Wednesday, January 19th 1944

I've been planning it for days, working it all out and screwing up my courage to do it. And today I did it. But it didn't work out at all like I had planned.

I'm getting really good at telling lies. I told Mum I just wanted to go out for some fresh air, that I was fed up with being cooped up. I nagged and nagged and finally Mum gave in, but only because it was a nice, sunshiney day, she said. She wrapped me up as if I was going out into the Arctic – gloves, hat, scarf, coat, the lot – and she told me to keep out of the wind, and I had to promise her I'd be back inside an hour. I promised… with my fingers crossed.

It wasn't that difficult to get through the wire. There was no one about to see me. I just wriggled my way through and made off across the field towards home, keeping behind the hedges so that I was always out of sight of Uncle George's house.

Home looked so empty and deserted when I got there: no hens scratching anywhere, no geese on the pond. I called for Tips as loudly as I dared. I looked in all the places I thought she might be hiding: the granary, the shippen, the milking parlour, the piggery. Then I remembered that one of Tips's favourite sleeping places was always up in the hay barn. I walked through the abandoned farmyard and was just climbing up the ladder into the hay loft when I heard voices outside the barn. It sounded like there were two of them, and they were American. That was when I felt a sneeze coming on, and there was nothing I could do to stop it. I couldn't help myself. I don't think I've ever sneezed so loudly in all my life.

I couldn't think what else to do. I lay down in the hay loft and pulled the hay over me so I was completely covered and tried to stop myself breathing. I heard them coming into the barn, heard them as they came up the ladder.

Then there was silence for a few moments. I was thinking I might just have got away with it, when suddenly I was grabbed by my wellies and yanked out. There were Adie and Harry staring down at me.

"Lily! Well, I'll be damned!" Adie said pushing back his helmet. "Look what we got ourselves here, Harry. Now, if I ain't mistook, Lily, you come looking for your cat, that right?" I nodded. "What you wanna do that for? Didn't I tell you we'd find her? Didn't I? Didn't I? Ain't you got no faith?" His whole face suddenly became very serious. "You got to promise me something," he said. "You got to promise you won't never come near this place again. You do what I say, Lily, or you gonna get yourself in real trouble. You gonna get yourself hurt bad, real bad, you hear me? Ain't worth it, not for no cat it ain't. Soon enough this here's gonna be a mighty dangerous place to be. You gotta stay outa here. You promise me, now." He was really angry with me. So I promised. They helped me down the ladder and together we ran through the farmyard, past the farmhouse and out over the fields to the perimeter wire, Adie holding my hand the whole way. I squeezed through. "Don't you never come inside the wire again." Adie said. "You just stay where you is, Lily. And don't you go worrying yourself. We'll find that old cat for you, and that's a faithful promise, ain't it, Harry?"

"Faithful promise," said Harry.

Then they walked away and I watched them go until I couldn't see them any more.

Mum met me at the door. She had her coat on. She was just coming out to look for me. "Look at the state of you," she said, and began brushing all the hay off my coat. "Where've you been?"

"In the barn," I told her. And that wasn't a lie, was it?

I've had such a supreme day, even though I didn't find Tips. I should be sad, but I'm not. I keep living it all again and again in my head, every exciting moment of it. I shan't sleep tonight. I know I shan't.

Monday, January 24th 1944

Back at school. Everyone else had been back for a long time of course and so they all knew each other and I didn't. All my friends from the village school already had lots of new friends from Kingsbridge School who I'd never seen before, and no one seemed that pleased to see me. I would have felt a bit out of it if Barry hadn't stuck by me like he did. He showed me round too, showed me where to line up, where to hang my coat. It felt a bit strange, a townie showing me round. But I don't think of Barry as a townie any more, not really. He kept telling everyone about Tips, and about how I'd been ill, so as a result everyone was very nice to me in the end. I'm going to make a promise to myself. From now on I'm never to be nasty to Barry again, even when I get irritated. He was really kind today. In playtime someone mistook him for my brother and I didn't mind at all. In fact I quite liked it, so I didn't say he wasn't.

I'm in Mrs Blumfeld's class which is supreme. We had a lesson about America, about all the states which are the stars on the flag, and she told us they've got a president instead of a king. She says it's this huge place, miles bigger than England, with great big lakes as big as England, with great high mountains called the Rockies, and they've got prairies and deserts, and canyons too. She didn't say what canyons were. She told us they play baseball not cricket, and how lots of different kinds of people live there from all over the world, how they all went there to find a place to live, to find freedom and to make a new kind of country, and how now they've come all the way back across the Atlantic to help us win the war against Hitler. I'd like to go there one day. I'm going to ask Adie more about it when I see him again. I'll ask him what a canyon is too.

At tea time Uncle George came in stamping his boots and told us it was snowing really hard outside. It was too. The sky was full of great heavy flakes that landed on my face and made me close my eyes when I looked up. I caught them on my tongue and let them melt. Then I thought of Tips out there in the cold and the dark and I started crying – I couldn't help myself. I called and called for her until Mum heard me and fetched me in. She was angry with me for going out, until she saw I'd been crying, then she was nice again. She put me in a hot bath to warm me through which was lovely, and made me drink a glass of hot milk with honey, which was not lovely at all. It was dis-gust-ing. Why can't cows make something nice instead? Like lemonade for instance.

I've thought of something. If the snow keeps falling like it is, if it doesn't melt, then there'll be footprints, won't there? Maybe tomorrow I could find Tips's paw prints and if I did, I could follow them and find her.

PS I've just woken up. Mum's got up and gone milking already. I'm looking out of the window as I write. It's early morning and still quite dark, only it's white all around because of the snow. It looks new and fresh, like the world's just been made. I can see Mum walking towards the milking parlour, leaving her footprints behind her across the farmyard. She's blowing on her hands; I can see her breath in the air. I've thought of something else: if Tips leaves her prints in the snow then I'll leave mine, won't I? And if I leave mine then someone could find them going through the wire and follow me. No good. I'll have to think of some other way. Back to sleep. I'm tired.

PPS I've woken up again. I just had this dream about Tips, and what's more it was a dream that came true in a way. I want to write it down now before I forget it. I dreamt she came looking for us through the snow, that she found her way in through the kitchen window, ran up the stairs, pushed open the door and jumped on the bed, and was purring in my ear. When I woke up just now I was so happy because my dream had come true. I could feel her warmth against my face. She was back, she was purring in my ear! But then I woke up properly, and it wasn't her at all. It was Uncle George's tomcat. He's still here and he's looking up at me out of his wide yellow eyes. I wish they were Tips's eyes. Uncle George's cat wants me to love him. But I can't.

Maybe Tips isn't ever going to come back. For the first time I'm beginning to think that perhaps she has gone for ever. I mustn't think like that. I mustn't. Once the snow's gone I'm going to go and look again and again until I find her. She's got to be alive, she's just got to be. If she is alive she'll be looking for food, won't she?

Stupid! Stupid! Why didn't I think of it before? I'll pinch some food from the larder, leftovers. No one will notice, not if I don't take much, not if I'm careful. I'll put it out for her in the hay barn back home. Then I'll watch and wait for her. She'll be hungry. She'll come. She's got to come. She must.

Thursday, February 10th 1944

I must have been in and out through the wire looking for Tips half a dozen times or more now. Every time the food I'd put out for her was gone, but I was never there when she came for it. I was so sure that sooner or later I'd get lucky, and she'd come while I was there, while I was waiting for her.

Then today the very worst happened. I went off as usual after tea, when everyone else was feeding up the animals. No one was about. As usual the food I put out in the hay barn yesterday had gone. So I put down some more and then waited up in the hay loft, hoping and hoping this time she'd come while I was there. That was when the dog came running into the barn, a huge Alsatian, as big as a wolf. He went straight to the food and snuffled it up. He knew exactly where it was. It was him! It was the dog who'd been taking it all along. Maybe I moved. Maybe he smelt me. I don't know.

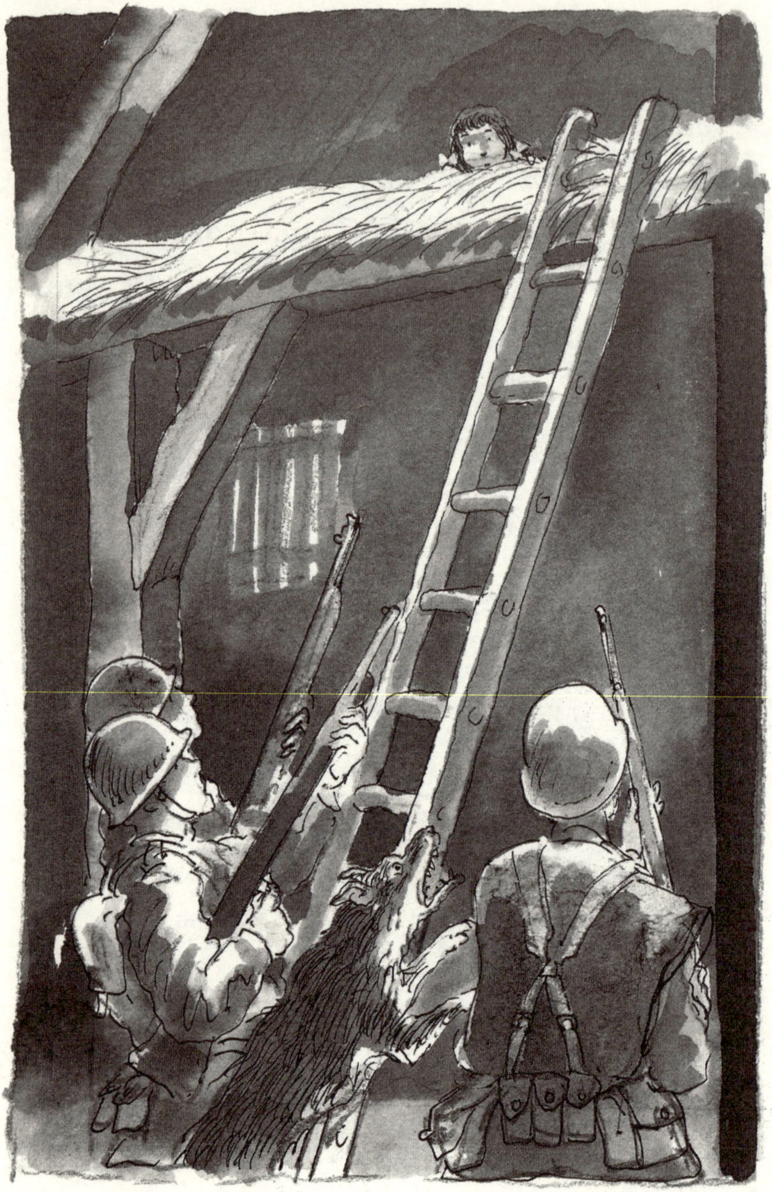

All I know is that he looked up and began barking at me, teeth bared, his hackles up, his whole body shaking.

Then there were sounds of voices and running feet, and the American soldiers came. They were looking up at me and pointing their rifles and shouting at me to come down. They couldn't see me, but they knew I was up there all right. They kept shouting and saying they were going to shoot unless I came down. So I did. I was hoping Adie would be there, or Harry, but it wasn't them. All their faces were white. The dog looked as if it was going to eat me, so I waited halfway up the ladder till they caught him and held him. One of them said, "Holy cow! It's a kid!" And then they walked me outside and bundled me into the back of a jeep. I kept telling them I was a friend of Adie's, but that didn't seem to make them any kinder towards me. They weren't rough with me, but they weren't exactly nice to me either. They said they were taking me to see the captain, that I was in real trouble.

The next thing I knew I was being marched into this room and there was this captain with a bald head, sitting behind a desk, looking up at me and asking me all sorts of questions, like what my name was, what I was doing there, and where did I live. So I told him and he shook his head and said didn't I know I could have got myself killed. I said no. Then he got angry at me, banged the table and told me I was never, never to go through the wire again, and did I understand. I said I did, but I just wanted to find Tips. And he said who was Tips and I said she was my cat. Then he said, "Jesus Christ Almighty," which he shouldn't have said, because you're not supposed to say things like that, unless you're praying, that is. Then he bawled out a command of some kind and in came another soldier and saluted. It was Adie. Was I glad to see him! "They say you know this kid, Soldier. That right?" the captain asked.

"Yessir," said Adie, standing very stiffly beside me and not looking at all pleased to see me. "She was just playing around, Captain, like kids do. She didn't mean no harm by it." Adie was told to take me home, to tell my mother and make sure it didn't happen again. "Yessir, Captain," said Adie and saluted again.

I smiled up at Adie as he took me out, to thank him for coming to my rescue. He didn't smile back at all. He walked me silently to the jeep and drove me all the way back home without a single word. He turned off the engine by the farm gate, out of sight of the house. "You're some crazy girl, you know that?" he said. He lit up a cigarette, and his face glowed in the dark and I could see now that he was really angry with me. "Here's what I'm gonna do, Lily," he said. "I'm not gonna tell your mama about what you done, if you promise me you won't do this no more. But you gotta promise like you mean it."

"I promise," I told him, but I didn't mean it.

"Now you listen to me real good. I been looking, Harry's been looking. We're gonna find that cat for you. Didn't I tell you? Didn't I say? But if you goes snooping about, I'm telling you, either you gonna get yourself blowed to bits, or they gonna catch you again. I'm serious here. We got patrols in there all day, every day. They'll catch you, Lily. Ain't no way they won't. Ain't no way I can save your hide next time." He told me I could go, so I got out of the jeep. He looked at me for a moment as I stood there and shook his head. "Just like my little sisters you is. Trouble. Nothin' but trouble. And stubborn as a mule. I knowed you were trouble moment I first saw you. You do what Adie says now. You be good, you hear." Then he drove off and left me there.

I think Adie knows I'm not going to be good. He knows I'm going back in to look for Tips. And I am too, because now I know for sure what's been stopping Tips from coming out of hiding and eating my food. That American guard dog, that Alsatian. I know what I'm going to do. I'm going to wake up early; I'll wait till Mum goes off to do the milking. No one will see me, will they? It'll still be dark in the early morning, so I should be safe enough if I don't take too long. And Tips always likes going out hunting when it's dark. She's probably hiding up somewhere by day, scared stiff of that guard dog. Don't blame her. That's probably why I haven't been able to find her all this time. But I'll find her now. She'll come out in the dark, I know she will. I'll find you Tips, I promise – I will.

I so want to tell someone everything that happened to me today. I think Barry's the only person I could tell. No one else would believe me. Maybe I'll tell him tomorrow.

Friday, February 11th 1944

I don't need to tell Barry. He already knows. Here's how.

I got up early this morning, while it was still dark, just as I'd planned. There was no one about. I heard the cows mooing in the parlour as I ran across the farmyard, and I could hear Mum singing to them. She likes to sing to them when she's milking. She thinks it makes them happy, and she likes them happy because they give more milk. I scrambled through the wire in my usual place, out of sight of the farmhouse, and ran across the fields. After a while I stopped to catch my breath and to call out for Tips, and to listen. That was when I heard the sound of panting coming from behind me. I thought it was that guard dog again, coming at me out of the darkness, coming fast, and I went numb all over with fear. But it wasn't the dog that came out of the darkness. It was Barry and he was angry at me, angry like I'd never seen him. He got hold of me and was shaking me. He said he knew I'd been up to something. He'd got up to go milking with Mum and he'd seen me running off. He was shrieking at me. "What do you think you're doing, Lily? It's dangerous. You shouldn't be here. It's going to be a battlefield. Live ammunition, Lily – shells, bombs, bullets. There's signs up everywhere. DANGER – LIVE FIRING. Can't you read? You're not allowed!" Then he stopped his shouting and suddenly let me go. "You've been in here before! You've been through the wire lots of times, haven't you?" he said. "You're looking for Tips, aren't you?"

When I began to cry he sat me down under the hedge. I told him everything then, all about Adie and Harry, all about yesterday, and how I'd looked and looked and couldn't find Tips anywhere, how I was sure she was still alive. Barry didn't say anything for a while, just picked at the grass. "You won't tell, will you?" I said.

"'Course not," he replied. "What do you think I am? But we've got to get out of here. Now!"

"Just one more look," I said. "Please, Barry. She could be waiting for us right now. Please." I knew he'd let me and he did.

As we walked across the fields together, the moon seemed to be floating on the sea. There were lots of ships in the bay, more than usual. In spite of the moonlight the sky was darker out there over the sea than over the hills beyond the farm. Dawn was breaking there. No sun yet, only the grey beginning of a new day. All was quiet. We climbed the gate and stood there, just listening. We began to call for her, softly at first, then a little louder, then as loud as we dared. There was no answering call, only an empty, eerie silence. But it was strange, because I felt the silence seemed to be waiting for something to happen, so when it did I wasn't nearly as surprised as I should have been.

Suddenly the sky was filled with bright orange and yellow flashes all along the horizon and then there came a great roaring followed by huge explosions, one after the other: down on the beach, in the village, explosions that were coming closer and closer to us all the time. I could feel the ground shaking under my feet. Barry took my hand and we ran, ran for our lives. But however hard we ran, the explosions seemed to be catching us up. I was screaming and screaming. I tripped and rolled over and over, and Barry fell half on top of me. Then the shelling stopped and we dared to stand up and look. In the thin light I could see there were landing craft coming through the smoke towards the beach, two or three at first, then dozens of them, the soldiers leaping out of the water and charging up the beach, firing as they came.

Barry pulled me to my feet and we ran. It seemed like miles that we ran, but we didn't stop till we reached the wire. I was in such a hurry I snagged my coat as I wriggled through and Barry had to stop and unhook me. As we walked home together, I was shaking and speechless and breathless. At the back door, before we went in, Barry made me promise never again to go through the wire. I promised, and this time I meant it.

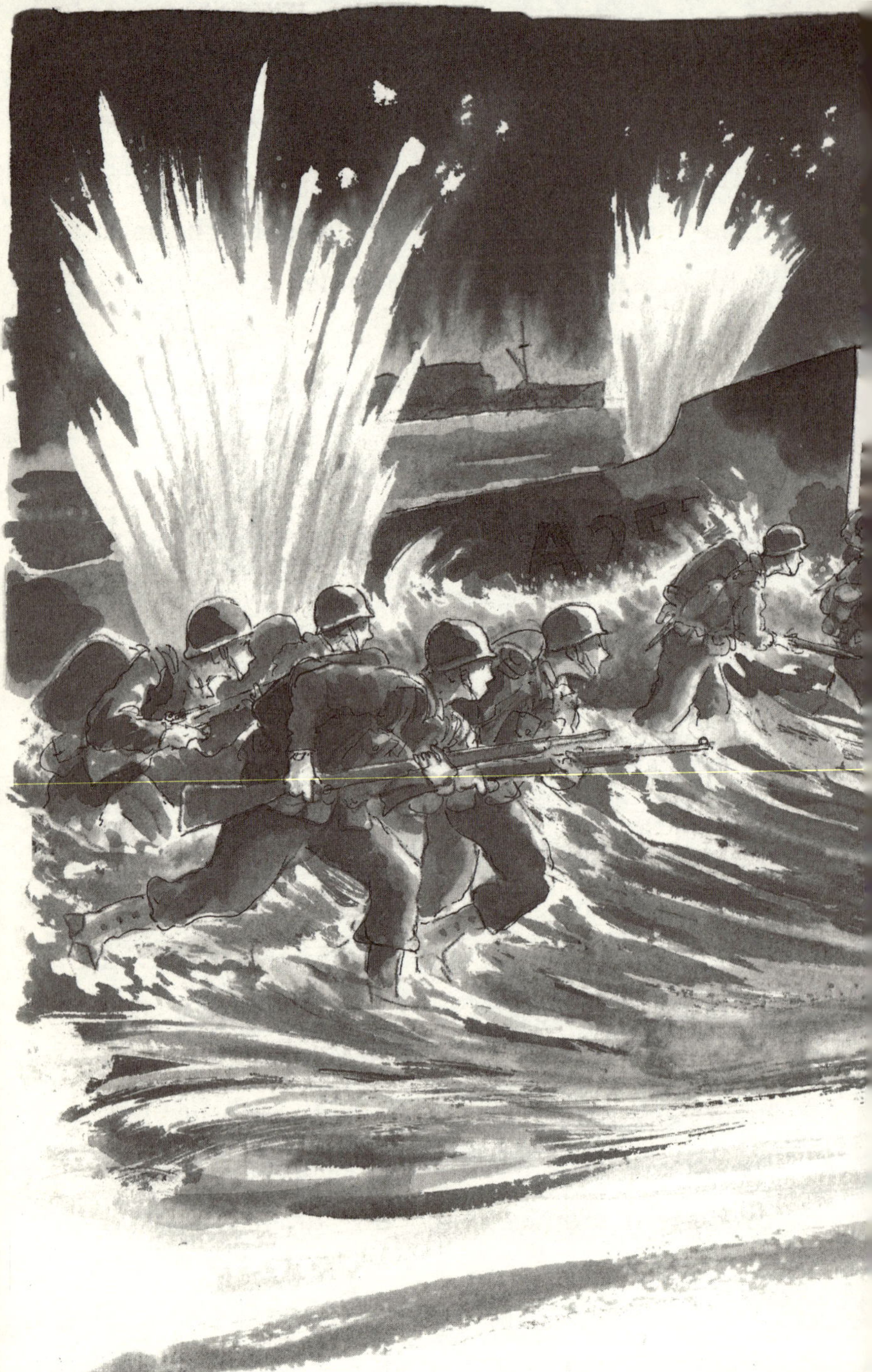

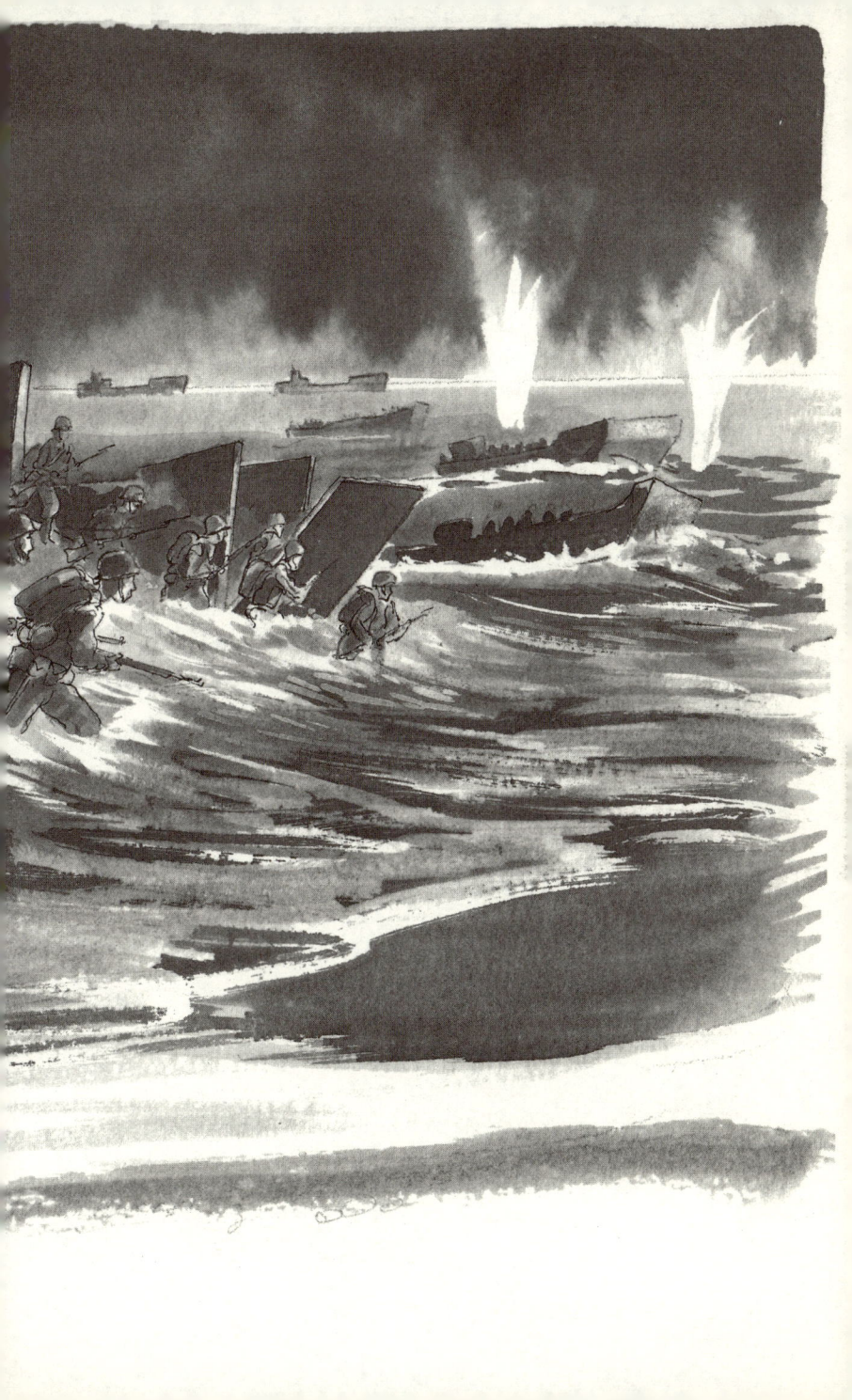

I really meant it. I was frightened out of my skin. I'm not going back in there, not any more, not for Tips, not for all the tea in China.

All day at school Barry and I kept looking at one another. Everyone was talking about the fireworks out at sea that morning. Everyone had heard it, or heard about it, but we'd *been* there. Mrs Blumfeld said she thought it was likely to happen again and again. "They have to practise." she told us. "It's like anything, children. If you want to do something well, you have to practise. And if we want them to win the war, if we do want Europe to be free again, then we want them to practise all they want, don't we?"

Uncle George's cat is back on our bed. He thinks he's taking Tips's place. Maybe he is, but only on my bed, never in my heart.

Thursday, February 24th 1944

Mrs Blumfeld was right. The Yanks are practising almost every day now. Most days now you can hear the whoosh and thump and crump of the bombs in the distance. I was coming up the lane with Barry after school today when we heard it again. It wasn't close enough to make the earth shake, not like before. But we were close enough to hear the cracking and spitting of rifle fire, and Barry said it sounded more like they were machine guns because they were firing so fast. It sounded to me like a whole orchestra of war. It was far away but it was still frightening, and the strange thing was the birds were joining in too. It doesn't seem to frighten them at all.

Friday, March 3rd 1944

It's like a miracle. We were just sitting in the kitchen having our tea when we heard a car outside. Uncle George's dog was going mad. Mum said to see who it was. By the time we went out Uncle George's dog was attacking the tyres, biting and snapping at them. It was a jeep. Adie was in it and Harry too. It was the first time I'd ever seen them without their helmets on. They looked even younger somehow, not men at all like the other soldiers. More like boys. "Got something for you, Lily," said Adie, and his smile seemed like a laugh waiting to happen. "Something that's gonna make you real happy."

I thought it would be some chocolate or something. But it wasn't. Harry reached into the back of the jeep and lifted out a cardboard box – a cardboard box which was mewing! "You said black and white, right?" Harry said, giving it to me. "We found this one hiding away in that old hotel down on the beach. She's blacker'n me and whiter'n you. Scratches some too."

Adie took her and held her out to me. "This the one you been looking for?" I knew her at once, from her green eyes, from her markings, her white paws, and from the deep roaring purr inside her as I took her into my arms and hugged her to my cheek.

I'm not sure how it all happened after that. I know I was crying a lot, then hugging Adie and Harry. I know they were about to get back in the jeep when Mum came out, and minutes later we were all sitting round the kitchen table, Adie, Harry, Grandfather, Uncle George, Mum, Barry and me with Tips sharpening her claws on my lap, and we were all having the happiest tea time of our lives. Mum got out the scones and clotted cream she had been saving for Sunday. Adie and Harry had never had scones before. Barry got some cream on his nose and tried to lick it off with his tongue and he couldn't, so he used the back of his hand and licked it and everyone laughed. And no one talked about the war, not even Uncle George. They stayed until it was dark.

I walked with Adie out to the jeep, Tips riding on my shoulder and clinging to me as if she would never let go. "Lily," he said quietly, "I gotta tell you there was other cats, young ones, a whole family of them down in that old hotel place. From the looks of her and the looks of them, I reckon they was her family, maybe too old to need mothering, but you'd better keep a good eye on her, else she could go right back to them, y'understand me?

She's here now. You keep her here." He stopped by the jeep and stroked Tips on the head. "I've had the best time, Lily, the best time since I left home," he said.

Then I asked him, "When you go out in those boats and do those landings, is it dangerous?"

He didn't answer for a moment. "They fire real live stuff over our heads, so I guess it is. But they do it so we can get used to it. They know what they're doing, I reckon. It'll be a whole lot hotter when we do it for real over in France, that's for sure."

"When will you go?" I asked him.

"Sooner the better," Adie said. "It's what we came over here for, Lily, so I just want to get on with it, get it done and get back home." Then he and Harry were gone. I realised too late that I never even said thank you.

Grandfather was sitting with his feet in the oven this evening when he turned to me and said, "Lily, I never thought I'd hear myself say it, but those gum-chewing Yanks are all right. They're all right."

Uncle George's cat hasn't been seen since Tips arrived. Tips is queen here now. She's taken over the whole house – and my bed. She's lying spread out on my feet, right now, flexing her claws and looking at me as I'm writing. She never takes her eyes off me. And Adie was right, she has had more kittens. It was some time ago but I can still tell. I just hope her kittens are old enough to do without her. I can't let her go back to them, I just can't. It's so good to have her back. I feel like I'm purring inside, purring with happiness.

I've been thinking. Next time I see Adie I'm going to ask him to bring her kittens home as well. Then Tips will be really happy like me. And she won't ever want to go running off to find them, will she?

Tuesday, March 7th 1944

Tips has gone off again. It was Barry's fault. He left the back door ajar when he went to fetch the logs. I told him. I told everyone she might make a run for it, that we had to be sure to keep her in. Tips must have slipped out behind his back and we haven't been able to find her since. Barry says he was only gone for a few moments. I try not to blame him, but in my heart I do. He should have been more careful.

I'm more cross than upset. At least I know where she must have gone: back to her kittens, back to the hotel. At least I know she's alive. As soon as I can I'll tell Adie, and he can go and fetch her back again, and the kittens too this time. He'll do it for me, I know he will.

Today was such a beautiful day too, clear skies and a blue, blue sea. There are primroses all under the hedges and celandine too. Why do sad things have to happen on beautiful days? And Barry's miserable too because he thinks I am angry with him. I'm not really, not much anyway. I'll make it up to him tomorrow. We heard lots more big explosions today – one huge one that shook the whole house. I hope Adie and Harry are all right.

Wednesday, March 8th 1944

Someone said it first on the school bus this morning. I couldn't believe it. I didn't want to believe it, but Mrs Blumfeld told us it was true. The Slapton Beach Hotel was blown up yesterday, blown to pieces during a landing exercise. She says there's nothing left but rubble. Barry picked some primroses for me on the way home this afternoon, because he thought they'd make me feel better, I suppose. But they don't. This time I know I won't see Tips again. There's no point in even hoping, not any more. She had her nine lives, I suppose, but her kittens didn't, did they? I can't even cry. I'm too sad. Uncle George's cat came in a few minutes ago. Maybe he knows what's happened, and he's trying to be kind. I've put him out now. I don't want any other cat, not ever.

Wednesday, March 15th 1944

Mum said this morning that she had a big surprise for me. I thought she was just trying to cheer me up. First she said Barry and I could stay away from school today, so we knew something was up. Then she cooked a special Sunday lunch, even though it wasn't Sunday, with roast chicken and apple crumble. The table was laid with all the best china and her best tablecloth, and she'd done her hair and put on powder and lipstick. Even Uncle George looked less like an old scarecrow than usual. He'd slicked down his hair and put a tie on. Grandfather wasn't there and no one would tell me where he was. Mum just tapped her nose at me and smiled mysteriously. Barry said he knew what it was all about but he wasn't going to tell me. So I pretended I didn't care anyway, which upset him a bit, which I shouldn't have. He was only trying to keep the surprise. And when the surprise came it was supreme, just supreme.

When we heard the dogs barking outside, I knew then it would be Adie. I was sure of it. I ran outside, but it wasn't an American jeep; it was a car, Grandfather's old Ford, still dusty from being kept in the barn. Someone was waving at me. I couldn't see who it was, not at first. Then he opened the door and got out. But he wasn't wearing an American uniform. It was a British uniform, with stripes on the right way up. Dad! Dad in his beret! Dad was home! "Hello Lil," he said. "Remember me?" I ran to him and we hugged there in the farmyard with Uncle George's dog chewing at the tyres of Grandfather's car. Then Mum did her hugging and cried a lot, and even Uncle George looked as if he was crying too as he shook Dad's hand. When I looked round a few minutes later to introduce Barry, he'd gone. He was there sitting beside me at lunch but he wasn't his usual chatty self, and he didn't eat much either, which wasn't at all like him. It was the *best* lunch. Dad ate as if he hadn't eaten at all in the two years he'd been gone.

He said right at the start he wasn't going to say a word about Africa and Italy and the army. He only wanted to know about home, about the farm and the evacuation, and how we'd all managed. We told him everything about the move, about Adie and Harry and about the Slapton Sands Hotel and Tips. He said how sorry he was and kissed me, which was nice because I knew he'd never really liked Tips all that much.

He did try to talk to Barry, but Barry had gone all shy and quiet and wouldn't say a word. After a while Barry asked to be excused and went out. I couldn't understand why he was behaving like he was until Mum said it. "He lost his father," she told Dad quietly. "In the RAF, over Dunkirk, wasn't it, Lil?" I felt so bad, so stupid not to have realised. I had my father back, but Barry could never have his back. I went out and found him sitting looking at the sea. He didn't want to talk. He didn't want to look at me even. He did want me to stay though, I could tell. I sat down beside him, and we said nothing to one another for a long time, which is what only true friends can do.

Barry cheered up that evening, but I wasn't that happy because Mum told me I had to move out of our room so Dad could sleep there. I'm sleeping on the sofa in the sitting room until Dad goes. He says he's got five days' leave. It's not so bad though, because with any luck I'll get to stay up late every night. They can't exactly make me go to bed, can they, if I'm down here? And anyway, it's not so bad, I've got the fire to look at and keep me warm.

I know I shouldn't say this. I shouldn't even have thought it. But I did. When Dad arrived, and I saw it wasn't an American jeep, I remember I felt a little disappointed. When I saw it was Dad I was happy, but I was sad too at the same time because it wasn't Adie. That's wrong, I know it is. But I am pleased my dad's back here and alive and well. I've missed him so much. I know that now he's come home. We're a real family again. He's thinner than he was and he's lost some of his hair, but I won't tell him that. He wouldn't like it.

Monday, March 20th 1944

I had to say goodbye to Dad before I went off to school this morning. He walked Barry and me to the end of the lane to meet the school bus, with Barry wearing his beret. He loves Dad's beret. Dad was in his uniform again, the first time he'd put it back on since the day he'd arrived, and I was very proud of him when the other children saw him. He's got three stripes on his arm, which means he's a sergeant and can tell other soldiers what to do. I think I didn't cry because I was even more proud than I was sad. He told me I had to be good. "I'll be home again soon, Lil," he said. "You look after your mum for me, and be good. The war'll be over before you know it." Barry handed him his beret. Dad ruffled his hair and we got on the bus. We ran to the back seat. Dad was getting smaller and smaller in the distance. Soon, all too soon, he was gone altogether. Then I did cry. But I looked hard out of the window so that no one would know.

It's been so strange having Dad back home. Somehow there didn't seem to be a proper place for him in the house. He spent most of the time with Grandfather and Uncle George on the farm, mending all the machinery, and a whole afternoon tinkering with the tractor engine with Barry, who loves getting his hands oily. Once he went off drinking in the pub with Uncle George and the others in the Home Guard, a sort of welcome home party I think it was, but we couldn't go of course because we're not allowed in pubs. Mum was so happy when he first came home, but then I'd see her gazing at him out of the kitchen window, and I knew what she was thinking. As the days passed and Dad's leave got shorter and shorter, we were all thinking the same thing. We didn't laugh like we had before. We were just waiting for the moment he had to leave, so we couldn't enjoy him being there as much as we should have done. It hung like a shadow over us. Now he's gone, and it's as if he's never been home at all. I'm going to pray for him every night he's away, starting right now, I won't miss once. Cross my heart and hope to die.

Wednesday, March 29th 1944

When we go to school now, we see more and more soldiers. Mostly they're Yanks, but some of them are ours too. We see them in lorries and in tanks, we see them marching along. They're putting up whole villages of tents all over the place. Every time I see a black soldier I look to see if it's Adie or Harry. I haven't seen Adie for ages now. I expect they've been doing lots more of their landing exercises. I know he's all right because Uncle George said he saw him only yesterday on patrol with Harry along the perimeter wire. Uncle George said he'd asked them to come and visit us again sometime. I hope they do. I really hope they do.

Thursday, April 20th 1944

The day of the Great Hot-dog Feast. That's what I'm calling today.

Barry and I were running up the lane, coming back from school. We were racing one another and I was winning, as usual, when we heard a car coming up behind us. It was Adie and Harry in their jeep. They said they were just coming to visit. Harry was carrying a bunch of daffodils. They gave us a lift home, which was good fun, but what happened next was SUPREME.

They were sausages really, but they called them hot dogs and they brought dozens of them. I've never seen so many sausages in my life. They said you just stick them between slices of bread and pour on tomato ketchup, and they brought that along too. So we had a great hot-dog feast, all of us together in the kitchen, and in the middle of the table were the daffodils Adie and Harry had given Mum. Barry said it was the best meal of his life.

He ate six! And got ketchup all over his face. I could only manage three. But they were supreme!

We only mentioned Tips once, when Uncle George's cat came in rubbing up against my leg and looking for a sausage himself. I told Adie what had happened, how Tips had gone off and about the hotel being blown up. He knew about the hotel, but he told me I wasn't to worry. "She'll come home," Adie said. "That cat's a real survivor, sure as my name is Adolphus T. Madison." And I said I wasn't so sad any more because I hadn't really thought about her since Dad came home, which was true.

Everyone talked about Dad a lot, and Mum told them she didn't know where he was exactly, but maybe he'd be part of the invasion too when it happened, and how maybe they'd meet up in France one day. And we all did a cheers to victory,

Barry and me in soda pop, which they'd brought along, and which is like a sort of American lemonade. It's nice, but not as nice as our lemonade. And the grown-ups did their cheers in beer, which Adie and Harry brought along too. They'd brought along the whole hot-dog feast – everything.

Adie's so tall he can't stand up straight in the sitting room without hitting his head. He keeps knocking his head and laughing at himself. And when Adie laughs, everyone laughs, the whole house seems to laugh. They didn't just bring us sausages, they brought us real happiness. Then they drove away into the darkness. Now they're gone the house seems empty and quiet. Barry's been sick, but he says it was worth it.

Friday, April 28th 1944

There was a thunderstorm out at sea last night. It woke me up. I knelt up on my bed and watched the lightening from my window. Mum slept through it, so did everyone else, but I heard it. I didn't imagine it. Tips used to hate thunderstorms. She'd burrow down my bed and hide. But they never frightened me, until this one. Or maybe it was the sudden blackness and silence which followed it that frightened me. I don't know. I hoped Adie and Harry weren't out in it doing one of their practice landings.

In school today Mrs Blumfeld read us a story. It was all about America. It's called *Little House in the Big Woods*. I like it a lot, but the people in it don't talk at all like Adie and Harry, not the way Mrs Blumfeld reads it anyway.

Uncle George's radio has gone wrong again. All you can hear is whistles and crackling. He's really cross but he still sits there all evening trying to listen to it, banging it from time to time, but all he gets is more whistling, more crackling. Barry and I got the giggles when Barry imitated Uncle George's grumpy face, and Mum told us off.

Monday, May 1st 1944

I wish today had never happened, that I'd never woken up this morning. It was all perfectly normal to start with: breakfast with Barry and Mum, off to school, lessons, playtime, lunch, more lessons, then the bus home. We walked into the kitchen and there was Adie sitting at the table with Mum. I knew there was something wrong at once. He was looking up at me as if he didn't want me to be there. Then he looked away.

It was Mum who told us. "It's Harry," she said quietly. "Adie came to tell us: he's been killed."

When Adie spoke, his voice was filled with tears. "We was told we gotta keep it quiet," he said. "But I ain't gonna keep it quiet, not for nobody. There's hundreds of us dead out there. What they gonna tell their folks back home? I tell you what they gonna say. Training accident or some such thing. But I was there and I knows. I knows what happened. I seen it with my own eyes. We had no way of fighting back, no way of defending ourselves. There were no one out there watching our backs, and that ain't right. That just ain't right." He cried then and couldn't go on. So Mum went on for him. She told us that three nights ago, the soldiers had been a few miles off shore in their ships, waiting to come in and do another practice landing on Slapton Sands, when suddenly out of nowhere came these German E-boats. The ships were like sitting ducks. They were torpedoed. They didn't stand a chance. They were all sunk. Hundreds of men were lost. Some of the soldiers, like Adie, did get picked up – but Harry wasn't one of them.

Mum gave him a cup of tea after that, and afterwards Barry and I walked him to the end of the lane.

"There's something I wanna tell you," he said. "Harry and me, we talked plenty. We was talking one day about what we was doing over here fighting in this white man's war. You know what he said? He said, 'I know why I'm doing it, because we ain't going to be no one's slaves never again, that's why. We got our freedom and we're not gonna let no one take it away. We gonna keep it.' That's what he said. But when I go over there to France, I ain't gonna be fighting for no one's freedom. I'm gonna be fighting for Harry, and they'd better watch out, because now I'm mad, I'm fighting mad." And as he put on his helmet he managed a smile. "Harry got no family back home. He told me after we was here last time that he reckoned you were about the only white folks that ever treated him like family. Right now that's just about how I feel too." Adie walked away from us and never looked back.

As we watched I wanted to run after him and hug him to me and never let him go. I wanted to tell him I loved him and that I'll love him to the day I die. Because I do. I love him more than lemon sherberts, more than mint humbugs, more than I love Tips or Mum or Dad, more than all of those put together. And that's the truth.

On the way home I picked a daffodil. I've put it in my diary on this page. So it'll always be here marking the day Harry died, and the day when I first knew I loved Adie.

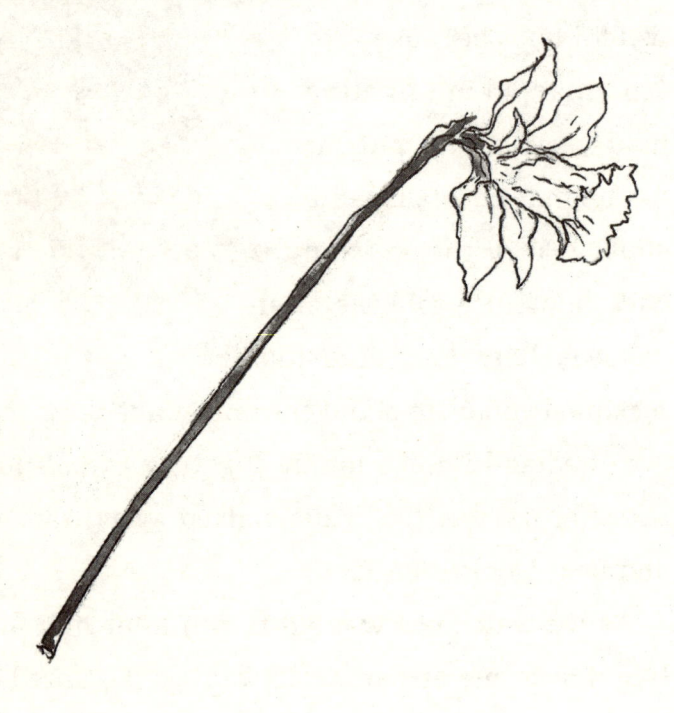

Wednesday, May 10th 1944

Adie still hasn't come back to see us again. I've been hoping and hoping every day. I wonder if he ever will. I can't stop thinking of him walking away down the lane, and that maybe it's the last time I'll ever see him. Mrs Blumfeld keeps saying the invasion must happen soon, any day now, she says – when the weather's right. They've got to wait till the weather's right. It's rough out at sea today. I hope it stays rough for ever, and then Adie won't have to go on the invasion, and he'll be safe.

I helped Barry and Mum pull off a calf this afternoon. The calf was walking inside ten minutes. I've seen lots of lambs born, lots of calves, and each time it surprises me how quickly they can get up and walk on their wobbly legs. What takes us a year or more, they can do inside an hour.

Mum's a bit down. It's because she hasn't had a letter from Dad since he left. We don't even know where he is. We think he's in England still, but we don't really know. We were kneeling there in the field, watching the calf trying out his first skip and falling over himself, and Barry was laughing. But Mum and me weren't laughing because our minds were elsewhere. If Barry hadn't been there I think I'd have told her there and then: "I know what it feels like, Mum, to miss someone you really really love."

I can't tell Barry that I love Adie, that's for sure, because he's too young and he wouldn't understand, and even if he did understand he'd be upset. He's never said it, but I know he wants me to be his girlfriend. I never will be, not now. Barry's more like a brother to me, more like a friend, a really good friend. With Adie, it's different, so completely different.

Saturday, May 20th 1944

Mrs Turner has come to stay, Barry's mum (she likes us to call her Ivy). Last Tuesday she just turned up out of the blue, to give Barry a nice birthday surprise, she said – that's in two days time. She gave him a surprise all right. She gave us all a surprise. We got back from school and there she was sitting with Mum at the kitchen table, her suitcase beside her. She hugged Barry so tight and for so long that I thought his eyes might pop out, and she pinched his cheek, which I could see he didn't like at all. She's got lots of powder on her face and bright scarlet lipstick, which Barry's always wiping off his face after she kisses him, and that's very often. And her eyebrows are pencilled on, not real, just like Marlene Dietrich in the films, Mum says.

Barry hasn't said much since she's been here, nor has anyone else. No one can get a word in edgeways. His mum never stops talking. She could

"talk the hind legs off a ruddy donkey" – that's what Grandfather says. And she smokes all the time too, "like a ruddy chimbley" – Grandfather says that too. Ivy's nice though. I like her. She came with presents for everyone, and told us again and again how kind we'd been to look after Barry for her. All through supper tonight she told us story after story about the Blitz in London, about the air-raid sirens, running to shelters and sleeping at nights down in the underground stations. She talks in a "townie" accent just like Barry does, only a lot louder and for a lot longer. She's very proud of her big red London bus. "I'm tellin' you. Ain't nothin' goin' to stop my number seventy-four from gettin' where she's goin'," she said this evening. "'Oles in the road, busted bridges, tumbled-down houses. They can send over all the hexplodin' doodahs they like. Will they stop my bus from gettin' where it's goin'? Not bloomin' likely, that's what I say."

Barry tries to stop her talking from time to time, but it's no use. In the end he just goes out and lets her get on with it. He spends even more time now out on the farm with Grandfather and Uncle George. Barry's mum makes no bones about it: she doesn't like the country one little bit, and farms in particular. "Smelly places. All that mud. All them cows. And the bloomin' birds wakin' you up in the mornin'." Yesterday she was washing up at the sink with Mum after supper when all at once she burst into tears. "What is it?" Mum asked, putting an arm around her.

"It's all that green," she said, pointing out of the window. "It's just green everywhere. And there's no buildin's. And it's *so* empty. I 'ate green. I don't know why, I just 'ate it."

She hardly ever goes out, just stays in the kitchen, smoking and drinking tea. Mum likes her a lot because she's good company for her and because Barry's mum loves to help out. She likes to be busy, fetching and carrying, scrubbing floors, ironing and polishing. She's black-leaded Uncle George's stove for him so he's happy too. Barry never actually says he wants her to go home, but I can feel he does. I don't think he's ashamed of her exactly, but you can tell he's uncomfortable with her around. He either wants to be at home with her in London, or down here with us, but not both. That's what I think anyway.

One good thing is that she's always teasing Uncle George, and no one else dares do that, about the holes in the elbows of his jacket, about how scruffy he looks. She sat him down a couple of days ago and cut his hair for him. She mended his jacket for him. And when Uncle George grumbles on as he does, about how he can never find anything these days with all of us living on top of him, how he used to have a bit of peace and quiet before we came, she just laughs at him.

"Go on," Ivy said (it sounded more like "garn"). "You'll miss 'em when they've gone back 'ome again, you know you will, you grumpy old codger you."

Surprisingly Uncle George didn't argue with her. He thought for a while and then he said, "Maybe I will, maybe I will." I think he really meant it.

Monday, May 22nd 1944

Barry's eleventh birthday. Barry's mum had brought down his birthday cake. She'd saved up her ration coupons for weeks and weeks. "I made it special," she said. And it was very special: fruit cake, with marzipan and royal icing with his name written on it in blue piping. Barry blew out the candles and closed his eyes to make his wish. Ivy had tears in her eyes and was trying not to cry. I think they were both wishing for the same thing, for the impossible: for Barry's father to be coming home.

I'll miss Ivy when she goes tomorrow. I think we all will. She makes us smile. She turns off Uncle George's crackling radio and we talk. She laughs a lot and never pretends. I like that. She means everything she says. I like people who mean what they say – a bit like Barry really. But I wish she wouldn't call me "ducky".

Friday, May 26th 1944

Mum's not been at all well. She's been coughing a lot for days now. She's very pale. The doctor came yesterday and said she had to have bed rest until she stops her coughing. Grandfather said that I could stay off school and look after her for a day or two, and help around the house with the cooking and cleaning. Barry said he'd stay home to help too, but Grandfather wouldn't hear of it and sent him off to school. Barry's not very pleased. He shouldn't grumble though. He's had lots of days off school to help out on the farm, specially at lambing time.

Mum had a letter from Dad today, so that cheered her up. He says he's somewhere in the south of England. He can't say where. Mum thinks he'll be going on the invasion when it happens. Maybe he'll meet up with Adie like we hoped he would. She keeps all his letters by her bed all the time, beside his photo.

This afternoon I went for a walk on my own up to the top of the hill. The larks were flying so high I could only hear them, but I couldn't see them. I did see the buzzards, two of them, floating on the air over the trees, mewing. For a moment they sounded just like Tips. Then I looked out to sea and saw the ships in the bay, dozens and dozens of them. I've never seen so many. It's the invasion. It must be. They're not gathered there for nothing, are they? There's one other thing I noticed today while I was up there. It wasn't only the sounds of the countryside I could hear about me. There was always a dull droning. I couldn't think what it was at first. Then I knew. It was the rumble of engines, jeeps, lorries, tanks. It was the rumble of war. I stood on the top of the hill with the wind blowing in my face, smelling the sea and all I could think of was Adie. I said a prayer out loud, then I shouted it into the wind. "Please, God, let him come and see me before he goes to the war. Please, God. Please."

Tuesday, June 6th 1944

We heard it on the radio. They've gone. The invasion began this morning. Adie's gone. Dad too probably. D-day they're calling it. I don't know why. We all knew something was going on before we heard it on the radio. Before dawn there was a distant thundering and roaring out at sea. Out of my window I could see flashes all along the horizon, and I knew then it wasn't just another thunderstorm. There must have been thousands of guns firing at the same time. And when Barry and me ran up over the fields after breakfast and looked out to sea, we saw all the ships had gone. So it was no surprise when on the radio this evening it said that we had landed all along the French coast: Americans, British, Canadians, French, all sorts. Uncle George said we'd show the Germans now. He and Mum drank too much cider together and danced a jig around the kitchen to celebrate and Uncle George's mad dog danced too, barking his silly head off. To start with, Barry and me sat and watched them. Everyone was laughing.

Mum still coughs when she laughs, but she's much better. But in the end we got up and danced with them. We did a conga round and round the table, till we all got puffed out. Then Mum gave Barry and me two mint humbugs each and some lemonade, to celebrate. Uncle George and Mum had a whisky each and we all clinked our glasses. "To victory," Uncle George said.

Grandfather came in from milking later and Mum told him what we'd heard on the radio. He said nothing, but went to wash his hands in the sink. Then all he said was, "Poor beggars. Poor beggars."

Mum said when she came up to bed a few minutes ago that today was the beginning of the end of the war, that Dad would be back soon, and then we could go back home to the farm and everything would be as it was before. But I don't think anything will ever be like it was again. Nothing stays the same, does it? Nothing is ever like it was, is it?

All I can think about as I write this is that Adie

might be lying out there tonight on some French beach, dead or wounded, and I'll never know, because no one will ever tell me because no one will ever know that we knew each other. I try closing my eyes and picturing him in my head. I try so hard to see him not dead and not wounded either. I try to see him alive and smiling at me. Whatever happens to him, wherever he is, that's how I'm going to remember him, for ever.

I know I should be thinking of Dad too, and I am. I'm trying. I'm thinking of them both now. I'm praying for them too.

This is me writing now, Boowie. This is your grandma. I wrote lots more in my diary after this but none of it is very interesting, and anyway the mice got some of it years later when my diary books were stored in a box up in the attic — mice or squirrels, I can't be sure. There are only two more entries I wanted to show you because they finish the whole supremely amazing story, in so far as my story finishes at all. And if you don't understand quite what I mean by that then you'll find out soon enough, but not until after the whole of the story has unfolded. Curiouser and curiouser...!

Thursday, October 5th 1944

My birthday and we've moved back home. It should have been the best birthday present I ever had. I was longing for today. And now it's come and I should be happy, but I'm not. This house isn't my home. It's an empty shell stacked with furniture, tea chests everywhere, and it's damp. When we arrived the front door was hanging off its hinges, so anyone could have been in and out, and by the look of it they have been too. It's a real mess. There's black mould on the ceiling, green in some places, and there are dead birds and leaves everywhere. The wallpaper's falling off above the chimney in the sitting room, and half a dozen of the windows are broken. The rain's come in and rotted the windowsill in my bedroom. The ceiling in Grandfather's room has come down in one corner: there's a hole in the roof where the slates have been blasted away by some shell.

The gutters are full of grass and one drainpipe

has fallen down into the garden and smashed the greenhouse. Not that you can call it a garden, not any more. You can hardly see a flower. Grass has grown up everywhere. You can't even see where the flowerbeds and the vegetable garden were. The granary must have taken a direct hit from a shell because there's nothing left of it but rubble.

Barry and me went off on a walk around the farm. There's nettles and docks head-high wherever you look. But the worst of it is that it's all so quiet. Only Grandfather seems truly happy to be home. "Never you mind," Grandfather said this evening, as we sat around the table in the kitchen in gloomy silence, "once we bring the animals back tomorrow, the place'll come alive, you'll see. We'll soon put it all right. Spick-and-span in no time. Few hens about the place and they'll cackle loud enough to drive out any quiet." I hope he's right. At least I'm back in my own room, even if it doesn't feel like it yet. All I've got so far is my bed, my chair and my lamp. My room smells. The whole house smells.

PS I can't believe this! I just finished writing my diary, and was reaching out to blow out the lamp, when I noticed some writing on the wall by the window, in pencil. This is what it says:

January 10th 1944. Harry and Adie were here looking for Tips. Welcome home Lily!

I just keep reading it over and over again. I can't stop crying and I don't know whether it's because I'm happy or I'm sad. I'm both. I'm not going to tell anyone about this, not tonight. It was written to me, so tonight I'm going to keep it to myself. I'll tell the others in the morning. I have to look at it again and again to believe it is real.

Friday, October 6th 1944

Supreme! Supreme! I feel supreme all over, because just about the best thing that could happen, has happened, and it happened at breakfast time.

I wondered where I was when I first woke up this morning. The window was in the wrong place. I was lying in bed, trying to work it all out, when I saw the writing on the wall. Then I remembered everything. I was home! I jumped out of bed and called everyone in to my room to show them the message Adie and Harry had left. Of course I told them as if I'd only just discovered it. Grandfather wasn't there. He'd already gone up to Uncle George's to milk the cows. All we talked about at breakfast was the writing on the wall, but we were in a hurry because Mum said we had to be up at Uncle George's as quick as we could, "lickety-split" she said, to help fetch home the cows after milking.

Anyway, we were washing the dishes when the

back door opened, all by itself it seemed, and in she came, meowing and purring all at the same time, wandering under the table, in amongst the chair legs, tail quivering with pleasure. Tips! Tips alive! Tips back from the dead! We were all crying, Barry too, and he doesn't even like cats. I put down some milk for her and she lapped till she'd licked the bowl clean. She's a lot thinner than she was, and there's a scratch on her face which wasn't there before. But she's definitely Tips, my Tips, green eyes, white paws and all her black patches in the right place. And she purrs the same too.

Mum said I didn't have to go with them to fetch the animals home, that she and Grandfather and Barry could manage without me. So all I've done today is cuddle Tips. I've played with her, fed her and cuddled her again. I think I gave her ten months' worth of cuddles in one day. She's come home, just like Adie said she would. I've looked back in my diary to be sure. These are exactly his words: "She'll come home. That cat's a real survivor, sure as my name is Adolphus T. Madison." So I've decided that from now on she's always going to be called Adolphus Tips. I asked her first of course, and she purred. So I know she's happy about it. Mind you, she's been purring nonstop ever since she came home! I think she's happy because she's got an important-sounding name, and she likes to feel important. I keep saying it, to get myself used to it, getting her used to it. Adolphus Tips. Adolphus Tips. It makes me smile every time I say it out loud, because it sounds so funny, and because every time I say it I think of Adie.

Just now I touched the writing on the wall before I turned down the lamp. I'm going to do that every night to bring him luck over in France. And I'm going to pray for him too, then maybe he'll come back like Tips has, like Adolphus Tips has.

And now, Boowie, over sixty years later, here's the beginning of the end of the story.

Adie didn't come back. But there has hardly been a day since I haven't thought about him, and about Adolphus Tips too. She was already quite an old cat by the time we found one another again, and she aged quickly after her miraculous return. I think that her struggle for survival on her own must have taken a lot out of her, and giving birth to all those kittens too. She died peacefully three years later and I buried her in the garden.

Gradually the people moved back into the cottages and farms all around us. As you can imagine, there had been a lot of destruction. Hardly a single building had survived unscathed and many were in ruins. The farms and farmyards were infested with weeds and rats, and there were rabbits everywhere, thousands of them. We ate a lot of rabbit stew! For a while it was a sad place to be, but bit by bit things improved. The houses were repaired, the farms tidied up. The church had been hit too, one of the walls blown out, so we couldn't use it for a while. I remember the first time the bells rang again. It was to celebrate the end of the war in 1945.

That was the year Dad came home, and the year the village school opened again. And it was the year we got our generator too. Dad had worked a lot on generators in the army, so he installed it himself. We were one of the first houses in the village to have our own electricity. Dad was always very proud of that. Later on, generators became his business. He took over one of the barns as his workshop and he supplied generators all over the country, all over the world. Mum and Grandfather and I went on running the farm together and we were quite happy to be doing it.

After the war was over Barry went back home to London, back to his mother. He wrote to me for a while, but then we lost touch. One of us didn't reply, I don't remember which. He came back to see us though several years afterwards. He had his new wife with him and wanted her to meet us, and to show her the farm I suppose. I remember I was even a little jealous. He still smiled the same, was still very sweet and kind. He told us over tea that his stay with us during the war had been the happiest time of his childhood. He's living out in Australia now near a place called Armidale in New South Wales. He became a sheep farmer. After his time with us down on the farm, he never wanted to be anything other than a farmer. We exchange photos of our grandchildren at Christmas. I hope to go and visit him one day. We'll see.

As you know, Boowie, Mrs Blumfeld never went back to Holland after the war, but stayed on in our village as the school teacher. You came with me to see her once or twice, do you remember? She's in the graveyard now, not far from Grandfather and Uncle George, and Mum and Dad too, and now your Grandpa as well. I keep all their graves as tidy as I can, and I often put flowers there too, snowdrops, primroses, bluebells, daffodils, fuchsia, whatever is in season, whatever I can find in the garden. Sometimes we've done it together, Boowie, haven't we?

Now to the end of my story. It was about three years ago. You had just gone back home, I remember, after spending your holidays with your grandpa and me. I was going for my usual walk along the beach, past the place where the old hotel had once been, when I saw a couple of men standing at the water's edge looking out to sea. I remember thinking it was strange because they looked a little out of place, not dressed for the beach at all. As you know, you can hear someone coming on those pebbles from a long way away. They must have heard me because they turned round to look at me at the same time. Both of them were very tall, and both were black. One looked much older than the other. He had white hair and was carrying a bunch of flowers. Maybe this was something I'd always believed would happen, because I knew who it was the moment I set eyes on him. It wasn't only my eyes that told me. It was my heart too. But he didn't recognise me. They turned away again, and as I watched, both of them began scattering the flowers into the sea, throwing them as far out as they could, which wasn't very far, so they soon floated in again on the waves and washed up on the beach. I knew the flowers were for Harry.

I waited a while before I approached them, not

wishing to disturb the moment.

"Adie?" I said. He turned and looked at me. It was him! It really was him. "Adolphus T. Madison," I went on. "That's T for Thomas, Private First Class, US Army?"

Then he smiled the smile I remembered. "Lily?" he said. And we each took each other's hands, unable to say another word.

So Adie and his son — he's called him Harry — came back to the bungalow and had tea with your grandpa and me. In between the scones and the macaroons Adie and I told one another the stories of our lives — there was a fair bit to catch up on, as you can imagine. We had a wonderful time together that day. Your grandpa took to Adie at once because Adie talked to him as if he wasn't in a wheelchair, as if he wasn't ill, and he always liked that, as you know. It was whilst we were talking that Harry told me that Adie had been wanting to make this trip all his life, to remember his old friend Harry and to visit the farm again where Lily, the little girl with the cat lived, and where they'd been made to feel so welcome.

Harry had grown up with the story all his life. Adie's wife had died a year or so before, and he didn't want to leave it any longer. "So we decided we'd just pack our bags and come right over," Adie said. "Say, d'you remember that day we came visiting with the hot dogs?" We laughed out loud then as we recalled the Great Hot-dog Feast and Barry's face covered in ketchup from ear to ear. I told him that Tips had come back home in the end just like he said she would, and that I'd renamed her Adolphus Tips. He said that it made him feel "real proud" to hear that.

They drove away after tea was over and went to see the farm on their way back to London. I should have liked to have gone with them of course, but your grandpa would have been upset if I'd left him alone again so soon after my daily walk. But Adie and I wrote to one another after that, often. He sent flowers for your grandpa's funeral and then wrote to me afterwards saying that if ever I'd like to visit them in Atlanta I'd be more than welcome.

So I went, Boowie, and that's where I am now, in Atlanta, in America. I don't think the two of us have stopped talking since the day I arrived — we have a lot of time to make up. And so when Adie asked me a week ago now, it seemed the most natural thing in the world to say yes. We got married last Tuesday. Second time around and I've married my childhood sweetheart. The church was full to bursting, and you never heard such wonderful singing in all your life. They sing with such joy over here, as if they really mean every word, every note. So I'm now Mrs Madison, and as soon as the honeymoon's over I'm bringing him home with me to live in Slapton. We'll be having our honeymoon in New York — neither of us have ever been there — and then we'll be flying back to London next Saturday evening. We arrive at Heathrow, Terminal Four at half past seven. I'm longing for you to meet him, Boowie. You'll like him, I know you will. I hope everyone else does too. Be there if you can.

I was there of course. We all were: uncles and aunties, the whole family. Some of them were still upset by the surprise of it all, but everyone was curious, me most of all. So we were all waiting for them at Heathrow, ready with confetti – that was my idea – as they came out of customs.

She looked so small beside him. They were holding hands and smiling like two cats that had got the cream and were blissfully happy to be sharing it. And then I was shaking Adie's hand. "Hi, there," he said, beaming down at me from a great height. "I reckon you've got to be Boowie. Yep. You're just like someone I used to know a long, long time ago, except you're a boy, of course, and you ain't got no pigtails."

After a while Grandma led me away, her arm around my shoulder.

"What do you think, Boowie?" she whispered.

"Supreme," I said. "Just supreme."

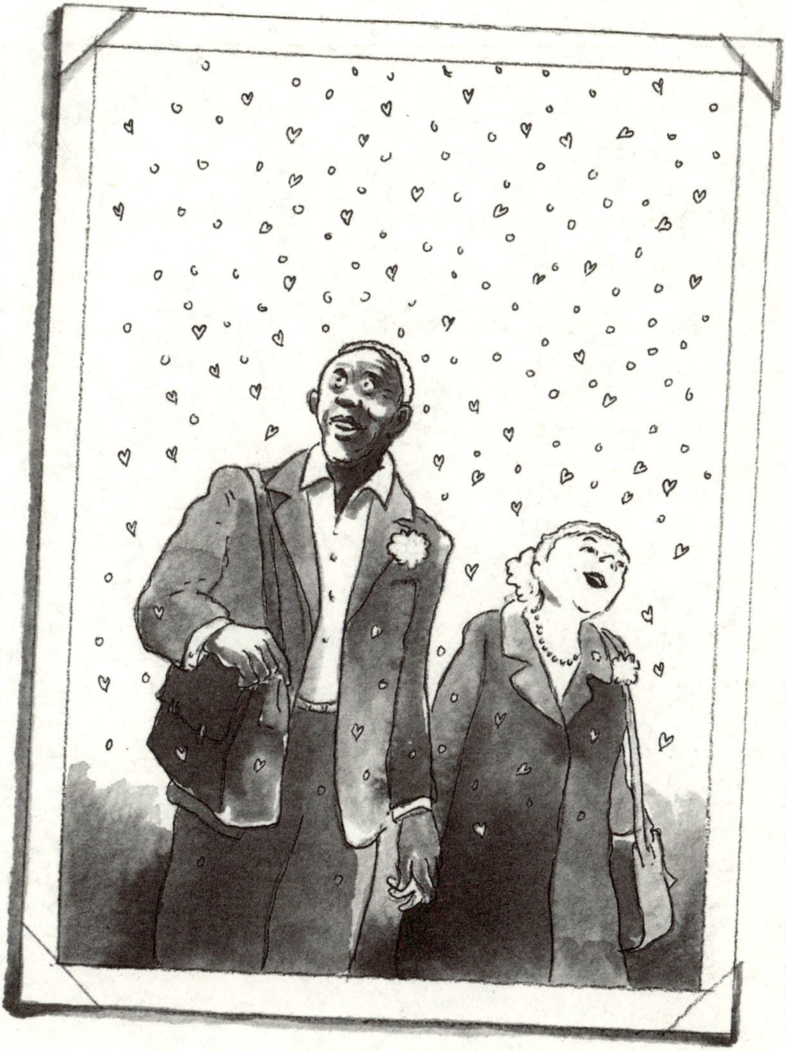

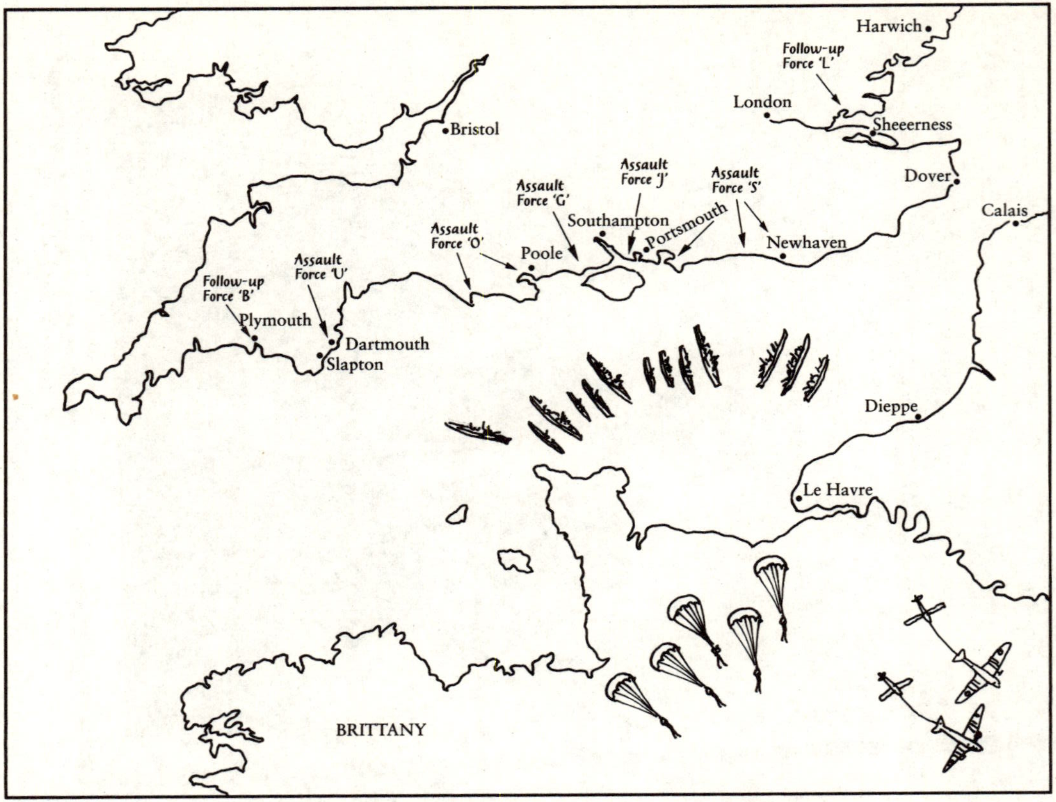
Harwich
Follow-up
Force 'L'
London
Sheeerness
Bristol
Dover
Calais
Assault
Force 'J'
Assault
Force 'S'
Assault
Force 'G'
Southampton
Portsmouth
Newhaven
Assault
Force 'O'
Poole
Assault
Force 'U'
Follow-up
Force 'B'
Plymouth
Dartmouth
Slapton
Dieppe
Le Havre
BRITTANY

POSTSCRIPT

In 1943, four years after the beginning of the Second World War, the Allies were making ready to launch an attack on German occupied France, in order to liberate Europe at last from Hitler and the Nazis. A seaborne attack on such a large scale had never been attempted before. The soldiers needed to practise, to exercise, and so they needed the training ground to do it.

The southern part of England became like a huge army camp, as the invasion force gathered and rehearsed. Many coastal areas had to be cleared so that simulated landings from the sea could take place, so that the soldiers were prepared when the time for the real invasion came.

The area around Slapton Sands in Devon was evacuated because the beach there was similar to the landing beaches in Normandy, across the English Channel. About 3000 inhabitants were given just a few short weeks to gather everything they had and move out.

Of course the disruption caused great hardship, and damage to the area during the landing exercises was extensive. There were casualties too of course, amongst the soldiers – and in Slapton they were mostly Americans.

During Operation Tiger in April of 1944, ships full of American troops preparing to be landed at Slapton were surprised by German E-boats in the channel and sunk. Many hundreds of Americans were drowned. This tragedy was deliberately kept secret for many years afterwards.

Then, on the morning of June 6th 1944, came D-day, as it was called, when the Allies landed on the French coast and fought their way off the beaches and inland, liberating French villages and towns as they went. Eleven months of hard fighting later, Germany surrendered and the Second World War came to an end.

Also by Michael Morpurgo

Private Peaceful
COOL!
The Dancing Bear
Farm Boy
Dear Olly
Billy the Kid
Toro! Toro!
The Butterfly Lion

For younger readers

Mr Skip
Jigger's Day Off
Albertine, Goose Queen
And Pigs Might Fly
Martians at Mudpuddle Farm
Mossop's Last Chance
Mum's the Word

Picture Books

The Gentle Giant
Sam's Duck
Wombat Goes Walkabout

Audio

Private Peaceful (read by Jamie Glover)
Kensuke's Kingdrom (read by Derek Jacobi)
Dear Olly (read by Paul McGann)
Out of the Ashes (read by Sophie Aldred)
The Butterfly Lion (read by Virginia McKenna and Michael Morpurgo)
Billy the Kid (read by Richard Attenborough)
Farm Boy (read by Derek Jacobi)
Adolphus Tips (read by Jenny Agutter and Michael Morpurgo)

ENJOYED THIS BOOK? WHY NOT TRY OTHER GREAT HARPERCOLLINS TITLES – AT 10% OFF!

Buy great books direct from HarperCollins
at **10%** off recommended retail price.
FREE postage and packing in the UK.

☐	**Private Peaceful** Michael Morpurgo 0-00-715007-5	£5.99
☐	**Cool!** Michael Morpurgo 0-00-713104-6	£4.99
☐	**The Dancing Bear** Michael Morpurgo 0-00-674511-3	£3.99
☐	**The Butterfly Lion** Michael Morpurgo 0-00-675103-2	£4.99
☐	**Toro! Toro!** Michael Morpurgo 0-00-710718-8	£4.99
☐	**Billy the Kid** Michael Morpurgo 0-00-710547-9	£4.99
☐	**Dear Olly** Michael Morpurgo 0-00-675333-7	£4.99
☐	**Farm Boy** Michael Morpurgo 0-00-675412-0	£4.99

Total cost _____

10% discount _____

Final total _____

To purchase by Visa/Mastercard/Switch simply call **08707871724** or fax on **08707871725**

To pay by cheque, send a copy of this form with a cheque made payable to
'HarperCollins Publishers' to: Mail Order Dept. (Ref: BOB4),
HarperCollins Publishers, Westerhill Road, Bishopbriggs, G64 2QT,
making sure to include your full name, postal address and phone number.

From time to time HarperCollins may wish to use your personal data
to send you details of other HarperCollins publications and offers.
If you wish to receive information on other HarperCollins publications
and offers please tick this box ☐

Do not send cash or currency. Prices correct at time of press.
Prices and availability are subject to change without notice.
Delivery overseas and to Ireland incurs a £2 per book postage and packing charge.

TORO! TORO!

By Michael Morpurgo

Alone on a Wide Wide Sea
The Amazing Story of Adolphus Tips
Private Peaceful
Cool!
The Dancing Bear
Farm Boy
Dear Olly
Billy the Kid
Toro! Toro!
The Butterfly Lion

For Younger Readers

Mr Skip
Jigger's Day Off

Picture Books

The Gentle Giant
Wombat Goes Walkabout

Audio

Alone on a Wide Wide Sea (read by Emilia Fox and Tim Pigott-Smith)
The Amazing Story of Adolphus Tips (read by Jenny Agutter
and Michael Morpurgo)
Private Peaceful (read by Jamie Glover)
Kensuke's Kingdom (read by Derek Jacobi)
Dear Olly (read by Paul McGann)
Out of the Ashes (read by Sophie Aldred)
The Butterfly Lion (read by Virginia McKenna
and Michael Morpurgo)
Billy the Kid (read by Richard Attenborough)
Farm Boy (read by Derek Jacobi and Michael Morpurgo)

TORO! TORO!

michael morpurgo

Illustrated by
MICHAEL FOREMAN

HarperCollins *Children's Books*

First published in Great Britain by Collins 2001
This edition published by HarperCollins *Children's Books* 2002
HarperCollins *Children's Books* is a division of HarperCollins*Publishers* Ltd
77-85 Fulham Palace Road, Hammersmith, London W6 8JB

The HarperCollins *Children's Books* website address is:
www.harpercollinschildrensbooks.co.uk

9

ISBN-13   978 0 00 710718 6
ISBN-10   0 00 710718 8

Text copyright © Michael Morpurgo 2001
Illustrations copyright © Michael Foreman 2001

The author and illustrator assert the moral right to
be identified as author and illustrator of the work.

Printed and bound in England by
Clays Ltd, St Ives plc

Conditions of Sale
This books is sold subject to the condition that it shall
not, by way of trade or otherwise, be lent, re-sold, hired out or
otherwise circulated without the publisher's prior consent in any
form, binding or cover other than that in which it is published
and without a similar condition including this condition
being imposed on the subsequent purchaser.

This book is proudly printed on paper which contains wood
from well managed forests, certified in accordance with
the rules of the Forest Stewardship Council.
For more information about FSC,
please visit www.fsc-uk.org

TORO! TORO!

As I was walking in the hills of Andalucia in the south of Spain last autumn, I came, quite by chance, upon a farm where they breed black bulls for the *corrida*, the bullring. The very same day I found myself on a wooded hillside looking down at the ruined village of Sauceda.

This remote village had been bombed and burned out in the early stages of the Spanish Civil War – the first time in Europe that deliberate aerial bombardment of a civilian population had ever happened. Since then, in Guernica, Warsaw, London, Dresden, Hiroshima and thousands of other cities, towns and villages all over the world, this practice has sadly become all too commonplace.

My first glimpse of that herd of magnificent black bulls, and then the sighting of Sauceda in ruins, served to inspire me to sit down and write *Toro! Toro!*. But I had some research to do first, into bullfighting, and into the Spanish Civil War. This terrible war, fought in the 1930s, was a struggle between the socialist left, the Republicans, and the fascist right, the Nationalists, for the control of Spain. After many years of vicious fighting, the Nationalists, under their fascist leader General Franco, won. Only on Franco's death, in 1975, did Spain become a democracy.

So here's *Toro! Toro!*, a story of children who lived through that war, a story of Spain, of bulls and bullfighting, of a grandfather (like me) and his grandson.

I hope you enjoy it.

MICHAEL MORPURGO
October 2001

*For
Eloise,
her book.*

PACO

I am the proud grandfather of a wonderful grandson – I have been for eight years. The two of us are very close. Somehow we know each other instinctively, like twins, in spite of the sixty years between us. We even share the same name. Nowadays they call me Abuelo (Grandpa), but when I was little I was always called Antonito, like him. It isn't only by his name that Antonito reminds me of me.

Until yesterday, being a grandfather had been a simple joy – all the pleasures of fatherhood, and few of the cares and woes. Then yesterday afternoon, up in his bedroom, Antonito asked me a question that had to be answered properly, honestly, and without circumvention.

It was a little enough thing that began it. It happened during the *siesta*. Antonito was bored. He was just messing around, as children do. All he did was kick a football through a window, by accident. When his mother came storming out into the garden, Antonito was standing there in his Barcelona shirt, looking as guilty as sin. He hadn't run off – he's not like that. There was no one else around except the cat and me, and we were having our afternoon nap under the mimosa tree at the bottom of the garden, well away from the scene of the crime. So, Antonio had to be the culprit. He was for it, and there was nothing I could do to help him.

"Antonito! How many times have I

told you?" I could see that chin of his was jutting already, and I knew there'd be tears welling up inside him. I could sense what he was going to say before he even said it. "I didn't do it. It wasn't me. Honest." And it was all said with such utter conviction, such determined defiance. Asked for an alternative explanation, he shrugged insolently at his mother, pursed his lips and refused to speak.

That one shrug was enough to send his mother into paroxysms of rage. He was "a careless, thoughtless, lying little toad and should be ashamed of himself". Antonito was banished to his bedroom. For some time afterwards, I could hear him crying, and then whimpering quietly in his misery and his shame. I longed to go up and console him, but had to bide my time until I was sure his mother had gone out (grandfathers have to be careful in such matters), before making my way into the house and upstairs. I knocked and opened the door.

Antonito was sitting on his bed, chin still jutting, until he saw it was me. "Hello, old fellow," I said, and went to sit down beside him. Neither of us could think what to say, so we said nothing. We often said nothing together. We were silent for some time. Then, out of the silence, came the question. "Abuelo, when you were little, did you ever do bad things? I mean, *really* bad. Did you ever tell a lie?"

"Plenty," I said. This was quite true of course, but I should have left it at that. Instead, seeking to empathise, wanting to make him feel better, I went on: "I'm telling you, Antonito, I was a whole lot better at bad things than you are. And as for lying, I was a pretty good at that, too."

He looked up at me with his wide eyes. "Honestly?" he said.

"Honestly," I replied. "Would I lie to you, Antonito?"

He smiled at that, and brushed the

tearstains from his cheeks. I felt I'd said the right thing.

"Are you going to come down now, and pick up that glass with me?" I asked him. "And then you can make your peace with your mother when she comes back, can't you?"

But I could tell he wasn't listening to me even as I was speaking.

"Abuelo," he said, "when you were little, what was the *very* worstest thing you ever did?"

I hadn't thought he would take it any further. I was on the spot now. I had a mountain of worstest things to choose from. But he'd asked me for the *very* worstest, and I knew at once what that was. I'd told no one else in near enough seventy years – not the real story, not all of it. It seemed somehow the moment to tell it; and it seemed too that if anyone had a right to know it, it was my grandson. I felt it was in some way his birthright, his inheritance. I knew too that he expected the truth from me. So I told him the truth, the whole truth.

"If I tell you something, Antonito," I said, "it'll have to be our secret. No one else must know, not until you're a father yourself, and then you can tell your own children. That's only as it should be. After all, it's our history I'm talking about – yours, and theirs too. Not a word till then, promise?"

"Promise," he said, and I knew he meant it. I could feel his eyes willing me on. So I began.

"I haven't always lived here in town, in Malaga. But you know that already, don't you? I've told you before, haven't I, how I was born on a farm, how I grew up in the countryside with animals all around me?"

Over the years I'd told him dozens of tales about my country childhood in Andalucia – he loved to hear all about the animals. But I'd promised him something much more exciting this time, and I could see he was full of expectation.

"This is not just another of my animal stories, Antonito – well, in one sense it is, I suppose. But this is the most important story I could tell you, because this story changed my life for ever. I'll begin at the beginning, shall I?"

* * * * *

I was born in a small farmhouse just outside the village of Sauceda on the first of May, 1930. There was my older sister, Maria – ten years older than me to the day – and Mother and Father. Just the four of us. We had uncles and aunts and cousins all around, of course. The whole village was like one big family. But we can skip all that. It was another birth about five years after my own that really began it all.

The farm didn't belong to Father. Hardly anyone owned the land they worked in those days – we just farmed it.

It was a hard life, but I knew little of that. For me it was a magical place to grow up. There were cork forests all around – we'd harvest the cork and cut it off the trees every nine years, to make corks for wine bottles. We had our little black pigs wandering everywhere, and dozens of goats for our milk and cheese, and chickens too. Never short of eggs for an omelette. We had mules too, for bringing the cork down from the hillsides, and horses. Everyone had horses or mules in those days. I could ride almost as soon as I could walk.

But mostly it was cows we kept. Not those lovely reddy brown Rositos you often see out in the countryside. Ours were black, black and beautiful and brave. My father bred only black bulls, bulls for the *corrida*, for the bullring. We must have had fifty or sixty of them, I suppose, counting all the calves. Magnificent they were, the best in all Andalucia, my father always said. As a small boy I'd spend hours and hours standing on the fence, just watching them, marvelling at their wild eyes, their wicked-looking horns, their shining coats. I loved it when they lifted their heads and snorted at me, when they pawed the ground, kicking up great clouds of dust and dirt. To me they were simply the noblest, the most exciting creatures on God's earth.

At that age though I had no real idea, no understanding of what they were kept for. They were just out there grazing in their corrals, part of the landscape of my life. I didn't ask such questions, not at five years old. Out in the cork forest I'd see the red deer in amongst the trees, the wild boar bolting through the undergrowth and the griffon vultures floating high up there in the sky. I didn't ask what they were there for either. Life seems simple enough when you're five years old. Then Paco came, and the war came, and the bombing planes came, and nothing was ever to be simple again.

There was a terrible thunderstorm the night Paco was born. Father asked me if I was frightened, I remember, and I said no, which wasn't true. And Maria said I was. She and I fought like cats sometimes; but I thought the world of her and she of me. So that's why I went outside into the storm with Father that night, to prove to Maria that I wasn't afraid. I followed Father's swinging lantern across the yard to the barn, hoping and praying the lightning wouldn't see the lantern and strike us dead.

The mother cow was lying down when we got to the barn, and two little white feet were already showing from under her tail. I looked on as Father crouched down behind her, took the calf by his feet, leaned back and hauled on him. There was some grunting and groaning (from both Father and the cow), but there was very little blood and it was quickly over. The calf slipped quite easily out into the world, and there he lay, shining black and steaming in the straw, shaking his head free of the clinging membrane.

"Bull," Father told me. "We've got a fine little bull." He knelt over him, lifted his head and poked a piece of straw down his nostrils. "It'll help him breathe better," he said.

The cow was trying to get to her feet. Father moved smartly away and took me with him. She was bellowing at us, and giving us the evil eye, making it very clear that she didn't want us anywhere near her calf. But try as she might the cow could not get up on to her feet. She just didn't seem to have the strength. Time and again she almost made it, but then her legs would collapse and she would be down again. In the end she gave up, and sat there breathing heavily and looking bewildered and frightened. Father did all he could to help her, but her only response now was to toss her horns at him angrily. He shouted and whooped at her, clapped her sides, twisted her tail – anything to panic her up on to her feet. Nothing would shift her.

"That calf has to drink, and soon," he told me, "or he won't live. And he won't be able to drink unless she stands up."

I joined in now, screaming at the cow to get up, slapping her, jumping up and down, but still she couldn't do it. She was stretched on her side now, completely exhausted by her efforts.

"Only one thing for it," said Father. Crouching down beside her, he stripped some milk from her udder into a bucket. Then he poured it into a bottle with a teat on it, lifted the calf's head and dribbled the milk down his throat until at last he suckled. All the time though, he was struggling against it, fighting the bottle, fighting Father.

"We've got a brave one here," said Father. "I'll hold him, Antonito. You feed him." And he handed me the bottle.

So there I was, feeding the calf

myself. I talked to him as I fed him, and he was calmer at once. I told him how beautiful he was, how he was going to be the finest bull in all of Spain. He sucked, and as he sucked, his eyes looked into mine and mine into his, and I loved him. After a while Father had no need to hold him any more. I told Father he should be called Paco, and Father said that it was a fine and proper name for such a brave bull. But I could see Father was becoming more and more anxious about Paco's mother. She was weakening all the time. Despite his best efforts, it was only a couple of hours later that she breathed one last sigh and died. In that one night I had witnessed my first birth and my first death.

THE DANCE

Paco was soon up and on his feet. I stayed there, crouched in a corner, to witness his first staggering steps. Every few hours after that we would go to the barn to feed him. I found I had to get on to an upturned bucket, otherwise he couldn't suck properly from the bottle. I'd stand up there, wave the bottle at him and call him over to me. After only a couple of days I didn't even need to do that. As soon as I opened the door into the barn he'd come trotting over, and he'd suck so strongly that it was all I could do to hold on to the bottle. Worse still, if the teat became blocked, if he couldn't drink the milk down fast enough, he would become impatient with me and butt suddenly at the bottle as if he wanted to swallow it whole, and the bottle would end up on the barn floor.

To begin with, Father or Mother or Maria would always be there with me. Maria said it looked easy and insisted on having her turn. To my great delight Paco went wild on her and butted her up the bottom. She never asked to feed him again. They very soon realised that with me Paco was always gentle, that I could manage him well enough on my own. After that, they just left me to it, which suited me fine.

I remember those days playing mother to Paco as the happiest of my young life. Paco followed me everywhere. I'd tie a rope round his neck and take him for walks up into the cork forests. I didn't have to drag him – not that I could have anyway, for he was already far too strong for me. He just seemed to follow along naturally. He was forever nudging me to remind me he was there, or to remind me it was feeding time – again. The two of us became quite inseparable.

Then one morning, after no more than a couple of weeks, it was over. Mother tried to explain to me why it had to end.

"You've done a fine job, Antonito," she said. "Your father's very proud of you, and so am I. No one could have given Paco a better start in life, no one. But if he's to make a proper bull, a bull fit for the *corrida*, then you mustn't handle him any more. No one must. We'd be gentling him too much. He's got to grow up wild. It's what Paco was born for, you know that."

I didn't. I had no idea what she was talking about, and cared less. All I cared about was that Paco was being taken away from me.

"And besides," she went on, "he'll be better off with a cow for a mother.

Father's picked out just the right one for him. She's got a calf of her own, but she's still got lots of milk to spare – more than enough for Paco. It might take a day or two for the cow to accept him, but Father'll see to that. Paco will be fine, don't you worry."

I argued of course, but I could see it was hopeless. It was Father himself, chewing on his bread that lunchtime, who had the last say. When it came to the farm and the animals, Father always had the last say. "From now on, Antonito," he was pointing his knife at me, "you keep away from him, you understand, or else he'll be no use to anyone. Keep away. You hear me now?"

It was the end of my world.

I cried for long hours in my room, and for at least a couple of days refused any food I was offered. I made up my mind I hated Father and Mother, that I would never speak to them again and that I would run away with Paco as soon as I could. I confided only in Maria. Without her I honestly think I might have starved myself to death. She took me out to see Paco in the corral with his nurse mother. I watched him frisking about with his new-found brother and all the other calves. She assured me that Paco was happy.

"That *is* what you want, isn't it?" she said. "Look at him. Doesn't he look happy to you?" I couldn't deny it. "Well then," she went on. "If he's happy, then you should be happy, too."

So it wasn't the end of the world after all. I decided Paco and I wouldn't need to run away. I decided instead that I would see Paco from time to time, but in secret.

Not quite in secret though, for Maria was my accomplice, my stooge. We'd wait until the coast was clear, until both Mother and Father were busy in the house or on the other side of the farm. Then we'd steal out to Paco's corral. Maria would keep watch and I'd stand on the fence and call him over.

I was fearful at first that he might have forgotten me. I needn't have worried. Whatever he was doing he'd come trotting over at once and lick my hand. I think he must have liked the salty taste of it. I'd let him suck on it like a teat and he loved that. It didn't seem to matter to him that no milk came out. Sucking was enough, and when Paco sucked he sucked hard. By the time he'd finished, my hand was raw, but I didn't mind. The other calves would be milling around but I wouldn't let them have even a taste. My hand was for Paco only. Once or twice his nurse mother came wandering over and shook her horns at me, but I always kept on my side of the fence and she soon lost interest.

I'd spend all the hours I could on that fence just talking to Paco, scratching his head and having my hand sucked off. Maria was forever fearful of discovery, and kept badgering me to come away. But luckily, Father and Mother never did find out about our secret meetings, not then, not ever.

Paco grew fast in his first year. He grew horns where there had been none, and often played at fighting with the other yearlings, mock battles which he always won. Sleek and fast, Father had already picked him out as the finest and noblest bull calf in the herd. Sometimes I would help Father move the herd to fresh pastures. We did it on horseback, with the brown and white Cabrestro bullocks in amongst them to gentle them as we drove them. I always rode Chica, the oldest, steadiest mare on the farm. She could have done it all with her eyes closed, I expect. Even then, when the bulls were running all together, you could pick out Paco easily. He would be at the front with the big bulls, the five-year-olds, the giants. I was so proud of him, but never spoke of him to anyone but Maria. She did warn me over and over again not to become too fond of him. I remember that. "All animals have to die, Antonito," she told me. "And you'll only be sad." But I was six years old, and death meant nothing to me. I never gave it a thought. I had some shadowy understanding that it happened, but it was of no interest to me, because it happened to old people, old animals. Paco was young. I was young. So I paid my sister's words of warning very little heed.

The dawning of the terrible truth was slow at first. I was walking back home from school one day when I came across some bigger boys hanging about by the well in Sauceda. A couple of them were playing at something in the street, egged on by the others. It was a game I hadn't seen before, so I stopped to watch.

One of the boys, my cousin Vittorio, was pushing a strange-looking contraption. It had a single wheel and two handles, like a wheelbarrow. However, the wheel did not push a barrow but a crude wooden frame with horns sticking out of the front, bull's horns. It was a simulated bullfight – I could see that now. I'd seen pictures in the village café of matadors with their capes, of bulls charging them. I'd always thought of it as some kind of dance. Vittorio was running at José with the bull machine, and José was sidestepping neatly at the last moment, so that the horns passed him by and charged only into his swirling crimson cape. And each time they all cried: "*Ole! Ole!*" It was balletic, mesmerizing, and I stayed for some while in the background, completely entranced.

Then José had a stick in his hand, and the chant went up: "Kill the bull! Kill the bull! Stick it in him! Stick it in him!"

Suddenly, in my mind, it was Paco charging the cape and the stick was a sword flashing in the sun, and there was blood in the dust and they were all cheering and laughing and clapping. I turned away and ran all the way home, the tears pouring down my cheeks. I would ask Maria. Maria would tell me it was all right, that this was not what really happened in the corrida, that it was just a game, just a dance.

I found her collecting the eggs. "It's a dancing game, isn't it?" I cried. "They don't really kill the bulls. Tell me they don't."

And I told her everything I had seen. She kissed away my tears, and did her very best to reassure me. "It's all right, Antonito," she said. "Like you say. It's a game, just a dancing game."

"And will Paco have to play it?" I asked.

"I expect so," she said. "But anyway, he won't know much about it. Animals don't think like we do, Antonito. Animals are animals, people are people."

I asked her again and again, but she became impatient with me and told me not to be silly. So I shouted at her and said *she* was the silly one, not me – a silly cow, I called her. At that she mooed at me and charged me, and I charged her back. In the scuffle we broke a lot of eggs, I remember, and Mother was furious with us both. But I went to bed reassured and unworried. We always believe what we want to believe.

Then we had news that Uncle Juan was coming to stay. Juan was the most famous person in our whole family. I'd only seen him once before at a christening, and remembered how tall and strong he stood, how wherever he was people seemed to be crowding around him. They called him *El Bailarin* (The Dancer). He was a matador, a real bulldancer. He lived in Malaga, miles and miles away over the hills. I'd never been there, but I knew it was a big and important town, and that my Uncle Juan had danced with the best bulls in Spain in the bullring there, and in Ronda too.

There was great excitement at his visit. Everyone would be coming and we'd be having a great feast. I told Paco all about Uncle Juan the evening before he came. Paco stood and listened, whisking his tail at the flies. "Maybe one day he'll dance with you in the bullring, Paco?" I said. "Would you like that?" I scratched him where he liked it, patted his neck and left him.

Uncle Juan came late the next day. We put up the long table outside, and when we sat down to eat our *paella* that evening there must have been twenty of the family there. I couldn't take my eyes off Uncle Juan. He was even taller than I remembered, and serious too. He never once smiled at me all through dinner, even when I caught his eye. He had eyes that seemed to look right through me. The talk was all of the *corrida* in Algar the next day, of how crowded it would be, how you had to be there early to find a place.

I was just about to ask Father if I could go too when he put his hand on my shoulder. "And Antonito will be coming too," he announced proudly. "It will be his first *corrida*. He is old enough now. He may be little, but he's a little man, my little man."

And everyone clapped and I felt very proud that he was proud of me. It was all laughter around the table that evening, and I loved it.

Darkness came down about us. The wind sighed through the high pine trees and the sweet song of the cicadas filled the air. They spoke earnestly now, their faces glowing in the light of the lantens. And the talk was of war, a war I had not even heard of until that night.

Everyone spoke in hushed voices, leaning forward, as if out in the night there might be enemy ears listening, enemy eyes watching. All I understood was that some hated General from the north, called Franco, was sending soldiers from the Spanish Foreign Legion into Andalucia to attack us, and that our soldiers, Republicans they called them, were gathering in the hills to fight them.

The argument was simple enough even for a six-year-old to understand. To fight or not to fight. To resist or not to resist. Father was adamant that if we went about our lives as usual, they'd be bound to leave us alone. Others disagreed vehemently, in raised whispers, talking heatedly across one another.

Through it all, Uncle Juan sat still, smoking. When he finally spoke everyone fell silent at once. "It is all about freedom," he said quietly. "A man without freedom is a man without honour, without dignity, without nobility. If they come, I will fight for the right of the poor people of Andalucia to have enough food in their bellies, and I will fight for our right to think as we wish and say what we wish."

Soon after, I became bored with all the talk, and I was getting cold. So I crept back into the house and upstairs. As I was passing the room we had prepared for Uncle Juan, I noticed that the door was open. A moth was flitting around the lamp, its shadows dancing on the ceiling. All Uncle Juan's clothes were spread out on the bed – his matador's costume, a wonderful suit of lights, glittering with thousands of embroidered beads, and beside it his shining black hat and his crimson cape. I crept in and closed the door behind me. I could hear the drone of their talk downstairs. I was safe. The costume was very heavy, but I managed to shrug it on. It swamped me of course, as did the huge hat which rested on the bridge of my nose so that I had to lift my chin to see myself in the mirror. Now the *muleta*, the crimson cape. I whirled it, I swirled it, I floated it and I flapped it, and all the while I danced in front of the mirror, using the mirror as my bull. *"Ole!"* I mouthed to the mirror. *"Ole!"*

Someone began clapping behind me. Uncle Juan filled the doorway, and he was smiling broadly. "You dance well, Antonito," he said, crouching down in front of me. "No bull would catch you, not in a million years. Bravo!"

"I have a bull of my own," I told him. "He's called Paco, and he's the noblest bull in all Spain."

Uncle Juan nodded. "Your father has told me of him," he said. "One day I may dance with him in the ring in Ronda. Would you like that? Would you come to see me?" He took the black hat off me, and the beautiful costume and the cape. I caught sight of myself in the mirror. I was ordinary again, not a matador any more, just Antonito.

He ruffled my hair. "You want to help me practise?" he said.

I didn't understand quite what he meant, not at first. Then he shook out the crimson cape and stood up straight and tall and near the ceiling, stamped his feet and flapped the cape. *"Toro!"* he shouted. *"Toro!"* And I charged. Again and again I charged, and each time I was swathed in his great cape and had to fight my way out of it.

At last he cast aside the cape, picked me up by the waist and held me high so we were face to face. "We dance well, little bull," he said, and kissed me on both cheeks. "Now we must both be off to bed. I've some serious dancing to do tomorrow. Wish me luck. Pray for me." And I did both.

I didn't sleep much that night. By the time I woke up, Uncle Juan had already gone. We set off early ourselves and rode in the cart to Algar. The road was full of horses and mules and carts all going to Algar for the *corrida*. Getting there seemed to take for ever. I sat with Maria beside me, who was strangely silent; she'd hardly said a word to me all morning.

The bullring was a cauldron of noise

and heat, the whole place pulsating with excitement. As the trumpets sounded, Uncle Juan strode out into the ring, magnificent in his embroidered costume. There were other men behind him, *banderilleros* and *picadors*, Maria told me. But when I asked what they were for she didn't seem to want to tell me. Instead, she took my hand, held on to it tight and would not let go. I was suddenly anxious. I looked up at her for reassurance, but she would not look back at me.

All around the ring the crowd was on its feet and applauding wildly. Uncle Juan stopped right in front of us and lifted his hat to us. I felt so proud at that moment, so happy. Another trumpet, and there was the bull trotting purposefully out into the centre of the ring, a glistening giant of a creature, black and beautiful in the sun. Then he saw Uncle Juan and the dance began.

TORO! TORO!

To begin with the dance was like the photo in the village café, much as I had expected, except that Uncle Juan did not do the dancing. He watched from the sidelines. One of the other men did the dancing, and his cape wasn't crimson like Uncle Juan's, but yellow and magenta. The bull charged him and charged him tossing his horns into the cape. And at each pass the crowd shouted *"Ole! Ole!"* just like in the game I had seen my cousins Vittorio and José playing back in Sauceda.

All this time Maria had my hand held tight. The bull was enjoying the game, I thought, pawing the ground before he charged, snorting, shaking his head. He looked so like Paco, bigger of course, but he held his head high and proud in just the same way. Still he kept charging and the man kept dancing. It was a good game. I was enjoying it too, and shouting along with everyone else.

Then came the third trumpet. I felt Maria squeezing my hand tighter. What followed in the next few minutes I remember as a nightmare of horrors.

The mounted picadors ride in, their horses padded up, and the bull charges. The first pike goes in, deep into the bull's shoulder, and he charges again, and again. And there's blood down his side, a lot of blood, and the crowd is baying for more. He feels the pain – I can see it in his face, but he knows no fear. He's a brave and noble bull. I see what I see through the mist of my tears – the *banderilleros* teasing him, maddening him, decorating his shoulders with their coloured darts, leaving him standing there still defiant, his tongue hanging in his exhaustion, in his agony.

Another trumpet, and there is silence now as Uncle Juan steps forward and takes off his hat. I cannot hear what he says, nor do I care. I know now what is to happen, and I hate him for what he will do. He stands before the bull, erect, with his crimson cape outstretched. "*Toro!*" he cries. "*Toro!*" And the bull charges him once, twice, three times, and each time Uncle Juan draws his horns harmlessly into the cape. It seems now that the bull no longer has the strength to do anything but stand and pant and wait. I see the silver sword held high in Uncle Juan's hand, produced as if by magic from under his crimson cape. I see it flash in the sun. But then I see no more because my head is buried in Maria's shoulder.

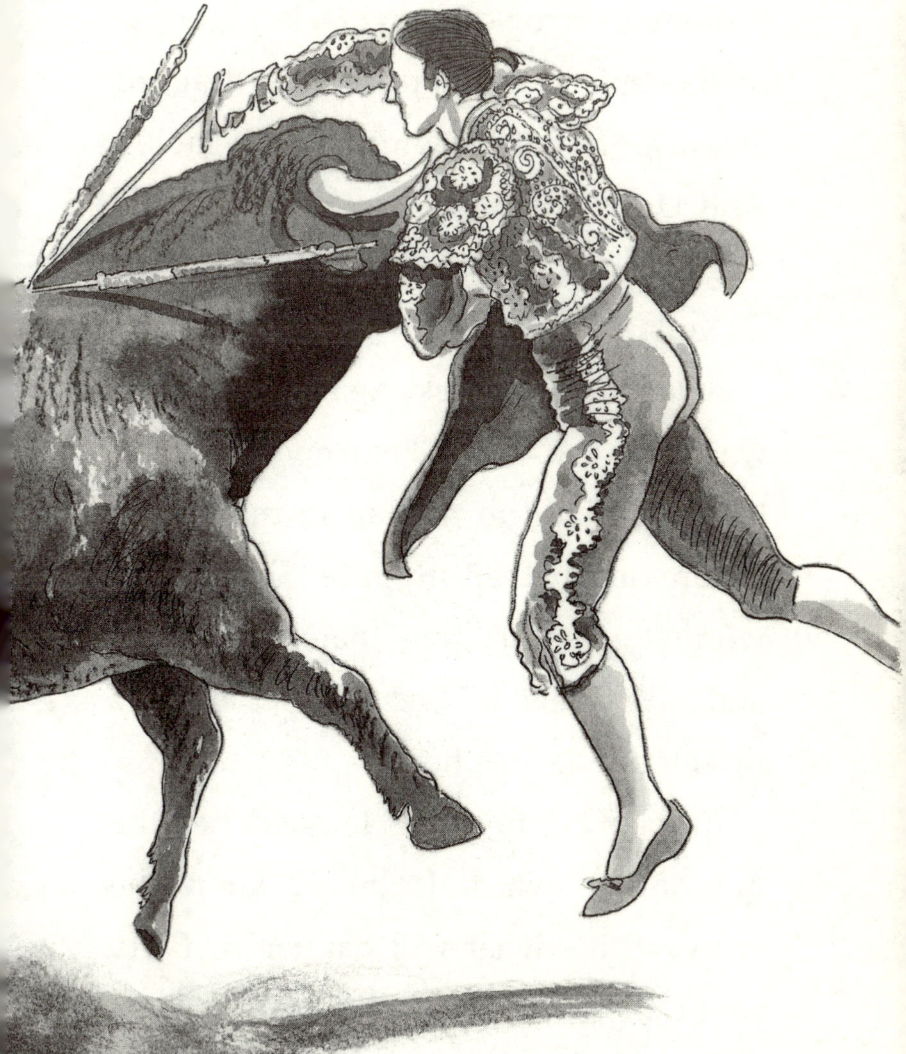

"Take me out!" I begged her. "Take me out!" As we struggled our way through the crowd I caught a last glimpse of the bull as his carcass was dragged away, limp and bleeding, by the mules. And Uncle Juan was strutting about the ring accepting the applause, catching the flowers.

Outside I was sick. Again and again I was sick, and Maria held my head. She took me down to the tap in the village square and bathed my face. She had no words to comfort me – there were none, and she knew it. She just let me cry myself out against her.

When I'd finished, I asked her the question to which I already knew the answer. "It's what will happen to Paco, isn't it?"

"Yes," she replied, and hugged me to

her. "Don't cry, Antonito," she went on. "Paco doesn't know it. Think of it like this: it'll be just a few minutes at the end of his life, and it's all so quickly over."

I pushed her away from me. "Never!" I cried. "I won't let it happen to him, Maria, I won't." And in that moment I made up my mind that somehow, some way, I would save Paco from the bullring. "I'm going to run away with him," I said, "and I'll never come back."

I committed myself to it that same evening by promising Paco face to face. He came trotting over as usual as soon as he saw me coming. I stood on the fence, smoothed his neck and spoke softly to him. I didn't tell him what I'd seen that day – I didn't ever want him to know. "It'll be soon," I told him. "I'll take you away so you can live wild up in the hills, where you'll be safe for ever and ever. I'll work something out, I promise you." But it was to be a long time before I was able to fulfil my promise.

There were other distractions. The war was no longer just talk around a dinner table. It was only weeks after the bullfight in Algar that the first soldiers came to the village, our soldiers, Republican soldiers. Some were wounded – I'd seen them on crutches, or with their heads bandaged sitting in the café. There was talk that others were hiding in the houses in the village or up in the woods. The war was not going well for them, for us, Mother explained. We had to feed the soldiers, she said. It was the least we could do. It would give them the strength to fight again. I still had no idea what it was they were fighting for.

Almost daily now Mother would send Maria and me up into the village with eggs and bread, ham and cheese for the soldiers. We delivered it to the café, and sometimes they'd be singing and smoking and drinking. I knew they were our soldiers, but they looked rough all the same and I was frightened of their eyes, even when they smiled at me. But they let me hold their rifles and pretend to shoot, and I liked that.

At home Father wasn't speaking. We all knew what it was that was troubling him. He was against taking sides in this war. Fighting an invader – he could understand that. But Spaniard against Spaniard, cousin against cousin? It was wrong, he said, plain wrong. Besides, it would only get us into trouble with one side or the other. He wanted us to stay out of it.

But in this Mother was adamant. She would send food to the soldiers in the village no matter what he said. They were defending us, defending freedom, and she would help them. She argued cleverly, talking him round, so that although he never agreed with her, he let her do what she wanted all the same. But he was grudging about it, and morose and silent. Thinking back, I suppose it must have seemed as if we were all against him. Maria and Mother were, it was true; but I just took the food up to the village because I wanted to hear the soldiers singing again and hold their rifles.

In all this time, Paco's escape was never out of my mind. I lay awake at night trying to work out how it might be done. Every time I went to church I'd pray to Jesus to tell me the way to do it. How could I separate Paco from the fifty others in his corral, and take him away up into the hills? How was I going to do it? I thought of confiding in Maria, of asking for her help, but dared not. There was just a chance that she would tell Mother – they were more like sisters, those two, always talking heart to heart. No, I would keep it to myself. Somehow I would have to work it out on my own.

The day the idea came to me, I was driving the herd with Father to the corral furthest from the house, where there was more grass. He seemed more talkative out on the farm with me than he ever was at home. It was because of his bulls, I think, his beloved black bulls. He was always at his happiest when he was amongst them. I was riding Chica, as usual, rounding them up from behind. The herd was drifting along easily – Paco going on ahead with the big bulls – when Father rode up alongside me.

"Well, Antonito," he said, "it won't be long before you can do this all on your own, will it?"

"No, Father," I replied, and I meant it too, because even as I spoke I realised at last how it could be done, how I could set

Paco free. I knew that what I was planning was terrible, the most terrible thing I could ever do to my father; but I had to save Paco, and this was the only way I could think of to do it.

That same night I lay in my bed forcing myself to stay awake. I waited until the house fell silent about me, until I was as sure as I could be that everyone was asleep. The sound of Father's deep snoring was enough to convince me that it was safe to move.

I was already dressed under my blankets. I stole out of the house and across the moonlit yard towards the stable. The dogs whined at me, but I patted them and they did not bark. I led Chica out of her stable, mounting her some way down the farm track, out of sight of the house, and then rode out over the farm towards Paco's corral.

My idea was clumsy but simple. I knew that to separate Paco from the others, to release him on his own would be almost impossible, and that even if I succeeded, sooner or later he would be bound to come running back to the others. He was after all a herd animal. I would have to release them all, all of them together, and drive them as far as I could up into the cork forests where they could lose themselves and never be found. Even if they caught a few of them, Paco might be lucky. At least this way he stood some chance of freedom, some chance of avoiding the horrors of the *corrida*.

The cattle shifted in the corral as I came closer. They were nervous, unsettled by this strange night-time visitor. I dismounted at the gate and opened it. For some while they stood looking at me, snorting, shaking their horns. I called out quietly into the night. "Paco! Paco! It's me. It's Antonito!"

I knew he would come, and he did, walking slowly towards me, his ears twitching and listening all the time as I sweetened him closer. Then, as he reached the open gate, the others began to follow. It all happened so fast after that. To begin with, they came at a gentle walk through the gate. Then they were trotting, then jostling, then galloping, charging past me. Paco, I felt sure, was gone with them, swept along in the stampede.

I don't know what it was that knocked me senseless, only that when I woke, I was not alone. Paco was standing over me, looking down at me, and Chica was grazing nearby. Whether Paco had saved me from being trampled to death, I do not know. What I did know was that my plan had worked perfectly, better than I could ever have hoped for.

I got to my feet slowly, amazed that nothing was broken. I was not badly hurt at all, just a little bruised, and my cheek was cut. I could feel the blood sticky under my hand when I touched it. I had no rope, but I knew I would not need one, that Paco would follow along behind Chica and me as if he'd been trained to it.

I had in mind to go as far as I could, as fast as I could, before dawn. Beyond that I had no thought as to where we would go, nor what I would do with him. As we climbed the rutty tracks up into the hills, I felt inside me a sudden surge of elation. Paco was free and now I would keep him free. I had no conscience any more about what I had done, no thought now of what it would mean to Father to lose his precious herd of cattle. Paco would not suffer that terrible death in the ring – that was all that mattered to me. I had done it, and I was ecstatic.

Chica seemed to know the path, and she was as surefooted as a mule. I never once came near to falling off, despite my exhaustion. Behind us, Paco was finding it more difficult, but he was managing.

I felt the damp of the morning mist around us before I ever saw the dawn. We climbed on, higher and higher into the mist, until the last of the night was gone and a hazy white sun rose over the hills.

We came suddenly into a clearing. On the far side was a stone hut, most of it in ruins, and beside it a circular stone corral. I hadn't seen this one before, but I had seen others. There were several like it scattered through the cork forests, built for gathering cattle or sheep or goats. Paco followed us in and I shut the gate behind him. Both Paco and Chica at once began nuzzling the grass. I lay down in the shelter of the wall, and was asleep before I knew it.

The warming sun woke me, that or the cry of the vultures. They were circling above us in the blue. The mist had all gone. Paco lay beside me, chewing the cud and licking his nose. Chica stood, resting her fourth leg, only half awake. I lay there for a while, trying to gather my thoughts.

That was when I heard the sound of distant droning, like a million bees. There

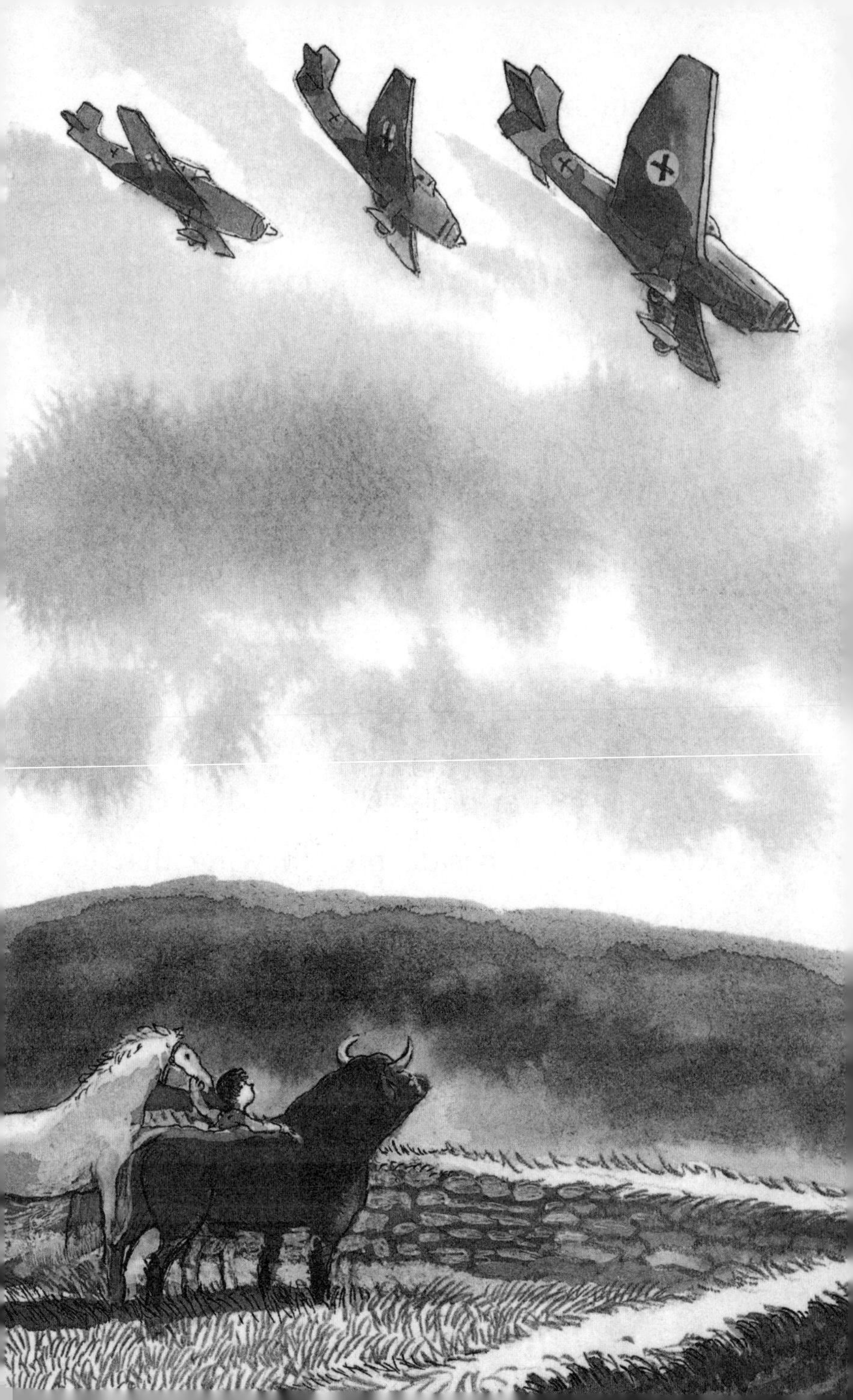

were no bees to be seen, and nothing else either. I thought I must be imagining things, but then Paco was on his feet and snorting. The vultures were suddenly gone. The droning was coming closer, ever closer, until it became a throbbing angry roar that filled the air about us. Then I saw them, flying low over the ridge towards us, dozens of them – airplanes with black crosses on their wings. They came right over us, their engines thunderous, throbbing so loudly that it hurt my ears.

In my terror I curled up against the wall and covered my ears. Paco was going wild and Chica, too, was circling the corral, looking for a way out. I waited until the planes were gone, then climbed up on to the wall of the corral. They were diving now, their engines screaming, diving on Sauceda, diving on my home.

I saw the smoke of the first bombs before I heard the distant crunch of the explosions. It was as if some vengeful God was pounding the village with his fist, each punch sending up a plume of fire, until the whole village was covered in a pall of smoke.

I stood there on the corral wall, trying not to believe what my eyes were telling me. They were telling me that my whole world was being destroyed, that Father and Mother and Maria were down there somewhere in all that smoke and fire. I don't think I really believed it until the planes had gone, until I heard the sound of silence again, and then the sound of my own crying.

SAUCEDA

Paco was still frantic, still circling the corral in his terror, so he paid me little attention as I caught Chica, led her out of the gate and closed it behind me. Only then did he seem to realise what was happening and came running over to us.

"I'll be back, Paco," I told him. "I'll be back, I promise."

I mounted up and rode away. The last I saw of him he was looking over the gate after us, tossing his head, pawing at the ground, and then we were gone down into the woods out of his sight. For some time I heard him calling for us, his plaintive bellowing echoing around the hills. Below us the smoke drifted along the valley, as if a sudden new mist had come down.

Chica seemed to understand the urgency, for she retraced her steps at speed the whole way down, stumbling often. Where the path was at its narrowest and most treacherous, I dismounted and ran on ahead, leading her. But running or riding, my head was filled with a gnawing dread of what I might find. I longed to be there, to see Maria and Father and Mother again, and yet I was reluctant to arrive in case my worst fears proved true. From time to time I was seized by fits of uncontrollable sobbing, but by the time we reached the outskirts of the farm I felt strangely calm, as if I had no more tears left to cry.

Perhaps because I had had so long to think about it, the sight of my home in ruins, in flames, came as no shock to me. The pigs snuffled about the yard as they always did, the goats grazed busily, scarcely stopping to look up at me as I passed. I stood in the yard and watched my house burn, the flames licking out of the windows. There was a terrible anger in those flames. I could hear it in all their roaring and crackling and spitting. I did not call for Father or Mother or Maria for I knew they must all be dead. No one could have survived in that inferno. How long I stood there I do not know, but I did not cry again until I saw the dogs. I found them lying dead near the water trough. I sat down beside them and wept till I thought my heart would burst.

In time, the flames had nothing more to burn and died down. Only the walls remained, charred and smouldering. I turned away, and with Chica following me, made my way along the road into Sauceda.

The village was unrecognisable. Hardly a house had survived. But I heard people, voices I knew. Then I saw them, faces I knew. My cousin Vittorio stood in the street with blood on his face. He was wailing, calling for his mother. There was so much wailing. Some were wandering about in a daze, mumbling to themselves.

Others just sat staring into space, tears running down their cheeks. I recognised some of the soldiers from the café. Several of them were filling buckets at the well and running across the street to a house that was still burning.

Only then, as I watched, did it occur to me there could be a chance that Mother and Father and Maria might still be alive. I began to ask after them. Vittorio didn't seem to know me. He just stared at me and kept saying over and over, "My mama. Where is my mama?" I asked everyone I saw, but no one had seen my family, no one could help me.

Then, as my thoughts gathered themselves, I wondered if I might have given them up too quickly. I should have searched for them back at home. They could have got out alive. Others had.

I rode home as fast as Chica would carry me, scouring the fields around me as I went. As I came into the farmyard I called out, but only the goats answered me. I looked in every barn, in every shed. I rode out over the fields, calling for them, calling for them, till my throat was raw, and I knew it was hopeless to go on.

I was sitting on the steps to the barn, my head in my hands, when I heard voices. I stood up. Soldiers. Hundreds of them were moving up the valley towards the farm, towards the village – not our soldiers, but other soldiers in different uniforms. If I ran for it, I would be seen before I reached the trees. The barn was my only chance.

I darted inside, and looked for somewhere to hide, anywhere. The voices were coming closer. I climbed the ladder to the hayloft, burrowed myself deep into the hay, curled myself up and was still. They were outside in the yard now, and laughing. I heard Chica whinnying and go galloping off. They were firing, whether at Chica or not I did not know. I curled myself up tighter and gritted my teeth to stop myself crying out loud.

I heard heavy footsteps in the barn below me, and a soldier's voice: "Let's burn the place down."

"Later," came the reply, "we've more important work in Sauceda. Let's go."

I lay where I was until I was quite sure it was safe. When at last I ventured out from under the hay, I found the whole farm deserted, except for Chica who was grazing contentedly with the pigs. I was down the ladder in a trice, and haring out across the yard. I scrambled under the fence and ran across the field towards Chica, scattering the pigs as I came. She stood still for me to mount her, and then we were away, galloping towards the hills and safety.

I rode up the same track I had taken the night before, but Chica was tired now and finding the going hard. She was breathing heavily, so after an hour or so I decided I must let her rest. I dismounted by a spring so that Chica could rest and have a drink at the same time. As she drank I looked down into the valley below, and saw the smoking ruins of Sauceda.

That was the moment the shooting began. I stood there and hid my face in my hands as the people of Sauceda were massacred. The sound of that shooting still echoes in my head all these years later. There was a terrible evil done that day. I didn't understand the nature of evil as a young boy, but I understood the loss. I understood that now I had no mother, no father, no sister, no family, no friends, no home. All were gone from me in one day. But I still had Paco. I had Chica, too. I wasn't entirely alone.

It was dusk before we reached the clearing and the stone corral again. I called for Paco as I rode up to the gate, but he did not come. He did not come because he was not there. I discovered a gaping hole in the stone wall. Paco had burst his way through and was gone. I was neither sad nor glad. Certainly Paco had been saved from the *corrida*. But all that had suddenly become very unimportant.

Exhausted, I lay down to sleep in the ruined shepherd's hut with Chica beside me for warmth. Like Chica, I had drunk from the stream nearby, but I ached with hunger, and with the pain of my loss. When I closed my eyes I saw Mother's face, and Father's and Maria's, and our home burning. I heard the shooting and the crackling of flames. I slept only fitfully, fearful of my nightmares, so that I was relieved to wake and find it was morning. But hunger was still gnawing at my stomach.

Looking back, I think perhaps it was the hunger that saved me in my early days in the hills, for it drove all other thoughts from my mind. I *had* to find food. I knew where to look – I had been out often enough with Mother or Maria picking the wild asparagus or mushrooms (I knew the good from the bad, or I thought I did), and thistles too, the thistles with the juicy stems. So, as we travelled that day, always higher into the hills, away from Sauceda, I gathered all I could find and ate it as we went. But try as I did, I could never find enough. I ate everything raw – I had no way of making fire, no means of cooking. I chewed on acorns, I plucked the fruit of the strawberry tree. I hated both, but they were better than nothing. I drank water whenever I could. When you're hungry, even water seems to fill you up, for a while at least. Worst of all, I saw food all about me in the woods – wild boar, red deer, fish in the streams. They came to tease me, I think. I tried tickling trout, but failed to catch any.

Chica of course had no problems finding all she needed to eat. She simply grazed as she went. It was she I talked to now, my only surviving companion. We slept on the forest floor, under the canopy of the trees, in limestone caves, wherever we could find shelter. I kept always to where the forest was thick, and as far as possible from all human habitation.

I do not know, because I really can't remember, how many days or weeks we wandered the hills together. But I do know that in the end, an infrequent diet of mushrooms and thistles and asparagus was not enough. It was all I could do now to find the strength to climb up on to

Chica, all I could do to cling on. My head was swimming, and I felt overcome by weakness and drowsiness. Time and again I slid out of the saddle, and then one day I fell off and just could not get up again. I lay there looking up at Chica, at the waving of the branches, at the shifting of the clouds. I heard the wind sighing through the forest and remembered, long long ago it seemed, a lantern-lit dinner outside the farmhouse, the time when Uncle Juan came, the day before the bullfight. I remembered his words: "A man without freedom is a man without honour, without dignity, without nobility." I could hear his voice speaking to me. I could see his face. And he was smiling as he had done in the bullring, lifting me up as he'd done when I'd danced the bull dance with him at home.

Now I could feel him carrying me. He was talking to me: "You'll be all right, Antonito. You'll be all right. I'll look after you now." I thought I must be dreaming, or that we were both dead and up in heaven. I reached out and touched his face. He was real. It *was* Uncle Juan.

THE BLACK PHANTOM

They told me later just how difficult it was to save me, to bring me back from the dead. It wasn't only that I was emaciated and wracked with fever when Uncle Juan brought me in. Uncle Juan and the others did what they could for me – but for weeks, they said, it seemed I had no wish to live. I don't remember being like that. There's not much I can remember, as I drifted in and out of sleep, but I do remember Uncle Juan being beside me. He would bathe my face with cold water. He would stroke my hair, talk to me, and try to feed me food I didn't want to eat.

I was lying in a cave, I knew that

much. I could smell the smoke of cooking, and hear the sound of people talking, moving about me, men and women and crying children. They would often come and peer down at me, close to my face. One day I heard one of them whisper to another: "It's Juan's little nephew, from Sauceda. Poor little mite. He's dying you know."

And I thought inside myself: "No, I'm not. I'm *not* dying. I won't let myself die. I want to see Paco again. I want to find him." So I started to eat for Paco, and very slowly began at last to regain my strength. And, as I did so, I began to take stock of what was going on around me.

I soon discovered that Uncle Juan was universally regarded as our leader. I could see that everyone looked to him for constant reassurance, and relied heavily on his strength of purpose and his unwavering optimism. Whenever he spoke, he inspired us and gave us hope. And hope was all we had. There might have been fifty people living up in the cave. Perhaps half were freedom fighters, like Uncle Juan. The rest were refugees hiding out in the hills, terrified to return home for fear of the soldiers, or the police, the *Guardia Civil*. Food was scarce; we had only what was brought up to us at night from the villages, or gleaned from the forest around.

I didn't have to tell Uncle Juan about the bombing of Sauceda. He knew about it, everyone knew about it, but there was no one else in the cave from Sauceda, and no word of any other survivors. I was the only one, and only I knew why that was. If I had not chosen that night to set Paco free, then I too would have been dead in the ruins of the farmhouse, or shot down trying to escape.

The more I thought of it, and I thought of it almost constantly, the less I felt I had the right to be alive. I hadn't survived just by good luck, but because I hadn't been there. I'd been away committing a dreadful crime. I'd been releasing all Father's beloved bulls into the wild, his whole pride and joy, robbing him of his lifetime's work. When I cried now it wasn't from hunger or grief, but from shame, from a deep sense of my own unworthiness.

Uncle Juan would hold me tight to comfort me. "I know, Antonito," he said one morning, wiping my tears away with his thumbs. "They were terrible things you saw. I know the pain you must feel.

Everyone here in this cave knows the pain you feel now. So cry, cry all you want. But when you've done crying, then be brave again, be my little brave bull, and come out fighting. Evil, Antonito, must be fought, not cried over. You understand me?" He smiled at me and laughed. "We are few, but we are strong. Even the beasts are on our side, do you know that? Have you heard about the Black Phantom of Maracha?"

Uncle Juan often told me stories to cheer me up, to take me out of myself. He told them well, too, and I loved to listen.

"This is not just one of my little tales, Antonito, this is true. There are patrols out in the hills – soldiers, *Guardia Civil*, looking for us. Don't you worry, Antonio. They won't catch us. We ambush them, we fight them. We send them running

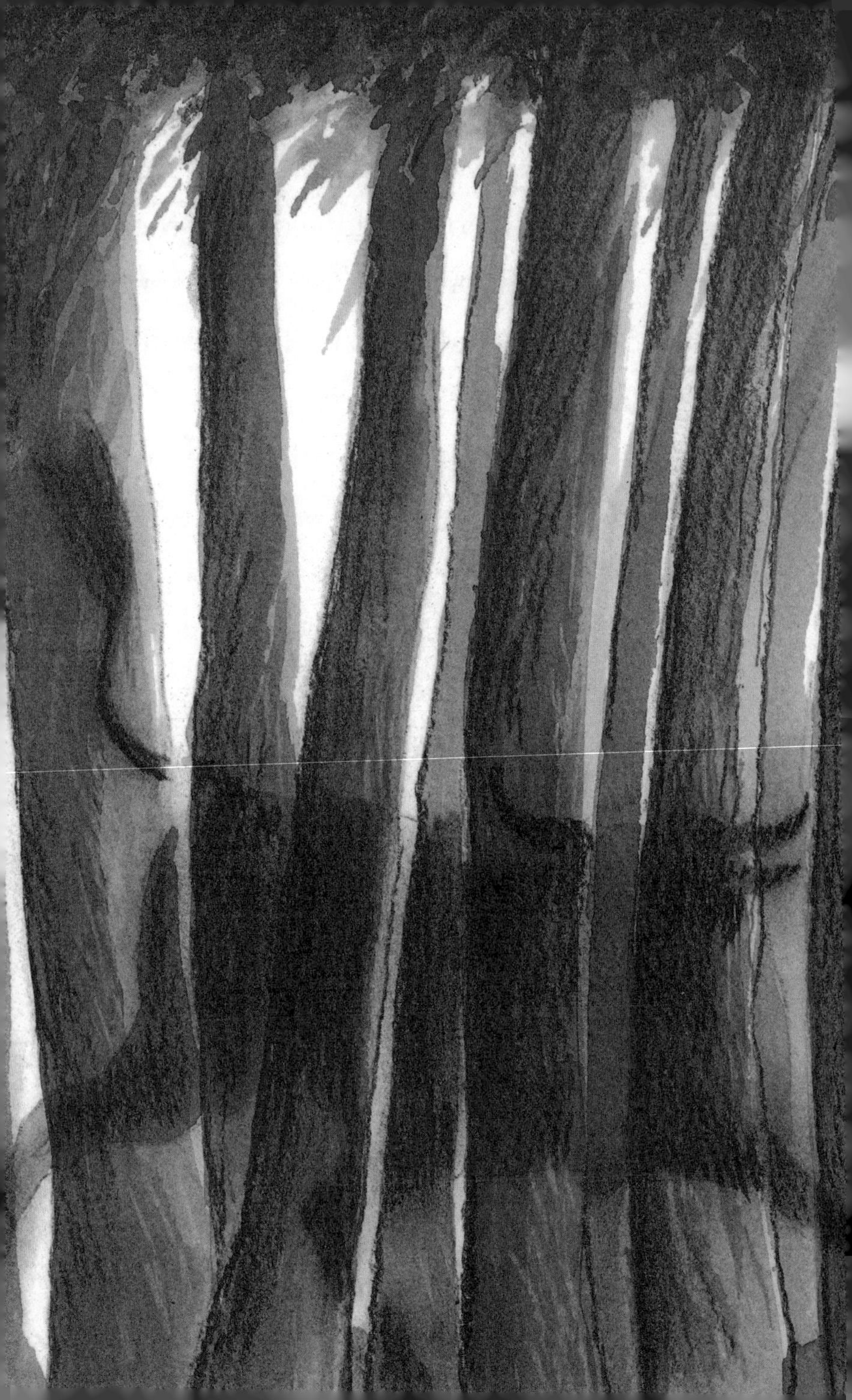

like the rabbits they are. But yesterday they sent out a patrol from Maracha – maybe twenty men from the *Guardia Civil*. They thought they saw something move in amongst the trees. They started shooting. Suddenly, out of the trees he comes, the Black Phantom! You know what he is, the Black Phantom?" I had no idea. "A *nobile*, a young fighting bull. He came charging at them. And what did they do? They dropped their rifles and ran.

"But one of them didn't run fast enough, and got himself tossed in the air like a pancake. Then the bull chased the others off, scattering them into the forest. When they turned to look, he had vanished, like a phantom, a Black Phantom. They went searching for him, but it was as if he had never been there. Yet he *had* been there. There were hoof prints, the hoof prints of a young bull. What do you think of that, Antonito?"

I could think of nothing to say. I had so much to say, so much I was longing to tell him, but I could say nothing without confessing all I'd done, without betraying myself. I knew, even as he was telling me, that it was Paco. It *had* to be Paco. Paco was alive! He was out there, somewhere. He was looking for me. One day we would find each other again, I was sure of it now.

After a while, because I had to say something, I said: "That bull, he must be the bravest bull in the whole world."

"You're right, Antonito," said Uncle Juan. "And if he can be brave against all the odds, then so can I. So can you."

The story of the Black Phantom lifted our flagging spirits – everyone knew about him by now. That evening the whole cave was suddenly a happier place. I heard the sound of laughter again, and when the children got together to act out the drama, I got up and joined in. I was the *nobile*, the young bull. I was Paco. I pawed the ground like he did, tossed my head like he did, and charged around the cave; and they all screamed and ran away like rabbits, like the *Guardia Civil* in the forest at Maracha.

But the fun and games were short-lived. Later that evening, there was the sound of shooting echoing about the hills. Danger was suddenly close again. Silent now, we huddled together in our fear.

The next morning Uncle Juan called everyone together. We all had to move deeper into the hills, he told us. The soldiers and the *Guardia Civil* were getting nearer each day. There had been fighting in the valley, and the soldiers were searching the forest. If we stayed where we were we could be discovered. So began our long march, some of the most terrible days of my life, days I shall never forget.

We only had two mules and Chica between all of us, and they were needed to carry what few blankets, what little food we had, as well as the younger children. The food very soon ran out, and then the rain came down, turning the tracks into streams and quagmires. We could only go as fast as the slowest amongst us, two old ladies, twin sisters, from Algar. Uncle Juan told the two old ladies they should ride instead of the children – I heard him – but they refused.

"It is the young that must live, Juan," one of them said, "not the old. We have had our lives. We have our sticks." And so they walked, and we children took turns to ride. Sometimes I rode Chica. Uncle Juan often gave me two small children to look after; one rode in front of me, the other clinging on behind. It was good to be riding her again, to feel her warmth and strength beneath me.

One morning, after yet another cold night in the open, we were readying ourselves for another day's march when I noticed that the two old sisters from Algar hadn't moved. They were lying together under a tree, hugging each other for warmth. Uncle Juan was crouching over them, trying to rouse them. I went over to him. I knew at once that they were dead. They lay so still, so absolutely still, one with her forefinger on her lips as if willing the world to hush. When Uncle Juan looked up at me, all the strength was suddenly gone from his eyes, and instead I saw only a deep sadness.

We buried them where they lay. Uncle Juan was never the same after that. I never once saw him smile again. All that great heart seemed to have gone out of him, but nonetheless, I still pinned all my faith, all my hopes on Uncle Juan. To me, to everyone, he was the one person who would bring us through somehow. He led us on, ever deeper into the hills, and from the top of every pass we saw always more hills, higher hills lost in the clouds. And still the rain came down. On we trudged, and as we went others joined us, more freedom fighters, more refugees, till our fifty was nearer two hundred.

One afternoon, as we came out of the woods into a narrow valley with a river running through, the rain stopped and the sudden sun warmed our backs and lifted our spirits. I remember we were singing as we came down into the valley. We saw ahead of us a cluster of farmhouses in a clearing, but it seemed as if the place was deserted.

From out of the houses they appeared, one by one at first, then in twos and threes, in their dozens, fearful, bedraggled and pale. But as they recognised who we were, as they realised we were friends, their faces lit up, and they came running. Uncle Juan and the freedom fighters were greeted like conquering heroes. Stranger hugged stranger. Friends found friends. Bound by common suffering, strangers became friends. We wept out of sheer joy that we were together, that we were alive.

Almost at once the talk was of the Black Phantom. Everyone knew of him, but only I knew who he was. Only I knew he was Paco. Every time I heard the name the Black Phantom, I felt so sure it was him, so certain that one day Paco and I would meet again.

I was making my way through the crowd of people, walking Chica down to the river for a drink, when I saw a girl standing in front of me, gaping at me wide-eyed. Maria! It was Maria! How long we clung to each other and cried together I do not know.

"And Mother? Father?" I asked her, but she shook her head and walked me to the river. There, on the river bank, as Chica drank her fill, she told me what had happened – how, when I couldn't be found that morning, she'd been sent out to find me, how the planes had come, and the house had been hit. She'd run back but there was nothing she could do. The house was ablaze. She couldn't get near it. She had looked for me everywhere, called for me, and the pigs and the goats and the chickens were running everywhere in a wild panic, and all the time the planes were bombing and strafing. All she could think of was getting away. So she ran and ran. She'd wandered the woods for days before meeting a charcoal burner, who had fed her and cared for her, and brought her here to hide up in the hills with all the others. They'd been here for weeks and weeks, she said, but there was very little food to go round and they were all terrified that the *Guardia Civil* might come.

"You won't have to worry about that any more," I told her, "because Uncle Juan is here with his soldiers, and they'll look after us."

"Uncle Juan is here!" she cried; and then she saw him and went running to him, throwing herself into his arms.

The three of us, Uncle Juan with an arm around each of us, sat together that night and we talked under the stars. After a while we fell silent, each of us wrapped in our own thoughts. That was the moment Maria asked me the question I'd been dreading. "You never told me, Antonito. Where were you when the planes came? I looked everywhere."

The lie I'd prepared came out easily. "I got up early and took Chico for a ride.

I wanted to see Paco. Then I heard the planes, and Chico just bolted. I couldn't stop her. I tried but she galloped off into the hills, and I clung on."

"Thank God she did. And thank God you went for a ride that morning," said Maria. "If you hadn't, then we'd both be dead, like Mother and Father."

Uncle Juan drew us closer. "I've decided," he whispered. "You take Chica, and you go tonight, now."

"Why?" I asked him.

"Because we are too many here. There's not enough food to go round. Because sooner or later we'll be discovered and will have to fight. We will fight, and fight as well as we can. But we are few and they are many. I don't want you to be here when it happens." Maria tried to interrupt. "No arguments, Maria. I have thought it all through. It's the only way.

"I want you to go to Malaga, to my mother's house – you've been there, Maria, you'll find the way. Kiss her for me, Antonito, and look after her. Be a son to her. Will you do this for me?"

"Yes," I said.

"Follow the river down into the valley. You'll join the road there. The *Guardia Civil* won't harm you. You are children. They have children of their own."

He led us to where Chica stood, white in the moonlight. He held us for a moment, kissed us both on the forehead, then picked us up one by one and sat us astride Chica.

"Go with God," he whispered, and we rode away along the riverbank and left him there. We kept turning in the saddle to see him, until the darkness took him from us and we were alone.

We did see soldiers, lots of them, but luckily they ignored us. Several times the *Guardia Civil* stopped and questioned us. Maria told them we were visiting our great aunt in Malaga, and each time they nodded us through. Wherever we stopped for the night people fed us and gave us shelter. If I learned one thing on that last journey, and while hiding in the hills with the refugees, it was that men and women have a capacity for kindness as great if not greater than their capacity for evil.

When at last, after many days' travel, we reached Malaga and Uncle Juan's house, I set about doing just what Uncle Juan had told me. I kissed his mother, and made myself a son to her. Together, Maria and I looked after her. I think she knew all along that Uncle Juan would not be coming home. She was strong and proud in her grief. We never did discover what happened to him. Like so many thousands of others in the Civil War, he just disappeared. But he's not forgotten.

Not forgotten, either, was the Black Phantom. Even in Malaga, in my new school, they had heard of him. There were stories of how he had been seen wandering the streets at night in Cortes, bellowing defiance, or spotted by a shepherd in the hills outside Jerez, even in the castle keep at Gaucin. He had surprised a column of soldiers, hundreds strong, near Cortes and put them to flight, and chased a *Guardia Civil* officer through the street of El Colminar. Even as a boy I knew the stories couldn't all be true – though I hoped they were, of

course. But the Black Phantom's survival and the tales of his triumphs kept hope alive even in the depths of our despair as the war was lost. I kept in my heart the hope that one day I might see Paco again, but as time passed it became only the faintest of hopes, based on a story I only half believed.

Great Aunt Nina was as good a mother to me as an old lady could be, and I had Maria, your Great Aunt Maria, who was always my soulmate, my great protector, and my dearest friend. She still is.

A few years later – I would have been nineteen or twenty by then – I had a job cutting cork in the forests near Maracha. I was on my own, and tired after a long day's work. I'd made myself a small fire, and after supper lay down beside it to sleep, the mules hobbled nearby. I fell asleep easily, and then I dreamed a strange dream, that Paco was lying there beside me, chewing the cud, licking his nose. He was so close I could smell his milky breath. I woke. Paco wasn't there. Of course he wasn't. It had been a dream. But as I got to my feet I noticed the grass nearby had been flattened. I felt it. It was warm. Then I saw hoof marks, the hoof marks of a massive bull. Paco had found me. We had found each other at last. The Black Phantom was no phantom. I called and I called for him, but he never came.

For years after that, whenever I worked the cork forests, I looked out for Paco, even though I knew it was quite impossible he could still be alive. But it didn't matter. Once was enough. I was a happy man.

* * * * *

My grandson's eyes had not left my face throughout the entire story, but after I'd finished he seemed to think there should be more.

"That was really the very worstest thing?" he asked. He sounded a little disappointed. "Didn't you ever break any windows?"

"I can't remember," I said. "I expect so."

The front door opened, and I heard his mother's voice. "I'm home," she called out. Antonito leapt off the bed.

"Secret, Antonito?" I said.

"Secret, Abuelo." He smiled at me, and was gone out of the room. By the time I reached the top of the stairs he was in his mother's arms, clinging to her.

"I'm sorry, Mum," he cried. "I'm really sorry." He looked up into her face.

"Mum, we won't ever be in a war, will we?"

"Of course not, Antonito."

"And you won't die, will you? You won't die?"

"Not for a while, I hope," she replied, and then she saw me standing there. "Abuelo, what brought all this on?"

I shrugged. "Who knows?" I said. "Who knows what goes on in the mind of a child?"

ENJOYED THIS BOOK? WHY NOT TRY OTHER GREAT HARPERCOLLINS TITLES – AT 10% OFF!

Buy great books direct from HarperCollins
at **10%** off recommended retail price.
FREE postage and packing in the UK.

☐ **Alone on a Wide Wide Sea** Michael Morpurgo 0-00-723058-3		£5.99
☐ **Adolphus Tips** Michael Morpurgo 0-00-718246-5		£5.99
☐ **Private Peaceful** Michael Morpurgo 0-00-715007-5		£5.99
☐ **Cool!** Michael Morpurgo 0-00-713104-6		£4.99
☐ **The Dancing Bear** Michael Morpurgo 0-00-674511-3		£3.99
☐ **The Butterfly Lion** Michael Morpurgo 0-00-675103-2		£4.99
☐ **Toro! Toro!** Michael Morpurgo 0-00-710718-8		£4.99
☐ **Billy the Kid** Michael Morpurgo 0-00-710547-9		£4.99
☐ **Dear Olly** Michael Morpurgo 0-00-675333-7		£4.99
☐ **Farm Boy** Michael Morpurgo 0-00-675412-0		£4.99

Total cost _____

To purchase by Visa/Mastercard/Switch simply call
08707871724 or fax on **08707871725**

To pay by cheque, send a copy of this form with a cheque made payable to
'HarperCollins Publishers' to: Mail Order Dept. (Ref: BOB4),
HarperCollins Publishers, Westerhill Road, Bishopbriggs, G64 2QT,
making sure to include your full name, postal address and phone number.

From time to time HarperCollins may wish to use your personal data
to send you details of other HarperCollins publications and offers.
If you wish to receive information on other HarperCollins publications
and offers please tick this box ☐

Do not send cash or currency. Prices correct at time of press.
Prices and availability are subject to change without notice.
Delivery overseas and to Ireland incurs a £2 per book postage and packing charge.